The Sound of Deception

SUSAN ANN WALL

The Sound of Deception

ISBN-13: 978-0692233115
Heart of Jupiter Publishing

ISBN-10: 0692233113

Cover
Foregound Image: © Yuri Arcurs | Dreamstime.com
City Image: © Susan Ann Wall
Design: Heart of Jupiter Publishing

Dedication

For Amy, my lifelong BFF.
Here's to another 37 years!! ♥

SUSAN ANN WALL

Prologue

Bryan Curtis watched his friends head south toward the condo where they lived. It'd been one hell of a night. He shouldn't have been surprised Owen's ex-wife had made an appearance at the bar. The woman was one manipulative bitch and she most likely had a plan to ruin Owen. Bryan wasn't about to let that happen.

"Can I crash on your couch?" he asked Morgan Landry as she stood beside him and watched her brother. Bryan worried she was going to go back into the pub and face off with Kristina, but he also didn't want to leave Seattle in case Owen needed him. Those two very valid reasons had kept his feet planted on the wet asphalt outside the pub instead of maneuvering him to the ferry.

"I'm sure you can find some willing blonde to shack up with for a night," Morgan teased.

Bryan sighed, wishing he could tell Morgan he wasn't interested in blondes, but he'd built that reputation all on his own, so he couldn't deny it without revealing the truth.

"Look, your brother's on edge, Stacie's on edge, and I'd bet the entire Pacific Fleet that if I walked away, you'd be back in that pub

1

finishing what Stacie started." Bryan still couldn't believe Stacie had confronted Owen's ex-wife, but she'd been drinking pretty hard, fueled by anger and what he guessed was jealousy before the evening even got started. It was a good thing Bryan had opted to stay sober. He was far beyond the years of bar fights and well into the years of keeping an eye on his friends when life got a little Whiskey Tango Foxtrot.

Morgan's hands landed on her hips, her chin lifting in sheer determination. "I don't need a babysitter."

"Sweetheart, I have no doubt you can handle yourself, but you know as well as I do any attempt you make to scare Kristina off is only going to fuel her ambitions."

Morgan's mouth slanted with mischief. "I was thinking more along the lines of murder."

Sounded like a good plan to Bryan, but he wasn't interested in spending the rest of his life behind bars. "Interesting idea, but it's probably better if we get out of here."

"Fine. Ruin my fun." Morgan stomped off in the opposite direction the others had headed.

"So, your couch?" Bryan called after her.

She threw her hands up in the air, but Bryan couldn't take his eyes off the tantalizing sway of her ass. "You practically live there anyway. I don't know why you bother asking."

He'd been spending more time there than he should, but Bryan figured if he was sleeping on her couch, then there wouldn't be a man sleeping in her bed – an idea he wasn't fond of. "My mother raised a gentleman."

"Is that what you tell yourself when you slink out of some bimbo's apartment at o'dark thirty?" she chided. Her tone was playful, but Bryan was getting tired of the jabs.

"Enough about my sex life."

Morgan laughed, a sound he usually loved, but Bryan didn't see the humor. He'd been dubbed a man-whore years ago. It wasn't a title to be proud of, but the fact was he liked women and wasn't interested in commitment. The math on that added up to a lot of short-term, no-strings relationships. His policy was pure honesty with the women he slept with and yeah, he suffered some guilt when they got attached and he sent them sailing, but it wasn't his fault what happened on their ends.

"You're not exactly the symbol of innocence," Bryan said after they got on the bus that would take them from downtown Seattle to the University District where Morgan lived.

"Excuse me?"

Now it was Bryan's turn to laugh. She obviously didn't like the tables being turned, but she'd started this game. "You go through men pretty quickly yourself."

"I date them. I don't sleep with them."

"Right," he drawled. He'd like to believe that was true, but women had a tendency to lie about their sexual escapades. Even Morgan, who could be brutally honest, would likely keep her numbers under wraps just to feed her brother's fantasy that she was still a sweet, innocent little girl.

"How many women have you slept with this year?" she asked.

Bryan shrugged. "I don't know. It's not like I make tally marks on my calendar."

"Safe to say a lot, though, right?"

"I guess." It was December, so yeah, it was safe to say a lot for the year, though admitting that to Morgan felt like taking a dull knife to his heart. He didn't care what other people thought of him, but Bryan didn't like Morgan knowing about the women he'd been with.

"Well, it's a big fat zero for me." She made a circle with her fingers, peering at him through the opening.

Had he been taking a drink, he would have choked on it. "Zero?" Bryan could hardly believe with all the men she'd brought around since she'd moved to Seattle last summer she hadn't slept with at least a few of them.

"None, nada, zero, zilch," she sang as though proud of her

numbers…or lack of.

"Why not?" Surely anyone with two eyes and a pulse would try to get her into bed. Hell, two eyes weren't even required. Even a blind man would know she was beautiful and sexy.

Beautiful wasn't a problem. Bryan had known plenty of beautiful women he hadn't wanted to get naked. In fact, both Stacie and Jenny ranked up there as beautiful. Sexy was the problem. Morgan was just about the hottest woman he'd ever known. Even hotter…she didn't have a clue. She was the perfect combination of girl next door and independent sass. If she wasn't his best friend's sister, he would have taken her to bed years ago.

She shrugged with an indifference that was a complete contrast to the way she dated. "It's not my thing."

"You're not telling me you're a virgin, are you?" Although the thought had him more aroused than he'd ever admit. He shifted in the seat, hoping the boner he was sporting wasn't as obvious as it was uncomfortable.

"God no. I'm not a saint. I just don't sleep with every guy who tells me I'm pretty."

Thank God for that. Bryan had a hard enough time keeping his cave man instincts under wraps when Morgan brought one of her dates around. She was overly affectionate, which was one reason he figured she'd slept with all of them. The way she kissed those men, he figured they had to be bumping uglies.

The bus maneuvered through the city, dropping off more people than it picked up. Only a few passengers remained as they hit the U-District.

"I don't get you," he admitted, shaking his head as he slouched in the plastic seat. The boner had softened enough that he wasn't at risk for pitching a tent in his loose jeans.

"What's not to get? I'm a strong-willed, independent woman who has no interest in relying on a man to get me through life."

"Yeah, but no sex in a year? Don't you, you know?"

Morgan laughed, one of the sweetest sounds he'd ever heard.

Fortunately, he heard it often. He'd never known someone who embraced life quite like she did, with fervor and humor...and passion. "Use your words, Bryan," she encouraged.

"Don't you ever get horny?" Morgan was always blunt, something Bryan liked about her, and he usually didn't have a problem speaking his mind, but it was a very personal question, and if he brought Owen into the equation, it was a completely inappropriate question. You didn't ask your best friend's sister, under any circumstances, if she ever got horny. You especially didn't ask her when she'd starred in more fantasies over the years than you could count.

Her spirited laugh drew the attention of a few midnight riders on the bus. After everyone turned their attention away, she whispered, "I'm horny now."

She may as well have commanded his cock to attention. He had to sit straight up again to hide his body's response. Damn her.

Bryan should drop the anchor on this conversation before he dove into waters that would lead straight to hell, but Christ, all the blood had rushed from his brain and the sailor in his pants demanded his curiosity be assuaged.

"And what do you do about that?" All kinds of visions played in his mind...Morgan with toys...Morgan with the shower massager...Morgan using her own hands.

"I'm not about to give away my dirty little secrets." And her smirk told him that those little secrets were very, very dirty.

He was going to kill her, or more likely he was going to pass out from the glorious sensation of her warm breath caressing his cheek mixed with the lack of blood flow to any part of his body other than the eager beast below his waist.

Bryan growled, whether in frustration or sexual hunger, he couldn't be sure – maybe both. They were treading in dangerous waters. Morgan turned to face forward in her seat, but in doing so, her thigh pressed against his. She probably wasn't even aware of it, but the heat emanating from her body had him ready to launch like a heat seeking missile and she was his locked-on target.

"You're a tease," he grumbled, scooting to his right half an inch to try and give himself some space. Unfortunately, the bus was no longer big enough for the two of them, never mind providing space between the plum seats.

Relief flooded him when the bus pulled up to their stop just a few blocks from her apartment. The December chill was a welcome contrast, but Bryan's libido didn't get the message, especially when Morgan started talking again.

"I've always wondered what you'd be like in bed," she cooed with a bounce in her step.

Bryan nearly tripped over his size thirteens. When he managed to right his steps, he wondered if she was being honest or playing with him. It was hard to tell with Morgan, but he decided to play along. "Define always."

"Since Norfolk," she admitted.

That stopped Bryan in his tracks. "When we met?"

Morgan gave him a look over her shoulder, a playful nod confirming her admission and a sultry smile heating his blood. Jesus, if she swung her ass any more in front of him, he was going to need to take a dip in Lake Washington.

He fell into step next to her, giving up the incredible view in order to keep his sanity. "That was twelve years ago."

She shrugged, bumping his elbow with hers as she did. Even that flirtatious touch had him turned on. "I know."

Or maybe her admission was the aphrodisiac.

Bryan, though he'd never admit it to anyone, had fantasized about Morgan ever since he'd met that innocent girl who'd just graduated high school. She'd spent the summer with Owen and Daphne in Norfolk, taking care of Owen's daughter during the day and living it up at night. Owen had tried to keep his sister on a short leash, but Bryan had learned quickly Morgan was her own person and wasn't about to abide by any rules her brother or anyone laid down. That's why Bryan had taken it upon himself to look out for her that summer. She was hot as hell, but the age difference had been enough of a deterrent. As they got older, his loyalty to his best friend had kept him away from Morgan. Of course, she always said he was like a big brother, so Bryan never imagined they'd have a conversation like this.

The bigger problem was that loyalty to his best friend was as strong as ever. Owen had made it clear time and time again that Morgan was off limits. Whatever game she was playing at, it wouldn't have a clean finish for either one of them.

"I've never had any complaints," Bryan bragged. To maintain control over this conversation and where it could lead, he figured the best strategy was to play up the man-whore reputation. He never flaunted it, but it had to be a sure-fire way to turn Morgan off.

"So you say," she teased as she unlocked the front door of her first-floor apartment.

It didn't take much to seduce Bryan. He liked women. He liked giving them pleasure as much as he liked finding his own pleasure with their bodies. If he'd been having this conversation with anyone else, any random woman in the entire world, he'd be naked and inside her by now, showing her exactly how good he was in bed.

But this was Morgan – his best friend's baby sister.

"What are you playing at, Morg?"

She hung the keys on a hook and did the same with her coat and Bryan followed suit, shedding his pea coat while waiting patiently for her to answer. When she turned to him that unbelievably hot mouth of hers curved, her intentions crystal clear in that piercing gaze. "I'm not playing."

He should leave, put his damn coat back on and take Morgan's advice by finding some random blonde to shack up with for the night. That'd be a hell of a lot less dangerous than staying within a fifty foot radius of the striking brunette who was testing his will power.

"You're drunk," he chuckled, remembering she'd done shots before they hit the pub, and then continued to drink during karaoke.

7

"Seeing Krisbitcha was a buzz-kill, actually. I sobered up pretty quickly." She held his gaze with those dark eyes sparking with something he should ignore.

"You know what happens to little girls who play with fire? They get burned," he warned in a voice so heated he barely recognized it as his own.

"I'm not a little girl."

Bryan had expected anger, had hoped for it because it was the only thing that was going to tamp his desire. Instead, Morgan's voice was as seductive as her gaze.

Her breaths were heavy and even though he kept his eyes locked on hers, he could see the hard rise and fall of her chest in his peripheral vision. He realized his own breaths matched hers and damn the room had just heated up to about a thousand degrees.

"I can see why Stacie was so upset earlier," she said before he could figure out his next move.

"What are you talking about?"

Her gaze shifted up and left and Bryan realized he had her wrists pinned against the wall. When the hell had he done that?

A smart man would have let go and stepped back. Bryan had never been accused of being smart.

"It is intimate, being held like this." When she licked her lips, the last ounce of Bryan's resolve evaporated like rain on the scorching steel of a ship's hull. Twelve years of denying himself the one woman he wanted engulfed him and he claimed her mouth like the selfish bastard he was.

God, she tasted good, something exotic and unique, the likes of which he'd never savored before. She moaned as their tongues dueled and Bryan was a goner. One kiss and they were at a point of no return.

Bryan didn't wax poetic about sex. Love, or even anything long term just wasn't his thing and he wasn't the kind of man who *made love* to a woman. Romantic gestures weren't in his repertoire and he certainly never heard birds singing or other crazy shit like that in his head when he was with a pretty and willing woman. Now, though, as Morgan's sweater dropped to the floor and his shirt followed, the feral tenor of that Drowning Pool song screamed between his ears, except instead of *let the bodies hit the floor*, he was screaming *let the clothing hit the floor*. Bryan had no intention of bodies hitting the floor. No, he intended to take Morgan right here against the wall next to her coat rack.

Her aggression only fueled his need and if he really gave a shit, he'd ask if she was always like this or if it was a year of celibacy that made her hot and crazed. But asking required speaking and Bryan preferred his tongue right where it was, diving into every corner of her mouth to savor her exotic flavor.

Except, damn, there were so many other places on her body to explore.

Her hands on his back were heaven, pulling him to her, those blunt nails offering a tantalizing scrape as they moved across his muscles. Putting his own hands to work, his deft fingers flicked open the front clasp of her bra with no effort. Her skin was as soft and hot on her breasts as it was everywhere else and finding her nipples hard and tight was like an invitation to taste them.

The shortest distance between two points is a straight line, but Bryan was more interested in tasting every inch of skin. He kissed her jaw line and spent a little time playing where her pulse throbbed wildly, all the while pinching and teasing those taut nipples between his fingers.

Her little mewls and moans were driving him mad, causing him to grind his erection into the sexy vee of her legs. He could feel her heat even through both of their jeans. When her hands slid down his back and came around to the button of his pants, he knew his mouth had to hurry. Once she made contact with his aching cock, he wasn't going to last long, but no way could he slow her down now.

Bryan claimed her nipple between his teeth, tugging gently and pulling a pleasured cry from her. Her deft fingers paused at the opening of his jeans as his tongue flicked and twirled the tight bud.

Yeah, that's right, sweetheart, let me have my way with you.

Her hands might have become paralyzed, but Bryan could multitask. It took both of his hands and all of his concentration, but he got Morgan's tight jeans open and pushed over her hips, along with what felt like a tiny little thong. He'd have liked to check her out in that, along with the lacy bra they'd already discarded, but the urgency exploding between them left no time for gawking.

Aw, hell. She was naked. There was definitely time for gawking. Bryan stepped back enough to take her all in, every gorgeous inch as she stood against the wall, her olive skin flushed with need. She didn't play shy and lord have mercy she didn't need to. He'd never seen any woman with such perfect curves, from her round breasts to the curve of her stomach and the flare of her hips.

He pulled his wallet out of his pocket, but had trouble getting a grip on the condom hiding inside. Christ, were his hands shaking?

"Give it to me," Morgan demanded and at first he thought she meant sex until she held out her hand, obviously wanting the condom.

While she tore at the package, Bryan rid himself of the jeans and boxers – the only obstacle left before he got to what he really wanted. Before Morgan could slide the condom over him, he took it from her. At this point, if her hands touched him, he was going to embarrass himself like a teenage boy right there in the foyer.

Fortunately the shakes had subsided and Bryan got the damn thing on without any drama. The fire in her eyes told him she was ready, more than ready, and the wetness he found between her legs proved it. Lifting her legs around his hips and using the wall for leverage, he slammed home with a loud grunt, hardly able to believe this was real.

Morgan.

Twelve years of fantasies didn't come close to living up to the reality of how good she felt.

"Don't stop," she pleaded and Bryan claimed her mouth again, cupping her perfect ass in his hands as he lost himself in the frenzy of their passion.

Her pebbled nipples scraped against his chest. Her incredible thighs strangled his hips. Her delicate hands clung to his deltoids. Everywhere their bodies met was a perfect union.

As he thrust in and out of her, her hips met him and retreated in a perfect rhythm, so perfect he couldn't even kiss her anymore. The need to watch, to see where they were joined shifted his gaze south and it made him harder, if that was even possible. Damn, that was hot. He'd commit the view to memory because as incredible as it was, something deep inside his mind echoed with the treachery of what he was doing.

It was easy to ignore all the wrongs and focus on what was so right, especially as Morgan's moans alerted him to her building orgasm. He was close too – too close – but tethered the rope, wanting to feel her pleasure before he lost himself in the sensations.

"Bryan," she moaned and he'd never heard anything hotter in his entire life.

Keep saying my name, he silently begged, unable to form the words. Whether it was the chemistry between them or just her own modus operandi in the throes of passion, Bryan didn't know and didn't much care because she continued to utter and moan his name as her sex clenched around him and the rest of her body went rigid with the intensity of her release.

"Morg," he bellowed before muttering who the hell knows what during the pleasure of his own release.

The aftershocks riddled their bodies as he held her there against the wall, their panting slowing as the seconds ticked by on the clock in the kitchen.

"Morgan," he sighed, forcing his bone structure to function so he could stop using her for support and actually stand upright to look at her.

She was a hot mess, her hair wild and her eyes sparkling. What was normally a beautiful olive tone was replaced by a pink flush. When his gaze found her smile, his heart kicked up more than a few beats and Bryan knew he was in a world of trouble.

That beautiful smile couldn't keep reality from crashing down on them as he realized what they'd just done – what *he'd* just done.

Morgan must have recognized that reality too because her smile faded, replaced with a stern expression. "Don't you even think about telling my brother."

Chapter 1

One fumble, two interceptions, and forty-three points later, the Seattle Seahawks had claimed the Lombardi Trophy. Bryan Curtis was ecstatic and a couple months ago, he'd be celebrating as hard as the rest of the Number Twelves in the downtown pub that was buzzing with the excitement of a first Super Bowl win. Tonight, however, he was more interested in seeing some of that sexy fan gear tossed on the floor while the woman who had worn it writhed beneath his body.

"Dance with me." Morgan Landry grabbed his hand and pulled him off the bar stool he'd been keeping warm for the last twenty minutes. Bryan wasn't much of a dancer, but Morgan was the one woman he could never refuse.

He went easily, sliding to the floor and moving to the back of the pub where the dance floor was filling up fast. Apparently, there were a lot of Bon Jovi fans in Seattle. Or maybe it was just the euphoria of the Super Bowl victory.

It was a natural reflex to complain about doing something he didn't particularly enjoy, but as he was about to voice a protest, Morgan did a little dirty dancing move right against his thigh. She was wearing a tattered denim skirt that had seen better days and damn him if he didn't wish he was in shorts so he could feel her skin rubbing against his. As it was, he could feel the heat of her legs through the denim. Maybe his own body heat had cranked up…along with a certain part of his anatomy.

Then the chorus hit and Morgan stepped back, rocking out to the 80's anthem as though she'd been born with big hair bands in her blood.

She sang along, her hips and arms moving to the beat. "Come on," she demanded, grabbing his hands. "I know you know this one."

You Give Love a Bad Name was a classic, he wouldn't deny that, but Bryan preferred Bon Jovi's more recent music. He moved with a little more rhythm, not because he was interested in dancing but because he was interested in seeing Morgan smile. He scanned the bar for Morgan's brother and found him at the pool table, shaking his head with an amused smile. Good, that meant he had no suspicions about what was really going through Bryan's brain.

If his best friend knew Bryan's main objective was to get Morgan naked, there'd be hell to pay. The Landry temper was like a Category 5 hurricane in a coastal town. Morgan controlled hers a hell of a lot better than Owen did. Add a good dose of betrayal – something Bryan had been guilty of for a good six weeks now – and the force would be immeasurable.

Bryan nodded at Owen before focusing on Morgan. He let his guard down since Owen didn't seem suspicious about them dancing together. The crowd swallowed them and the pool table was lost from view. Morgan spun around, grinding her perfect ass into Bryan's groin and if he hadn't already been speeding toward a painful erection, her little move guaranteed that destination. Bryan gripped her hips because what the hell else was he supposed to do.

And just that quickly, she stepped away and spun around, singing along and smiling as though she was having the time of her life. There was a time when Bryan had enjoyed being out on the dance floor with her, but that was before he'd crossed the line a couple months back. Now all he could think about was getting her alone, getting her naked, and making her scream his name.

The song faded out and a new one amped up. "That was fun," Morgan said, patting him on the chest and spinning away. She gave him a quick glance as she left him standing there. The little temptress had just teased him into oblivion and by the smile on her face and the sway of her ass, she knew it. If Owen wasn't across the room, he'd toss Morgan over his shoulder and carry her out of there and straight to the nearest bed. Bryan, however, didn't have a death wish. No way could he go all cave man on his best friend's sister – at least not when said best friend was watching. He'd find a way to get her back later.

Morgan reached the pool table before Bryan finally decided to head back to the bar. He needed a tall cold one to cool him off. Otherwise, he was going to act on those cave man urges, Owen's wrath be damned.

"Don't let Owen catch you looking at Morgan like that," Ty Sullivan warned, holding out a sweating pint glass as Bryan hit the bar. Bryan not only took the glass, but drank the amber down like a parched sailor stranded on a desert isle. He grunted, knowing that's exactly where he'd like to be right now, but not stranded alone. He imagined tattered clothes abandoned on a sandy beach while the woman who had worn them sought shade and something a little less innocent beneath Bryan's body.

"What are you talking about?" Playing dumb was his only defense and he prayed it was better than the defense the Broncos had played today in the Super Bowl. Leaning his six foot two frame against the mahogany bar of his favorite Seattle pub, Bryan continued to watch Morgan with more than just interest. He had to figure out how to blow this party and get the brunette alone.

"I get the impression he's a little protective of his sister," Ty rambled on in that heavy Boston accent Bryan still hadn't gotten used to. "I don't know, maybe that doesn't extend to you."

Bryan snickered as he finally turned his attention away from Morgan. "Oh, it extends to every man with or without a pulse." The status of best friend didn't exclude Bryan from the population of men who weren't allowed to lay a finger on Owen Landry's little sister. "But it's not a problem. I'm not interested."

It was Ty's turn to snicker. "Really? Because you were just looking at her like she's the only woman on earth."

Ty was obviously spending too much time with the women and jumping to conclusions based on hopeful romantic notions. "I think you're mistaken," Bryan insisted, focusing on a group of women on the other side of the pub.

"Listen, it's none of my biz. I just figured you'd want to keep it on the down low if you don't want your buddy castrating you."

That was good advice. Owen trusted Bryan. Until a couple months ago, Bryan had never betrayed that trust. Now he was betraying his best friend once or twice a week. Even now, Bryan's brain was formulating a plan to get Morgan into bed tonight.

Owen was a nice guy, the best friend anyone could ask for. Bryan couldn't count the number of times Owen had had his back when he found himself in a tight spot. The man didn't judge and didn't question. His only expectation was to not have his trust betrayed – when it was the man could be mean and vengeful. Bryan was sure his Cajun buddy had learned a few moves from some nasty old gators on the bayou.

Those moves didn't usually extend to Bryan. In fact, the two of them always had each other's backs. They'd walked away from bar fights, sports brawls, and drunken idiocy together. Bryan stood by Owen while his bud went through two divorces. Of course, Morgan had been there too. She and her brother were tight. Growing up with an abusive, drunk father would do that.

To Bryan's annoyance, Ty nudged his shoulder. The guy was tall, but swam to stay fit so didn't have the size Bryan did. Hitting the weights four days a week for the last ten years had really pumped Bryan up. The only guy he wasn't confident about taking down was Owen. "Just a heads up, I'm not the only one who's noticed."

Bryan had hoped the conversation was over. A blonde made eye contact with him and even though he wasn't interested in the slightest, she would make a good cover. Too bad Ty seemed to want to talk this topic to death. The guy was definitely spending too much time with the women in their circle of friends. Since Bryan was interested to know who else had noticed his glances so he could take the appropriate countermeasures, he kept the conversation rolling. "What do you mean?"

"Carter thinks there's something going on with you two."

Stupendous. If Ty's girlfriend Jenny Carter had suspicions, she'd blab to her best friend Stacie. Then Stacie would tell Owen because those two love birds didn't keep secrets from each other. "There's nothing going on. She's like a little sister to me." Which made Bryan a complete pervert. The sister card had been an easy play until a month and a half ago when their relationship took an unexpected turn. Now it just made him sound like a sick bastard. Add that to disloyal friend and he was building quite the resume.

Unable to resist the allure of Morgan's presence, Bryan turned his attention back to where it wanted to be. "I was just checking her out. You gotta admit, she looks damn good in that skirt."

The tattered denim frayed at mid-thigh. Morgan was all legs, slender at the calf, enough to grab onto at the thigh, and hips that had the perfect amount of curve. That denim skirt looked like a thrift store toss out and the tight-fitting raglan Seahawks shirt would have been right at home in Bryan's box of rags he used while tinkering on an engine, but damn if the woman didn't look hot as hell in them.

Ty laughed. "I'd like to lie and say I didn't notice, but yeah, she does."

Morgan and Owen were playing a round of pool in the corner of the pub. The siblings were ruthlessly competitive, so Owen was focused on the table. When he wasn't, Stacie held his attention, so Bryan wasn't too concerned about being caught gawking by his buddy. Apparently, he should have been concerned about everyone else catching him.

When Morgan's next play brought her to the bar side of the table and she bent over in the denim rag, Bryan choked back a moan as Ty abruptly turned to the bar. Yeah, if Jenny caught Ty checking Morgan out, he'd be the one facing castration.

Morgan nailed the seven in the corner before sashaying around the table to line up another shot. This time, Bryan got a clear shot of rave green lace and cleavage – until Morgan lifted her lids and locked eyes with him.

Aw, hell, that look meant one thing: he wasn't going to get a wink of sleep tonight. He was good with that. Waiting, though, might just kill him.

Normally Bryan didn't mind the wait or the chase. The women he usually hooked up with didn't offer much of a challenge, so when one did, the change of pace was welcome. All that had changed with Morgan. He wasn't supposed to want her, wasn't supposed to have her, but he did and the having only made the wanting stronger and made the waiting hell.

Life had been so different a year ago. Owen and Bryan would hit a club. Owen would go home alone, Bryan would go home with the hottest woman who'd buy his cheap pick-up lines. Things took a turn for crazy when Owen brought Stacie home one night. Bryan had never thought that one night could change life so drastically, but it'd happened more than once in the past year.

Once Owen and Stacie fell in love, which was almost immediately, the club outings morphed into pub gatherings where Jenny would join the three of them when she'd finally allowed her workaholic self to close up shop for the night. Then Morgan moved from Louisiana just before Ty transferred from Boston. More often than not, six became seven when Morgan dragged along one random guy after another. Bryan had continued to seek out the kind of company that suited his needs, but for the first time in his life, casual sex with random women had gotten old. Unfortunately, his reputation was well-known and to keep from doing something stupid, like sleeping with his best friend's sister, he'd kept on keeping on.

Well, at least until that first night with Morgan.

"What are you stewing over?" Ty asked, rescuing Bryan from his reverie.

"Clan Landry has been monopolizing the pool table. Someone should do something about that." One or both of the siblings had been at the table since the big game ended. It wasn't the first time they'd done this and honestly Bryan didn't give a shit, but Morgan wouldn't leave while Owen still owned the table and the only way to get him to give it up was to beat him. Morgan seemed to be the only one capable enough, but she wasn't consistent. She'd beat him one game and lose to him the next. Bryan could likely beat Owen if Morgan wasn't around to distract him. Tonight he was more interested in her playing with his cue stick than shooting pool, so he wasn't confident in his pool-shooting skills.

"It's the wrong kind of pool for me," Ty echoed Bryan's thoughts, only the swimmer likely wasn't thinking about where he wanted to sink his cue stick. "You're going to have to talk Carter into it. She can be a shark if she sets her mind to it."

Bryan had no doubt about that. Jenny was a shark about everything.

"Next round's on me if you make an attempt."

"Hit me," Ty said, the Irish in him not prone to turn down a free beer. "I'll see what kind of damage I can do at that table."

Five minutes later Bryan was nursing another beer at the bar, Ty was whispering in Jenny's ear in the corner, and Owen and Morgan were still trying to best each other at the pool table.

Would this night never end?

He'd kill for something other than post-game analysis on the big screen. The only options were to watch Morgan or pretend to be interested in the blonde on the opposite end of the pub.

Choices.

"Buy me a drink?" the blonde asked, sidling up on the stool next to where Bryan leaned on the bar. Well, that decision was made.

"Whatever the pretty lady wants," Bryan signaled the bartender.

"Sex on the beach," she purred. Bryan nearly choked on his beer. Months ago it would have been a pick up line he'd welcome. Now, not so much.

"Great game," she said, trying to keep Bryan's attention. He wasn't particularly fond of small talk, but it seemed to be a necessary evil. It'd be so much easier just to walk up to an attractive woman and ask her if she wanted to go somewhere private and have sex, but he couldn't imagine that would work in his favor. So he'd played the game for years, buying women drinks, flirting, making small talk, doing the whole get to know you thing. It hadn't actually been all that bad when he was interested, but interested was not a state he was in tonight – at least not in this woman. The one playing pool across the bar held that honor.

"Awesome game," Bryan agreed because he really was ecstatic the Hawks had taken the title.

"So…are you here alone?" she asked with less confidence than when she'd ordered the drink. Playing hard to get wasn't Bryan's MO and he rarely backed down from an advance after making eye contact. Unfortunately, with his well-earned reputation, if any of the crew saw him ignoring a pretty blonde, there would be questions.

Bryan nodded at the pool table. "I'm here with friends."

"Oh," she said, likely doing the math. "Is one of them your girlfriend?"

Bryan wanted to say yes, which was the craziest thought he'd had since taking Morgan up against her foyer wall. Then again, he hadn't been thinking at all that night, just acting on pure sexual need.

Even though he wanted to claim her, the truth of their relationship was that it was casual. That's what they'd agreed to and it seemed to work for Morgan as well as it had been working for him. He could lie to the pretty blonde to deter her interest, but that also wasn't his MO. Besides, one lie typically led to another and he

He could picture it

already felt neck deep in it by keeping his hook-ups with Morgan a secret.

"No," he finally muttered, opting for honesty so he wouldn't risk getting caught in the lie later. He could picture it now, the blonde saying something within earshot of Owen about Bryan having a girlfriend. Owen would do the math and wonder why the hell he was using Morgan as cover instead of taking the spoils. It was Bryan's own fault for building the *man-whore loves blondes* reputation over the years. No one knew his true reason for pursuing blondes and it wasn't something he was about to admit to now.

"Well, maybe you want to join me and my friends," she suggested, batting her mascara-thickened lashes as the fruity drink hovered in front of her bright pink lips.

"Maybe later," he offered without committing. Dammit, he didn't want to deal with this shit right now.

"Okay, well, don't take too long. We might be hitting another bar soon, but I could be talked into staying." She held up her glass as she slid off the stool. "Thanks for the drink."

"Sure thing." He watched her walk away to put on a show for any of his friends who might be watching, but her rave green stretch pants only reminded him of the lace under Morgan's worn-out shirt.

When the blonde glanced over her shoulder, Bryan gave her a quick nod and smile. *Shit.* This was going to complicate the night. There was nothing Bryan hated more than complicated entanglements. That's why he generally avoided them.

Shifting his gaze back to the pool table, he knew shit was going to hit the fan when he caught Morgan's searing stare.

***

"Damn, girl, looks like you're gonna score tonight and I'm not talking about pool."

Given the stare down she was locked in with Bryan, it didn't take a genius to know what Jenny was referring to.

"Bryan likes blondes," Morgan uttered obstinately, "and he's a man-whore. He's looking for an easy lay and I'm just letting him know it's not me." What Morgan was trying to tell Bryan was that she wanted to strangle him for checking out that blonde bimbo. She wouldn't say the words out loud, though, not to Jenny and especially not to Bryan. Their arrangement was casual and he could look and touch if he felt so inclined.

Morgan was actually more annoyed with herself for getting pissed off when she'd caught him looking. Everyone knew he liked blondes. Since she had no ownership of him, he was free to do whatever he wanted. Up until now she thought Bryan would be going home with her tonight. Now she wasn't so sure. If Jenny was making assumptions, maybe it was better if she and Bryan didn't hook up tonight.

"Is that how you define the non-verbal communication going on between you two? Because from my perspective, wow." Jenny fanned herself with both hands. "It'd be hard to say no to someone who was looking at me like that."

Morgan liked Jenny, most days. She was strong-willed and opinionated, not unlike Morgan, so occasionally their personalities clashed more easily than they melded. "I guess that's the difference between the princess and the realist," Morgan said without mirth. She wasn't worried about offending Jenny. The woman had thick skin and even if she didn't, Morgan needed to turn the conversation away from the way Bryan was seducing her with his burning gaze.

Jenny laughed. "Damn, girlfriend, you don't hold back, do you?"

"I could say the same for you, princess." This time she added a bit of sarcasm to the label she often used for the woman who was living what she called her happily ever after.

"Touché," Jenny said with a curtsy. "On that note, I'm going to go find my handsome prince. You might say no to a sure thing, but that's not my style."

Morgan resisted the urge to breathe a sigh of relief. She'd managed to sink the eight ball before the rest of her solids thanks to Jenny's distraction, so she popped the cue stick into the rack and found her way to the bar for a drink. It wasn't a coincidence the spot she occupied was right next to where Bryan had been holding vigil for the last twenty minutes.

She spoke without looking at him, hoping the intentional avoidance didn't look so obvious to their friends. "If you don't stop looking at me like that, we're going to have a lot of explaining to do." Had they not been out with their friends, Morgan would have encouraged rather than deterred him. His heated gaze had her skin practically burning through her clothes and she was uncomfortably aroused.

"You make it hard for a guy not to look at you, Morg. Bend over in a short skirt and a low cut shirt. See how many men don't look."

"I dress like this all the time," she said.

"And I look all the time. It's never bothered you before."

"Yeah, well, Jenny's never commented on you staring before. If she's making comments to me, you know she's making them to Stacie. Then guess who'll be invited to the party."

"We could just tell him," Bryan muttered. He'd wanted to since that first night. She both loved and hated the loyalty between him and Owen, but no way did she want her brother to know what was going on between her and Bryan.

"He'll either drag us to the courthouse to get married or he'll lock me away and do who knows what to you. I'm pretty sure you want to keep your *little* sailor fully attached."

"Big sailor," he corrected when she teased him about his size. There certainly wasn't anything little about Bryan, but she didn't need to stroke his ego. "This is the twenty-first century, we're free to do whatever we want. Besides, I betrayed him. I'm willing to suffer the consequences."

Morgan rolled her eyes at his noble gesture. Men were such

idiots. "Are you willing to give up the fun we're having? Because that's what will happen if he finds out."

"Morg," he groaned, but not in that pleasurable way that she loved.

"I'm serious. If he finds out, we're done. We both know this isn't a long-term thing anyway and I'm not willing to put up with his crap for a little nookie."

She wasn't ready to give Bryan up. Her teenage crush had turned into full-blown fantasies years ago. Unfortunately, Bryan had always treated her like a little sister, so she'd never thought he was interested. He'd proved otherwise six weeks ago on the rock my holy world scale. She'd never had such wild, unabashed sex in her life. Morgan didn't have a lot of experience to compare it to, but being with Bryan was amazing. Plus, it just kept getting better. Even though they'd been together at least a dozen times now, she had yet to live out all those fantasies she'd developed over the years.

"Fine," Bryan snarled. "I won't tell him, but throw me a bone here. Are we hooking up tonight?"

Morgan turned around to scope out their friends. Owen had Stacie pinned in the corner near the pool table, probably whispering dirty things in her ear given her smile. Jenny and Ty were racking up the pool table, taking turns glancing at the bar where Morgan stood with Bryan. "Probably not a good idea the way we're being watched. In fact, I'm calling in my back-up plan."

Morgan reached in her pocket for her phone, but Bryan grabbed her wrist. "What the hell is your back-up plan?"

She didn't like the anger in his voice, nor the way he held her wrist. When she eyed where he held her, then shifted her gaze to meet his, Bryan dropped the hold as though she'd burned him. He'd obviously read her expression – the *let go of me now or you'll be choking on your balls* look was an effective deterrent for any man who liked his parts where they were.

Morgan took a deep breath to ease her racing heart. Bryan had never touched her aggressively like that. He could be aggressive in bed, but it wasn't possessive. The way he'd just held her wrist had spoken volumes from a book she'd read from as a kid. She learned a lot from that schooling, watching her father beat her mother to a pulp if she didn't do what he demanded.

Given the way Bryan's eyes had softened, she didn't need to tell him to never touch her like that again. She could already read his apology loud and clear which was better than verbalizing what had just happened. She didn't like talking about the past or dwelling on it and since Bryan was in the know on her childhood, it was best to steer clear of the topic.

"Derek is my back-up plan," she announced, reaching for her phone again.

"Who's Derek?"

"One of my classmates. Don't worry, he's gay, but he can pull off straight. We do this for each other all the time."

"Do what for each other?" His grumbly question made it clear he didn't like the idea of a back-up plan that involved another man, but since he'd been eying that blonde bimbo earlier, he lost the right to dislike it.

"Pretend to be on a date so neither one of us gets hit on. You want me to call my friend Holly? She's hot and blonde." Morgan hated how much he liked blondes but Holly was anti-men at the moment, so while she'd distract him from the bimbo across the bar, she wouldn't go home with him.

Dammit, she realized she was nurturing her own possessive streak and that was a bad sign. She and Bryan were just messing around, no strings, no commitment, just the way they both preferred. Morgan wasn't sure why Bryan was anti-marriage, and he never asked about her reasons, though given his knowledge of her childhood, he probably had more than half a clue.

"No, thanks. If I thought I needed reinforcements, I'd hit up that blonde over there. In fact, I think I will."

Bryan ordered another beer and…Sex on the Beach? Seriously?

Figures the courtesy-of-bleach blonde would drink something completely slutty.

Morgan sipped her beer and kept her trap shut as Bryan leaned on the bar and waited for the drinks. He gave her a quick nod before heading across the bar to where a group of bimbos, including the blonde he'd been talking to a few minutes ago, were sitting at a table.

And sure enough, he handed the blonde the slutty concoction in the tall glass. Her ridiculous giggle echoed throughout the bar. Morgan's skin prickled as though her sixth grade teacher had just scraped her long, nicotine-stained fingernails down the chalkboard.

It wasn't jealousy surging through Morgan's veins. She only wore green when she was rooting for one of Seattle's teams. Even though it was a strong color in the Landry family, she'd made the decision years ago not to act on any of the emotions she'd inherited from her abusive father. Instead of chasing Bryan across the bar and telling him to stay the hell away from that blonde and any other woman, she found Derek's number and hit send. He answered on the first ring and said he'd be there in twenty.

"Oh, and Derek, when you get here, your name is Alex and you need to kiss me with tongue."

Chapter 2

If Bryan was going to be an asshole, she could play that game too. She'd blown the Derek card letting Bryan know he was gay, but who's to say she didn't have a back-up plan to her back-up plan. Derek liked role-play.

Jenny came over to the bar and ordered another round for the four still hanging around the pool table. "Just FYI, girlfriend, you're shooting daggers."

"He's an asshole," she said without thinking. Dammit, why couldn't she keep her emotions under wraps and her big fat trap shut?

"No shit. Everyone in this bar knows you feel that way. What'd he do?"

Morgan couldn't make this be about his chicken shit loyalty to her brother or the slutty blonde he was clearly interested in taking home. She had to make it about something else if she hoped to keep their friends with bennies status under wraps. "He said you look like a twenty-cent whore in that shirt. He had some choice things to say about Stacie too." Jenny looked fantastic, as always, classy and sexy in a Number Twelve jersey that hugged her curves.

"Where the hell does he get off saying that shit?" Jenny spat.

"That's what I said. When I stuck up for you two, he said I

looked like a fat slut."

Jenny's eyes were as round as a full moon. "Are you serious? He said that? To your face?"

Morgan nodded to affirm the lie.

"You gonna sick your brother on him?"

That's exactly what Morgan was trying to avoid. "Nah, that'd be too easy," she quipped. "I've got better ways of getting back at him."

Morgan realized a little too late she'd riled Jenny's temper at the expense of protecting herself. Regretting the lie was an inconvenience she'd have to live with. Short of admitting to something she didn't even want to own up to in her own head, she couldn't back out now. "Oh, hey Jenny, I'm sorry. I shouldn't have said anything."

"No, believe me, I'm glad you did. I'm going over there right now."

Shit. Morgan should have thought this out. She thought about stopping Jenny, but then again, it'd be fun to see her go off on Bryan. Since Morgan couldn't do that, in public or otherwise, this was the best she could dish out.

Teach him to flirt with a blonde bimbo and buy her a slutty drink!

Jenny stormed with grave purpose across the large room. Physically, Bryan had nearly half a foot and eighty pounds on her, but the petite woman was undeterred. She poked her beautifully manicured finger into Bryan's chest, causing him to wince before he stood in stunned silence. Jenny's head bopped back and forth as she apparently chewed Bryan a new one.

"Where'd your friend go?" The bartender asked when he delivered the last of the drinks.

"I got it," Morgan offered. It was the least she could do after stirring the pot.

She'd waitressed during college, so knew how to carry four glasses across a crowded bar. Ty met her on the near side of the pool table, relieving her of two glasses. After she delivered the other two to the lovebirds, she glimpsed across the room to see Jenny's head still bopping around. Reading Bryan's lips and body language, she saw his denial.

"What's going on over there?" Ty asked.

"Bryan was being an ass so Jenny's giving him a piece of her mind."

Ty laughed. "Looks like it's more than just a piece."

When Jenny finished her tirade, Bryan's gaze lifted to Morgan, a furious fire in his eyes.

Shit. She was going to have to face the music of her little lie. Bryan started across the bar, the blonde watching him with a dollop of horror plastered on her pretty face. Morgan steeled herself for Bryan's wrath, but before he made it across the bar, Derek swooped in and swept her off her feet.

***

There was nothing that boiled Bryan's blood more than seeing some guy, any guy, shove his tongue down Morgan's throat. Worse, she didn't seem to mind.

"So that's Derek, huh?" Bryan asked as he settled at the bar again. His voice was steady but he couldn't hide all the angst that'd been stewing ever since that guy walked in and started playing tonsil hockey with Morgan.

"No, that's Alex."

Who the hell was Alex? "What happened to Derek?"

"He was busy."

Bryan grunted and took a long drink. Morgan was playing it cool and maybe he deserved that for the performance he'd put on with Serenity over in the corner. Morgan was the one who insisted they keep their relationship a secret, so she shouldn't be pissed if he was playing by her rules. Then again, maybe she was pissed because he'd physically removed Alex from her body.

"Alex is gay too, right?" Damn, the guy better be for the way he'd been touching Morgan.

"No," she laughed. Bryan didn't like the humor in her voice. "Alex is definitely not gay."

Okay, enough was enough. Bryan pushed off the bar and faced her. "What the hell are you playing at, Morg?"

Oh, yeah, she was playing him. It was written all over that mischievous smile. "I'm sure I have no idea what you're talking about."

"First you sick Jenny on me and then you let some guy stick his tongue down your throat and put his hands all over your ass."

"I didn't sick Jenny on you and Alex, well, he's just really...affectionate."

What Alex had done was about three million steps beyond affectionate. "Why'd you invite him here? You going home with him tonight?"

The amused look faded "I invited him here because we need to redirect Jenny and Ty's suspicions. Besides, you were all over that blonde bimbo. Looks like she's a sure thing for you, so I don't know why you've got your tighty whiteys in a bind."

"I wasn't all over Serenity–"

"Oh, she has a name," Morgan snarled. "Serenity. Perfect."

It was his turn to be amused. "Green isn't your color."

"I'm not jealous," she countered, but Bryan recognized the emotion because he was wearing his own shade.

"You suggested I find company with someone else," he reminded her.

"I did not."

Hadn't she? Hell, she'd even offered to call in her friend when she'd called Derek. How the hell had she ended up with Alex? Was there more going on with them than Bryan really wanted to know about?

It was unheard of for Bryan to get possessive with someone he was sleeping with and he'd never had an issue with women carrying on with someone else. He always used a condom and if a woman was involved with someone other than just him, the chances of her getting attached and asking for more were significantly reduced.

Morgan, though, he didn't want to share her with anyone and wasn't that going to cause problems.

"What's going on here, Morg? First you say we're not on for tonight, then you get jealous because I'm trying to keep the cover *you* insisted on?" At this point, Bryan would rather face Owen's wrath than keep up this deception.

She sat on the stool with one leg crossed over the other, revealing a whole lot of tempting thigh and her arms folded across her breasts, accentuating some inviting cleavage. Her body language signaled she was shutting him out, but damn if it wasn't turning him on. "You're the one who practically tossed Alex across the room."

"The guy had his hands on your ass." Alex was lucky to be alive. Of course, he was probably hating life right now with Owen reading him the riot act.

"So who's jealous?" Morgan cooed.

"Jesus, Morgan. If you're gonna start playing games, I'm done." He didn't want to be done. Hell, they'd just gotten started, but Bryan didn't do complicated relationships. He liked women. He liked sex. That was it.

"I'm not playing games. I'm just trying to keep what we're doing under wraps. You're the one going all alpha male here."

She had a point. Bryan wasn't sure what had possessed him to get all possessive, but he couldn't reel it in. He wanted Morgan. He didn't want to share her. How could something so simple be so complicated?

Bryan grunted, not willing to admit his part but also not willing to apologize.

"Do you really want to be done?" she asked, her voice softening as her arms dropped and she gripped the bar stool. "Because I

31

thought we were having a good time."

"I was having a good time until tonight." The situation with Jenny was uncomfortable but it was seeing Morgan with another man that had him mental. "Maybe we need to establish some rules."

"Rules?" Bryan played by the rules while in uniform, but when it came to women, there weren't many rules he followed. "Like what, we don't see anyone else?"

Fear flashed in her eyes and Bryan was surprised he wasn't feeling it himself. He hadn't been exclusive with anyone in almost a decade. That wasn't the way he rolled, but shit, had he really not been interested in anyone since he started messing around with Morgan? That revelation was interesting.

"We see who we want, do what we want, just like always, but maybe we just don't do it in front of each other."

That was a perfect arrangement. Bryan maintained his freedom but kept things going with Morgan. So why wasn't he excited about her solution?

"That works for me if it works for you," he said, unwilling to explore his internal motives for keeping her away from other men.

"It works for me."

"Great. Now can you go fix things with Jenny?" He didn't like being in her sights. He hadn't said anything about her looking like a whore and given the smirk on Morgan's face when Jenny had been tearing him a new one, he knew she'd set him up.

"Sure. Sorry. I'm not really sure why I went all psycho on you."

"Because the thought of missing out on some quality naked time with me had you frustrated."

"Yeah, you just keep telling your ego that." She patted him on the shoulder as she slid off the stool. "I'm going to go rescue Derek from my brother."

Derek? "Wait, I thought you said that was Alex."

Morgan winked as she walked away.

***

For Bryan, a night out usually ended with him in bed with a woman. Lately that woman had been Morgan. Not tonight.

No, tonight had been a complete debacle. They'd set some ground rules – that was just great. Rules usually had him saying good-bye and moving on to the next willing body, but for whatever reason, Morgan's rules didn't scare him off. No, instead they pissed him off.

He didn't want her seeing anyone else, whether he was in the know or not and how fucked up was that? Christ, he was getting in over his head with her and yet he had no desire to grab a life jacket.

What the hell was happening to him?

After Morgan left with Derek, Bryan felt compelled to leave with Serenity just to keep up the rouse. They'd hit another bar and he found an excuse to leave after the first drink. Serenity had programmed her number into his phone and Bryan let her just to avoid any further discussion, but had no intentions of ever calling.

Yeah, he was *that* guy.

So here he was, about to board the ferry for a riveting night alone in his bed. *Outstanding.*

His phone beeped with a text message. A moment of panic made his stomach lurch before remembering he had not given his number to Serenity. The last thing he needed was to field unwanted phone calls. Relief and frustration did the tango when his phone displayed Morgan as the sender.

Whr r u?

Bryan was tempted to ask her why she wanted to know, but it wasn't in his nature to play games, so he answered her straight up. *About to board the ferry.*

Her response was quick. *Last 1?*

Great, had she changed her mind about hooking up? There weren't a lot of options. This was the last ferry to Bremerton. If he boarded, he was in Bremerton for the night because he'd had too much to drink and couldn't drive. If he missed this boat, he was homeless for the night unless she took him in or he swallowed his pride and called Owen.

Sometimes living on the other side of the sound really sucked.

His response was answered with a call instead of another text.

"Your timing stinks," he told her. "I've got five minutes before the last boat leaves."

"Good thing I didn't wait five more minutes then." He could hear the smile in her voice and he was glad she was more relaxed than earlier in the night.

"Good thing. Where are you?"

"Behind you, top of the stairs."

Bryan turned to find her just where she'd said. She was wearing jeans now, so she'd obviously gone home. It was cold enough that he got the change in wardrobe, but he wished she was still in that skirt.

"What happened with Derek?" he said into the phone. She held her ground at the top of the stairs and Bryan remained in his spot at the other end of the terminal.

"He took me home."

"Home to your place or his?"

"I told you, Derek's gay. Besides, we're not supposed to ask. I didn't ask you about *Serenity*." The sarcasm – or was it jealousy – kicked in on Serenity's name, spurring Bryan to poke the bear a little more.

"No, you didn't. What if I hadn't answered my phone?"

"I'd be standing in the ferry terminal alone." The amusement was back in her voice and he could see a smirk.

"Come here," he commanded, done with this game and needing to feel her body pressed against his.

"You come here," she countered.

It felt like a power play and Bryan wasn't sure he wanted to give up any more power to her than he already had. Unfortunately, she was stubborn. She'd stand there until dawn just to prove a point.

"Meet in the middle?" He saw her smile brighten and was happy they'd found a compromise. She closed up her phone and he followed her lead, stepping out when she did, careful not to run even though his instincts were screaming for him to sprint.

The terminal was empty. What few people had been lingering were now boarding the ferry. "You're a tease," he said when they were close enough for conversation.

"Not the greeting I was hoping for." She stopped just inches in front of him. "You just going to stand there or are you going to kiss me?"

She'd been playing with him all night. He was done with the games but that didn't mean he was going to make this easy. No, she'd have to work for what they both wanted. "Someone might be watching."

"No one important," she shrugged.

"How did you know I was alone?" he teased.

"I took a chance."

"That wasn't very smart." Morgan's ground rules basically granted him permission to go home with Serenity. As far as Owen, Stacie, Jenny, and Ty knew, he had and Bryan was sure Morgan would hear about it at some point. He could preempt any issues by explaining himself now, but explaining himself was like admitting there was more to this relationship than there was.

No complications, man, he reminded himself.

"Nothing about what we're doing is smart, but it's fun."

And that was Morgan. She embraced life, lived by her own rules. It was one of the things Bryan really liked about her, but damn if it wasn't messing with his head.

"You like living on the edge, don't you?" he teased, focusing on the moment rather than the drama playing out in his head.

"No more than you." She leaped into his arms and kissed him with absolutely no reserve or subtlety. Her open mouth was warm, her tongue demanding as she took and gave. It was exactly what

Bryan wanted and more specifically, it was what he needed. Her warm tongue and hot body was the perfect reminder of what they were both in this for. Sex. No strings, no commitment. Just a couple of friends finding what they needed with each other.

Hell, they needed to get back to her place. Screw the busses. Bryan planned to hail a cab and over-tip the driver if he could break a world speed record for getting them back to Morgan's apartment in less than ten minutes.

But then, to hail a cab he had to extract his tongue from her mouth and his hands from her ass and he was enjoying all that a bit too much to stop just yet.

Her little moans jacked him up so he was painfully hard, but Bryan was willing to endure the pain because the pleasure would be worth the wait – his and hers.

When her phone rang with what he recognized as Owen's ringtone, Bryan wanted to curse. She never ignored her brother's calls.

"Hold that thought," she said, pulling away from their kiss with more ease than he would have managed. When she dug around in her bag and cursed looking for the phone, he knew she was affected as he. Good. It was her turn to suffer a little.

"Hey, Owen. What's up?" She said joyfully when she finally found the damned contraption, but her smile quickly faded. "Is she alright? Tell me what happened."

***

Morgan hated the frantic tone in Owen's voice. In most situations, he was as calm and controlled as she, but not when it came to Stacie and her head injury.

As a nurse, Morgan was trained to be calm in tense situations, but she'd learned the skill as a child. Crying while dear sweet Daddy beat the shit out of her mom only angered him more. Her father demanded obedience and self-control, and Morgan complied. She had hoped it would protect her mother, but that was futile. The woman didn't protect herself, how could her kids do it for her?

"I can be there in ten minutes, but I think you should take her to the emergency room."

"She's refusing to go, but she agreed to let you have a look at her."

Morgan was no neurologist, but she'd done her fair share of reading on brain injuries since last summer and could check vitals. Maybe Stacie would go to the ER at her insistence.

"I'm on my way. Sit tight and stay calm."

"You didn't see it. She's never had one this bad before."

"Everything's going to be fine," she assured him with a confidence she had learned to fake a long time ago.

Morgan disconnected the call and made note of the time. One A.M. It was about a ten minute walk to Owen's condo, but she could be there in just a few minutes by taxi.

"What's up?" Bryan asked as she tossed her phone in her bag.

"Stacie had a seizure. Owen said it's the worst one he's ever seen. She claims she's fine and won't go to the ER. He wants me to check her over."

"You going to get her to the ER?"

"Yep. I'll convince her. I can be very persuasive."

"Don't I know it," he said playfully. "Come on, let's catch a cab."

He put his hand at the small of her back and guided her outside. She was surprised to see a couple cabs parked near the terminal. It was late, but she supposed there might be one more ferry coming in. "You can't show up there with me," she said when the cab got moving. She pulled her keys out of her bag and held them out to him. "Why don't you head back to my apartment and I'll meet you there in a little while."

"I'm not letting you traipse all over the city by yourself after midnight."

Oh, the noble gestures of men. Morgan typically found such behavior a bore, but coming from Bryan, it warmed her. He'd always tried to protect her in that *you're like a little sister to me kind of way* – which annoyed the hell out of her. She had an older brother who thought he was her keeper; she certainly didn't need his caveman best friend to play the part too. All that shifted after they hooked up though. Now Morgan thought it was sweet. She didn't like the possessive behavior, but Bryan's protective nature was starting to grow on her. "I'll be taking a taxi, not traipsing."

"I'm not leaving. I'll wait downstairs."

Oh, the stubborn mule. She squeezed his thigh, high, her fingers grazing the bulge in his jeans as she did. The move elicited a sexy grumble from him and that only made her want to tease him more. She nipped his earlobe and whispered, "I was looking forward to going back to my apartment and finding you naked in my bed."

The grumble morphed into a groan that vibrated through his entire body. She caught a quick glance from the driver in the rearview mirror, but that didn't deter her. Hopefully the guy was professional enough to keep his eyes on the road and not on the show in the back seat.

"I can just picture you stretched out on my bed, watching as I strip out of my clothes." And she could. The man was gorgeous, all toned muscle and firm skin. He had the perfect amount of chest hair and a thin line from chest to groin. She pictured him with his hands folded behind his head, propping him up just a little bit so that confident, if not cocky, gaze could focus on her.

With a growl, he gripped her at her nape and pulled her to him. The seat belt kept her somewhat restrained, but it didn't prevent Bryan from claiming her mouth, lips firm and possessive. When his tongue swept across her lips, it was her turn to moan. Holy wow, did the man know how to kiss.

"We're here," the driver said as the car came to an abrupt stop. Bryan paid as Morgan scooted out. She needed a moment to cool down before facing her brother and morphing into medical mode.

Before she entered the building, Bryan grabbed her and pulled her back against him. His body was hard and strong and the heat it emanated penetrated her skin even through the layers of clothing. "We're going to do all that," he said in a commanding voice, "every little thing you just said in the cab."

She couldn't suppress the smile. God, he made her so hot. He kissed her again, as if sealing the deal and she was looking forward to getting back to her place.

"But I'm still waiting here for you." His voice was still commanding and Morgan could waste precious time arguing, but she knew his underlying reasons for staying had more to do with the situation than leaving her to navigate the city alone. Like her brother, Bryan was the big, strong, heroic type. She figured that had a lot to do with his service in the navy and she admired him for it even though he'd never admit to it. That's also why he wouldn't admit to being worried about Stacie, and as a result, being worried about Owen too.

Morgan simply nodded to agree with his terms before they went inside and she got on the elevator alone.

Though she was worried about Stacie, Morgan took advantage of the short ride to compartmentalize her personal feelings and draw on the professional demeanor which kept her grounded during an emergency. When she got in there her nursing instincts would kick in, pumping the adrenaline through her body and allowing her to completely focus on the situation. Stacie was brave, but the traumatic brain injury she'd suffered nearly a year ago had forced her to have brain surgery last summer and she was still dealing with the aftermath.

In addition to the headaches and seizures and impulse control issues, Stacie still had memory loss. She was in therapy trying to cope with both the psychological and physical trauma surrounding the accident and she probably didn't want to go to the ER out of fear. A TBI opened the door to so many unknowns and often had chronic symptoms. At this point, Stacie may never get her memory back or be able to get off the meds that helped keep her impulses on a leash.

Owen nearly ripped the door off its hinges after she knocked. "Where's your medical bag?" he asked without saying hello.

"I wasn't at home. I came straight here from downtown."

"You left the pub hours ago. I thought you were going home?" Having an older brother was a double-edged sword. Morgan loved Owen. He was more than just her brother, he was her best friend, but he'd taken it upon himself to be her protector, and too often her keeper, even when she didn't need protecting. Owen was well aware of her perspective on marriage, so didn't like when she dated. *All men want is sex*, he'd told her too many times, and he didn't approve of her sleeping around.

Of course, he didn't know she didn't sleep around. She enjoyed torturing him, so kept that little fact to herself. She didn't consider what she had with Bryan to be sleeping around. Their friends with benefits status was the perfect arrangement for two people who weren't looking for anything permanent. Even though she hoped he wasn't sleeping with anyone else, she preferred not knowing, preferred leaving that door open to him. It was safer.

"The whole city is celebrating the Seahawks win. I wasn't about to miss out on that." Celebrating the Seahawks wasn't just about fitting in to her new home. Their father had been a Saints fan, so when the Seahawks beat the Saints on the road to the Super Bowl, Morgan had been ecstatic; celebrating their Super Bowl win was almost as good as hammering a few more nails in the long-ago buried coffin.

It was a lie Owen would easily buy. He'd been just as ecstatic about the Saints losing and the Seahawks claiming the Lombardi trophy. "Where's Stace?" she asked, putting the focus where it needed to be.

"Sofa," he said, taking her coat and letting her get on about her business. Stacie was sitting upright, flanked by Jenny with Ty sitting across from her in the matching chair. Stacie had an icepack resting on her forehead.

"Hey, Morgan," she said without opening her eyes. "Sorry to drag you out so late. I told Owen not to call."

"Don't be ridiculous," Morgan said, taking her wrist to check her pulse. "I was still out." Out again, actually, but no one needed accurate details.

"Oh, well, sorry for ruining your fun."

It wasn't ruined, just on hold. Bryan would wait, maybe not patiently, but he'd wait.

"Tell me about the seizure," Morgan said when she finished getting a read on Stacie's pulse. It was within normal limits, so that was good.

"I don't remember it. We were on the elevator, I got a little dizzy, and then everything went black. When I woke up, I was here on the couch."

"No other symptoms leading up to it? Headache, nausea, chills, hot flash?"

"Nothing that I recall. Just the dizziness."

Morgan looked at Jenny, "Did she hit her head?"

"No. Owen caught her. She was out for a couple minutes."

"One hundred and thirty-four seconds," Owen added. He'd gotten in the habit of timing the seizures and they documented all the details in the journal per her neurologist's advice.

"Look at me," Morgan commanded and Stacie complied, taking the icepack off her forehead as she lifted her head from the back of the sofa. Her eyes were spasming, a common symptom with seizures, but it still worried Morgan.

"Your eyes are wigging out. Is that typical for you after a seizure?"

"Not since before her surgery," Owen said, looming over Morgan's shoulder.

"How long has it been since you had a seizure?"

"Months," Stacie sighed.

"November 18. She's had a migraine since then, but that was

stress when Kristina was in town," Owen informed her. He was such a mother hen.

"You should go to the ER," Morgan suggested. "I can't take your blood pressure and a doctor is going to be able to evaluate you better than I can." Morgan was confident in her skills, but TBIs weren't something to mess around with.

Before Stacie could answer or argue, a knock sounded at the door.

"Who the hell is that?" Owen muttered, but Morgan knew exactly who it was.

"Hey man, what are you doing here?" Owen asked when he opened the door and found Bryan standing there. Morgan wanted to ring his neck. He was supposed to be waiting outside.

"Morgan texted me. How's Stace?"

Nice lie.

"Not sure. Morgan's trying to talk her into the ER. You didn't have to come. I know you were probably getting busy with that blonde."

Ah, so he had left with *Serenity*. Morgan fought back the jealousy because it was a completely ridiculous emotion which shouldn't be rearing its ugly head anyway. She'd blame her inability to control her emotions on stress and worry. Yeah, that was perfect, blame Owen and Stacie.

Bryan only grunted in response which irked Morgan even more. Was he really expecting her to sleep with him tonight now that she knew he'd been with that bimbo? God, he really was a man-whore.

"ER, Stace," Morgan commanded, channeling her disgust into something more productive.

Stacie didn't argue, and Morgan hoped the angst in her voice was interpreted as medical concern rather than man-whore annoyance. Morgan helped Stace off the sofa and walked next to her to the elevator. In the parking garage, they climbed into Stacie's Jeep Grand Cherokee.

Bryan drove and Morgan rode shot gun while Owen sat close to

Stacie in the back. Jenny and Ty drove Owen's Mustang since neither of them owned a car. Harborview Medical Center was a just a short ride up the hill and Bryan dropped them off at the emergency entrance before going to park the car. The emergency room was a flurry of activity, likely due to the hordes of people who'd been out celebrating the Seahawks win. Hopefully there wasn't anything too serious and Stacie would get bumped to the front of the queue.

Ten minutes later, Bryan, Jenny, and Ty joined them in the waiting room. Owen sat next to Stacie, his arm around her as he stroked her hair. Ty and Jenny sat holding hands, both of them keeping a close watch on Stacie. Bryan stood in the corner, arms crossed over his chest and one ankle crossed over the other. If he wasn't such a pig, he'd look sexy as hell, but Morgan didn't like swine.

The tension in the waiting room was like a dense fog, creating a thick void where fun and laughs usually existed. Morgan couldn't blame it all on the worry they all shared for Stacie. From her peripheral vision, she could tell Bryan was watching her. He probably didn't like being called out in front of her about sleeping with that bimbo. Yeah, maybe they'd established some rules, but a part of her she didn't like to acknowledge had hoped he'd keep it in his pants unless he was with her. Morgan's only option now was to get over it, but not before she made Bryan suffer.

Chapter 3

Wednesdays were usually busy, but tonight the neighborhood clinic where Morgan volunteered was practically a snooze-fest. She loved the opportunity to keep her emergency skills up and reveled in all the hands-on learning opportunities, something she preferred to text books and classrooms. Since volunteer hours were a requirement of her scholarship, it was good she enjoyed it. She only worked Tuesday and Wednesday evenings, but would have taken more hours if there were more hours in the day. With a full load at school and thirty hours a week at Dr. Merrill's family practice, there wasn't much time to spare.

The clinic catered to low-income women and families and was typically busy. The unusually slow shift was a good thing for the people of the world but made for a boring evening for the medical professionals. Most of the city was celebrating the Seahawks victory. Owen had messaged her earlier, inviting her to join him, Stacie, and Bryan for the parade, but Morgan's schedule forced her to decline.

What got her panties in a bind was that the invitation came from her brother and not Bryan. A busy night at the clinic might have kept her mind from wandering to places it had no business venturing to, like thinking about the fact she hadn't heard from

Bryan since they parted ways at Harborview early Monday morning after Stacie had been discharged.

With work, the clinic and classes, she'd been too busy to think about him and that blonde bimbo. Now that life was putting on the breaks, her mind was free to fester like an open wound that hadn't been cleaned.

Bryan was busy too, she guessed. He had work and navy responsibilities and most likely had a long list of women to fill his bed. He was probably with *Serenity* right now.

Gah, Morgan couldn't even think of her name without rolling her eyes.

The fetal monitor beeped, drawing Morgan's attention where it should have been anyway. Amelia Costas was thirty-two and this was her second pregnancy. Her SUV had been rear-ended earlier in the day. It had been a low impact collision, but after talking to her insurance company, Amelia freaked out about the health of her baby and decided to come in for an exam.

The risk was pretty low given the type of collision, but it was still smart to get checked out. Doctor Sisco had instructed Morgan to hook Amelia up to a fetal monitor. It was standard protocol and Morgan had done this countless times, but the machine was high-tech, so as long as it wasn't beeping, her job was pretty boring.

"Does that beep mean something bad?" Amelia asked, a tear in her eye. Morgan gave the woman's hand a gentle squeeze while offering a reassuring smile. "It's just the timer. You're baby looks incredibly healthy. He has a strong heartbeat. We'll keep an eye on you for another hour or two and as long as his heartbeat remains steady, we'll let you go home for the night."

"But I have to come back tomorrow?" Amelia asked.

Morgan reset the timer. "Yep, but it's just routine. We'll monitor him again tomorrow for a couple hours just to be sure there's no delayed trauma."

"I can't believe this happened. I was just trying to be courteous and let another car in. The guy who hit me said he was reaching for

45

his coffee at that exact moment and didn't see me stop. So stupid."

Morgan finished programming the monitor before turning back to Amelia and giving her hand another squeeze. "Accidents happen, but it's good that you came in to get checked out." Morgan pointed to the monitor where the heartbeat was displayed as an analog signal. "See that, that's his heartbeat. Nice and strong."

"Thank you," Amelia sighed.

"Can I get you some water or a snack? We have quite a selection in the vending machine?"

"That'd be great. I'll take a muffin if there are any."

"One muffin coming right up."

Morgan grabbed a couple dollars out of the Sunshine Bucket the staff contributed to for situations like this.

"We have a trauma coming in," Cathy, the charge nurse told Morgan as she passed the nurse's station. "We need you. Holly can take over in eight."

Morgan knew what that meant. Some asshole had beat up his wife or girlfriend. Holly was an intern, just like Morgan, but she was also a survivor. She'd been nine weeks pregnant when her boyfriend beat her up and caused a miscarriage. That was a year ago and even though Holly hadn't known she was pregnant, she was still dealing with the emotional aftermath. She didn't handle domestic violence cases well, so she was kept off them.

"I was just getting the woman behind curtain eight a muffin and water. Her name's Amelia and she's pretty shook up even though the baby appears to be fine."

"I got it," Holly said confidently. Holly was studying to be a nurse-midwife in the same master's program Morgan was enrolled in at the University of Washington.

Even though Morgan had her own personal experience with domestic abuse, she'd learned to compartmentalize it as a survival mechanism years ago, so she could handle these cases when they came in, which was far too often in her book. She stopped to scrub and grab a pair of non-latex gloves on her way to the ambulance entrance, mentally preparing herself for the situation. Not all women were like her mother. Some actually fought back or at least defended themselves. Unfortunately, many went back to their abuser, just like her mother always had.

Morgan didn't understand it, nor did she want to try. As far as she was concerned, if a man laid his hands on a woman in anger, he belonged in jail. Her father had ended up six feet under instead of behind bars. Maybe it made her a bad person, but she was glad for that. Any jail time wouldn't have been long enough, not that her mother ever would have pressed charges anyway.

When Morgan met the ambulance, she inhaled a deep breath. He looked to be around thirty, thick brown hair, a day or two worth of stubble and arms covered in tattoos. Morgan didn't even have to get close the catch the stench of bourbon.

Perfect. Bourbon had been her father's poison.

"Aren't you a pretty one," he slurred. The look in his eyes made Morgan's skin crawl and reminded her of being a developing teenage girl living in a house with a frightening man.

"Mr. Welch," Morgan addressed him while looking at the chart the paramedics had started in the ambulance. "How much have you had to drink?"

"It was just one."

Morgan nearly laughed but reeled in the sarcasm and focused on being a professional. "One shot? One highball? One bottle?" Morgan had heard the just one comment enough to know it didn't mean just one drink. "I need specifics if we're going to treat you."

"I can't say I remember, honey, but it couldn't have been a bottle because I can't get it up when I've had a bottle and you've got me harder than a redwood."

A beat up drunk with a boner – great. And Morgan had been annoyed that the night was slow?

She focused on the chart to prevent her childhood from invading the present. She was a medical professional and no matter how much of a sleaze ball this drunk was, she was obligated to treat his injuries.

"Okay, Mr. Welch, we can't give you any pain killers without knowing how much alcohol is in your blood, so we're going to have to run some tests."

Derek met her at the door as the paramedics pushed the gurney inside. It was standard procedure to assign one male and one female nurse to domestic violence cases, especially when the patient was a man. Sometimes it caused issues when the victim was a woman, but men were stronger and even a woman could be hard to restrain. When they got Mr. Welch parked behind curtain four, Derek started checking his wounds while Morgan focused on his vitals.

"Tell me about your injuries." Morgan commanded.

They avoided asking what happened, as that typically triggered a rant, but sometimes even the best practices didn't work.

"That bitch came after me with a baseball bat. And not just any bat, that one was signed by Ken Griffey, Jr. Now it's got my damned blood all over it."

Morgan wouldn't care if it was signed by Hank Aaron. This wasn't personal, it was just her job and she needed information from her patient. "Your injuries sir. Where were you hit with the bat?"

"She clocked me in the head first. Then in the knee. She even tried to nail me in the balls, but I got a grip on it before she could. She oughta know better 'n that. She mighta been first to strike this round, but you can bet your pretty little ass she'll get what's coming to her."

An image of Morgan's mother flashed through her mind. The woman never fought back. Not once. She...

"Morgan, can you get me a needle kit and betadine. I'll draw some blood so we can get a tox screen started." Derek didn't know about her childhood. No one in the clinic did. In fact, Owen, Stacie, and Bryan were the only ones privy to that knowledge. Owen had lived it and even though he didn't talk much about their father, he'd fought his own demons a couple months ago and told Stacie everything. Morgan wasn't sure how much Bryan knew, but just knowing was enough as far as she was concerned. She didn't ever bring up her father's tirades because it was better to let dead dog's lie.

Morgan sucked in a couple deep breaths to steady her shaking hands as she reached for a wrapped syringe and bottle of antiseptic from the cabinet on the wall. She'd learned a long time ago to keep a tight hold on her emotions and it was time to put that skill to work. Fortunately Derek was handling the blood draw, though she wouldn't mind stabbing Mr. Welch a few times trying to find a good vein.

Derek may be a bit flamboyant at times, but he certainly was efficient with a needle. Their lunatic patient seemed to settle down, the alcohol finally acting as a depressant. Morgan managed to get a grip on her emotions and tuned out Mr. Welch's sporadic rants while they got his wounds cleaned and bandaged. He'd refused any x-rays and Morgan nearly flipped her lid when his wife came into the clinic looking for him. Mrs. Welch looked to be in her third trimester and had a shiny collection of bruises, and not just fresh ones.

Maybe she was overstepping her bounds, but Morgan had to say something. She pulled the woman aside, claiming there was paperwork to be done. Morgan pulled out a folder from behind the circulation desk and handed the woman a card. It was more discreet than a brochure, which battered women tended to turn away from.

"This is the number and address of a women's shelter just north of the city. If you call them, they'll pick you up and get you to a safe place."

"It's not what you think," the woman insisted, her head hung in shame. A knot grew in Morgan's chest as she fought back the memories from her childhood.

The woman had uttered words that Morgan had heard more times than she could count. "I'm sure your life is perfect," she responded, unable to lock down the sarcasm. Like so many others, this woman obviously didn't want help and Morgan wasn't going to waste her time. She could take blood pressure and bandage an open wound like no one's business. Dealing with battered women who didn't want help? Nope, not one of Morgan's strengths and not particularly a skill she was looking to develop.

Morgan walked away before making a scene and opted to check on Amelia. Finding the woman had been discharged and the clinic was overstaffed, she opted to call it a night.

It was just after ten o'clock when Carol, the shift supervisor, told Morgan to go home. Exhausted from dealing with Mr. Welch the lunatic and fighting off memories of the nightmare that had been her childhood, Morgan nearly jumped out of her skin when someone *hey'd* her across the parking lot.

Bryan leaned against a tree, much in the same stance he'd held in the ER the other night, but way more relaxed.

"What are you doing here?" she snapped, both startled and annoyed.

"I was in the city, thought I could give you a ride home."

Morgan narrowed her eyes at him. "I live two blocks from here."

Bryan responded with a clothes-melting grin. "Yeah, well, why walk when you can ride the Ducati?"

"It's February," she laughed, rolling her eyes. She wanted to be mad at him for leaving the bar with that bimbo the other night, but something about him was irresistible.

"No snow or ice. Perfect riding weather."

Maybe it was or maybe he was warm after coming from some woman's bed. The image of Serenity hanging all over him flashed through her mind, reminding Morgan she wasn't going to be his sloppy seconds. Since they'd established some ground rules, Morgan couldn't ask him about other women, so she opted for a more reasonable cop-out.

"It's been a rough night. If you're here for a booty call, I hate to disappoint you, but I'm not in the mood."

"Are you okay?" She appreciated the concern in his voice because if he'd showed disappointment, she was going to have to kick him in the nuts and she didn't have the energy for that.

Since he asked a question she couldn't answer honestly, she chose not to answer it all. The later part of the evening had been a replay of her worst nightmare. Somehow Morgan managed to hold it together and remain the consummate professional but now, outside the walls of the clinic, she was ready to lose her ever-loving mind.

"I need a hot bath and some herbal tea. Then I'm going to watch Friends on DVD until I laugh this day away and fall asleep."

Bryan fell in step behind her and put his hands on her shoulders. "How about a massage too? You know I'm good with my hands."

A massage sounded fantastic, but she knew what that would lead to and the last thing she wanted was a man in her bed. Right now she didn't even want one in her life.

"Your massages always lead to sex."

"I promise to keep my clothes on."

She ignored his suggestion and kept walking. Maybe he'd take the hint and go back to his motorcycle, get on the ferry, and stay on his side of the Sound.

"You know you can talk to me. I'm a good listener."

He was a good listener. Even though their friendship had tacked on some benefits in recent months, they still talked a lot and Morgan was grateful for that. She hadn't wanted to lose her friend just because she'd given in to her fantasies, but Bryan was mature enough to take what they were doing at face value. She did not, however, want to talk about her day.

Bryan walked the two blocks with her despite claiming to have his bike. When they reached Morgan's place, she realized even though she didn't want him in her bed, she didn't want to be alone. Her apartment was dark and scary and though it was a world away from the nightmare she'd grown up in, it had plenty of dark corners where the demons could lurk and threaten.

"You want to watch Friends with me?" she asked, hoping he would say yes and not expect anything more.

"Yeah, that sounds like fun."

"Just the episodes, though. I'm serious about the booty call. Not tonight."

"There's more to me than just a sex fiend. I also know how to make popcorn," he bragged.

Morgan laughed and for the first time in hours, felt the tension fading. He really was one of the good guys even if he did sleep with any blonde bimbo who looked his way. "Popcorn sounds good."

Morgan made tea, though Bryan opted for a Coke. He tossed the popcorn in the microwave and got the Friends DVD loaded. She settled into a corner of her couch and Bryan took the opposite end. It was a good, safe distance, completely platonic.

Yet she yearned to have his arms wrapped around her.

This wasn't unlike many of the nights when she'd hung out in her brother's room while their dad went ballistic on their mother. They didn't have a TV, but they'd do homework together or play cards or read books. It was safe. It was comfortable.

But Bryan wasn't her brother. He was just as honorable, but she would never really know for sure what he was capable of. He'd been possessive the other night and Morgan hadn't forgotten how he'd grabbed her wrist. Despite that, she found herself wanting to touch him, wanting him to touch her back. For years Morgan had been determined not to turn into her mother. She would never let a man possess her, control her, demand things of her. She would never let a man touch her in anger. If it happened that he did, she certainly wouldn't hang around long enough for him to do it over and over and over.

An episode played through, but Morgan barely noticed. She was surprised when the credits began rolling and Bryan hit pause on the remote.

"Do you want me to call Owen?" he asked, the concern in his voice even heavier than it'd been when he'd asked if she was okay.

"Why?"

"Something obviously happened today. I'm guessing you don't want to be alone, but I'm probably the last guy you want hanging out on your couch."

Actually, Bryan was the only guy she wanted hanging out on her sofa. He knew about her childhood, about what an asshole her father had been and wouldn't offer empty words of reassurance if she told him about her day.

"A husband and wife beat each other up tonight. The husband was my patient. He tried to hit on me. It was disgusting."

"That sucks, Morg."

Morgan wasn't sure if he was referring to the couple or her own post-traumatic stress. And that wasn't even the worst of it.

"It usually doesn't bother me, but the woman was pregnant and when I gave her a card to a nearby women's shelter, she went into denial."

"You can't save people if they don't want to be saved."

Wasn't that the truth. That's one of the reasons she was going into midwifery. Bringing babies into the world was a better calling than trying to fix what was already broken beyond repair. "I just don't get it. Why are women so stupid? She's going to end up dead. And what is going to happen to that poor child?"

"Maybe she won't. Maybe your gesture will get her thinking. You did your job, but you can't make people's decisions for them. You can't feel guilty when they don't do what you think they should."

"I know. It just stirs up a lot of memories."

"I get why you volunteer at that clinic and why you deliver babies, but that stuff won't make the memories go away. All you can do is not let them have a negative impact on your life."

"So says my shrink," she laughed, but Bryan didn't smile.

***

Bryan was a far cry from a shrink. Hell, he didn't even have any real life experience with what Morgan experienced and it pissed him off beyond measure about what she had gone through. "Listen, I've never been through what you and Owen grew up with, but you're a strong woman, Morg. You have a good head on your shoulders. Don't let that bastard of a father haunt you. He can't hurt you anymore."

Morgan chortled and Bryan would give anything to hear the fun in her laugh again. "He never laid a finger on me, not once. He beat the shit out of my mother and Owen, too, a few times. But he never touched me."

Thank God for that. If the man had assaulted Morgan, Bryan would dig up the rotting body and kill him all over again. There was no excuse for touching a woman like that, especially as a father. "The abuse doesn't have to be physical to make an impact."

Morgan knew that as well as anyone. As a nurse, she saw all kinds of crazy shit that people put each other through. He reminded her, though, because it was obvious she was hurting and she needed to talk it through.

"I know. It wasn't even really abuse. It was more of a threat. I remember how he looked at me after I hit puberty. It was creepy and wrong. That guy at the clinic looked at me like that tonight."

"He's not coming after you, sweetheart." Bryan would hunt him down and kill him if he did.

God, he just wanted to take her in his arms and hold her until she wasn't scared anymore. The last thing she needed, though, was to feel like she was being pawed at, so he kept his distance, sitting on the opposite side of the couch and wishing her worries away.

"I know, but that doesn't mean I won't have nightmares about it tonight. It also killed me to let his wife leave with him. She has a choice, but the baby she's carrying doesn't."

Bryan's stomach lurched. He couldn't fathom how a man could hurt a woman, never mind a child, even one still growing in the womb.

He wished he could wash the whole night away for Morgan, keep the situation at the clinic from scaring her like this. She was a good person, generous and caring. She didn't deserve this. Even though he couldn't take the day back, maybe he could keep her from having nightmares. "Hey, why don't you go get in the bath. I'll stand guard out here and sleep on the couch tonight. I'm pretty good at chasing ghosts away."

"They teach you that in the navy?" she laughed and he was glad to see some of her humor coming back.

"Yeah, they do. It's a required class in boot camp."

"Thanks for hanging out but you don't have to spend the night. My sofa isn't very comfortable."

"I've slept on worse. Besides, if I don't leave in oh," Bryan glanced at his watch, "five minutes ago, the chances of me catching the last ferry are pretty slim. I don't feel like driving all the way around. It's too cold for that."

"Then why'd you take the Ducati?"

Because he was hoping to give her a ride and be sandwiched between her thighs, even if it was only a few blocks. "Navigating the city streets isn't so bad. Opening her up on the interstate is another story."

"Okay, well, you probably want to move your bike. I wouldn't trust it at the clinic overnight."

"You gonna be alright for a few minutes if I run out?"

She smacked his shoulder. "I'm not a damsel in distress. Go get your bike, the bath is calling my name."

Bryan would have loved to join her in a steamy bath, but sometimes the best thing a guy could do was keep his clothes on. Morgan had been his friend before they started messing around, so he wasn't going to abandon her needs just because he'd been hoping to get a little tonight.

He ran to the bike and was back in her apartment in just minutes. A subtle fragrance filled the apartment and given the faint flicker he could see beneath the door jam, she had candles burning in the bathroom. Bryan positioned himself on the couch so he could see her when she came out. A half hour after he got back from getting his bike, the water slurped down the drain. He pushed off the couch, deciding to flick on the water kettle in case she wanted another cup of tea. After grabbing the entertainment magazine off the side table – not his typical reading, but he didn't just want to be lurking – he once again got comfortable on the couch.

"I put the water on if you want another cup of tea," he said as she came out of the bathroom wearing a thick terry cloth robe. She'd pulled her partially wet hair into a clip except for the rogue strands that framed her flushed cheeks. She looked more relaxed than she had before the bath.

When she smiled, Bryan's heart nearly melted. "Thanks, I would like some tea. I'm just going to get my PJs on."

She disappeared down the hall and Bryan wondered what she wore for PJs. When he spent the night, she slept naked unless she happened to slip on whatever shirt he'd been wearing. He liked her in his clothes and loved putting them on the next morning with her scent still lingering on them. That coconut perfume she wore drove him crazy. That wasn't what he was catching tonight though. Whatever she'd used in the bath smelled citrusy but still sexy as hell.

When she came out from her room, hair still clipped, she sported a giant purple University of Washington sweatshirt that fell loosely over black stretch pants. The outfit shouldn't have turned him on, but she looked beautiful, so comfortable and relaxed.

"You want a cup too?" she asked as she maneuvered around the small kitchen.

"Yeah, sure." Bryan wasn't much of a tea drinker, but if it meant Morgan would keep him company, he'd do anything. He watched her go through the process of steeping the tea and adding honey. When she finally brought the two cups over to where he'd been holding vigil on the couch, she sat in the middle, her knee brushing his as she curved her leg in and faced him.

"How was the parade?" she asked.

Bryan, Owen and Stacie, along with a million other Puget Sounders had flocked downtown to see the Seahawks ride down Fourth Avenue to CenturyLink Field with the Lombardi trophy.

"Intense. I've never seen so many people all in one place. The energy was incredible."

"It was. I thought the clinic would fill up with overflow from the ERs, but it was actually slow considering how many people were in the city."

Bryan would have loved to celebrate the Seahawks victory with Morgan, but public display of affection – especially in front of Owen – was against the rules and given the energy downtown, he doubted he would have been able to keep his hands off her. He thought it had been a good thing she hadn't given up her shift at the clinic, but after hearing about her night, he wished she wasn't so dedicated.

Celebrating with her would have been fun. Morgan had only been in Seattle for half a year, but she loved everything about the city, including its sports teams. She didn't do anything without fully embracing the moment, so she would have absorbed the celebratory energy and had the time of her life. On top of that, being at the celebration meant she wouldn't have had to deal with that douche biscuit at the clinic and the memories he'd conjured.

"So…" Morgan started as she put her empty cup on the table at the end of the couch. Bryan knew this was going to be interesting because she usually didn't ease into any conversation. She was the type of person who dove head first into the deep end, yelling Geronimo just for fun.

"So?" Bryan prodded when she left the thought hanging.

"I, uh, I have a strange request," she finally managed to say.

"Hit me."

"You know I'm not the snuggling type, and you're not really into it either, but could we make an exception for tonight?"

She wanted to snuggle? It was a strange request because she never wanted to do that. Bryan wasn't much into cuddling either, but with Morgan he found himself wanting to. Her body was soft and warm and having sex only fueled his desire to keep touching her. With other women, he'd never had to try. When the deed was done, the woman he was with usually clung to him like a leach. Morgan was different. She'd give him a quick kiss and roll away. The only way he could get close was to spoon with her and she always elbowed and kicked him until he finally gave up and gave her some space.

"I think I can handle it," he said, glad for the opportunity to be close to her, but he was curious about her change of heart. "You sure you can?"

The apprehension was gone from her face, replaced with a bright smile. "It was my idea, I think I can handle it."

"Come here," Bryan said, putting his cup on the makeshift end table and opening his arms to her.

Morgan crawled across the couch to Bryan. Her body molded right against him as she squeezed between his body and the back of the couch. She splayed one hand on his chest and Bryan wrapped his arms around her, holding her firmly. He had to put one foot on the floor for leverage, but he didn't care. She felt so good and right, her body soft and warm.

He synchronized his breathing with hers, something he always did when they shared a bed. He loved the connection it offered, knowing they were drawing in the same air at the same time. It wasn't until her breathing deepened in sleep that he would allow himself to drift off.

Bryan realized now that Morgan had fallen asleep, quicker than he could have imagined.

She was obviously exhausted, both from the emotional turmoil of her job and the physical demands. She'd often told him how wired she was after a shift, that it could take hours for the adrenaline to stop pumping. That's why she liked her herbal tea before bed. Bryan was sure the bath also helped to calm her nerves tonight. And maybe, just maybe, the security of his arms added an extra layer of comfort that allowed her to finally come down from the rush.

The fact she'd fallen asleep in his arms shouldn't have boosted his ego as much as it did, but trust was a big issue for Morgan. It made him happy that she finally trusted him enough to fall asleep like this.

He didn't want to disturb her, or ruin the enjoyment of holding her like this, but the couch wasn't that comfortable and it was better to disrupt her sleep now rather than later.

"Morg, let me get you into bed, sweetheart."

"Huh?" Her body stretched with the grace of a cat and it made him hard having all those soft curves tighten against him. "Oh, did I fall asleep?"

"Yeah. Come on, I'll tuck you in."

He eased away from her body and lifted her off the couch. She stayed plastered to him like a second skin and lifted her sleepy eyes. God she was beautiful. When she smiled, Bryan's heart thumped with joy. Then she gave him a slow kiss.

It was soft and sweet, not filled with the same intensity they usually shared when they couldn't get each other's clothes off fast enough. He figured such a gentle kiss was her way of thanking him but the sweet gesture rocked him just as hard as her passion-filled kisses.

He got her tucked in and started for the bedroom door. "You don't have to sleep on the sofa," she said quietly.

Sleep in her bed and keep his hands off her? That was going to be a personal challenge, but he was willing to give it a try to stay off the couch and be close to her.

Bryan stripped out of his jeans, but left his boxers and t-shirt on. After he climbed under the covers, Morgan moved back against him, molding her body to spoon with him.

There was no way Bryan could do this. "This isn't a good idea. How about you roll over."

She chuckled, probably because it was more a demand than a question, but Bryan didn't find any humor in the moment. On a normal day, he wanted her with a ferocity he'd never felt for another woman. Tonight, knowing she'd had a rough shift at the clinic, he wanted to pound her worries away.

"Having trouble keeping the sailor in your shorts?"

"You make it very hard…and difficult."

Now she was laughing. "I wore the least sexy thing I could find so I wouldn't come across as a tease."

"You'd look sexy in a garbage bag."

"Such flattery. Is this better?" She nestled against him, her head on his chest and one arm resting on his abs. He wanted those long fingers to play around with the hair on his chest, but the stupid t-shirt prevented that. He had to remind himself this wasn't about his needs. Morgan needed a friend right now, not a lover. Bryan was determined to be whatever she needed, even if it turned his balls blue.

Wrapping his arms around her, he held her close but not too tight. "You comfortable?"

"Yeah," she sighed. It wasn't long before her breathing changed to the deep sleeping rhythm. He could have lay awake all night smelling her hair, touching her skin, but the comfort of holding her close and keeping her safe lulled him to sleep almost as quickly.

***

Morgan bolted upright with a gasp. Bryan wasn't sure if they'd been asleep for minutes or hours. Regardless, it was obvious she'd had a nightmare.

"Morgan, it's okay. Wake up, sweetheart." He turned on the

bedside lamp and she stared at him, confusion tensing her pretty face.

"You're alright Morgan, it was just a dream."

Her breaths were quick, labored, her eyes holding the kind of panic you'd see on someone in a horror movie.

"What were you dreaming about?" As a kid, Bryan's youngest brother Blake often had nightmares when their mom was deployed on a ship. Blake would climb into bed with Bryan, who always found his little brother fell back asleep more quickly if he talked about the dream. He wasn't sure if the technique would work on Morgan, but it was all the experience he had to pull from.

"Spiders," she said, a shiver racing down her spine. "Really big, hairy wolf spiders. They were in their webs in the corners, just staring at me, their legs all twitchy like they were going to spring from their webs."

Brian wasn't an expert in dream interpretation. Hell, he wasn't even a novice, but he could go a million places with an analysis of that dream. The staring, the multiple legs. He imagined that was her subconscious brain turning her dead father into a creepy creature that could stalk her even in her sleep.

Morgan shivered, like she had the heebie jeebies and she looked around the room, inspecting every corner. There were no spiders, no webs. The room didn't even have dust in it. He imagined she kept it very clean specifically for this reason.

"You've had this dream before."

She sighed in obvious resignation. He was glad she wasn't going to try to hide the truth. "Yeah."

"That's why you don't like to share a bed while you're sleeping." It all made sense. Morgan didn't like being rescued. This was the first time Bryan had ever seen her be vulnerable. She obviously wasn't comfortable with people seeing her that way, but was she making an exception for Bryan or was she just too drained to fight it back?

She folded her arms around her knees, tucking them tight

against her chest. Bryan rubbed her neck and shoulders, which were tight with tension and fear. "Sweetheart, there's no spiders, no ghosts. Nothing's going to get you."

"You think I don't know how ridiculous I am!"

"That's not what I meant. Your fears aren't ridiculous at all."

"I'm not afraid."

"But you're picking a fight with me."

She pulled away from him and nearly leaped out of bed. She gripped her elbows so firmly that her knuckles paled, all the while shaking her head.

"You shouldn't even be here." Bryan flinched at the disgust in her voice, unsure sure what he'd done to inspire that emotion.

"I can sleep on the couch," he said, hoping like hell she didn't take him up on that. He'd liked holding her, but it obviously hadn't been enough to protect her from the demons swimming around in her mind.

"No, you shouldn't be here at all. Why aren't you with Serenity?" There was more disgust as she said the name, and Bryan realized she'd steered down a completely different road. Maybe it was her way of avoiding the fear. He probably shouldn't enable that kind of behavior, but he remembered how angry she'd appeared at the hospital after Owen had mentioned him leaving with Serenity, so he figured the topic would come up sooner or later.

"I left the bar with her the other night to keep the cover you so adamantly insisted on. I didn't go home with her. I didn't even lay a finger on her."

"Why not? She seemed to be your type?"

"Yeah, and what type is that?"

"You know, blonde and easy."

He deserved the blow, but that didn't mean he liked it. For years he went for blonde and easy, but now that he'd been with Morgan, his old ways just didn't appeal to him.

"I prefer you," he admitted.

Morgan huffed as though she was going to tell him he was full of shit, but instead she just paced the room. Bryan watched her wear a hole in the old carpet, wondering what the hell he should say now. He didn't do well with conflict, at least not when it came to women. He could handle fights with his brothers and he'd been known to throw a punch every now and then, but since he tended to avoid complicated entanglements, he had no experience to pull from.

"We're not a couple," she finally said, stopping her back and forth to pin him with a deadly stare.

"I'm still not clear on why you're picking a fight with me."

Morgan started pacing again, snapping Bryan's patience like a frayed roped reeling in a heavy anchor. He pushed off the bed and crossed the small room. When he came face to face with her, he felt like he was looming and that only seemed to spark her anger. So Bryan did the only thing he could think of…

When he claimed her mouth with his, she didn't resist. She wrapped herself around him like a pretzel, her body warm and pliant. As quickly as it started, it was over, Morgan pulling away abruptly and forcing some space between them.

"I'm not sleeping with you if you slept with her. I know I'm not supposed to ask, but I just can't do it. I saw you looking at her."

Bryan had been looking at Serenity, but not because he was interested in her. It was all to keep this deception going. Trying to explain that to Morgan seemed lame, though, so he kept the facts simple. "I didn't sleep with her."

Her lips pursed as if she was mulling over his response. "I swear it, Morg. I didn't touch her." He wished he'd been an Eagle Scout so he could give her a scout's honor, but all he had was his word. She was going to have to choose whether or not to believe him, and ultimately, trust him. He worried that was the bigger issue.

"I think you should go. I'm a wreck and I'm just going to keep taking it out on you."

"I can handle it," he said, not wanting to leave her alone for his own selfish reasons as well as for her wellbeing.

"Yeah, but I can't."

Bryan didn't want to argue with her. She'd had one hell of a night and maybe being alone wasn't the best thing for her, but neither was having an asshole around who was only fueling her anger and fear.

"I'll call you in the morning," he said, grabbing his jeans off the floor and slipping them on. One of the many skills he'd learned in the navy was to dress quickly. He never thought the skill would be useful when he was leaving Morgan's bed.

Morgan didn't stop him. She simply followed him to the door and closed it behind him. The click of the deadbolt was followed by the chain sliding home. Bryan stepped off the porch and into the cold Seattle night, wishing his old truck had been running so he didn't have to take the Ducati. It was going to be a long, cold ride to Bremerton.

***

Her apartment sparkled, her closet was reorganized by style and color, and all of her monthly statements that had been stacked under the TV were now properly filed. With nothing left to distract her, Morgan was forced to get back to the fifty page research paper which was due tomorrow.

The computer screen mocked her, the words she'd written making perfect sense but the void of white left to be filled creating an intimidating foe. She had gone into nursing knowing tests were a necessary evil, but didn't think research papers would be such a core part of the curriculum. Morgan was good at her job, but the academics required to be a nurse didn't come easily. She'd never been a gifted student. She got straight A's because she worked her ass off to get them. Test anxiety forced her to study hard. Unfortunately, she didn't take that approach with papers. Fortunately, she performed well under pressure. She might have avoided writing the paper, but once it was done, she had no doubt she'd earn an A.

All the necessary research was complete, but since she'd rather have a pap smear with a first-time intern than write the damned paper, she'd procrastinated until she couldn't possibly procrastinate any longer. Her chosen topic, holistic pain remedies during labor and birth, was fascinating and she learned so much, but organizing that knowledge into something readable – gah. Morgan had toyed with the idea of hiring Stacie to write the paper, but knew she had to earn her grade and degree. There would be no cheating, not if she expected to live with herself.

The knock on the door was both welcome and annoying. She wanted the distraction, but needed to focus. Balancing the wants versus the needs was like deciding between a hot fudge sundae and a garden salad. One was good for you but the other was so, so good.

She'd even turned her phone off to avoid distractions. Owen knew she'd gone off grid and if there was an emergency, he'd have to show up at her door. She hoped that wasn't the case now.

She finished the sentence she was typing because God forbid she lose the thought. With a quick save of the document, she was padding across the room hoping whatever this distraction was would be fabulous.

It was like a wish come true when she opened the door to find Bryan leaning against one of the posts holding up the roof over her doorway. Damn, he looked good, dressed in leather chaps over jeans and a leather jacket. Totally hot fudge sundae. He held his helmet in one hand and a paper bag in the other. Didn't the man realize it was February? It was a bit chilly to be riding the Ducati. Again.

Morgan hadn't bothered to tell Bryan she wasn't available since he'd annoyed her and she was embarrassed by her psychotic behavior a week ago. She'd managed to avoid his calls and text messages, but that was probably because he wasn't one of those needy guys. He left one voice mail and one text and when she hadn't responded, she hadn't heard from him again.

"I heard you're holed up writing a big paper. Thought you might need some sustenance."

Morgan had been snacking all day, but hadn't had an actual meal. It was part of her routine – snack, clean something, write a few sentences, repeat. She eyed the bag and her stomach rumbled on cue. "You brought food?"

"Just subs. Nothing to get excited about."

A sub sounded fantastic and Bryan looked fantastic. She hadn't considered sex as a distraction, but it seemed like a good idea now. "You like it when I get excited about your sub."

"How's your paper going?" His sexy smirk didn't match that big brother tone in his voice. Oh, how she abhorred that tone. She already had a big brother. She had other needs Bryan was stellar at fulfilling.

"It'll get done," she shrugged, knowing she might have to pull an all-nighter, but it would get done.

"I didn't come here to be your distraction. I wanted to make sure you were eating."

"I hate it when you do that," she said even though she didn't. She loved that he looked out for her, but wished he didn't do it with that brotherly tone.

"I appreciate the food. If this isn't a booty call, you can just leave it and go."

Bryan handed her the bag but instead of leaving, pushed his way past her and made quick work of shedding his leathers. Holy cow, he was wearing Levi's. He normally wore loose-fitting jeans, but every once in a while graced the world with faded denim that molded to his muscular legs.

Hot fudge sundae with a cherry on top. Yum.

"So how much do you have left to write?"

Morgan shrugged again. "Thirty pages," she said as though it was no big deal.

"Thirty pages? That's one hell of a paper."

"It's supposed to be fifty to sixty pages. I'm on schedule to get it done on time." She would, because she always did, but that didn't mean she would get any sleep.

"When is it due?" he asked with doubt in his voice.

Morgan shrugged again. "Tomorrow at two."

Bryan looked at his watch and laughed. "You're going to write thirty pages in twenty hours?"

"Hey, if I write two pages an hour, I'll have it done in fifteen." She put the bag on the table in front of the sofa and went to the fridge to pour them each a glass of water from the filtered pitcher before meeting Bryan back in the living room.

"Anything I can do to help?"

"Not unless you're an expert in holistic pain remedies during labor and birth."

Bryan laughed. "I was born, that's about the extent of my experience with birth. Since I don't remember it, I'm not much of an expert."

Morgan settled onto the sofa next to him, letting her leg rub up against his. Based on how much she had left to write, she didn't need the Bryan's distraction, but her inner procrastinator welcomed it. God, she hated writing papers.

"You know it's February, right?"

"Yeah."

"So why are you on the Ducati?" Morgan loved his motorcycle. When she'd first moved to Seattle last summer Bryan had taken her out on some great rides. Now though, it was a bit cold.

"My truck needs a new exhaust."

"Didn't you just put in a new carburetor?" She had heard Owen talk about doing that over the weekend. Morgan figured that was one of the reasons she hadn't seen or heard from Bryan in a week.

"Yeah, and then we discovered the exhaust was shot."

"Seems like it'd be easier just to trade it in for something that's less of a POS."

"She's not a piece of shit. She just needs a little TLC. I've been through a lot with that truck. I'm not tossing her aside just because she's a little worn."

Funny how he referred to his truck as a female, especially considering how quickly he usually did toss women aside. Morgan opted not to point that out since it might deter him from distracting her from her paper.

"Isn't it a bit cold to be on the Ducati?"

"The leathers keep me warm enough and I'm only riding around the city, not on the freeways."

"You're crazy," she said as he unpacked the subs.

"So I've been told. Now dig in. I bet you haven't eaten in days."

Bryan knew her habits. He'd been around during the last quarter when she was getting ready for finals and had brought her food a couple times when he realized she'd only been snacking.

"Is this from Randy's?" she asked, although she could tell by the brown paper wrapping it had to be from the small sandwich shop just a couple blocks from her apartment. Bryan nodded as she unwrapped the sub in her lap.

He'd gotten her a turkey sub with all the fixings she liked – spinach, olives, hot peppers, provolone. He'd even gotten the whole wheat bread she liked. Randy's made the best subs she'd ever had and she nearly had an orgasm with the first bite.

"You moan like that again and this courtesy visit will be more than I planned."

She put a little more effort into her next moan, hoping to entice him out of those snug jeans.

"Knock it off," he said before tearing off a huge bite of his sub. She guessed he was having roast beef with everything. The man liked his meat and his vegetables.

Morgan rubbed her leg against his. "You usually like it when I moan."

She waited for him to toss aside the sandwich and have his wicked way with her right on the sofa, but instead, he just shook his head. "You have a big paper to write and I figured you weren't eating. As much as I'd love to get in your pants, I don't want to encourage your incessant procrastination."

Such a romantic. Now Morgan wasn't just frustrated with the paper, but her loins were burning. Bryan in leathers. Bryan in Levis. Bryan smelling good and looking sexy and emanating sex even as he ate a sub. "How did we go from having sex twice a week to not at all?"

"Life," he drawled between bites. "Since I can't tell your brother to piss off so I can bone his sister, I have to work on the truck and the Mustang when he shows up."

"If you told him you wanted to bone his sister, he'd tear off your bone and toss it in the deepest part of Elliot Bay."

"Don't even joke about that," he said with a mouth full of sandwich. So charming.

Despite his table manners, she still wanted him. She'd gotten used to having him and right now his body was so much more appealing than the white screen on her computer. "You could bone me now."

Bryan smiled and shook his head. "Miss me?"

She hadn't had time to think about missing him, but now that he was here, she realized she had. What did that say about their relationship? She wasn't interested in getting attached. Bryan was a friend with benefits and that's how she intended it to stay until he was simply a friend again. Missing him made things awkward.

"I miss your little sailor more than I miss you," she teased.

"Big sailor," he corrected. "He's missed you too. You need to get that damned paper done so we can do something about this loneliness before it becomes chronic. I don't want to have to resort to cold showers or worry about growing hair on my palms."

If she didn't have a mouth full of turkey sub, she'd remind him of his blonde ambitions, but she wasn't really in the mood to tease him about his man-whore status. The night of the Super Bowl they'd agreed not to flaunt whatever extra-curricular activities they were engaged in. If Bryan was seeing any other action, she didn't want to know. Ignorance was bliss.

They finished their subs in a comfortable silence. It was one of the things she really liked about Bryan. They'd known each other long enough that they didn't have to ramble on with meaningless banter. They could enjoy their food and not feel awkward about it because they weren't making small talk.

Bryan cleaned everything up and Morgan let him. He was a sight to behold in those muscle-hugging jeans. He disappeared in the kitchen and Morgan stretched out on the sofa, letting her shirt ride up so some skin was showing. Had she known Bryan might stop by, she would have put on something sexy, but she'd learned from their time together that it didn't matter what she wore.

When Bryan came out of the kitchen, he stopped abruptly, giving her a once over that felt like a warm caress. Bryan just shook his head and headed toward the foyer.

Morgan rolled over to find him putting his leathers back on. The frustration she'd already been feeling doubled. Not only did she have to write a ridiculous paper, she was going to have to do it while all hot and bothered.

"You're not even going to kiss me good-bye?"

"If I kiss you, there won't be a good-bye." His voice had changed in that sexy way that revealed he was aroused.

Morgan licked her lips. "I can live with that," she tried her most seductive voice but since Bryan continued to put his leathers on, Morgan knew it wasn't effective. Since when did Bryan say no to sex?

"Do you have a hot date?" she asked even though she wasn't supposed to.

"No. If you want to know the truth, I'm going to go home and most likely jerk off. You're killing me, Morg."

Maybe it made her a pervert, but the thought of him with his hand wrapped around himself turned her on even more. "You don't have to leave."

He zipped up the jacket and grabbed his helmet. "I'm not going to be the reason you don't get your paper done."

Morgan sighed. "I told you, it'll get done."

"I know." He paused with his hand on the door handle. "You want to do something tomorrow night?"

"What'd you have in mind?" she asked playfully.

"Dinner. It's Valentine's Day."

All the warmth left Morgan's body in a rush as a shiver raced down her spine. "I absolutely do not want to do anything with you on Valentine's Day."

Chapter 4

Bryan knew immediately he'd said something wrong. Shit, maybe he shouldn't have mentioned Valentine's Day.

He'd never met a woman with so many aversions to romantic notions. Not that he was all into them himself, but he'd had girlfriends around Valentine's Day and even though he didn't buy them jewelry or flowers, dinner and a box of chocolates seemed to guarantee he'd get lucky. With Morgan, though, it wasn't just about getting into her pants. He wanted to take her out, had even set up a flower delivery. Shit, was that going to get him in trouble?

"Come on, Morg, dinner will be fun."

"No. That's something couples do. We're not a couple."

"So I can have sex with you, but I can't take you out to dinner."

"I don't need that kind of foreplay," she said.

"Maybe I do."

She laughed. "Oh, come on, Bryan. You're not going all soft on me."

Was he going soft? He didn't feel obligated to do something nice for her to recognize the romantic holiday. He *wanted* to do something nice, to let her know she meant a lot to him. Christ, maybe he was going soft.

"You know what, forget it. I'm just trying to be a nice guy, but I forgot who I was dealing with."

"What the hell is that supposed to mean?" Bryan felt satisfied that he'd poked the dragon. It was a little less lonely when you weren't pissed off alone.

"Little Miss Anti-Relationship," he snarled.

"And you're Mr. Anti-Relationship."

Actually, he wasn't, at least not anymore. That realization surprised him. "You're the one who insists we keep this under wraps." The guilt had been getting to him. Owen had asked about the blonde from the Super Bowl a couple times, giving Bryan more than one opportunity to confess. Of course, the truth was he was more afraid of Morgan's wrath than her brother's, so he'd kept his trap shut.

"You know why."

"He's my best friend and you're forcing me to lie to him."

"If you can't handle it, then maybe we should go back to just being friends."

"As opposed to what?" Bryan wasn't even sure how to label their relationship.

"Friends with benefits."

Is that all they were, friends with benefits? Bryan was a damned fool for thinking it was more. He was an even bigger fool for wanting more. Any day orders would come in for him to go out on a ship. The navy was the only commitment he'd ever wanted and with only three years left until he retired from service, he didn't need the hassle of a woman demanding more of him than he could promise. Morgan was right, he was getting soft. Morgan offered exactly what he wanted – incredible sex with no strings attached. Bryan needed to take it for what it was and enjoy the fact it wasn't complicated.

"Sorry," he muttered. "You're right. Friends with bennies is exactly what I want. See you later. Good luck with your paper."

Bryan walked out the door, careful not to slam it behind him even though he had the sudden urge to break something.

***

The lingerie she'd bought begged to be worn. The flowers she'd received screamed for her to run far and fast.

Morgan had always strategically ended her relationships to avoid things like birthdays, Christmas, and especially Valentine's Day. With her research paper looming, she'd completely blanked on the nauseating holiday this year. Not that she'd thought she needed to end things with Bryan to avoid any uncomfortable exchanges. She figured since they were just friends with benefits, they didn't need to do anything special.

That's why the flowers surprised her. She'd never been given flowers before and these were so incredibly beautiful. Bryan had done well, choosing an arrangement of yellow and orange roses. She knew yellow roses symbolized friendship, but she'd had to do an Internet search to learn that orange roses symbolized attraction and desire.

It was the perfect bouquet, and Morgan was trying to convince herself it meant nothing more than the message symbolized by the flowers.

She also had to ignore the warning in her heart the flowers sparked. Her father would sometimes send her mother flowers. Never as an apology. No, Emmanuel Landry never apologized. He'd send her flowers for no apparent reason. They were always red. Sometimes roses, sometimes carnations, but always red. He only ever signed his name on the card. There was no other written message, but the warning became apparent. The red symbolized blood in Morgan's mind because whenever he sent them, he beat the crap out of her mother.

These flowers weren't red though, and Bryan was nothing like Emmanuel Landry. Morgan didn't even think Bryan had a temper. She'd never seen it and though he acted possessive at times, it was more charming than scary. Of course, maybe that was the lure.

Charm the pants off her and when she was least expecting it, boom, unleash the horror.

But Morgan wouldn't be with Bryan long enough to risk that. She didn't know exactly how the military worked, but she knew every few years people got moved around. Bryan had been stationed at Bremerton for about five years. It was likely he'd be going somewhere else soon. Morgan tried not to let that thought sadden her. She and Bryan were friends. They'd stayed in touch over social media and with an occasional phone call. Of course, that had always been to check up on or report Owen's status, especially after his last divorce. Their "benefits" status had made their friendship more personal, so she hoped Bryan would want to stay in touch when he'd moved on. Maybe that's what the flowers were an indication of.

Yeah, that was it. Friendship and desire. It was that simple. They'd ignored the second part for years, but now they'd both owned up to it. She wanted him. She always had and it was obvious he felt the same. No, she didn't want a romantic dinner, but she did want to spend the night in Bryan's bed.

Morgan slipped into the lingerie, a black lace bra with embroidered red lips and matching panties. It was as playful as it was sexy and she knew Bryan would have fun peeling it off her. Dressing up was one of the things couples did, so she wasn't going to go there. He seemed to like it when she wore tight jeans and a t-shirt, so that's the look she went with.

When she called him, the call went straight to voicemail. She left a flirty message, thanking him for the flowers and letting him know she wanted to see him. To cover all her bases, she decided to text him too. Maybe it seemed desperate, but he'd been pretty pissed off when he left her apartment last night. She hoped he wasn't ignoring her on purpose.

She'd been a total bitch last night – again – and was determined to make it up to him. That's why she'd hit the lingerie store after she turned in her sub-par paper.

75

While she waited for Bryan to call or text back, she dove into her studies. She used to read suspense novels to fill her time, but ever since she'd gone back to school, fiction only made an appearance during the week between quarters. A master's degree required a tremendous amount of reading and to prepare for finals, Morgan read every chapter twice, once as a read-through and once to take meticulous notes on important points.

When her phone buzzed with a text message, she nearly leaped off the sofa. She shouldn't get this excited about seeing Bryan, but she did like spending time with him and especially liked the naked time they spent together. She'd never been with anyone so sure of himself and able to translate that confidence into pleasure for her. The orgasms were always mind-blowing and now that she was done with that damned paper, she really needed a full-body release.

Instead of finding a text from Bryan, it was from Holly, asking what she was up to. It had been two hours since she'd called and texted him, and Morgan wasn't the type of woman to wait for a man, not even one who was a genius in bed, so she sent a text to Holly inviting her over to watch horror movies. It was a long-standing tradition for Morgan. The only time she ever watched horrors was on Valentine's Day. It just seemed appropriate given she wasn't into the lovey-dovey romantic crap.

Holly said she'd bring chocolate, so Morgan changed into stretch pants and a sweatshirt and dug out her horror collection from under the bed.

***

"You going to ignore that beep forever?" Owen asked from under the truck. Bryan had ignored Morgan's call a couple hours ago and knew the text that followed was likely from her. He was still a little pissed off about her attitude yesterday and he didn't want to hear her bitch about him sending flowers on Valentine's

Day.

Bryan placed a wrench in Owen's extended hand. "We need to get this broke-dick truck fixed. I need something other than the Ducati to get around." Bryan liked the motorcycle, but Morgan was right, it was a little ridiculous to be riding it in February.

"So you are going to ignore the beep."

Grabbing the second creeper, Bryan rolled under the truck. Owen was a hell of a lot more skilled than he'd been when they first bought the 'stang they were restoring, so Bryan didn't need to check his work, but maybe the audience would steer Owen's focus back to the truck and away from Bryan's personal business. "Is it annoying you?"

"Not really, I'm just curious why you'd ignore it." He tightened the bolt and looked over, a sardonic smile revealing his amusement. "Women troubles?"

Bryan took the wrench and rolled back out, fighting the chill that tried to race up his spine. The garage was warm thanks to the electric space heater they'd been running all day. "I never have women troubles." He didn't let women troubles happen. As soon as he caught a whiff of an issue, he'd end a relationship. Bryan was never in for the long term and he'd always been honest about that. When women wanted more, it wasn't a problem, it was just over.

Owen rolled out from under the truck. "Then why are you ignoring the text?"

Bryan sighed, a habit he'd adopted since he'd been messing around with Morgan. He never had a reason to expel deep breaths before her. His laid back attitude was the result of incredibly low-key parents and a lifetime of living with the navy. Service demanded patience and he'd felt as though he'd mastered the skill. Morgan tested all of his limits. Even though he hated when Owen tried to beat a dead horse, the simmering frustration had nothing to do with his best friend and everything to do with the man's sister. "What are you my mother?"

"No, but you've been acting like a little bitch all day, so I know something's up. Are you sad you have no one to spend Valentine's Day with?" Owen's mocking tone should have made him laugh but he didn't find any humor in the comment.

Worried he might feed Owen's suspicions, so Bryan forced a chuckle. "Hardly." Bryan definitely wasn't sad. Pissed, yes, but sad was for pussy-whipped Romeos who succumbed to the rants of women. That wasn't Bryan.

That didn't stop him from wanting to help Morgan get over her relationship issues. He wasn't sure what had come over him, but he definitely wanted to make their situation exclusive. Then again, if he was going to be going out on a ship soon, and he hoped that was going to happen, he didn't need the complication of leaving a woman behind in port. Not that Bryan thought Morgan would cheat, but distance made people do crazy things. "I'm not a pussy-whipped Romeo. I don't need a woman to fill some void on a holiday targeted to get people to spend their money when what they should be doing is acknowledging their love every damned day of the year."

"So says the man-whore."

Bryan hated being called that, but to admit it might open a door to a conversation he couldn't have. "So says the man-whore," he mumbled as he wiped his greasy hands on a rag.

Owen leaned against the truck and took a long drink from the water bottle he'd brought. His narrowed gaze prickled Bryan's nerves. He didn't like being assessed, especially when he was keeping a secret from his best friend. "You should do what Morgan does on Valentine's Day."

Bryan simply wanted to do Morgan on Valentine's Day, but that wasn't looking promising. "What's that?"

"She watches horror movies all night. Has her own little movie marathon."

Bryan laughed. "That is why I have so much more respect for your sister than I do for you."

"Yeah, well she does it because she won't acknowledge her real issues."

Bryan knew that. Her father's abuse and her mother tolerating that abuse had left a mark on both Morgan and Owen. Bryan had watched Owen battle those demons a few times, after each of his ex-wives cheated on him, and again just a couple months ago when one of those ex-wives showed up to manipulate him again.

"Can't be easy for her," Bryan crossed his arms, hoping he was showing neutrality. Owen knew he and Morgan were friends. He'd go ballistic if he knew Bryan had crossed that line.

"It's not easy, but she doesn't even try. She needs to realize not all men are like our old man." Owen chuckled and Bryan understood the paradox of that statement. The last time Owen had battled those demons, he'd been convinced he couldn't avoid the Landry legacy. It'd taken the love of a good woman for him to realize he wasn't anything like his father. "Being a husband doesn't equal controlling and abusive. Why do you think she dates a different guy every other week?"

She wasn't doing that anymore – was she? Bryan was sure she hadn't been seeing anyone since the two of them had hooked up. When she had a date, she was obvious about it. The only time she'd ever snuck around was with him.

Right?

The thought of Morgan with someone else made him want to propagate all the ships from Naval Station Everett and launch a full-blown strike on every man in Puget Sound. Christ, he was acting like a sailor with channel fever, except he hadn't been out on a ship that was finally approaching port after months at sea.

Owen pushed off the truck. "I'm out of here. You might not have anything going tonight, but I have a beautiful woman to wine and dine."

Bryan had never been jealous of what Owen and Stacie shared before, but suddenly, he didn't want to be alone. Morgan had shot him down about dinner and she was likely fuming because of the flowers. As soon as his buddy left, Bryan finally checked his messages. He was obviously a glutton for punishment since a ridiculous hope that Morgan wanted to see him bubbled in his chest.

The thank you message made him smile. When he listened to the voice mail and heard her sweet Cajun accent and the tease in her voice, he was intrigued by her proposition. A million images played through his dirty mind thinking about the kind of special lingerie she wanted to show him. He wasted no time in calling her back.

"You have the worst timing in the world," she said by way of greeting.

"Hi to you too," he chuckled.

"Hi, but seriously, why didn't you answer? What have you been doing? No, wait, don't answer that."

Bryan laughed again. "I've been with your brother, fixing my truck."

"Oh." He could practically picture her delicious lips forming a tight circle at her wrong assumption. Damn, he wanted to kiss the tension right out of them and make her melt into his arms.

"So, you coming over?"

"I can't. When you didn't call back, I invited Holly over for a movie night."

Dammit. He shouldn't have ignored her call, but couldn't she even give him a chance to get back to her. It'd only been a couple hours. "Horror movie marathon?" he asked, letting his amusement win over his frustration. Frustration would get him nowhere.

"Uh, yeah. How'd you know that?"

"Owen told me. You ladies probably need a big strong man there to protect you from all the horror." It was desperate, yeah, but Bryan was pulling out all the stops.

Morgan laughed. "You wish. Having a hot guy here defeats the purpose."

"You think I'm hot?" he teased.

"You know I do." Her voice was breathy and the sound went all the way to his cock. Damn, it was going to be a lonely Valentine's Day.

"Yeah, but I just like to hear it."

"Now that I'm done stroking your ego…"

"Sweetheart, I've got something else for you to stroke," he reminded her.

"Down boy. It's not going to happen tonight. I'm not blowing off Holly for a little nookie."

Bryan could respect that. He didn't make it a habit to blow off his friends for that kind of action either. "Just for the record, it'd be a lot of nookie. You free tomorrow night?"

"No. A bunch of us are going out to celebrate turning in our papers. I get out of work at noon, so I'm free all afternoon until six."

"I'm meeting Owen and Ty to work on the mustang."

Her sigh matched his. "So I guess I'll see you when I see you," she said. Sunday was out because she had a study group and since Monday was a full day of work and classes for her and he had a twelve hour shift starting at 0700, they really couldn't make any plans.

"Damn, Morg. All I can think about is you in Valentine's lingerie. It's going to be hard having that fantasy in my head and not knowing when I'm going to see you again."

"You'll survive. It gives you something to add to your spank bank."

"Nice. You talk like a sailor, you know that?"

"Must be all the time I spend with you."

He loved her sailor's tongue. The woman spoke her mind and didn't worry about being judged for the way she spoke it. "You know, I haven't needed to masturbate for a long time. I like to save it all up for you."

"Oh really," she purred.

"Really. But tonight, I just might have to close my eyes and imagine your hands on me."

"Maybe I'll do the same." There was that breathy voice again and Bryan was grateful he was alone in the garage.

"Don't tease," he scolded, adjusting the erection so it wasn't so uncomfortable. Christ, picturing Morgan with her hands...oh, God, talk about a fantasy for the spank bank. "I can still catch a ferry and be there in less than two hours."

"You can tease me, but I can't reciprocate?"

"Not when you're the one shutting us down for the night."

"I told you, I'm not blowing off my friend. Speaking of, she'll be here any minute, so I should go."

"Call me after she leaves. We can have phone sex."

"Not as satisfying as the real thing," she laughed. "Anticipation is good for the loins."

Yeah, well his damn loins were going to turn blue.

"Anticipation sucks. Have fun with your horror flicks."

"I will. Bryan?"

"Yeah?" And there was that hope bubbling in his chest again.

"Thank you again for the flowers. They really are beautiful."

Just like you, he wanted to say, but kept his trap shut so he didn't ruin the moment. "I'm glad you like them."

"I love them and I'm sorry for being such a bitch last night about Valentine's Day."

"Apology accepted. I'll talk to you later."

He hated to hang up, especially not knowing when he was going to see her again, but he was happy she enjoyed the flowers and hoped maybe she'd think of him every time she looked at them.

Chapter 5

"Yo, bro. What's doing?" Bryan asked as he pressed the phone between his shoulder and ear.

"Megan left me," his brother said without greeting. Bryan's heart dropped into his stomach as he dropped onto the couch. The laundry he was folding could wait.

Megan and Beau had met in the navy but Megan had opted not to make it her career. She'd been discharged after her initial enlistment. Meanwhile, Beau had reenlisted just a month ago and was approaching thirteen years, well over the hump to retirement.

"Dumb question, but are you alright?" Bryan asked.

"No. She warned me, you know. Told me if I re-up'd she was gone. I didn't believe her. But hell, even if I did, I couldn't give up the navy. It's all I know."

Bryan understood. He was married to the navy, which was why he wasn't interested in the kind of marriage that would bind him to a woman who didn't understand the commitment the navy required.

"What do you need?" Bryan asked. He was tight with his two brothers. Moving around a lot as kids, they'd formed a strong bond, one that got stronger each time they had to leave their friends behind. Now all three of them were in the navy and rarely saw each other, but they always had each other's backs.

"I have to move off post. Housing has given me two weeks to vacate. I also need to get totally fucking trashed and have meaningless sex with countless babes. I don't remember how to pick up women. Can you come out for a week or two or even a long weekend?"

Bryan wasn't interested in giving his brother lessons in picking up women, but he'd be there for him nevertheless. "You bet. I'll talk to the skipper as soon as I get off the phone with you. There's nothing pressing going on, so it shouldn't be a problem and I have plenty of leave saved up." Being on a three on, four off shift schedule afforded him plenty of time off. Even when he had navy duties to attend to on his off days, it didn't demand too much of his time. Things had been pretty slow lately, which was why Bryan had left early today. He had planned to get some things done around the house so he could see Morgan tomorrow.

"Did you call Blake?" Bryan asked. Beau, who was stationed at a joint military installation just outside Denver, was the middle brother, four years younger than Bryan. Blake was two years younger than Beau and currently stationed in Connecticut. Since Blake was a master at arms, it might not be as easy for him to get away.

"Not yet."

"You want me to do it?" Bryan didn't have a lot to offer. There was nothing he could say to make Beau feel better, but maybe he could ease some of the logistics for him.

"I appreciate the offer, but it's my issue, I should deliver the news."

Bryan put his feet up on the table and leaned back on the cushions of his old couch. Maybe if he relaxed a little bit, it would alleviate some of Beau's tension. Energy of the universe, or some shit like that. "Then I take it you haven't told Mom and Pop?"

"Haven't figured out how to tell them their son is a failure yet," Beau droned.

He wasn't a failure. Obviously Megan had issues and Bryan

wondered if she was stepping out on his brother and using his reenlistment as an excuse to leave. "We both know I'm their favorite son, but that doesn't mean they'll think you're a failure," Bryan explained, hoping to add a little humor to the horrible situation.

"No, no, I'm their favorite. That's while they'll be disappointed."

"Of course they'll be disappointed, but not because you're a failure. It takes two to make a marriage work and obviously Megan wasn't willing to compromise."

"Apparently, neither was I."

"Mom and Pop will understand. They love you, and you know they respect your commitment to the navy."

"I know, it's just tough. They're going to give me all that parental advice about trying to work it out. That's why I called you first. You never offer up bull shit."

"Yeah, well, I do what I can." Bryan did want to talk more, find out if Beau thought Meagan was stepping out, but that could wait until he got to Colorado.

"I might need to call you back after I tell them, just for one of your reality checks."

"Not a problem. I'm always got your back."

"I know, you're the best."

"Damn straight. That's why I'll always be Mom and Pop's favorite. It's all about being the wise first-born. Nothing you can do to change that, so don't get your boxers in a bunch."

Beau laughed and Bryan was glad he could ease the situation, even if only for a few minutes.

"Maybe I'll start going commando just to avoid any bunching. Women like that right?"

"Not as much as men do, but you can see if it works for you."

"I'll do that. So how are things with you?"

"Good. Things are good." Bryan wasn't sure what to say. He couldn't talk about Morgan since it was just a friends with bennies thing, but she seemed to be the only thing he did want to talk about. "We'll catch up when I get there. I'll call you as soon as I have the details. In the meantime, stay sober and stay sane. Wait until I get there to lose your shit."

"I'll try. The last few days have been pretty fucked up. I'm looking forward to letting it loose."

"Call Blake and Mom and Pop. If you need to, call me too. Anytime. Day or night."

"What? To cry on your shoulder? Ain't gonna happen."

"You never know, you might like it."

"Later asshole."

"Later, bro. I'm serious, stay sane until I get there."

"Is that an order?" Beau quipped.

"You bet your ass it is and since I outrank you, you better follow it."

Bryan wasted no time in calling the skipper and asking for leave. Fortunately, the man was compassionate, unlike some leaders Bryan had served under in his seventeen years in the navy. All he had to do was fill out a chit and get all the appropriate signatures and he was good to go.

Two hours later Bryan had a flight booked for the next day. When laundry was done, he'd pack up a sea bag and be ready to go first thing in the morning. A jaunt across the sound on the ferry and the light rail to the airport and he'd be on his way. All that was left to do was let Morgan know. The question was, did he call or text?

By definition of their relationship, he didn't even have to tell her, but he wanted to. She was working her normal Wednesday shift at the clinic, which meant she wouldn't answer her phone. He could leave her a voice mail, but figured she'd be more likely to check her text messages first.

A knock on his door shifted his attention. Bryan opened it to find Owen on standing there.

"Hey man," Owen said as he walked in. "Rumor has it you're taking leave."

"News travels fast." Bryan wasn't surprised. The computer security office wasn't that big and Owen was a supervisor, working directly for Bryan.

"Things are slow, not much else to talk about. What's up?"

"Beau's wife left him. I'm going to help him move out of base housing and move on, if I can."

"Well, if anyone can, it's you. You've got a lot of experience with that."

Too much. Bryan hadn't been stationed with Owen during his two divorces, but when Owen had called, Bryan went. His buddy was as much a brother as his own blood.

"How long are you going to be gone?" Owen asked.

"Two weeks. I fly out tomorrow morning, back on the eighth." Two weeks away. It'd been that long since he last hooked up with Morgan. Another two weeks was going to be a lifetime. Shit, maybe he should have scheduled his flight for Friday so he could spend some quality naked time with her before he left.

"Anything I can do?"

Bryan shook his head. He wasn't even sure what he could do, but just being there for his brother was important. "Got any words of wisdom for my brother?"

Owen chuckled. "No wisdom. He's got to move on in his own way, his own time. Did she cheat on him?"

"He didn't say. Apparently she told him if he re-up'd they were through. Beau thought it was an idle threat."

"Would he have gotten out if he believed her?"

It was Bryan's turn to laugh. "The navy is all us Curtis' know. It's been our life since we were born."

"Then I guess they weren't meant to be."

It sounded lame, but it was true. Their parents had been an exception to the norm, married for forty-five years, both of them serving in the navy for nearly thirty years. Bryan had always known what his parents shared was rare and he was proud of their commitment to each other and the navy. He, however, never believed he'd find a woman who respected his commitment. A career in the navy was like being married and most women didn't want to share their husband with another wife. Bryan also never wanted to be in the position where he had to put his wife second. It was inevitable as a sailor. Duty came first, then family.

"You going to work on the Mustang while I'm gone?" They'd bought a '67 junker nearly a year ago. Restoring it was a slow process, but it gave them something to do on their off days.

"It's no fun doing it alone."

"That statement applies to so many aspects of life," Bryan quipped.

Owen laughed along with him. "So what does your girl think of you leaving town so suddenly?"

Woman, he mentally corrected, but didn't take the bait. Bryan recognized the question for what it was. Owen was digging.

"I don't have a girl," Bryan said. It was mostly true. Even though lately he'd been wanting Morgan more and more, the fact was she wasn't his. Plus, she was no girl. Morgan was a red-hot, passionate woman.

"I'm going to find out who she is, you know that right?" Owen sounded pleased with himself, but Bryan knew the truth. His buddy wouldn't be happy at all if he found out. The real problem was Bryan doubted the *if* of that statement. He'd always believed it was more likely a *when*, but he'd do his damndest to meet Morgan's demands, especially if it meant staying in her bed.

"Nothing to find out, man. Absolutely nothing."

***

Two weeks? Bryan was going to Colorado for two whole weeks?

Morgan wished she had checked her messages before leaving the clinic. If she had, she might have been able to catch the last ferry to Bremerton to see him, or at least invite him to spend the night at her place. Now it was too late and his flight was early enough that she wouldn't be able to see him tomorrow either.

Why two weeks? And why so suddenly?

Oh, God, was there some sort of emergency? One of his brothers was stationed in Colorado – had something happened to him?

Morgan wanted to call, to see if everything was alright, but it was after midnight. Since he had to get an early start tomorrow, he was probably already sleeping.

Since she was so wired, Morgan logged onto her computer. Grades should be posted and she was anxious to see how she'd done on her paper. She'd also check Facebook to see if Bryan posted something. She didn't spend a lot of time on social media and neither did he, but he often referred to one of his brothers as a social media whore, so maybe there was something about the sudden trip.

Shit. The lines between friendship and something more were starting to blur. Would she have been this worried two months ago?

Hell yes, she would have. Bryan was her friend, always had been. So what if she'd finally acted on the burning crush she'd had for twelve years. That didn't change their friendship.

Did it?

Morgan didn't like the race of her heart or the fluttery feeling in her stomach. If she didn't know better, she'd think she was coming down with something. But no, this was not the flu. She was pining – pining!

She'd rather have the flu!

Before she'd hooked up with Bryan it had been more than a year without sex. She certainly hadn't pined after anyone during that time. Since their arrangement was simply friends with benefits, she shouldn't be pining now either. Two weeks was hardly the end of the world. There was work and classes and her volunteer time at the clinic. Two weeks would fly by. In no time at all Bryan would be knocking on her door for a booty call.

Morgan went to her room to change out of the scrubs and into something less antiseptic. Her uniform was comfortable enough, but she didn't like hanging out in it. Instead, she slipped into one of the giant t-shirts Bryan had left behind on one of his sleepovers. She loved wearing his shirts, especially this one that had his name on it. She wasn't sure what the reference meant – *What About Bryan* – but it was cute with the cartoony image and made her think of him.

A large sigh escaped as she realized wearing his shirt was probably only feeding the issue.

Two weeks was good, actually. Pining was a bad sign. She'd never done it before. Usually her relationships ended when whatever guy she was seeing started pining or acting possessive or asked for more from their relationship. Morgan wasn't in for the long haul. She had no interest in marriage. Her career came first, especially now with the career change she was making. It was important to focus on her studies and become the best mid-wife she could be. Pining over a hot guy who also had no interest in a permanent relationship was a waste of precious energy.

It was okay to miss him, she reassured herself while filling a glass with ice and water. They were good friends, after all. In fact, the last few times they'd hung out had been purely platonic. Missing him would be like missing her brother or Stacie if they took off for a couple weeks. It was no big deal.

She sent him a text asking if everything was alright before returning to the laptop.

Morgan's fingers lingered on the keyboard as she stared at the log in page to access her grades. She was hopeful about the research paper, but not confident. Since Bryan had left her hanging, a good part of the night was spent stewing instead of writing. She was convinced she'd have been more productive if they'd just gotten down and dirty.

Well, there was no time like the present. Morgan logged in and nearly sent the computer flying off her lap. She got a C. A flipping C!

Oh, for the love of Pete that was bad. Her scholarship was dependent upon a 3.5 GPA. A C would send it plummeting.

Her heart raced as she clicked on the icon to view her instructor's comments. Joan Forrest was a practicing mid-wife and while Morgan liked her teaching style, it was no secret that she was difficult to please. Still, a C!

Morgan read the comments and wished she could disagree, but the truth was she'd been distracted...distracted and sexually frustrated. The comments were right on the mark, stating the topic was interesting and relevant, but Morgan had only scratched the surface of holistic pain remedies during labor and birth. She'd achieved the minimum page count, which was only a guide, and Joan would have liked to have seen more in-depth statistical data and analysis of each of the methods.

Had Morgan not been distracted, she would have done better. She'd never gotten a C in her life. Not once!

Dammit, she couldn't afford to be distracted. If she lost her scholarship, there was no way she could afford to stay in school. The master's program was expensive and Morgan had normal bills as well. She was making ends meet now, barely, and she didn't have much savings, certainly not enough to dip into if she lost the scholarship.

Logging onto Facebook, she checked her study group page to see if anyone shared their grades. She could use a little encouragement right now. If everyone scored low, Morgan wouldn't blame this little infatuation with Bryan.

No comments about the paper. She wasn't sure she wanted to post her horrid grade, but she wouldn't get any encouragement by keeping it to herself. She typed a quick message, sharing her disappointment. With any luck, a few others would have received a low grade too. Not that she wished bad grades on them, but it would indicate the instructor's ridiculously high standards were the problem rather than Bryan being a distraction.

Since it was after midnight, Morgan didn't expect any

immediate responses, so she stalked Bryan's wall to see about his sudden trip. His brother Blake posted a very telling message.

Can't wait to see you and Beau Curtis. The babes better brace for impact with the Curtis brothers on the loose.

Great. Why had she logged onto her computer again? All it seemed to deliver was bad news.

It couldn't be an emergency if Bryan planned to troll for *babes* with his brothers. Still, the trip seemed sudden. Then again, he didn't have to report to her.

Maybe it was a sign. Not that Morgan believed in that stuff. She took life as it came because she didn't know any other way. It could just be good math. Her low grade plus Bryan going out to scout for babes with his brothers equaled a message Morgan shouldn't ignore. It seemed as though it might be time for her to move on.

It's not like her arrangement with Bryan was permanent anyway. She'd learned a hard lesson as a kid, that a woman couldn't trust a man to take care of her and love her. There were a few rare times, when she was very young, that she could remember her father actually being happy and affectionate. As time passed, those times became few and far between until they were non-existent. She attributed his anger to the addiction her denied. Since her father denied having a problem with alcohol and preferred to blame everyone around him and the world for his troubles, he'd never sought help. Neither had her mother.

Morgan refused to end up like that. Just as she knew her mother couldn't control dear sweet Daddy, Morgan knew she wouldn't be able to control any man in her life. Nor did she want to. That's not what relationships were supposed to be about. Even though she'd seen her sisters in healthy relationships, Morgan lived with too much fear from what she'd seen as a child. Her sisters hadn't experienced what she and Owen had. They'd gotten only a small taste of it, not the years that Morgan and Owen had to endure. Morgan never wanted to be in a position where someone who claimed to love her was a threat to her safety, so she'd opted against marriage. She'd never been interested in having children of her own. Being an auntie was enough. Bringing babies into the world as a mid-wife would be an added bonus.

***

"Why are you wearing Bryan's shirt?"

Morgan hadn't been expecting her brother. It was only eight in the morning, for the love of Pete. She had class in a couple hours, so was taking her sweet time getting ready. It'd been a shock to hear a knock at the door so early, and an even bigger one when she found Owen on the other side.

"What makes you think this is Bryan's shirt?" she asked, trying not to sound like she was scrambling for an excuse.

"I bought that shirt of some guy's back in the laundry room of the barracks at Ft. Bragg. Apparently What About Bryan was a local band in Atlanta. I saw it and knew Bryan had to have it."

Okay then, she wasn't going to be able to pretend it didn't belong to him. "Oh, that's cool. I had no idea."

"So why are you wearing it?" Now suspicion sparked in his voice. Morgan was going to have to put out this fire before it exploded.

"You know Bryan crashes on my sofa on occasion. He must have left it here on accident. I didn't even realize it was his." That made her sound a little slutty, but she liked to tease her brother with that prospect.

"Who else would it belong to?"

"It could have been Erik's or Derek's or–"

"Enough. I don't need a laundry list. Maybe you should stop dating guys whose names rhyme with ick."

Mission accomplished. She'd successfully steered Owen away from any suspicions of Bryan and of men completely. "I'll date whomever I want, no matter what his name sounds like. So why are you here?" No point leaving the discussion open. Plus, Morgan was curious what had her brother here so early.

"Stacie made cinnamon buns this morning." He held up a bag. "I'm willing to share if you make coffee."

Morgan had already had her yogurt, but who was she to say no to cinnamon buns. "Does she have a deadline?"

Owen laughed. "Yeah. I don't want to complain about her procrastination because she can bake like no one's business, but she gets a little moody. I figured I'd better give her some space this morning."

No one ever accused her brother of being stupid. He had a tendency to be overly trusting when it came to women, but he definitely wasn't stupid.

Since she lived alone, Morgan had invested in a single cup coffee brewer. "Pick your poison," she said as she opened the drawer that held a variety of flavors of single serving pods.

"I forgot you had this. I should get one for Stacie. She can't make coffee to save her life."

After he picked a pod, Morgan took it because the deal was she'd make the coffee. A minute later they each had a hot cup of flavored java and a cinnamon bun on a plate. Owen settled onto the sofa and Morgan took her spot in the papasan chair.

"Holy Moses, this is good," she moaned after taking a bite. "Are these from scratch?"

"Yeah. Like I said, she's stressed and procrastinating."

"Good lord, these are the best thing I've ever tasted. If you don't marry her, I will."

Owen shifted on the sofa and got a funny look in his face.

"What?" Morgan asked.

He took another bite. "I bought a ring," he grumbled with a mouth full of cinnamon bun.

"No way!"

It shouldn't have been a surprise, but she knew Owen was trying to take things slow with Stacie, something he'd failed to do with his two ex-bitches. "Ohmigod! Is she pregnant?"

A spark of anger flashed across Owen's face before his shoulders slumped. "I'm never not going to get asked that question, am I?"

"Sorry, big brother. You made your bed."

"Technically, Kristina wasn't pregnant."

"Yeah, but you thought she was and you married her. So, when are you going to pop the question. And when do I get to see the ring?"

"I don't know and after it's on Stacie's finger."

Morgan was happy for her brother. She adored Stacie and thought she was the right person for her brother. Even though Morgan didn't believe in love for herself, she was happy her brother, who felt strongly about love, had finally found the right woman for him.

Despite all that, Morgan threw a pillow at him. "How can you not know? You bought the ring, for the love of Pete!"

"She's on deadline and stressed. It's not a good time."

Morgan was pretty sure there was never a good time, but she didn't want to get into that debate. "Is it a story deadline or illustrations?"

"Illustrations. The stories come to her easily. She has a whole stockpile of them. She tends to obsess over the illustrations though. She has them sketched out and CC loved 'em, but Stacie isn't so sure about one of them, so she's avoiding painting it."

Stacie didn't like to share her work, so Morgan hadn't read the stories, but she'd seen some of the paintings and they were incredible. She was anxious to see Stacie's first book, which was scheduled to be published in a few months.

Owen finished off the cinnamon bun and grabbed another out of the bag that was conveniently placed on the table in front of him. "So do you know who this mystery woman is that Bryan is seeing?"

Morgan choked on her coffee. Where the hell had that question come from? Hopefully it was just a deliberate yet random change of topic to avoid further inquisition about the ring. Bryan's mystery woman wasn't a topic Morgan was interested in discussing.

"I'll take that as a yes," Owen continued as Morgan tried to clear her throat.

"Bryan has a mystery woman?" she asked between coughs.

"So you don't know who she is?"

You're looking at her, Morgan thought, but no way was she telling her overprotective brother she had a friends with benefits arrangement with his best friend. "Uh, no idea. I thought Bryan was a many women kind of guy."

"He usually is."

"So what makes you think there's *a* mystery woman?" She had to know so she could tell Bryan to do a better job of covering his tracks.

"He's been acting weird. He checks his phone a lot when we're at the garage. One day it beeped a couple times and he ignored it. I've never seen him do either of those things before. It's gotta be a woman."

There could be a million explanations for both of those things, but Morgan didn't want to act too defensive and steer suspicion her way. "Well, he hasn't mentioned a thing to me," she offered.

Owen chuckled and nodded at her. "When I saw you in that shirt, I thought it might be you, but Bryan knows better."

"What's that supposed to mean?" Morgan tossed her empty plate on the table and wiped her hands on Bryan's shirt. She should have been expecting the comment but it still pissed her off. She didn't need her brother's permission to sleep with anyone, not even his best friend.

"There's a code, Morg. Guys don't covet their buddy's sister."

"Guys covet," she threw out some air quotes because it was such a ridiculous term, "their buddies' sisters all the time. This is the 21st century, not the stone age."

Owen paused before taking another bite of cinnamon bun. "Good guys don't."

Morgan just shook her head. "How can you refer to Bryan as both a good guy and a man-whore?"

"Good guy doesn't mean nice guy. There's a difference."

It was difficult to argue with that logic. Bryan would go to the ends of the earth for his family and friends. He did not, however, make such noble gestures for the many women who had occupied his bed. Morgan wondered where she fell in that spectrum now. First and most importantly, she considered Bryan her friend. Yeah, the benefits were nice, but that didn't define their relationship. However, if Owen thought Bryan was acting funny, that might be cause for concern. The last thing she needed was Bryan shifting the rules.

The most logical explanation was that Bryan was seeing someone else, or maybe a few someone elses. Morgan didn't like that idea, but it wasn't her business. She and Bryan had an agreement, a sort of don't ask don't tell kind of thing. So really, the mystery woman could be anyone.

Her gut started to churn. She probably shouldn't have eaten the cinnamon bun. All that sugar was going to wreak havoc on her stomach for the rest of the morning. Maybe an antacid would do the trick.

Morgan rolled out of the papasan and looked at Owen. "I gotta get to class," she said, hoping to get him to leave. Otherwise, she might sit here and stew about Bryan with other women while indulging in another cinnamon bun. All that would get her were extra pounds and an ulcer, just what she needed!

Chapter 6

"Men are such pigs," Jenny scowled as she peered at the computer over Morgan's shoulder.

"I don't know, it looks like fun," Stacie said from Morgan's other side.

"Sucking alcohol off a stranger's body does not look fun," Jenny retorted. Morgan was surprised. The woman liked having sex in public. What made body shots so revolting?

"Well, I wouldn't do it with a stranger, but I bet it'd be fun with Owen."

"Owen was a stranger the first time you slept with him," Jenny reminded her.

"Yeah, that was fun too," Stacie said merrily.

Listening to the two women made Morgan feel like she had a devil over one shoulder and an angel over the other, except the roles were confusing. She'd have pegged Jenny for the devil over Stacie.

The three of them were sitting on Jenny's sofa. Morgan was in the middle while Jenny lounged on her right and Stacie sat on the edge of the cushion on Morgan's left. Stacie's laptop sat open on the table in front of them, displaying the picture that had prompted the body shot debate. Apparently Bryan was having the time of his life with is brothers in Colorado. The stripper was blonde – no surprise there – and Bryan looked perfectly content with his mouth attached to her belly.

Meanwhile, Morgan's heart pounded furiously against her rib cage and she had to focus on her breathing to keep it within normal limits. Never mind the fact her anger was blazing like a wildfire.

"How can you not have a problem with him doing that?" Jenny asked.

Morgan ignored the question. Pretending she didn't know it was directed at her was as good a defense as any.

"Morgan?" Stacie prodded, continuing the back and forth banter that was starting to make Morgan's head spin. She wouldn't blame the crazy vertigo on the pictures she was looking at because that was a reality she didn't want to explore.

Morgan shrugged. "Why would I have a problem with it?" The truth was, she wanted to kill him, but that was her own personal issue. She had no claim on Bryan, nor did she want one. Friends with benefits was all they were.

"Come on, there's obviously something going on between you two," Stacie said.

"Actually, there's not," Morgan asserted.

"The way you two look at each other, there ought to be laws," Jenny quipped.

Morgan had been careful not to look at him any more than she had before they'd started messing around. It wasn't difficult since she'd always thought he was hot. Of course, now she knew what he looked like naked, which only served to make the man even hotter. "Bryan's hot, so sue me."

Jenny clicked her tongue. "You don't look at him like he's hot. You look at him like he's dessert."

"And he looks at you like you're charcoal grilled steak tips," Stacie added.

That was a great analogy. Morgan was just a piece of meat in Bryan's eyes. Perfect.

"Bryan's a man-whore. He's probably just going through a dry spell and thinks I'm available."

"Aren't you?" Stacie asked.

"Not to him." That mostly wasn't a lie, not anymore. She knew about his man-whore ways, but as long as it wasn't in her face, she could ignore it. Seeing a picture of him drinking who knows what off of some stripper's belly was repulsive. She'd bit back the rage and feigned indifference for the sake of keeping their hook-ups a secret, but she wanted to castrate him.

"You're so full of shit," Jenny said, pushing away from the sofa. "Who wants a drink?"

Need had replaced want halfway into this conversation and Morgan was ready to focus on the point of girl's movie night – fun. Jenny was hosting, Stacie got to pick the movie, Morgan brought the drinks, and Holly, a new addition to their girl's nights, was bringing the food. What she hadn't expected was being cornered about Bryan. It all started with the way he'd been watching her at the bar after the Super Bowl. She'd warned him, but apparently the man didn't know how to be subtle.

Or maybe he'd been trying to sabotage this whole thing. He kept saying he wanted to tell Owen, but maybe he was just looking for an out. That'd explain why he let his brother post those pictures of him and that stripper.

"Just for the record, I don't believe you either," Stacie informed her before turning to Jenny. "I'll have a drink."

Morgan had brought all the necessities for frozen daiquiris, including a couple varieties of flavored rum. Jenny was the master of making frozen drinks, so Morgan let her work her magic while she tried not to stew over Bryan's escapades in Colorado.

A few thumps at the door had Morgan making a brief escape from the inquisition. Holly was due to arrive with food and that'd be a great distraction.

When Morgan opened the door, several cloth shopping bags hung from both of Holly's arms.

"Want me to take some of that?" Morgan asked.

"Nope, just clear the way so I can put them on the table."

Morgan followed and when Holly was unshackled, the two of them started emptying the bags.

"I brought everything we need for fajitas. The beef, chicken, peppers, onions are already cooked. We might want to reheat it and I have a few different types of tortillas. I also brought sour cream, refried beans, lettuce, Mexican rice, salsa, and guacamole."

"You're a rock star," Stacie said, helping them get the fajita buffet set up.

When they were all settled in the living room with food and drinks, Holly's eyes opened wide as she stared at the computer.

"Is that your friend Bryan?"

"He's in Colorado helping his brother adjust to single life," Morgan explained, still pushing for indifference. Bryan had called when he'd arrived at his brother's and explained the situation. Morgan had never met Beau, but she was still sad for him. She'd seen her brother go through two divorces so understood how difficult it could be. According to Bryan, his brother was wrecked and determined to do something stupid. Morgan thought if anyone could keep Beau walking a straight line, it was Bryan, but after seeing the photo his other brother posted, she wasn't so sure. "Looks like he's having a good time."

"I bet he goes home with her," Jenny said between bites. "We should start a pool, how many women he sleeps with while he's there."

"That's a horrible game," Stacie countered. It seemed the two of them had gone back to their normal roles of Jenny being the devil and Stacie being the angel.

"Three," Morgan said.

They both looked at her like she had three heads, so Morgan held up three fingers as she took a drink to further confirm she was in on the pool. Thinking about Bryan with three women only fueled her temper, but she focused on the opportunity to steer Stacie and Jenny's suspicions away from her and Bryan.

"Three," she sang in a sickly-sweet tone. Stacie just shook her head, but Jenny shook off her surprise.

"He's at a strip club. I bet he goes home with two tonight and I bet he's already been with one. He's still got a week there. I'm going with five."

Morgan swallowed hard at Jenny's analysis.

"Just because they're dancers doesn't mean they sleep with the customers," Holly said.

Jenny's dark eyes rolled. "Right. They take off their clothes and let strange men lick exotic drinks off their bodies."

"Don't forget lap dances," Morgan added. She had no doubt Bryan had received his share of lap dances over the years. He was probably getting one right now, if not more.

"It's a job. They have a boss who dictates what they do while at work." Holly turned to Morgan. "Do you enjoy administering enemas or removing catheters?"

"No, but those aren't sexual acts."

"Believe me, just because it's sexual doesn't mean it's enjoyable."

"Are you speaking from experience?" Jenny asked, raising a brow. Morgan wondered the same thing. Holly was being awfully defensive.

"I've had a few friends who were dancers. They didn't sleep with the clientele. In fact, they took hot showers to wash all that nastiness off every night."

"If it's so nasty, why'd they do it?" Jenny's voice was filled with disbelief.

"It pays well. I have one friend who paid for college with the money she made as a dancer."

Life without student loans. That sounded appealing, but no way could Morgan take off her clothes in front of a bunch of gawking men. She couldn't even bring herself to wear the sexy nurse outfit Bryan had nearly begged her to get. It just seemed too sleazy.

"What are we watching tonight?" Morgan asked, hoping to steer the conversation to safer waters. Holly seemed a little defensive about the whole stripper thing and Jenny could be ruthless. Morgan liked them both, but she felt a stronger bond with Holly who had survived the abuse of an ass-hole boyfriend. It seemed the only thing Jenny had survived was an excessive wardrobe.

"*Much Ado About Nothing*," Stacie said proudly. Of course it would be Shakespeare. Stacie always chose something literary when it was her turn to pick.

"I'm making another batch of daiquiris," Jenny said as she trolled to the kitchen.

"Maybe I'll join the boys," Morgan groaned. "They've gotta be watching something better than Shitspeare."

"Hey, don't diss the classics," Stacie said, pointing at Morgan. "You have to stay, you had a daiquiri."

"And I'll have another if thou is going to punish thy friends with a language no one speaks or even understands."

"People understand it. Entire student bodies study it." Stacie's words were a little slurred, so the margarita was obviously working its magic on the lightweight. Not that Morgan considered herself a heavy weight when it came to drinking, but she was sure she wasn't slurring yet.

"Fine. We'll watch Shitspeare. But what are the boys watching?" So she could fantasize about being across the hall with her brother and Ty while she was forced to endure nineteenth century literature transformed into twentieth century cinema.

"They were going to watch the Band of Brothers series during our movie nights, but they didn't want to start without Bryan so I think they're having an Avengers marathon." Jenny explained.

Morgan would prefer any of the Avengers movies over tonight's selection. Talk about some hubba hubba eye candy. Man, they really needed to make a Hawkeye movie. Maybe Morgan would pick a Jeremy Renner movie when her turn rolled around again. Hansel and Gretel offered almost a full frontal. He wasn't quite as hot or *reach out and touch you* as Bryan, but he also probably didn't suck body shots off blonde strippers when he was supposed to be helping his brother adjust to single life.

Men really sucked. In bad ways. Best not to think about the good ways because then she might stop stewing and even though he wasn't there to see it, Bryan deserved a good, long stew.

***

"I swear, I did not hook up with that stripper," Bryan said as soon as she answered the phone.

Morgan laughed because she had a bit of a buzz from the rum and because he hadn't even said hello. Guilty conscience much?

"I didn't ask," Morgan informed him.

"No, but that picture makes me look bad."

He was bad. So, so bad. "Are you? Bad? Bad, bad Bryan."

"Are you drunk?" He didn't seem amused by her playful question. Party pooper!

Morgan giggled as she settled back on the sofa, resting her head on the cushion, which seemed to be spinning a little bit. Her head, not the cushion. See, this was why she'd done crappy on that paper. It wasn't the distraction of bad, hot Bryan. It was her weak grasp of English. Well, she was Cajun, so technically it was her grasp of ESL. Never mind the fact she knew hardly any Cajun French. It had been dear sweet Daddy's language of love, so Morgan had avoided using it her entire life. Still, she was drunk and from Louisiana, so she could claim it.

"It was chick flick night." She explained as the room started to spin. "I had a few, tres, trois daiquiris, mucho heavy on the rum because Jenny was making them."

"Rum? Where are you now?" his voice was all macho sailor man, going into hero rescue mode. He sounded sexy as sin, but damn, she hated his stupid hero complex.

"I'm home," she sighed, closing her eyes to stop the spinning.

"Alone?"

That was a sobering question. He'd spent the evening with a stripper and he was worried about her having company? Big, hypocritical, alpha jerk. "For now," she teased.

"Where's Owen?" Bryan was familiar with chick flick night. Owen took it upon himself to drive everyone home. No wonder he and Bryan were best friends, what with their big muscles, stupid hero complexes, and monster egos.

"He drove my drunk little patootie home and left. He's probably getting some right now."

"Are you planning to get some tonight?" Bryan asked.

"That, my friend with benefits, is none of your business," Morgan reminded him. "We have an agreement. Don't ask, don't tell."

At last a laugh. He was being so serious. Morgan didn't like serious Bryan. She preferred the fun guy. Ha, fun guy. Well, he did like dark, wet places. Yeah, she definitely preferred fun, naked Bryan.

"That was President Clinton's solution to gays in the military. Our agreement isn't quite as ambiguous."

Oh, but it was. Not knowing what the other was doing left a very gray area that Morgan didn't like to think about but couldn't get out of her head. "I won't be sucking body shots off anybody, if that's what you're worried about."

"What I'm worried about is you being drunk on rum. It makes you very friendly."

Did it? She hadn't noticed. When Bryan was around, she didn't need rum to feel friendly. "You're worried I'm going to screw someone because I've had a few drinks? I have more self-respect than that." She tried to keep her voice playful, but he was starting to irk the hell out of her. He was the one who got personal with a stripper. Did he think she'd seek revenge? There were better ways of doing that than disrespecting herself.

"I miss you," he said, surprising her. Was she really so drunk she couldn't keep up or had he just pulled a complete 180 on this conversation?

Morgan missed him too, but she wasn't drunk enough to blurt out that little ditty. "I suggest you get over it. I noticed that stripper was blonde. Just your type."

"Blondes aren't my type," he growled.

"Really? Because I've only ever seen you with blondes."

"You're not blonde."

"I know. Makes me wonder what you're doing messing around with me." It wasn't the first time she'd wondered, but it had never been something she wanted to explore.

"Morg–"

"No, you don't have to explain," she interjected.

"What if I want to explain?"

"What if I don't want you to?" she countered.

"You're being difficult," he sighed.

Was she? All she was doing was trying to keep things simple. He didn't owe her an explanation and she wasn't going to demand one. That would complicate things between them, something she was trying to avoid.

"I didn't want to do the body shots, but my brothers were asking questions. I couldn't exactly tell them about you and I couldn't be vague about being involved with someone. Blake is a social media whore and he's friends with Owen on Facebook. Anything I said would have been all over the Internet, then I'd have to lie to your brother more than I already am. Doing the body shot was the easiest solution."

That was convenient, but there was one little problem. "We're not involved."

Chapter 7

"Like it or not, we are. I'm not with anyone else and have no interest in being with anyone else." Morgan's heart kicked up a few beats. Anxiety or excitement? A healthy serving of both, probably, and didn't that just take this simple arrangement and throw in a heavy dollop of complication.

"How do you know I'm not?" she teased, hoping to lighten the mood and get her heart back to a normal rate. Maybe that would alleviate the flutter in her belly too.

"Are you?" he asked.

"No," she admitted, choosing not to play games. She was a master at talking in circles, but for some reason, it didn't seem fun at the moment. No, nothing about this conversation was fun. In fact, it was turning into a real buzz kill.

"I'm not saying we need to label it or make promises to each other or anything like that, but you can't deny that we're involved."

No, she couldn't. "How's Beau doing?" she asked.

"Admit we're involved and I'll tell you," he said.

So much for her attempt at changing the subject. "Fine. We're involved. How's your brother doing?"

"He has good days and bad. I've been trying to keep him away from women, but he seems determined to do something stupid."

"Are you going soft?" she teased. Bryan, the reputed man-whore, trying to keep his heartbroken brother away from women seemed like a paradox.

"Sweetheart, nothing about me is soft, especially with your voice in my ear." His voice was playful with a hint of that seductive rasp that made her girl parts all gooey.

Morgan laughed. She wished Bryan was right there on the sofa next to her, showing her just how soft he wasn't. Unfortunately, he still had a week in Colorado. "I meant with your brother, you perv."

"Beau was never the type to sleep around. He's the kind of person who commits himself to a woman before he sleeps with her. I don't want him doing something he'll regret."

"So if Beau's the good boy and you're the man-whore, what does that make Blake?"

Bryan released a heavy sigh that she could nearly feel through the phone. "I hate that title, by the way."

"Man-whore?" It was a surprise to hear him say that, the sailor who had carried the title as proudly as he did his military rank.

"Yeah. I also hate that everyone thinks I have a thing for blondes. I don't."

Morgan laughed. "What are we playing now, true confessions?"

"I'm not playing anything. I'm just saying." The frustration in his voice spun up some guilt as Morgan realized just how difficult she was being.

"Bryan–"

"Right, I know. I'm getting too personal for you. Look, it's late. I'm going to go. I just wanted you to know there's nothing going on with me and that stripper. It was one body shot to keep my brothers off my back, that's all."

Morgan stared at the phone after it went silent. Bryan hadn't even said good-bye. If she wasn't ready to pass out, she'd call him back and apologize because above all else, they were friends. Maybe Bryan was just frustrated with his brother though, and he didn't need Morgan pouring gasoline on that fire. She'd wait until she was sober and check in on him.

***

"What's her name?" Beau picked up the phone off the floor and tossed it on the bed before he dropped onto the mattress next to Bryan. Pelting the phone against the door probably wasn't smart, but smart was one of those things that seemed to be more and more elusive.

"Who?" Bryan had been playing dumb so often he was worried he might start losing brain cells. Probably already had given how defeated he felt at the moment.

"You hate phones and you check that thing every five minutes." Beau grabbed it off the blanket and started inspecting it. "Looks like it survived. Heavy duty case, that's smart."

Bryan grabbed the thing before Beau could identify the source of his angst.

Shaking his head as though he understood the stupidity of throwing a phone against a door, Beau mumbled, "Has to be a girl."

Woman, Bryan silently corrected. One who cranked his otherwise mellow demeanor to full boil and thought he was a man-whore. He was ready for that title to swallow the anchor.

"I've gone through six phones in the past year." Beau leaned back against the pillows, his hands folded casually behind his head. "Two of them I threw at a door just like you did. One I ran over with my truck, six times. The other two casualties were courtesy of the floor."

Bryan was quickly learning that Beau and Megan's marriage hadn't been a bed of roses. Bryan still wasn't convinced she hadn't been stepping out on his brother, but it wasn't a subject he wanted to push with Beau. The guy was hurting enough and the marriage was over, so there was no point finding more reasons to be miserable.

"Maybe I got called back from leave," Bryan suggested, looking for any viable excuse for throwing the phone.

"Nah. That wouldn't make you throw your phone. Only a girl can have that impact."

Woman.

Growing up, he and Beau had spent countless hours lounging on each other's beds and talking about the things that trouble boys. Sometimes it was sports, agreeing on how much the Yankees sucked or commiserating when Army beat Navy. It was usually girls, though, with Beau droning on about his broken heart and Bryan trying to offer sound advice. Never once had Bryan been on the receiving end of that kind of advice.

"I'm treading in foreign waters," he admitted, realizing he needed to talk to someone about Morgan. Beau could keep a secret, unlike Blake who would plaster it all over Facebook while simultaneously calling their mother to rat Bryan out. He loved Blake, but man, he didn't know how to keep his trap shut.

Beau nodded. "Must be serious then."

Bryan scrolled through the phone to find his pictures and tapped on one of his favorites of Morgan. It was the night of the Super Bowl, right after Malcolm Smith returned an interception for a touchdown. Her smile was so natural, so full of life, just like the woman. "I don't know what it is," he grumbled, clearing the picture before tossing the phone to the end of the bed. He was starting to want serious and had no idea what to do about that. Being married to the navy, Bryan had never wanted to commit to a woman. Morgan, though, she tempted him to want things he'd never considered. That would all be fine if she wasn't so averse to relationships.

"So, her name," Beau coaxed.

Bryan wasn't sure he was ready to give that information out. Beau had never met Morgan but he knew Owen and might make the connection. But hell, he'd kept it a secret for so long it was starting to eat away at him. His head might be a jumbled mess after talking to Morgan, but he did know without a doubt he could trust his brother.

"Morgan," he surrendered, her name like a lover's caress across his lips. Damn, he missed her, even with her damn *we aren't involved* attitude.

"Why is that familiar?"

"She's Owen's sister." No point making Beau think too hard.

"No way!" Beau's eyes were wide with disbelief. "Wait, isn't she the one you've had a thing for since Norfolk?"

How the hell – "What makes you say that?"

"Uh, because you told me."

"When?" Bryan had no recollection. His ridiculous lust for Morgan had been locked away in a vault for as long as it had existed.

"My bachelor party. Blake was trying to hook you up with a couple girls, brunettes. You said blondes only. I asked why, you confessed. The only brunette you wanted was your best friend's sister, and since she was off limits, you'd never be with a woman who even remotely resembled her."

Shit. If he'd confessed to Beau, had Blake heard too? No, no way. Blake couldn't keep a secret to save his life and since he'd never said a word, he clearly didn't know.

"We hooked up once," Bryan said with a smile, remembering how he'd taken Morgan up against the wall just inside her apartment door. It had been the most incredible experience of his life. "That's all it was supposed to be, except then it happened again and again and now – shit, now I can't get her out of my head."

"What does Owen say?"

"He doesn't know." Bryan shook his head and realized he was wringing his hands, his knuckles turning white and aching. He made an effort to stop, flexing his fingers to push the tension out, but it did nothing to alleviate the ache in his chest. "Morgan doesn't want anyone to know."

Beau laughed. "What happens if he finds out?"

"He kicks my ass and Morgan secures the first life boat she can find. She doesn't do relationships – can't even say the damned word."

Beau laughed some more. Not a chuckle or a chortle, but a gut-wrenching, teary-eyed laughter that echoed throughout the room and shook the queen-size bed.

"Fuck you, bro," Bryan spat, backhanding his brother with a love-pat. The pucker factor had increased exponentially. He should have just kept his damned trap shut.

"Listen, you know I've got your six, but you have to admit, this is, well, it's a soup sandwich. You've got it bad for a woman for the first time in your life and she doesn't feel the same."

Didn't she though? Feeling it and admitting to feeling it were two different things. Bryan knew she felt something, but breaking down her walls to get her to admit she felt something, that was a battle he wasn't sure he was equipped to fight.

"It's complicated," he sighed, hardly able to believe he was in this predicament. "I've always lived by the rule that there's nothing I need that I can't put in my sea-bag."

"Love bites, bro," Beau advised, nudging Bryan with his elbow. "It bleeds. It'll bring you to your knees."

Bryan raised a brow at his brother. "Seriously? The best advice you can give me is Def Leppard lyrics?"

"Love lives, love dies. It's no surprise. Love begs, love pleads. It's what you need."

Bryan might laugh at his brother's off-key rendition of the song, but love was the last fucking thing he needed. With any luck, his detailer would get him assigned to Carrier Strike Group Three and Bryan's ship would sail soon – very soon. Just him and his sea-bag, as it had always been. He wasn't going to leave a PACFLEET widow behind. Not only was it not his style, but Morgan wasn't the type either. That's why things had been so great the last couple months. They were friends with benefits, to echo Morgan's words. Bryan should be satisfied with that. What the hell was he thinking trying to push the envelope?

"She's your kryptonite," Beau muttered.

"Fuck, you're not going to sing me another song are you?" Obviously Beau wasn't the one to go to for advice on women, but he was the lesser of two evils. If he'd been talking to Blake, the situation would be headlining World News Tonight.

"I think I need to clean out my iPod. I've been listening to Megan's playlists."

"You know that's a modern form of a torture, right?"

"Yeah, well, what's a guy to do? I love her. I know I have to get over it, but it's not going to happen today or tomorrow."

"No one expects you to, but you shouldn't actively torture yourself either."

"I know you think I've been one of those pussy-whipped Romeos, but when love doesn't bite, it's pretty damn fantastic."

"Which makes you a pussy-whipped Romeo," Bryan pointed out.

"I know you say you're married to the navy, but you're about to swallow the anchor. Do you really want to spend the rest of your life alone?"

"I've got three years until retirement and I'm hoping to spend that time on the pond. I'm not planning that far in advance." The truth was, though, he wanted Morgan in his life. She'd be done with school by the time he retired and they'd be free to do what they wanted. Bryan planned to stay in Puget Sound and wanted to start his own computer security business, hopefully partnering with Owen. Morgan would be delivering babies, but without school, she'd have more time. Bryan wanted her to spend it with him, but acting now, when he knew his ship was going to sail, would be foolish. Better to stick with the arrangement they had.

"Ladies," Blake said as he padded into the room. "What am I interrupting?"

He had a guitar slung over his shoulder, his fingers strumming lazily. Blake had always had a talent for music. He'd been in choir and band in high school and had even won some talent contests.

"Bryan's in love," Beau chided.

Blake immediately stopped strumming and raised a brow. "Seriously, bro?"

"No, not seriously," Bryan countered. "Never known you to play guitar in the middle of the night." Yep, it was a blatant subject change and he wouldn't be surprised if one or both of his brothers called him on it, but no way in hell was he talking about Morgan within earshot of Blake.

"Yeah, well, haven't seen you in the middle of the night for nearly two decades."

Fair enough. They saw each other once a year if they were lucky. Though they stayed in touch by phone and computer, Bryan really had no clue about his brothers' routines.

"Shit, I didn't get you in trouble with your girl, did I? I can take that picture down."

Bryan had never known his youngest brother to be apologetic or serious. "You alright?" Bryan asked.

Blake strummed his fingers across the strings a couple times. Bryan didn't know a thing about music, but the sound Blake was making sounded good.

"I'm getting out." Blake focused on the guitar as he dropped onto the end of the bed.

"Getting out?" Beau and Bryan asked in unison.

"Of the navy. When this enlistment is up next winter, I'm out."

"Why?" Okay, asking the same questions in harmony was starting to get weird.

"You love the navy," Bryan pointed out, thankfully solo.

"I like the navy. I've never loved it."

"But twelve years. Dude, you're more than halfway to retirement." Beau was shaking his head as though he couldn't even fathom what Blake was contemplating.

"The navy isn't my lifelong dream. It's been okay, but it's not what I want to keep doing."

"Did something happen?" Bryan asked. Blake had been unusually mellow this trip. Bryan had thought the baby of the family was just being low key to support Beau, but that had never been Blake's style. Something had to be doing with him.

"Nah, nothing worth talking about." He upped the beat on the notes he played on the guitar, producing a harsher sound.

Damn, there was definitely something going on with him, but Blake wasn't the type to be pushed. While Beau put it all out there, Blake was more like Bryan, keeping his shit close to his sleeve. Unlike Bryan, Blake couldn't be pushed into talking. The more you pushed, the more he retreated. "So what do you want to do?" Bryan asked, opting to give his brother space.

Blake turned, crossing his legs Indian style and sitting between Beau and Bryan's feet. He looked at the two of them for a long minute, as if debating whether or not to give up his plans. Then he held up the guitar and said, "This."

"Music?" Bryan and Beau were back to their synchronized song.

"Don't give me any shit about it, okay? It's what I want."

Christ, when the hell had Blake decided this? Bryan never knew him to want anything except a career in the navy. Just like Mom and Pop, just like he and Beau. It was the family business, so to speak, and Blake had always been all in.

"Where you gonna do that?" Bryan wanted to ask how, but that wasn't very supportive and it was obvious by the way Blake's shoulders sagged that he needed his brothers to support him on this.

"I was thinking Seattle," he said as he looked up.

Bryan smiled. He didn't give a shit if it was the navy or music that motivated his brother. Having him nearby was more than he ever could have hoped for. "Good choice."

"I'm no Nirvana or Jimi Hendrix, but the scene is pretty good there. I figure I can play some local venues while I'm recording an album, put it out on the indie network."

"You're serious about this?" Beau sounded as stunned as he

looked.

"As a heart attack."

"Well, fuck, both of you are going to be in Seattle and I'm going to be wherever the navy decides to send me next."

"I told you I'm trying to get on a ship." But if Blake was making a permanent move, when it came time for Bryan to retire, his brother would be there.

"I've had enough of that to last me a lifetime," Blake mumbled. Even though Blake had the least amount of time in the navy, he'd spent more time on a ship than Bryan and Beau combined.

"You keep me posted," Bryan commanded. "I'll help you get set up in Seattle. And if you want to talk about whatever shit is going on with you, you know we're here for you."

"Always, man," Beau agreed.

"Roger that," Blake said and strummed another note.

***

Her feet were all buffed and her toes just needed to dry. Morgan used a light peach polish, nothing flashy, but a color that made her feel pretty. With the mud mask and the hair conditioning treatment working their magic, she'd soon feel like a new woman.

Just in time for Bryan to come by and make her really feel like a new woman.

The self-spa treatment and pending orgasms were just what she needed after living at the library for nearly three weeks studying for finals.

Her test anxiety had to be genetic because she'd always had it. Morgan wasn't the type of student who crammed the night before an exam. She prepared, studying with manic commitment for weeks. For two weeks leading up to exams and then every moment between the first test and the last, she'd reviewed her meticulous notes, textbooks, journal articles and written assignments. Just as she'd done the previous quarters, Morgan had even organized study groups with her fellow classmates. Of course, she'd maintained her work schedule at Dr. Merrill's office and her volunteer hours at the emergency clinic because she needed the break from studying, a break that wouldn't cause her any guilt.

All that meant she hadn't seen Bryan in over a month. When he returned from Colorado, he'd called, but Morgan was already in study mode. He'd sounded disappointed when she said she couldn't see him until after finals, but after promising an entire weekend of naked fun, he'd agreed to let her study and wished her luck.

The knock at the door surprised her. Bryan wasn't due for two more hours and if it was her brother showing up uninvited, she was going to kill him.

Morgan waddled to the door, careful not to smudge her still-wet toenails. She didn't have a peep-hole, so she turned her ear to the door. "Who is it?"

"Open the door and find out," Bryan said.

She smiled, excited to hear his voice until she realized her current state. "You're early."

"I couldn't wait. You going to let me in or what?"

"I'm not ready."

"Ready? You do realize I'm going to strip you naked as soon as the door closes behind me, right?"

She'd been hoping for just that, but his timing was horrible. "I'm in the middle of a spa treatment."

"I've seen you with that mud stuff on your face before," he said with a chuckle. He had, but that was before he'd seen her naked. For some reason, it seemed awkward for him to see her like this now. Of course, that was completely ridiculous. She didn't have to impress him. They were friends, after all, and just because there were benefits didn't mean she had to get all freaked out by him seeing her all mucked up.

"Consider yourself warned." She slid the chain from the door and opened it wide, revealing her glorious state.

One corner of his mouth lifted in a delicious smirk. "You look great."

"Shut up." She likely looked like something out of a horror movie with her hair slathered in conditioner and piled on top of her head while the mud on her face dried and cracked.

Everything about him exuded confidence as he walked into her apartment and kicked the door closed. He looked her up and down before nodding at her. "Are you naked under there?"

Morgan crossed her arms defensively across the terry cloth robe and returned the smirk. "Wouldn't you like to know."

"I would. That's why I asked."

"Yeah, well, I'm not going to tell you. That'll teach you to show up early."

He reached for the tie at her waist. "Showing is so much better than telling."

Despite the heat in his gravelly voice, Morgan swatted his hand. "Hands off Petty Officer Curtis or I'll make you drop and give me twenty."

"It's *Chief* Petty Officer and believe me, I'd be happy to drop and give you twenty."

"I was referring to push-ups," she laughed.

"You'd enjoy what I have in mind way more than push-ups."

Of that she had no doubt. "I need to get in the shower and rinse all this off," she said, signaling to her face and hair.

"Take your time. I'll get dinner started." He bent to pick up a couple cloth grocery bags off the floor. She hadn't even noticed him carrying them, but the way he'd been looking at her when he walked in had her a little distracted.

"You're cooking?"

Bryan never cooked when they hung out because Morgan enjoyed unwinding in the kitchen. Occasionally, though, it was nice to be pampered.

"You've been studying your ass off for the past few weeks. You deserve a nice meal and a long massage."

Massage. That sounded even better than dinner.

"So you don't want me to get dressed after my shower?" she teased.

Bryan dipped his head and raised his brow as if she'd said something completely off the wall. "I never want you dressed."

That sounded good too. How long had it been since she'd seen him naked? Too long.

Morgan took her time rinsing her hair and face and lathering herself up with the shower gel Bryan seemed to like. He was always telling her she smelled good and she didn't wear perfume, so it had to be the gel.

When she was at risk of evaporating like the steaming water, Morgan forced herself to leave the sauna-like shower and dry off. Giving a quick peek out the door, she confirmed Bryan was nowhere in sight before disappearing into her bedroom. He said not to get dressed, but she still had the flirty lingerie from Valentine's Day to wear for him. That wouldn't hinder a massage.

She tossed her robe back on and combed out her thick hair before seeking out the sexy man in her kitchen. A couple dozen candles illuminated the small space that made up her living slash dining room. She was lacking a dining table, but a small bouquet and two tapers served as the centerpiece on the table in front of her sofa.

She wandered into the small kitchen. "Wow that smells good. What is it?"

"Chicken curry. My brother Blake – you know, the Facebook whore – he has a whole slew of recipes he's collected on the Internet. He claims they are all ridiculously easy."

"Are they?" Morgan was intrigued by a slew of easy recipes. Yes, she liked to cook, but with her crazy schedule, easy was often necessary.

"So far, yeah. This is the fifth or sixth one I've tried. All easy, all delicious."

Sounded kind of like Bryan. He was so incredibly easy to be

with and delicious. Hell yeah, that about summed him up.

Suddenly Morgan didn't care about dinner or the massage. She just wanted the man standing in front of her. She dropped her robe and gave a little whistle to get his attention. When he turned around, his jaw dropped as quickly as the spatula.

Chapter 8

Bryan had just died and gone to heaven. Damn she was beautiful, an angel in devil's clothes. Hell – maybe he was actually in hell because it was suddenly really hot and all the blood seemed to be rushing south.

He swallowed hard. *Hard.* What the hell had he been doing?

He'd seen Morgan in her underwear before. He'd seen her naked. Maybe it was because he hadn't seen her in weeks, but she'd never looked hotter than she did standing there in black lace spattered with red lips. Little red lips. Every-damn-where.

He had every intention of kissing every single one of them. At least twice.

The smell of curry drew his attention away from the beautiful woman in front of him. He'd been doing something before she walked in – what the hell was it?

Oh yeah, dinner. Bryan grabbed for the spatula, but it wasn't on the counter. Morgan's giggle brought him back around.

Damn, it was hot in the kitchen.

Dinner. He needed to tend to dinner. If he stood there and stared at Morgan, or acted on the impulses raging in his pants, dinner would burn and his plans for the evening would sink like the Titanic.

Except the fire in her eyes made it hard – *very hard* – to focus on anything else.

"Morgan," he swallowed again, her name a sweet, intoxicating honey on his tongue.

"Dinner can wait." Her voice echoed his desire but if he took her now, right here in the kitchen, well, damn, that was an idea.

She stepped in to his body, her hands resting on his chest, practically searing the cotton.

"You are so hot," he groaned.

"Everywhere," she whispered, pressing into him a little bit more.

She lifted onto her toes, her hands moving behind his neck and pulling him to her lips. He went easily, a sailor seduced by the Siren's song, and when her tongue danced against his, Bryan gave up caring about dinner and his evening plans.

Then he heard the burner click off and knew he could do better than a quickie in the kitchen while dinner burned.

"Anticipation." his voice was more gravel than baritone, so he cleared his throat and made a second attempt at modern communication. "On Valentine's Day you said anticipation was good for the loins."

"We've had weeks of anticipation." Her voice was practically a purr, making her very hard to resist.

"I don't want to rush. The weeks have taught me patience." More accurately, he wasn't going to last two minutes once he was inside her, so better to make foreplay a long-lasting event for her benefit.

"Patience is overrated." She stuck her bottom lip out in a pout, but it was a tease and temptation Bryan couldn't resist. He kissed her again, nipping at the plump bottom lip before swiping his tongue across it.

When he managed to pull away, he said, "I'll prove that theory wrong." After grabbing a new spatula out of the drawer, Bryan flipped the chicken, scraping it off the bottom. Another minute or two and it would have burned. As it stood, it was on the crispy side of brown.

The timer was showing less than two minutes until the rice was ready. "Have a seat. I'll serve you."

"You know I'm not interested in food, right?"

"Me either, but we're both going to need our strength."

She chuckled, a seductive little sound that made his heart beat faster and his knees go weak.

"Go sit."

She gave him an abrupt salute, but picked up her robe and shrugged it back on. Bryan let out a sigh, both relieved and disappointed that she'd covered up the playful lace and exquisite body. As she padded away, Bryan adjusted himself to ease the discomfort of his erection and focused on the task at hand. He was going to feed her first. Then he'd relax her with a thorough massage. Finally, he intended to ravish her body until neither one of them could walk.

***

Dinner was fantastic. The massage, complete bliss. Even though she was putty in his hands, Bryan was not taking advantage of that and Morgan was about to start making demands.

"Roll over," he commanded.

Morgan moved slowly. If he could tease her with dinner and magic hands, she could take her sweet time too. Bryan shifted as she rolled over so he was still perched between her legs. On her back, she reached for the button of his pants, but he grabbed her hands and stopped her from opening the denim.

"You're overdressed," she informed him.

His gaze scorched her skin with its slow tour of her body. She still wore the flirty bra and panties, at his insistence. If she'd had her way, they'd both have been naked before dinner. "I'm not done with your massage."

"I'm more relaxed than I've ever been." Finals had been stressful, but she was confident she'd aced every exam. Bryan had worked all the tension out of her muscles. Now all she wanted was to feel him inside her.

"I know how to make you even more relaxed." his hands pushed at her thighs, spreading her legs wider and opening her up to him. His gaze focused on her panties and it was a complete turn on how he looked at her.

"I want you," she said.

"You'll have me, just not until I finish the massage."

His strong hands caressed her inner thighs before he started a firm, slow knead. The massage was starting to be a form of carefully executed torture. Why wasn't he attacking her? They hadn't seen each other in a month and it'd been longer than that since they'd had sex. Unless...

"Why'd you just tense up?" he asked.

"Yes or no. Did you have sex in Colorado?" She really didn't want to know, but need seemed to trump want, at least in this case.

"No."

She propped herself up on her elbows, studying his face. "Since you've been back?"

"Morg–"

"Yes or no."

"No."

"Are you lying?"

"No."

"Would you tell me you were lying if you were lying?"

"I don't lie."

She was sure that was true. She'd never known him to lie. "Have you kissed anyone? Gotten anyone off by any means?"

"Not since the last time I got you off."

She wanted to make him swear it, but that was ridiculous. Honesty was in his nature and even though they'd avoided the subject since that night on the phone when he'd been to the strip club, she and Bryan were exclusive.

Morgan fell back on the bed, pushing her arms flat at her side. Bryan slowly lowered his body between her legs, kissing her through the panties. The affectionate caresses teased her body and taunted her mind. She didn't want to let him do this as much as she did.

Before the battle between her mind and body produced a winner, Bryan abandoned the gentle kisses and tugged the panties from her hips.

"Relax," he drawled, his breath warm against her thigh. "This'll feel good, I promise."

"I thought you were going to finish the massage," she reminded him.

"I am, with my tongue." He kissed her thigh, warm lips, wet tongue, hot breath and Morgan nearly came from the anticipation.

The man was good at everything he did. She'd never been kissed with such passion, never been touched with such care. Whether they were having sex or just making out – or giving a massage – he was meticulous with his attention. She shouldn't be nervous with what he intended to do next, but this wasn't a common thing for her. She'd only ever let one boyfriend go down on her, and it was so long ago, it was hardly worth a memory. And technically speaking, Bryan wasn't her boyfriend. He was just a friend, with benefits.

"We haven't done this before." Stating the obvious. Great. Way to play it cool.

"If you don't want me to, then just tell me, but I promise you, you'll enjoy this as much as I will."

She didn't doubt that, but it was such an intimate connection. She didn't let such personal connections happen.

"Stop thinking and just feel, Morg."

He was right. She was thinking too much. Thinking would get her to one of two places. Since she wasn't willing to venture down the commitment road, ultimately she'd end up alone and she wasn't ready for that. She'd been alone for the past month and her skin was prickly with need.

Relaxing back on the bed, Morgan focused on the physical sensations, his breath, his skin, his mouth. Oh, god, yes, his mouth.

Her hips bucked at the first caress of his tongue. She thought she heard him chuckle, but before it registered, he was teasing and tasting and she was lost in the sensations, no longer putty, but completely liquid and his for the taking.

She looked up to find his blue eyes focused on her and the connection was like being struck with a bolt of lightning. Gripping the comforter in her fists, she tried to breathe normally, but that was completely shot. He was tying her in knots, like a cherry stem on his tongue and even if she hadn't been willing to sink into the abyss, it would have taken her.

Hopefully the wall between her bedroom and her neighbor's was well insulated because Morgan cried out like a banshee being tortured. Except this wasn't torture, it was the most glorious pleasure she'd ever experienced. Bryan gave no indication of letting up until her body, panting with the exertion of taking everything he had to give, went completely lax. He'd reduced every cell to a puddle of bliss.

He kissed her thighs and hips and belly, working his way up with a cocky smile. Then he focused on her bra, kissing all of the little red lips embroidered over the lace with warm caresses. When he seemed satisfied that he'd kissed every single inch, his hands eased beneath her and released the hooks before easing the straps off her shoulders.

"You're so beautiful," he said, the reverence in his voice as convincing as his gaze.

It was Bryan who made her feel beautiful, if not by the focused gaze, then by his affectionate touch. No one else had ever made her feel the way he did.

Morgan loved the scrape of his stubble as she kissed his chin.

Her freshly manicured nails scraped over the hair on his chest and found his nipples, giving them a brief squeeze before she continued south. His pants had to go.

Bryan offered no resistance, letting her hands roam and release the button then the zipper of his jeans. He cooperated in getting both the pants and boxers pushed over his hips and finally took the reins in getting them the rest of the way off. From somewhere he produced a condom and tore it open, wasting no time in getting it rolled over his thick erection.

"I don't know if I can make you come again before I lose it. It's been too long." his voice was rough with need, making her even more desperate for him.

"I just want you inside me," she confessed. Bryan was the only man she'd ever been with who had made her multi-orgasmic, and after what he'd just done, she'd be content without an orgasm for another year.

Okay, maybe a week.

He eased between her legs and slowly pushed inside her, his groan making her even hotter.

"So good," he said with another slow thrust. When Morgan squeezed her muscles around him, he lost the control he'd been clinging to and pounded into her with the kind of passion she'd grown accustomed to from him. God, he felt so good, his mouth hot on her neck, chest rough against her breasts, and his hands pinning hers to the bed. He was hot, oh so hot inside her, she thought she might spontaneously combust from the friction.

He said her name again and again between groans and grunts and kisses and nips. All the while, another orgasm sparked to life causing her to moan his name. It was the perfect harmony, sexual desire mixed with the affection they shared, bringing them higher and higher until he was cursing and she was crying out with the pleasure they brought each other.

As their bodies seemed to float back to the bed, Bryan kissed her neck and breasts, his tongue leaving wet hot trails all over her skin.

"I missed you," he finally said in her ear.

Morgan could ignore the words or over think the situation, but instead she channeled her inner Han Solo, looked at him with the cockiest smile she could conjure and said, "I know."

**

The woman made him mental. He should leave, teach her a lesson for trying to keep her distance, but Bryan couldn't bring himself to do it. He hadn't seen her in weeks and was determined to wake up next to her in the morning.

"It was supposed to be funny," she called after him as he disappeared into the bathroom.

Bryan took his time, disposing of the condom and washing up, but mostly taking stock of the man in the mirror. He should be relaxed now, but instead he was all keyed up and not in a good way. "First it's Def Leppard lyrics and now Star Wars. I'm not sure what I did to deserve this special kind of hell."

He couldn't hide in there forever, so he reminded himself what it was he was doing with Morgan – just messing around – and forced the tension out of his body. He nearly leaped out of his skin when he opened the door and found Morgan blocking his path. "Def Leppard lyrics?" she asked, obviously confused by his rant. It hadn't been intended for her ears. He needed to remember how small her apartment was.

"Never mind." His gaze shifted down her naked body, firing up his libido again. Yeah, she made him mental, but she also made him hard. "You want me to stay or what?"

"My eyes are up here, perv," she chided.

"You're naked. Don't expect eye contact." No, because there were too many gorgeous curves for him to enjoy. Damn, he wanted to stay. He hoped she was done playing games. "So, am I staying or going?"

"Staying. The whole Han Solo thing was a joke."

He and Morgan had a good time together, always. He shouldn't let one little comment get to him, but damn if he hadn't been hoping for her to reciprocate.

"Maybe I can return the favor, give you a full body massage."

Her hands on him for an undefined amount of time? He was down with that. "Okay, I'll stay, but only if you throw in breakfast." Yeah, two could play this game and if she was going to keep her distance, it was time for him to stack the cards.

"All I have is yogurt."

"Lucky for you I picked up bacon and eggs when I hit the store today."

"So you're making breakfast."

"I made dinner. Breakfast is all you. But now, tell me more about this massage."

Her smile lit his libido on fire. The woman had him in a constant state of arousal.

"Go lay down on the bed and I'll show you."

That was a command he could follow.

He plopped down in the middle of her queen-size bed and made himself comfortable. Morgan, in all her naked glory, straddled his thighs and caressed his back, a gentle tease that was more arousing than relaxing. When her hands disappeared, he heard her working the cap of a bottle, then felt the cold drizzle of oil on his back. It was something he'd picked up at one of those stores in the mall that sells all the soaps and lotions and the smell would forever remind him of Morgan.

She spread the oil all over his back with both hands and started a slow knead of his muscles. All of her attention was focused on his neck and shoulders, but Bryan was focused on the way her hips moved over his thighs.

He was uncomfortably aroused but Morgan's hands managed to coax some of the tension from him. He began to relax again, but couldn't let go of the fact she hadn't reciprocated his affection. Revealing her innermost feelings was difficult. Bryan knew that before he'd smacked into her brick wall again. He wasn't the let's-talk-about-our-feelings kind of guy either, but telling her he missed her seemed harmless enough.

"That feels good," he said as she used her knuckles to work out a knot he didn't realize he had.

"Have you been working on the mustang?" she asked, her voice a smooth elixir.

"Yeah. Engine's done, so we started the body work."

"Mmmm...I like doing body work with you."

And she did it well, too.

Her hands started massaging his ass and Bryan's already painful erection jerked beneath him. Then he felt her teeth nipping at him, first one cheek, then the other.

"Did you just bite my ass?" he asked, turning to see her mouth curved with a mischievous smile.

"You have a great ass," she shrugged. Her hands worked their way down his thighs and calves and back up. He expected her to bite his ass again, but she didn't. Instead, her bare breasts pressed into his back and he felt her warm breath across his ear.

"I missed you too," she whispered.

And that was his undoing. Four simple words, the exact words he'd wanted to hear. Now that she'd said them, he needed her, *all* of her. Rolling over, he managed to keep her straddled over his thighs. "Get a condom," he demanded.

"But I'm not finished with the massage," she teased in an overly sweet voice.

"Yes, you are."

She didn't argue, just reached across to the bookshelf next to the bed and grabbed a condom out of a basket. She rolled it on painfully slow and when she was done, Bryan took the reins.

They both gasped as he entered her, Morgan's head lolling back before she focused her gaze on him. He reached up to cup her breasts, thumbing her nipples and drawing a sexy little mewl from her. She rode him slowly and Bryan knew this was heaven.

"I love having you like this. I have the perfect view." He could see where they were joined, the curve of her soft belly and pert breasts, the nipples that were so responsive to his touch. And when she came, he'd be able to watch the pleasure spread across her face as she cried out and lost all control.

"So beautiful," he murmured, taking her all in, every inch of skin, every curve.

She pushed her hands against his chest, giving herself more leverage to ride him harder and faster. Damn, she was so fucking hot. He wanted to stay like this forever, on the edge of release, hearing her pleasure, seeing it.

But more than that, he wanted to make her come. There was nothing sexier. He reached down between her legs and started working her with his finger. "Oh god," she moaned and Bryan knew she was close. Good, he was too and he didn't want to have to visualize computer code to keep himself from coming before she did. No, he preferred to stay right there with her, feeling her, hearing her, tasting her.

Then she called his name and no amount of computer code could have stopped him from coming with her.

***

"Why are you up so early?" Bryan asked, rubbing his hands across his rough chin. Normally he was a morning person too, but it was Saturday and he'd ravaged Morgan's body into the wee hours of the morning. It should be a day to sleep in.

"I have to work."

"It's Saturday."

"Yeah, and I work every other Saturday from eight to one. Today's my day."

Okay, fine, she had to work. The alternate Saturday schedule was no secret, but she didn't have to be in until like eight or nine. Why was she up so damned early?

"It's only six," he grunted.

She smiled at him over her shoulder. "You wanted breakfast."

"I want you, naked, back in bed."

Her laugh melted his heart and fired up the big sailor between his legs. Or maybe seeing her in his t-shirt did that. "Have breakfast and then you can go back to bed and wait for me."

His arms came around her, pulling her back against his morning wood. "Because I have nothing else to do," he drawled with a fair amount of sarcasm. He really didn't. He'd planned to tinker on the car today, but Owen wasn't going to be around, so it wasn't all that much fun on his own.

She moaned as his hand slid down her belly. "I don't care. *I* have something else to do, like pay tuition. Grad school isn't free."

"Oh, Christ, you don't have panties on," he growled, his fingers finding that soft, wet spot between her legs.

Bryan shoved down his shorts, thankful he'd thought to grab a condom on his way out of the bedroom. He clicked off the burner and moved Morgan away from the stove.

"Breakfast."

The word meant nothing. The surrender in her voice and the way her back arched, her legs moving slightly apart, well, that meant everything.

"You're breakfast." He lifted her shirt and slid into her from behind and oh, yeah, she felt good. Bacon and eggs had nothing on being inside Morgan's hot body.

Her nipples were so tight between his fingers, her breasts warm as he cupped the soft swells and teased her. And hell, those little moans, those might just drive him over the edge sooner than he wanted.

But hell if he could stop, or even slow down. Moving in and out of her like this as she pushed her perfect ass against him, bracing herself against the counter for leverage. Yeah, this was why he couldn't get enough of her.

She gazed at him over her shoulder, a sexy smirk lifting one side of her mouth. Damn, he loved the way she smiled, whether her mouth was curved with happiness, humor or sarcasm it didn't matter. Morgan had the kind of smile that could start wars or end them.

"Bryan," she beckoned and he slowed his thrusts so he could lean in and kiss those luscious lips. Even though his body demanded he take, he forced himself to a slow exploration of her mouth. His tongue roamed the luscious curve of her lips before he found her tongue. The connection was explosive, a combination of tender and urgent which melted his heart and fired up the rest of his body.

She undid him. Thoroughly and completely shattered every reason for keeping this a casual acquaintance. Bryan had never wanted more from anyone. In fact, he ran from more, ran as fast as his legs and lungs would take him.

Before he said something stupid in the throes of passion and sent her running, he kissed her more and moved one hand to the sweet V between her legs. He wanted her to come, wanted to feel it and hear it and taste it. He wanted to take her to that place where they didn't need to exchange words to understand the power of the connection they shared. Yes, she had admitted they were involved, but they were so much more than that. He knew it beyond a shadow of a doubt. Morgan knew it too. Bryan didn't need her to say the words. He just wanted to feel it.

Her breath was warm, so damn warm on his cheek as she broke from his lips. Her ass writhed against him, shattering his control and he pumped into her harder, faster, until he was breathing as hard as she.

"Morg," he groaned.

"Yes," was her whispered response before she cried out his name again and again, taking Bryan right over the edge with her.

Chapter 9

Morgan liked hot Seattle days. They were like cool Louisiana days, which meant they were tolerable. She didn't miss the heat or humidity of her hometown. She also didn't miss the lingering memories that continued to haunt her long after her father had died.

She watched Owen and Stacie on the other end of the gazebo where her brother was getting the built-in grill cleaned up. The whole crew had decided it was warm enough for a cookout at Gasworks Park and Morgan was happy for the warm, fresh air.

Stacie and Owen chatted back and forth, a natural and easy affection shared between them. Both of them smiled with every exchange and it was clear how much they loved each other. Morgan was happy for her brother. After the calamities of his two marriages, she was sure he'd finally gotten it right. Stacie was smart and kind, something neither of Owen's ex-bitches had going for them. She didn't seem to have a manipulative bone in her body, which really made her the polar opposite of Krisbitcha and since Stacie was the least selfish person Morgan had ever met, she was also the polar opposite of Daphbitchne.

Morgan had no intentions of ever getting married, but Owen wanted that kind of relationship, longed for it. She wondered how long it would be before he popped the question to Stace.

The two shared an affectionate kiss and even though Morgan should look away and let them have their privacy, she couldn't help but stare. She didn't believe love was in the cards for him until she'd seen Owen and Stacie together. Their love was real, soul-deep; strong enough to survive anything.

"What are you smiling at?" Owen asked after Stacie made her way across the park and he joined Morgan at the picnic table where she was unpacking all the grub.

"You're happy," she pointed out.

"I am," he agreed, still smiling like a love-drunk fool. "You could have that too. You just need to let go of the past."

"I'm focused on my career right now."

Owen eyed her with speculation, recognizing her cop-out for what it was. In high school she'd been focused on getting a full scholarship to college since there was no Landry family wealth and she didn't want to go into debt. She was even more focused on her studies in college, not just to keep her free ride, but to ensure a decent job after graduation. She got to use his bad marriages as her next excuse, but now that he was in a good, solid relationship, her new cop-out was her career.

"Just don't let Dad haunt you forever."

"Dad doesn't haunt me," she said honestly. It was her mother, still alive and well, who haunted Morgan.

Owen simply grunted, which probably meant he didn't believe her. The only way to convince him their father wasn't a problem was to admit their mother was. Talking about that would only dredge up the past, making it seethe like a fresh wound. Morgan could stanch a bleeder like nobody's business. Letting a wound bleed out was not in her skillset.

When he grunted again there was a little chuckle mixed in. Morgan recognized that sound as surrender and was relieved he wasn't going to push her. Then again, Owen didn't like to be pushed when it came to the past either.

"You think she's the mystery woman?" Owen asked as he

grabbed the charcoal.

Morgan followed him to the grill. "What are you talking about?"

"Holly," he said, nodding to where Bryan and Holly were engaged in what looked like a pleasant conversation. "You know Bryan's into blondes. Has been ever since I've known him."

If he was so into blondes, why was he currently spending all of his free nights in her bed? Morgan's dark hair was closer to black than blonde, yet Bryan seemed to love it, always breathing it in and putting his hands in it.

And Holly, well, she was off men at the moment. Ever since the fiasco with her ex, she tended to be skittish around men. She didn't look wary now though, and Morgan didn't like the way that thought made her heart race in panic.

Was Bryan lying when he'd told her he wasn't into blondes? She'd never followed up on that given his hasty end to their phone call that night. Mostly, she didn't want to re-open the door he'd nudged. Yes, they were involved, but she didn't like admitting it. That practically forged a path to admit other feelings she wasn't at all interested in acknowledging.

"She's gotta be the mystery woman. They look like they're into each other," Owen said after he got each briquette positioned just so.

"She hasn't mentioned anything." Morgan tried to sound indifferent. She'd invited Holly for two reasons. First, she really liked her and Holly didn't seem to have any other friends, so Morgan wanted to do what she could to fix that. Second, Jenny and Stacie were drawing dangerous conclusions about her and Bryan and since Morgan and Bryan were the only singles in their crew, she worried her two friends were going to try their hands at matchmaking. So best to bring in a seventh wheel.

Just one itty-bitty-tiny-little problem – she brought Holly along for her own benefit, not for Bryan. The way Holly smiled at him – and he smiled back, trudged up insecurities Morgan didn't like to acknowledge. Plus, she had no claim on Bryan. Being *involved*, as he'd insisted on labeling it, covered a very broad spectrum.

The whole friends with benefits thing worked really well for both of them. Neither was interested in anything serious. Being involved really wasn't a big deal, except with this crew. If their secret got out, there would be expectations for another happily ever after. Morgan didn't do fairy tales. Neither did Bryan.

Owen posed a whole other problem. Brother Dearest had a 1960's mentality when it came to Morgan and men. How he could get away with having a one-night stand with Stacie but expect Morgan to be a virgin was beyond her, but that was Owen's thing. He'd been telling Bryan for years that his little sister was off limits. Morgan had teased Owen a couple times about hooking up with Bryan, to which her brother reminded her about Bryan's habits. Morgan wasn't his type. Bryan liked blondes.

Her stomach churned looking at Bryan and Holly sitting at the bottom of the hill, laughing like they were long lost friends, maybe even lovers. Usually when Holly was around men, she was tense, guarded. There was nothing guarded about her now.

So what...it was fine. Morgan had struggled during finals, a little distracted thinking about Bryan. Her classes were just as tough this quarter. Letting Bryan go, though, was something she wasn't quite ready to embrace. For reasons she didn't want to explore too deeply, or even shallowly, she didn't like the idea of Bryan and Holly together. She didn't like the idea of Bryan with anyone.

Well, except her.

"I'm going to go find Stacie," Owen said. "The coals need to warm up for a while."

Morgan plunked herself down on the picnic table closest to the grill. The coals needed to burn, but they still required supervision. Since everyone else was busy in couple land, Morgan decided to keep watch over the coals.

Jenny and Ty were at the top of the hill, flying a kite. Stacie and Owen disappeared around the front side of the hill overlooking Lake Union. When Morgan turned her attention back to Bryan and

Holly, the object of her annoyance had disappeared and Holly was making her way to the gazebo.

"Bryan's cute. You didn't tell me he's your boyfriend."

"He's not," Morgan said.

"Really? He wouldn't stop talking about you."

Leave it to Bryan to blow their cover. "We're just friends. He's my brother's best friend."

Holly laughed. "Well, it's pretty obvious he has a thing for you."

"I don't think so."

"So you're not into him?" Holly asked with hope. Morgan felt compelled to keep her blonde friend away from Bryan, but the only way to do that was to own up to what they were doing. Or…play up his reputation.

"Bryan's a man-whore," she announced with distaste. "That's not my idea of safe sex."

Holly maneuvered her way between Morgan's legs. That was strange enough, until she ran her fingers over the denim on Morgan's leg. "What is your idea of safe sex?"

Before Morgan answered, Holly kissed her. It was just a light caress of lips, an experiment, she guessed, but it stunned her stupid. What the hell was she supposed to do? Kissing back wasn't an option, but she didn't want to pull away and hurt Holly's feelings either.

"So you're not into me either," Holly said matter-of-factly, no hurt in her voice.

"It's not you Holl. I'm just not into women."

Holly just shrugged, backing away from the table.

"I didn't know you were…geez, Holl, I'm sorry if I led you on."

"You didn't. You're just really fun and adventurous and I took a chance you might want to, you know, with me. I'm not so much a lesbian as I'm anti-men and lonely right now. Women seem to be the safer sex."

"Have you been with women before?" Maybe it was prying, but

Morgan was dying to know. If Holly was bisexual, she'd kept a closed lid on it. Morgan prided herself on being able to read people, but she'd never once caught this kind of vibe from Holly.

"Once, when I was nineteen. I definitely prefer men, but right now I'm just lonely."

"I'm sorry, Holl."

"Don't be," she said and Morgan knew she was sincere. "I'm a horrible judge of character, so the only way to know for sure is to try. I suppose I should have asked first."

"Matchmaking is fun." It had to be since she dated a new guy every time it rained. At least, she had been until she hooked up with Bryan. Maybe she could use her skills on someone else instead of herself. "I could help you find someone."

Holly held up her hands as though she was trying to stop a Mack truck. "No. Seriously, I like you enough to, you know, put the moves on, but I wouldn't be comfortable trying that with anyone else. I just need to get over my man issues."

"I could probably help you with that too. I know lots of guys."

Holly smiled. "Like Bryan?"

If Morgan hadn't witnessed how relaxed Holly had been when talking to Bryan, she'd never believe her friend could be interested in a man who was so alpha. After what she'd been through with her ex, Morgan couldn't imagine Holly ever being interested in someone so confident and in charge. Everything about Bryan wreaked alpha man, sometimes to the cave man level. He wasn't the type of man Morgan usually took an interest in either, given her childhood, but Bryan was different somehow. His alpha wasn't scary like her father had been. No, Bryan wore his alpha ego like a sexy second skin.

Of course, if Morgan could be attracted to him given her aversion to domineering men, it wasn't a big stretch to think Holly could be too. Or maybe Holly was just a glutton for punishment, always going after the bad boy. Fortunately for Morgan, not only was Bryan a bad boy, but he was a good man. One she wasn't willing to give up yet.

She was willing to match Holly up with anyone, just not Bryan. "Believe me, you don't want him," Morgan said even though she wanted to scream at Holly to keep her paws off him.

"I know," Holly laughed. "You are so easy."

"What are you talking about?"

"I'm just teasing. It's pretty obvious you want him. I wouldn't be surprised if you've already had him."

"What?" Morgan choked. She and Bryan were discreet. Maybe they'd had a few moments of weakness, letting their private affection bleed into their social personas, but they'd gotten that under control.

"Don't worry, you're secret is safe with me – but only if you give me some details. Is this just a crush or do you two have something going on?"

Morgan debated what she should say. The arrangement was safe as long as no one knew about it but she was dying to share with someone how good he was. God, was he ever! Her cheeks flushed just at the thought of Bryan's hands, his mouth, his...

"Ladies, am I interrupting something?"

"No, not at all," Holly answered in a flirtatious purr. "In fact, I was just going to head up the hill. I brought a tub of bubbles and the wind is just right. Catcha."

And with that, Morgan was alone with Bryan.

"You two looked cozy," Bryan said, waggling his brows.

Morgan rolled her eyes. She'd hoped no one had seen Holly's advance, but of course, Bryan of all people had to bear witness. "Pervert."

He shrugged as though it was common knowledge. "I'm a guy. The girl on girl thing is hot."

Of course he'd think that. If Bryan was nothing else, he was a typical guy. "Yeah, well, it's not my thing." She wiggled her fingers and pointed at his head. "That little fantasy will just have to play out in your imagination."

"It already has."

Another eye roll. She was going to give herself a headache. "Predictable."

Bryan settled into the spot between Morgan's legs that Holly had vacated. This time, Morgan was turned on, especially when she felt Bryan's erection push between her legs.

"What are you doing?"

"No one can see us." his fingers slid under the frayed hem of her t-shirt. They were warm and rough and strong and she wanted him to explore every inch of her.

Except, here in the park, someone might see them. She wasn't sure what would be worse, getting caught by her brother or getting caught by Stacie or Jenny.

Letting her brain take control of the situation, Morgan pushed Bryan away and hopped off the table. "Someone could mosey around the corner any moment and spot us. Stop being stupid. Think with the head on your shoulders, not the little sailor in your pants."

"Little?" Bryan quirked a brow.

Okay, yeah, he wasn't little.

"You know what I mean."

Crossing his arms, his expression grew serious. "I'm not sure I do."

Great, now she was going to have to stroke his ego.

"Okay, the *giant* sailor in your pants. Better?"

His arms fell to his sides as his face relaxed. "I prefer ginormous, but I'll settle for giant.

Morgan walked across the gazebo to the path that looked toward Lake Washington. It was such a beautiful day, not a cloud in the sky. But for some reason, she wasn't feeling the sunshine. She felt more like she was trapped in a gloomy day. She wanted to blame Bryan or even Holly, but the foreboding feeling had been haunting her even before she got out of bed this morning.

"Let's get out of here," Bryan suggested, wrapping his arms around her.

She wriggled out of his hold. "You really need to stop touching me in public."

"Morgan, no one's watching. No one cares."

"I care."

He stepped back, giving her the space she demanded. "Fine. Let's go somewhere where no one can see me touching you."

"We can't just ditch our friends because we want a quickie."

"Need is a better descriptor. Quickie isn't what I had in mind. And yes, we can ditch our friends. You don't think they'd ditch us?"

They would. In fact, they had. "I'm not going to be the person who does that." She never had been and wasn't about to start now. Men were not a priority in her life. Even when she had gone as far in a relationship to consider someone her boyfriend, she never put him first. Ultimately, that was what ended the relationship. That's why it was so much easier to date with wild abandon rather than settle on one guy. Or why having a friend with benefits worked out so well.

"Fine. Then can we at least cut this party short? I've got my bike. After lunch, let's catch the Kingston ferry and head up to Deception Pass."

Morgan hadn't been up there yet, but she'd seen pictures and it was on her list of places to explore. Plus, she loved riding on the back of Bryan's Ducati. "That sounds like fun. We probably shouldn't pass up a day like this. It might rain for the next two months."

Two hours later, the party was breaking up. Holly had to work and surprise, surprise, Jenny and Ty had disappeared, probably somewhere nearby to have a quickie. Stacie was on the hillside sketching and Owen had taken up residence on the blanket next to her with a book. Bryan and Morgan said their farewells and headed north.

It was cooler on the bike than it had been at the park, but it gave Morgan an excuse to hold on tight and absorb the heat of Bryan's hot body. She wasn't much of a snuggler, but hanging on to him like this, with the inside of her legs pressed against the outside of his, her arms wrapped firmly around his waist, and the air moving past them in thick drifts, it was invigorating. She felt so alive and free, ready to conquer the world. She made a note to have Bryan take her for a ride during finals next quarter so she could take this feeling and maybe conquer some of her test anxiety.

In the meantime, she was just going to enjoy being pressed up against this incredibly sexy man. For the first time all day, she didn't feel that impending doom hovering around her. This was good therapy, being on the back of the bike. She'd have to remember that the next time the world got to be too much.

That didn't happen often; once a year, sometimes twice. It was always linked to something, like the anniversary of her father's death when she knew she should be celebrating but instead couldn't stop replaying the horrible events of her childhood. Mother's Day typically triggered it too because it was one of those times when she was obligated to call her mother and pretend they didn't have a dysfunctional relationship.

Morgan thought it would be easier to deal with her mother now that they weren't living in the same town or even the same state, but nothing had really changed. If anything, her mother was more critical, accusing her of not calling often enough, yet the woman herself never picked up the phone except on Morgan's birthday. Any other time, Morgan was expected to take the initiative. Why would she want to do that when the calls made her feel like an inadequate daughter who could never live up to her mother's expectations?

She was earning her master's degree, for Pete's sake. Her mother couldn't even be proud of that. No, Morgan needed a husband, needed to settle down and have children. She wasn't getting any younger. Soon men would stop looking at her because she'd be too old to bear children.

So old fashioned. Didn't her mother know it was the twenty-first

SUSAN ANN WALL

century? Women didn't have to get married or have children. They were allowed to have a career, a life. They didn't have to succumb to the demands and abuse of a drunken asshole who thought the world owed him something and beat the crap out of his wife to prove it.

Ugh, how the hell did she get moving like a freight train down this line of thought? She was on the back of a motorcycle, the wind in her face and Bryan between her legs. It didn't matter that they were fully clothed and speeding down the road, she was still irrevocably aroused. He did that to her. Just a quirk of his mouth or the promise of something more in his eyes turned her on.

So why did her mother keep popping into her head?

"Everything okay back there?" Bryan asked over his shoulder.

How did he do that, always sense when something was bothering her? "I'm fine. How long to Deception Pass?" she asked, hoping to avoid further inquiries.

"About half an hour."

They'd decided to drive to Mount Vernon and hit Deception Pass from the north, then take the ferry back from Clinton. Morgan had been looking forward to making out on the ferry, but she'd just have that to look forward to on the return trip.

She leaned into his back, tightening her grip around his waist. One hand slid across hers, his skin warm despite the cool air. The quick caress sent a shiver of need through her. He wiggled a little bit and she wondered if he felt the same spark.

***

Brian saw the clouds moving in. They were too far north to turn back and miss the storm, but Oak Harbor wasn't far and happened to have a fantastic little B&B.

As they stood on the bridge overlooking Deception Pass, he pointed at the incoming doom. "We're going to get wet."

Morgan crossed her arms as she turned to him. "It didn't occur to you to check the weather before we left?"

"I was excited about the sunshine." And getting Morgan on the back of his bike. You had to love a Ducati. The Superbike was the kind of motorcycle that was great to ride alone, full of power and speed. It was even better if you had a hot body on the seat behind you. She was forced to wrap her arms around his waist to hang on and Morgan was enough of a tease that she'd rest her hands high on his thighs when they slowed down. Despite the two layers of leather separating them, her breasts were pressed against his back, her perfect female form against his hips.

"I know a B&B in Oak Harbor. It's probably safer to get off the road."

"You planned this," Morgan said.

"No, but I like the thought of getting you naked sooner rather than later."

"Let's head to Oak Harbor then."

They locked hands as they headed back to the bike. Bryan was always surprised at how easy they did the couple thing. But then, they'd been friends for years, and each harboring a secret attraction, so it shouldn't have been a surprise at all now that they'd acknowledged it.

They hadn't gotten a mile from the bridge when the rain started dumping on them. It didn't even start out as a subtle sprinkle. When it rained in Puget Sound, it really did pour.

In good conditions, the ride to the B & B was only about fifteen, maybe twenty minutes. In a downpour, it took them twice as long and they were soaked to the bone by the time they got there. That worked for Bryan. His plans didn't involve clothes.

There were plenty of rooms available in mid-April, so they got checked in quickly. Bryan practically attacked Morgan when they were in their room.

"Down boy. I need to use the bathroom."

"Okay, but make it fast. I have plans for you."

Morgan smiled as she sashayed to the bathroom. Bryan started to strip out of his wet clothes. The leather chaps and jacket had kept him mostly dry, but the rain pounded them hard enough that even the leather couldn't fully protect them.

"Oh, wonderful," Morgan said from the bathroom. The tone in her voice didn't sound happy.

Bryan knocked lightly on the door. "Everything okay in there?"

"Dammit," she hesitated for a minute. "I have a little problem."

A woman in the bathroom with a little problem. Bryan bit back the groan, hoping he was wrong.

"I hate to do this to you, but I didn't bring my purse and I need some products. Can you go to the store?"

No, no, no. Absolutely not. He was a sailor in the U.S. Navy. A Chief Petty Officer. Buying, quote – products – unquote, was below his pay grade. "I can take you to the store so you can buy your own products." And he could pick up a six pack to drown his sorry ass libido.

"I'm already bleeding. I can't leave this bathroom."

"Morg," he groaned through the door. No way did he want to do this. He didn't even know *how* to do it. Bryan had never bought products in his life. Growing up with brothers didn't lend to such opportunities and obviously his mom had been discreet about such things because he couldn't even recall ever seeing such products in their house growing up. Hell, he couldn't even remember her buying that stuff when she'd drag him to the commissary to go grocery shopping.

"Come on, Bryan. You're a big boy. You can do this." There was humor in her voice, as though she was teasing him and didn't that just make him feel like an idiot.

"I don't think I can. I don't know what to buy."

"Get me some paper and I'll write a very detailed list."

"List?" How many products did a woman need?

"I need tampons and Pamprin. I'm going to get hit with cramps in the next hour or two and believe me, you want me to be taking

Pamprin. Otherwise, I'm a bear – not the teddy kind. I'm talking grizzly. I also need clean underwear and pants."

Bryan grumbled as he walked across the room where a small pad of paper and pen sat on a desk. When he returned, he knocked lightly on the bathroom door. Morgan reached her hand out and grabbed the pad and pen.

"Can you go to the front desk and see if they have any tampons? I really don't want to sit here waiting for you."

Bryan wasn't comfortable doing this either, but what could he do, leave Morgan stranded in the bathroom while he shopped for her products?

Fortunately, the lady at the desk was sympathetic and had what Morgan needed. She also offered extra towels and explained the closest store was the Walmart in downtown Oak Harbor, and called for a cab when he explained he was on a motorcycle.

When Bryan returned, he handed Morgan what she needed and she gave him her list. She was detailed, with the color of the box, as well as sizes for jeans and underwear.

Bryan didn't like shopping for himself. Shopping for woman products was a true test of character. "I'll probably be gone an hour. You going to be alright?"

"Yeah. I'll grab a shower and see if I can't wash my clothes up a little bit. Bryan?" she opened the door again. "I'm really sorry about this. I'm usually prepared but this is a couple days early. I'm never early."

Bryan shrugged like it was no big deal. "Don't worry about it. I'll be back soon." He wanted to make some snide remark about her owing him – big – but he imagined this was just as uncomfortable for her. She talked a good game, but that was part of her confident persona and the fact she was a nurse studying to be a midwife. He didn't want to make her feel bad for something she obviously had no control over.

The shopping adventure wasn't as horrible as he thought it'd be. Morgan's list was detailed enough that he knew exactly which box of lady's product to grab. The medicine she requested was easy enough to find too. And shopping for panties, well, that was a special treat.

At first Bryan felt like a perv in the underwear section of Wal-Mart, but there were some sexy little numbers on display and he enjoyed imagining how Morgan would look sporting a variety of the get-ups. He'd only ever seen her in cotton panties and satiny thongs. Oh, and that sexy number with the lips all over it. He figured something sexy wasn't the best option for a woman who was having her monthly visitor, so he grabbed a package of cotton panties. He also added a set of boy shorts and matching bra that looked like a rainbow. Morgan wasn't really into lacey undergarments and frankly he'd seen enough of those in his lifetime that they didn't do much for him. This colorful cotton number, though was just what Morgan would wear and he was eager to taste the rainbow.

After locating a pair of jeans in the size she specified, Bryan also grabbed a package of boxers, socks for both of them, a small bottle of laundry detergent, deodorant for each of them, toothbrushes and toothpaste, and a backpack to get the gear back to Seattle. He considered getting a bottle of wine, but if Morgan was going to be taking pain killers, or whatever that Pamprin stuff was, he figured she wouldn't want to mix alcohol. So he hit the herbal tea aisle and spotted a box of the stuff she kept in her cupboard. Maybe that'd help her feel better.

He hit the in-store Subway on the way out, got a foot long sweet onion teriyaki for him and a six inch turkey for her. Then he called the cab service. The same driver arrived within five minutes.

Was this what married couples did? Buy products for each other? He could picture his brother fumbling along the lady products aisle in Wal-Mart and that made Bryan chuckle. His brother was a softy. If Megan wanted him to run to the store to get her products, he'd do it without question or complaint. Well, Bryan supposed Beau wouldn't be making those trips for Megan anymore, but it probably wouldn't take him long to find new love and be just as pussy-whipped as he had been before.

In their room, Morgan was curled up in a ball on the bed. Her hair was wet and the room felt humid, like she'd had a really hot shower.

"Morg? You alright?" he asked in a whisper. It looked like she was sleeping and if she was he didn't want to disturb her.

"Cramps," she groaned.

"I got everything you asked for." He came around the bed to find her face contorting in pain. Bryan felt the caveman come out, a desperate need to protect her. What the hell could he do to get rid of menstrual cramps?

He opened the Pamprin and handed her the bottle before moving into the bathroom to fill a cup with water. When he returned, she was rifling through the bag. She had found the cotton panties, jeans, and box of tampons, all of which were laid out on the bed. Then she pulled out the rainbow bra.

"This wasn't on my list," she said with a smile that made his heart skip a couple beats.

"It was on mine."

"I'm not wearing this for you tonight."

"I know. I'm not expecting you to. Maybe you can surprise me with it sometime. There's matching undies too." She put the bra back into the bag and didn't bother to inspect the undies. Maybe he'd made a mistake buying her underwear. Morgan got weird about stuff like that. She was adamant they were friends – with benefits – and friends didn't buy romantic gifts for each other. He'd managed to get away with the Valentine's Day flowers and bringing her food on occasion, but the underwear might be pushing it. He braced for her wrath, his brain working overtime to come up with a reason to justify the gift.

She grabbed the bottle of water from the bed and after swallowing three big pills, she grabbed his hand. "I'm sorry you have to see my like this. I usually lock myself up for the first two days of my period."

Well, wow, that really wasn't what he'd expected. He took a step closer and cupped her cheek. "You're fine. I don't mind. Honest." That was no lie. Morgan wasn't the damsel in distress type. In fact, she was more apt to swoop in and be the rescuer. He'd never seen her be vulnerable, not once. The only other time he'd seen her like this was that night after the abusive asshole at the clinic. Maybe he was a bastard for liking her this way, but he couldn't help it.

Morgan turned into his hand, first nuzzling it, then caressing his palm with her soft lips. Yeah, hell yeah, he liked her vulnerable. Damn her monthly curse though because he couldn't act on the impulses raging through him. "I got you some of that herbal tea you like. Want me to make you a cup?"

Her eyes widened with surprised. "You're the sweetest guy I know."

That was kind of sad. All he did was buy her tea and undies and woman products. Truth be told, he was still dying to get her naked.

"Yeah, well don't let that secret out. It'd ruin my reputation as a perverted caveman."

"Well, you know I can keep a secret," she said before lying back on the bed. "The Pamprin has an antihistamine, which I'm really sensitive to, so they're going to knock me out pretty quickly, but I'd love a cup of tea before I pass out."

The room came complete with a microwave, so he heated up the water and dropped a tea bag in. That was about all he knew about making tea. He'd been an instant coffee man until he got stationed in Bremerton. Living in the Pacific Northwest, famed for its consumption of coffee, he'd quickly turned into a java snob. He wouldn't touch the instant stuff now even if it was the only option. But he'd never made tea before. He'd seen Morgan and Stacie and Jenny do it plenty of times. It didn't seem all that complex.

When he handed the cup to Morgan, she breathed in the fragrance and sighed. Perfect. Score one for him on tea making.

After she'd taken a few sips, Bryan mustered the courage to ask the question that'd been niggling at him since she'd explained why she wasn't prepared.

"So, Morg," he started, settling on the bed next to her. "I know I'm going to sound like an ass, but I need to know. Is you being early something I need to be concerned about?"

Morgan laughed and he knew his question was stupid, but just as he didn't know anything about buying woman products, he didn't know if being early was an issue. "No. You need to worry if I'm late, not if I'm early."

"Okay, just checking." That's what he figured, but really knew zip about a woman's cycle. They hadn't had any condom mishaps, but he'd heard a long time ago that swimmers could get through even a pin-size hole and he'd never spot that when he peeled the damn thing off.

She nudged him with her elbow, a flirtatious gesture that washed the tension of his question away. "I'm on the pill. Even if we had a condom mishap, the chances of me getting pregnant are slim." Morgan settled in against his chest. She was under the covers, he stayed on top, but the gesture was still a shock. Morgan didn't snuggle, not even after sex or when they slept. Bryan had never been much into cuddling either, but when there was a warm, soft body in bed next to him, he liked to have at least a hand on that body. With Morgan, though, the more he was with her the closer he wanted to get. It'd started out as a physical need, but it was quickly gaining ground in other areas. His attempts to ignore that need were doing nothing to tamp it.

The first few times they had sex, he woke up the next morning to find Morgan sleeping on the couch. She claimed his snoring kept her up, but he'd suspected it was more than that. After about the umpteenth time he asked her about it, she'd finally admitted she didn't like sharing a bed when she was sleeping. It was her problem, leftover demons from her childhood.

Bryan saw it as a personal challenge. It had taken countless tries, but he finally coaxed her into staying in the bed. She always rolled onto her side and curled into the fetal position, much like she'd been when he returned to their room here. But at least she was there next to him, so that, you know, if he wanted to wake her up in the middle of the night, it was convenient.

Now though, it wasn't just about satisfying his carnal middle-of-the night urges. He wanted more, way more than he'd ever wanted from any woman. It was another personal challenge. He tried to hold her after they had sex, but she always resisted. It had never occurred to him to try it before sex, or on a night like tonight when they weren't going to have sex at all.

She finished her tea, then slipped out from under the comforter. She was wrapped up in two towels, one around the top, one around her waist. "I need to get a pair of these on before I fall asleep."

Bryan reached into the bag and grabbed the package of t-shirts he'd bought. "Do you want one of these?"

"Yeah, that'd be great. You thought of everything."

When she came back out, dressed in black cotton panties under the extra-large white t-shirt, Bryan had to recite the phonetic alphabet backwards to keep blood flowing to his brain and not rushing to the sailor coming to life below his waist. She wasn't just sexy, she was beautiful, with her dark brown hair swept over one shoulder and her brown eyes masked in a sleepy haze.

"Well, at least I know why I was so bitchy at the park today," she said as she climbed under the billowy comforter.

"And here I thought it was because we couldn't get any privacy."

"You're such a guy. Is it always about sex with you?"

No. Not anymore. If he told her that, would she run? Because of the storm they were stranded, so there was nowhere for her to run, but it'd be selfish for him to corner her now, in her current predicament. So he went for the lie. "Pretty much. Especially after seeing you kiss your friend like that. That was hot." Okay, half lied. Seeing Morgan and Holly so intimately close had fired up his libido and sparked some new fantasies.

"You're such a pig," she laughed, nudging him a little more aggressively this time. "And for the record, she kissed me. I didn't kiss her back."

"You didn't pull away either." Yeah, he'd watched the whole thing unfold. When he came out of the bathroom, Holly had moved between Morgan's legs and Bryan was stunned fucking stupid. He just stood there on the other side of the gazebo and gawked like a pervert – because he was one.

"Honestly, I didn't know what to do. Holly's been through a lot. Her last boyfriend beat her up and caused her to have a miscarriage. I was afraid I'd hurt her. I really had no idea she was interested in me like that."

"Well, you know, if you wanted to experiment with that sort of thing, I'm willing to watch. You know, just to see if it works for you." *Please say yes, please say yes.*

Morgan laughed and hit his chest. "You just want a threesome."

Duh. "Hey, doesn't make me a bad person."

She nestled against his chest, causing Bryan's heart to leap again. He made a mental note to swoop in with that Pamprin stuff and herbal tea the next time the curse hit her. "Have you ever had a threesome?"

Her voice was casual, but this wasn't the kind of conversation he wanted to have with Morgan. He'd had a lot of women, and she knew that, but being with her was different. She'd been his friend first, still was. She knew his reputation and they'd often joked about it. It wasn't something he wanted to joke about anymore though, but he also couldn't lie to her. "Uh, yeah. Couple of times."

He searched his memories but couldn't even come up with faces. Christ, what did that say about him? Either he was an asshole for not remembering the women or he was an even bigger asshole for being with so many women the memories got all mixed up in his head.

Morgan groaned and Bryan knew that wasn't the answer she

wanted to hear.

"Hey. You asked. I'm not going to lie. We both know I'm not a saint."

Maybe the lack of memory just meant all those hook-ups weren't of any significance anymore. He'd had his fill of women and had always thought that'd be his lifestyle. He wasn't about to apologize for it.

Now, though, with Morgan, that lifestyle didn't seem so appealing. Bryan wanted her – only her. If he could only figure out a way to tell her how he felt without it blowing up in his face.

Chapter 10

Morgan had to remind herself one of the things that was safe about Bryan was the fact he wasn't a saint. This was a short term, uh, arrangement. She wouldn't even classify it as a relationship and that worked for her.

As if sensing the need for a topic change, her belly roared like a lion that hadn't eaten in weeks. "I suppose this place doesn't have room service?"

"Oh, I forgot. I got subs." Bryan got up and pulled a couple Subway bags out of the back pack he'd been carrying when he returned from the store. "Turkey, right? Everything green? Light on the oil."

Either she was overly predictable or Bryan really was the sweetest guy she knew. He had her sub nailed, just like he had when he brought her one from Randy's. If the sub was on Italian bread, she was going to think of a really fantastic way to show her appreciation. Just not tonight. Unwrapping it, she found the sub was indeed cased in her bread of choice.

"How'd you remember all this?" she asked before sinking her teeth in and moaning at the delicious carb and veg overload.

Bryan laughed, whether it was at her surprise or her lack of finesse with a big sandwich she didn't know. Since her belly was demanding more, she didn't really care what he found so amusing. This was delicious. Perfect. Just what she needed after such a trying day.

Bryan got to stuffing his own face after offering her a shrug for an answer. Either he was hungry or avoiding the topic. Fine with her. They didn't need to explore any personal issues like why he knew exactly how she liked her subs prepared from different sub shops.

But the thought tugged at her heart. What was going on? Why was a stupid sandwich so important? Stupid hormones. Having her period sent everything into flux and she was obviously making a mountain out of a mole hill. It was just a sandwich. It was no big deal.

"Why are you looking at me like that?" Bryan asked after a couple bites.

"Like what?" she played coy.

"Like I have three heads?"

Morgan laughed. "Because you do. I should have eaten before I took the Pamprin. I think it's going to my head."

"You wanna see what's on the tele?"

Good, good, good. He wasn't going to pursue it. Sometimes he tried to get her to own up to things she had no business feeling. She didn't even like it when he owned up to his own feelings – again, things he had absolutely no business feeling.

"You can turn it on if you want, I'm going to finish this and pass out."

Bryan reached in the bag again, this time pulling out a book.

"You really did think of everything." She felt bad. This wasn't what Bryan had in mind when they set off on their ride, especially not when he checked them into this romantic little getaway. "I really am sorry."

"Don't worry about it, Morg. It's not like you asked for Mother Nature to rain on the party. Besides, it doesn't always have to be about sex. I like just hanging out with you."

She gave him a quick kiss on the cheek. "You're good people. I like hanging out with you, too."

She always had, ever since he'd tried to babysit her out on the town in Norfolk. Daphbitchne was being MegaBitch and wouldn't let Owen go out, and Owen had tried to keep Morgan on a short leash, but she was eighteen and free to do what she liked. So she went out and had the time of her life. All the while, Bryan tagged along. He claimed he just wanted to hang out, but even then she'd known he was keeping an eye on her for Owen.

"You're good people, too." He nudged her a little, offering her an affectionate smile. Morgan forced herself not to read too much into it. They were friends – friends with benefits – and she didn't want to blur the lines of their acquaintance. Of course, it was ridiculous to think the man-whore had deeper affections. He didn't do love, one of the things that made him super appealing.

"Let's keep this between us, though. I wouldn't want my reputation ruined."

"If I were to ruin your reputation, we'd have to give up our little secret."

Bryan laughed. "Yeah, wouldn't want anyone to know about that."

"Owen would kill us," she pointed out. "And you know it."

"No, he'd kill me. He'd just lock you up."

"Which is exactly why this is better kept a secret." She needed to reaffirm it to herself as much as to him. Morgan didn't do love, she didn't do forever. She was not going to turn into her mother, not sooner, not later. Bringing babies into the world was her calling. She didn't need to be married to do that.

Bryan's phone rang and he grabbed it off the table next to the bed. "Speaking of the devil," he said, then answered. "Hey man. What's up?"

Bryan rolled his eyes a few times as he listened to Owen. "Yeah, she's with me. I don't think she packed her phone…Well, we weren't expecting to be gone so long. Right now we're waiting out the storm." Bryan listened some more, then laughed. "Don't worry, man, she's in good hands…" Next came a snort as he shook his head. "You know what I mean. Morg's not my type anyway…yeah, yeah, I'll tell her. Lata."

"Tell me what?" It had to be something important if her brother had called Bryan to track her down. He knew they were going for a motorcycle ride when they left the park, but yeah, they should have made it back to Seattle by now.

"Tomorrow is your mother's birthday," Bryan informed her. "Owen wanted to remind you to call her."

All of a sudden, a very bright light came on in Morgan's mind. That feeling of impending doom she'd been wrestling with all day, well, now she knew where it came from. "Jerk," she muttered.

Bryan held up his hands in surrender. "Hey, I'm just the messenger."

"I meant Owen." She hated him being the voice of reason between her and her mother. Then again, there'd be hell to pay if Morgan forgot to call. She did have a reminder on her phone, so she'd have figured it out tomorrow before it was too late. "But you're a jerk too."

"What'd I do?"

She raised a brow. "Not your type?"

"You were just preaching about keeping our dirty little secret. What was I supposed to say, don't worry man, I can't bang your sister tonight anyway because the monthly curse disrupted my plans?"

She knew it! "So you are mad."

"Disappointed, Morg, not mad." He caressed her cheek as she fought back the rush of emotions. "I meant what I said. It doesn't always have to be about sex. So, you wanna talk about your mother?"

"What?"

"That's the real reason you're picking a fight with me, isn't it?"

Sometimes she really hated him.

"Why do you hate her so much?" he asked.

"I don't hate her." She definitely didn't hate her mother. After all, the woman had brought Morgan into the world. Their relationship had been strained for as long as Morgan could remember. Her mother was submissive to a fault, something Morgan never wanted to be.

"You sure act like you do."

Yeah, she probably did, but no one could understand, not Owen who had been there through all the abuse, and certainly not Bryan who grew up with two loving parents. Morgan didn't want to talk about her mother, but something about Bryan's imploring eyes pulled the words from her. "It's just, it's *him*." Morgan knew she didn't have to explain who *him* was. Bryan and Owen had been friends since Morgan was in high school. Her brother kept their horrid childhood as close to the cuff as she did, but Owen was close enough to Bryan to clue him in on their history. "I just don't understand how she could love him, after everything he did to her. She stood by him."

"I'm sure she had her reasons." Bryan brought his arm around her shoulder, giving her a gentle squeeze. "He's been dead, what, almost fifteen years? Don't you think it's time to let it go?"

"I do let it go. Then her birthday rolls around and she gets all delusional, talking about him and how he proposed to her on her birthday."

"It's probably tough for her, Morg. I mean, the man abused her. The emotional abuse probably took a bigger toll than the physical stuff."

"You think I don't know that? I was there, what I didn't see, I heard. She should have called the police, or at the very least left. He worked every day and finished off the workday at the bar. She had hours every day to pack up our shit and get us the hell out of there."

"I don't think it's that easy."

No, not for a woman who loved her abuser. That's why her mother never left and continued to expose Morgan and Owen to their own personal hell.

"He came after me once," Morgan admitted.

Bryan shot off the bed and she wished she hadn't confessed that little secret. She's not sure why she did. No one knew. Not even Owen.

"What?" he demanded, fury pouring off him in waves.

"Don't tell Owen," she pleaded. What the hell was she doing, opening up like that? Bryan didn't need to know about her horrid childhood, especially the single most frightening moment of Morgan's life. Now that the words were out, she wished she could take them back. Better to keep her big fat trap shut and keep Bryan a safe distance.

"What the fuck? Owen doesn't know?"

One little problem though. Bryan looked angry enough to kill the dead.

For whatever reason, she'd opened the gate. Bryan was always honest with her. She was always honest with him. He knew enough already that she could trust him with her darkest secret. Maybe if she did talk about it, the memory would lose some of its power.

"Owen would have killed him." Of that, Morgan had no doubt. He'd always been protective of her. She didn't know if that was a natural affection or if it was nurtured by their environment, but by the time she was fifteen, it was clear Owen would never let their father near her. "It wasn't long before he died. Owen had a wrestling match. I usually went to the library after school and waited for him to come and get me, but I'd forgotten a book at home, so I just figured I'd hide in my room."

Bryan fisted his hands. He stood on the other side of the small room, but it still felt like he was looming over her, ready to protect her from anything. "He didn't touch you did he? So help me Morgan, if he touched you I will figure out a way to bring him back to life so I can kill him."

No, Emmanuel Landry had not touched her. She may have been young and guarded by her brother, but she'd learned early on how to protect herself from the evils that lurked in every corner of that house. "I kicked him in the groin before he could get to me."

"Good. Oh, thank God." Bryan released his fists and cracked his knuckles as he paced the room. She watched him with a curious eye, wishing she could read his mind.

"You can't tell Owen," she said again. "Dad beat the shit out of him when he got home that night. It wasn't the first time, but usually it was because Owen stepped in to give mom a break. It was the first time he'd taken a beating for me."

"Why didn't you tell him?" Bryan asked, clearly confused.

She laughed without any humor. "Because Owen would be serving a life sentence in prison."

"I know your brother. He's smart. They never would have found the body. I imagine he knew all the perfect places to covertly feed the gators."

That was probably true, but Morgan hadn't been thinking about that when she was just a teenager. As much as Owen had tried to protect her, she protected him too.

"So you didn't tell your mom?"

Morgan nearly choked on that. "When I first developed boobs, she told me to wear lose shirts so he wouldn't notice. For a long time I did, but at some point I wanted to stop hiding. The first time I wore a shirt that showed how developed I was, she said if he came after me, it wouldn't be her fault."

He dropped onto the bed and pulled her to him, holding her so tight she could hardly draw a breath. His affection caused her to melt, exhausted from the confession and the antihistamine and the thought of having to call her mother tomorrow, but also comforted by the strong arms that would protect her from anything.

"She's never hugged me. Not once. Not when I got my period the first time. Not when I turned sweet sixteen. Not when I graduated high school. It's amazing I'm as well-adjusted as I am."

Bryan chuckled, a deep rumble vibrating against her ear. "You're pretty incredible."

"Flattery isn't going to get you anywhere tonight."

When he put some distance between them, albeit only inches, Morgan felt cold, but then his strong yet gentle fingers turned her chin so she was facing him and the warmth from his expression filled her. "It's not flattery. You're incredible, Morgan. I've always thought so."

Most days she'd counter with something flirtatious or sarcastic to downplay the emotions she saw rolling off him like steam. Not tonight though. Whether it was the exhaustion or the hormones, or something else she didn't want to consider, his affection was what she wanted, what she needed. But what did she say to that? Thanks seemed inadequate. Without giving it any further thought, she kissed him, a slow, warm kiss that spoke volumes more than words ever could.

Bryan pulled away, his look too serious. "Just because she didn't hug you doesn't mean she doesn't love you."

"Maybe not, but I'm a disappointment to her." Morgan had grown accustomed to her mother's disappointment, but verbalizing it to Bryan gave it a painful sting she hadn't acknowledged in years.

"Why do you say that?" Bryan asked.

"It's the same every time I call her. She asks if I'm seeing anyone. I tell her no. She lectures me that I'm not getting any younger, I should find a nice man and settle down, have a few kids."

"She just wants you to be happy, Morg."

What a joke. "Like I need a man to be happy," Morgan huffed. She'd never agreed with her mother's philosophy of marriage.

"Hey, I agree. I have the same issue with my mother. But we're social, sexual beings. We need companionship. That type of need is typically satisfied by a member of the opposite sex. For our parents' generation, that comes in the form of love and marriage."

"You've been watching Dr. Phil again," she chuckled.

"Actually, my mother told me that."

"Yeah, well, I don't need love to be happy. I certainly don't need marriage."

"Amen," Bryan murmured, giving her shoulder a squeeze before letting her go.

She was glad they were on the same page with that. But then, that's why he was safe. She didn't have to worry about Bryan falling in love with her and demanding the same thing in return.

They finished their subs and Morgan settled back into the pillow, pulling the comforter up to her shoulders. She was super sleepy, but that was a good thing. It meant the Pamprin was working and she wouldn't be pummeled with cramps.

"Come here," Bryan said softly, pulling her into his body.

"What are you doing?"

"Holding you."

"Why?"

"Because I want to."

Normally she'd fight him, but it felt nice to be held like this. It was a new sensation, comforting and comfortable.

"Sleep well, Morg."

"You too," she sighed, unable to keep her eyes open any longer.

***

"Can I use your phone?" Morgan wanted to get the call over with. It was early in Washington, but Louisiana was two hours ahead and she wanted to catch her mother before she got busy.

"You want privacy?" Bryan asked, handing her the phone.

"Nah. It'll be quick." She dialed the number, the same number she'd grown up with. Her mother had never moved, not even after her father died. If it was Morgan, she would have sold the house to get away from the memories, but her mother likely stayed for that exact reason, to hang on to the memories. How she could love a man who beat her was beyond Morgan, but nothing she could say would ever change her mother or the past. So it was time to put on her happy face and play nice.

"Hi Mom," she said when Candace picked up.

"Oh, Morgan." Candace sounded relieved and confused. "Where are you? I didn't recognize the number."

"Oh, I'm out with a friend and my phone died. Happy Birthday."

"Thank you. So is this friend a man?"

Nothing like cutting right to the chase. If Morgan admitted to being with Bryan, her mother would jump to conclusions, especially this early in the morning. "Uh, no, just a friend."

Bryan looked at her and shook his head, but the smile on his face showed his humor. She put her finger over her lips to remind him to be quiet.

"Are you doing anything special today?" she asked, trying to focus the conversation on her mother's birthday and not Morgan's lack-of-love life.

"Yes, actually. I have news. Fantastic news."

"Really?" Morgan asked, surprised. "What's up?"

"I'm getting married," Candace sang in a giddy voice.

"Right. Nice one, Mom." Candace had never once dated after Emmanuel died. She'd spent all these years mourning the one man she'd ever love. It made Morgan sick.

"I'm not kidding, Morgan. His name is Will Crepeau and he's a truly wonderful man."

"A truly wonderful man? You wouldn't know one of those if he smacked you in the face." Morgan caught Bryan's expression from the corner of her eye and turned away, embarrassed he'd heard her. Her mother brought out the absolute worst in her.

"Morgan Landry, I am your mother–"

"Right, so that makes you an expert in truly wonderful men."

"You can either be happy for me or you can let that chip on your shoulder continue to mold you into a miserable and lonely old woman. I love Will, and I thank God every day for a second chance at love."

164

Because she'd done so well the first time. "Oh, Mom, please tell me he did not propose to you today?" Morgan was horrified at the thought of history repeating itself all over again. This time she wouldn't be a little girl, hiding in her brother's bedroom while her father took his aggressions out on the woman he demanded proclaim her love as her face met his stiff hand.

Her mother laughed, but that didn't ease Morgan's horror. "He proposed last week. Today he is taking me shopping for a wedding dress."

Candace did sound happy in a way Morgan wouldn't have recognized. Her mother had always seemed to live on the edge of happiness, as though it was within her grasp, but for some reason she refused to take the leap of faith. Just as Emmanuel had felt the world owed him something, maybe Candace balanced that out by feeling she didn't deserve happiness. That certainly would explain a lot.

It had been so many years. Maybe Bryan was right, maybe she did need to let it go. Morgan couldn't begrudge her mother the happiness that had always eluded her. Maybe her second chance at love would serve her well this time.

"Does he," Gah, she was afraid to ask the question. Not that her mother would answer honestly anyway. "Does he treat you well, Mom?"

She felt Bryan's hands rest on her shoulder and she nuzzled her cheek against one hand as her mother rambled on and on about what a truly wonderful man Will Crepeau was.

When Candace had finally said her fill, Morgan asked, "Does Owen know?" Is that why he'd searched her out or was it really just so innocent as to remind her about the birthday?

"No, dear. He hasn't called yet. Don't tell him and ruin my surprise. I know he'll be happy for me." Her voice held a hint of disdain, filling Morgan with guilt for her inability to truly be happy for her mother.

"I'm happy for you," Morgan insisted even though her voice

wasn't convincing. "I just worry about you. You didn't even tell us you were involved with someone."

Ha, wasn't that the pot calling the kettle black! Morgan's situation was different, though. She and Bryan weren't heading down Forever Road. So they were involved – it was no big deal. They had both agreed it was a temporary thing and that was working. It'd work better if her damn period hadn't been early.

"I wanted to be sure before I let the cat out of the bag. Beth and Janie met him last night and they seem to really like him. We're going to get married in Las Vegas this summer. I hope you can come."

"In Vegas? You're leaving Louisiana?" Morgan couldn't hide the shock in her voice. Her mother had never been out of the state.

"As a matter of fact, I'm selling the house. Will bought an RV and we're going to travel the country, maybe even go to Canada."

"He bought an RV or he's buying one with your money?"

Candace clucked her tongue, obviously disappointed in Morgan's assumption. "Such a cynic, just like your father." The comment was like a slap in the face and Morgan felt every muscle in her body tense with anger. "It's no wonder you're not married. Will has his own money and he wants to take care of me. I see no point in keeping the house. When we're tired of traveling, we'll find something a little more modern."

Morgan shook off the sting of the insult and focused on this new chapter in her mother's life. She couldn't picture it, her mother traveling like that. She hardly ever left Lafayette and now she was going to travel the entire continent? And selling the house? After all these years and all the horrible memories, she was selling it now? Because of a man?

"Will you be able to come to the wedding? I'd really like you to meet Will."

Morgan had absolutely no interest in watching her mother walk down the aisle to marry another man who would either use or abuse her, or both. No, she wouldn't be going to the wedding. Since she'd already played the bitch card once during this conversation, Morgan opted to lay down the non-committal card. "I'll try, but I'm taking a full load of classes this summer. I'm not sure I'll be able to get away."

"Certainly the world won't end if you miss a few classes. I seem to remember you missed a lot in high school."

Morgan only ever missed school when her period hit and the cramps were too crippling to even move. Her mother had never offered any sympathy and certainly hadn't taken Morgan to the doctor for a medical intervention. It wasn't until her senior year of high school, when she'd gone to Planned Parenthood to go on the pill that she stopped missing school because of cramps. There was no point rehashing that old battle. She hadn't won back then and bringing it to the surface now would be moot. "Grad school isn't high school," was all she had to offer, but her mother wouldn't understand that. She never furthered her education. No, she'd married Emmanuel Landry soon after high school and started having babies right away.

"Well, I can see there's no point trying to convince you. You've already made up your mind."

"I haven't–" she started, but she was tired of this conversation. Arguing with her mother got her absolutely nowhere. Candace was stubborn as hell, a proud woman who never owned her mistakes – like staying with a man who only offered a lifetime of abuse and fear. "Congratulations, Mom. Have fun shopping for a dress. Let me know when the wedding is and I'll see if I can be there."

They said their stiff good-byes and when Morgan ended the call, she gripped the phone tightly in her hand to keep from hurling it across the room.

"Let me take that," Bryan said, prying it from her hands. He tossed it on the bed and put his hand back on her shoulder. His touch was comforting and some of the tension dissipated as though he'd extracted it with some fancy voodoo. "So your mom's getting married."

"Apparently," she murmured, wishing she'd taken him up on the opportunity for privacy so she didn't have to talk about it. "Can we get out of here?" she demanded, the room suddenly a suffocating cavern that pummeled her with memories of a man hitting the woman he'd vowed to love and honor.

"Let's go," Bryan said. They'd already packed all their gear into the backpack. Morgan strapped it on her shoulders as they approached the bike. It was another sunny day, no remnants of last night's sudden storm lingering in the blue sky.

She was surprised when Bryan turned the motorcycle north, heading back the way they came. They were supposed to ride the ferry back. Twenty minutes later he parked on the south side of the bridge that spanned Deception Pass. "Let's hike down to the beach."

The man was amazing. Morgan hadn't grown up near the ocean, but the few times she'd visited it, she'd found it so incredibly soothing. The path from the road was winding and steep and required total concentration to maneuver. Bryan led the way, keeping a slow but steady pace and looking over his shoulder on occasion to check on her. A couple times she wanted to remind him she didn't need a babysitter, but she recognized his intentions as good. Everything about him was good. She'd never met a more empathetic person in her life and she could see why he was so skilled at talking Owen off the ledge when his ex-bitches had screwed him over.

"Why aren't there more people down here?" she asked, surprised at the near-empty beach.

Bryan grabbed her hand and held it loosely as he led her toward the water. "It's early on a Sunday. People are probably at breakfast or church or sleeping in."

The cold sea air was refreshing, the blue sky calming. The water rustled as it washed over the rocks, turning the small pebbles as the waves rescinded.

She needed this, more than she'd realized. "Do you come here a lot?" she asked, wondering if this was a guaranteed score zone for him. It was romantic, if you were into that sort of thing, which she wasn't, but it also had a peaceful allure, seducing her with a subtle tranquility.

"I've been through on my bike a couple times, but I've never been down here. It's nice."

It was more than nice. It was perfect.

She stopped their slow stroll across the sandy part of the beach and pulled him back to face her. "Thank you." Morgan lifted onto her toes to give him a quick kiss, but his lips were so strong, so sweet, she found she didn't ever want to let go of him.

Gah. She broke the kiss, feeling ridiculous at the sentiment. This is what girls did when they fell for a guy. She wasn't like that. She'd never once gotten all googly-eyed over being kissed or sleeping with a guy. Attraction was a natural thing that didn't require love. That's what she and Bryan had – a crazy attraction. She wasn't falling for him and the only reason she was being so emotional was because of the hormones. Sometimes being a woman really sucked.

She'd have preferred he look at her like she had three heads because the concern that washed over his expression had her heart beating a little faster.

"Aren't you and Owen working on the car today?" she said.

"Yeah. I guess we should head back."

Morgan started toward the path which would lead them back to the motorcycle. Bryan kept pace a couple steps behind. She was grateful for the distance.

***

"So who is she?" Owen asked

"Who's who?"

"The girl."

"What girl?" Bryan asked, playing stupid.

"Every time that damn phone beeps, you drop what you're doing to check the message. So knowing you, you're waiting on confirmation of a sure thing."

"If it was a sure thing, I wouldn't be waiting on a call, now would I?" Bryan knew it actually wasn't a sure thing, given Morgan's current condition, but that didn't mean he didn't want to see her. When he'd dropped her at her apartment a few hours ago, he'd asked about watching the Sounders game together. She was non-committal, said she'd let him know after she took a nap and a long shower. Given the distance she'd suddenly put between them on the beach, and kept between them, he wasn't confident she'd call, but he was hanging on to hope like it was a lifeline.

"Touché. So who is she?"

"If you must know, I'm waiting to hear from my detailer. I'm trying to get Beau assigned to the Pacific Northwest." It was as good a story as any, holding a truth he could share with his buddy.

"Does your brother want a babysitter?"

It wasn't about babysitting. After Blake's big announcement, Beau admitted to being jealous his brother's would be living near each other. Bryan was doing what he could to bring them together. Besides, despite giving it his best effort, Beau was not adjusting to single life very well. Bryan wasn't about to stand back and let his brother implode. "He needs a change. He's been in Colorado almost as long as I've been here. Plus, he needs to be somewhere where Megan isn't. She's staying in Colorado and when she finds herself a new man, Beau isn't going to take it well. And since Blake is moving out here, well, it'd be nice to have Beau around too."

"I get that," Owen said, having way more experience in the divorce department than Bryan, or even Beau. "Doesn't your brother have a different rating though? How can your detailer help?"

"All the detailers are in cahoots and I introduced Philmore to his wife, so he owes me."

"Your detailer's name is Philmore?" Owen laughed.

"Philip Morton. The nickname was a no-brainer."

Owen nodded and laughed. "Never known you to play matchmaker. You usually keep the pretty ones for yourself."

He didn't know the half of it.

"Heather was looking to be a navy wife. As soon as I figured out her end game, I put her in the right hands."

"Was that before or after you banged her?"

"Before." He'd recognized her as a base bunny almost immediately, so hadn't even laid a finger on her. Plus, he wasn't the kind of asshole who had a good time with a woman then handed her off to his buddies. There were lines Bryan didn't cross.

Things had worked out well for the couple. They'd been married seven years and had a couple cute boys with a baby girl on the way.

"Is that how you've managed to stay in Bremerton so long, by holding your matchmaking effort over his head?"

"Staying here's just dumb fucking luck," Bryan laughed, unsure how he'd managed to stay in Bremerton for so long. He was grateful though, because he loved the area and had finally found a place to call home when retirement hit. "I think I've just gotten lost in the shuffle, but I'm also working with Philmore to get reassigned to Carrier Strike Group Three before my luck runs out." It was a different assignment, but relatively same location since the Kitsap Naval Station and Bremerton Naval Yard had merged years ago.

"Clever. You PCS but don't have to move. You up for deploying though? With the tensions igniting again in Iraq, I don't imagine those ships are going to stay in port too much longer."

"Getting on a ship is the point. I've been a land-ho for too long."

"You've been a ho, that's for sure."

"Fuck you, man," Bryan didn't have a better retort because it'd been true and to admit he didn't like being reminded of that would force him to own up to other things, things he wasn't sure were to his benefit.

"So detailers keep hours on Sunday?" Owen asked.

Man, the guy wasn't an idiot.

"Probably not. I'm just anxious, that's all. Beau needs out of Colorado and I've been here almost five years. I've never been anywhere that long, not even as a kid. I'm itchin' for a change."

"You're itchin' for something, but I don't think it's a change."

"There's no girl, man. I don't have time for that shit. Don't need the hassle, either."

"Last one bit you in the ass, huh?"

The current one was biting him in the ass, too. "You know, it's not like I lie. I don't know why these babes think they can change me."

"That's how most women operate."

"Yeah, but you got lucky. Finally. Things still going well with you and Stace?" Bryan was sure if he got the pussy-whipped Romeo focused on Stacie, he'd stop riding Bryan's ass about his sex life. Bryan didn't like lying to his best friend. If it ever came to a head, he was afraid the damage would be irreparable. Owen didn't deal well with betrayal. The only thing worse than sleeping with his best friend's sister would be tagging Owen's girlfriend.

"Yeah, nearly perfect. I keep looking over my shoulder, though, wondering when I'm going to get hit with the shit storm that's been following me my whole life."

"I'm not an expert, but I think you might have finally beaten it. Stacie's great."

"Yeah." Owen didn't sound convinced which threw Bryan for a loop. Usually the man lit up like a beacon when he talked about Stacie.

"What?" Bryan asked, hoping there wasn't trouble.

Owen put the wrench down and wiped his hands on a rag. Then he went over to his backpack and pulled out a little box. It was small enough to hold a ring.

"Ah shit, you serious?"

"Yeah. You think I'm an idiot, don't you?"

Bryan went to the cooler and grabbed a couple Cokes, tossing one at Owen. "Actually, with Stacie, no. I think you finally got it right this time. Congratulations, man. So when you gonna pop the question?"

"I have no clue. I've never done this before. With Kristina and Daphne, well, there was a baby involved, at least I thought there was. So it was more of an agreement than a proposal. I don't want to fuck this up. Plus, I'm not convinced she'll say yes."

"She still having nightmares?"

"Yeah. They've been pretty frequent the last couple of weeks, since the anniversary of her accident. I wish I knew what that bastard did to her."

"It's probably better you don't. You wouldn't do well as someone's bitch in jail."

"You'd know, sailor. You'd hook me up with some soap on a rope, right?"

"Maybe an anchor in your ass. So, is she still getting counseling?" Bryan asked.

"Yep. Her therapist even suggested hypnotherapy, but Stacie's pretty freaked out by that. I don't think she wants to remember."

"Post-traumatic stress is tough. You know that better than anyone."

"Unfortunately. I'm mostly over all that garbage though." Owen's phone rang from the bench next to where he was perched. He eyed the caller ID and gave Bryan a wry glance. "Mostly," he muttered before answering with a simple hello.

Bryan was curious because the only calls Owen ever received when they were holed up in the garage were from Stacie or Morgan. He took on distinct personalities when he talked to each of the women in his life, neither of which he was showing now.

"I just want to help. I know you need the money. There are no strings. Just take it." Owen's face was tense. Whomever he was talking to obviously wanted nothing to do with what Owen was offering.

"Of course we'd love to see him, but that's your call. No

pressure." There was another long pause, the tension coiling like a snake ready to strike. "Take your time, Shannon. I know this must be a difficult time. Just consider my offer."

When Owen disconnected, he let out a long sigh. Bryan raised a brow in question and after Owen stewed for a minute, Bryan finally gave him a verbal shove. "Shannon?"

"Logan's mother," Owen sighed.

"Logan? As in the kid Kristina left at your front door and claimed was yours?"

"Yeah," he sighed. "Stacie was devastated when Child Services took him. Shannon isn't getting any support from her ex now that he's awaiting trial, so I'm just trying to help."

"But *you* weren't devastated at all, you know, not saying good-bye to the little guy because you were too busy drowning in bourbon." Maybe he shouldn't call Owen out on it, but this wasn't just about Stacie and it wouldn't do the man any good to keep his personal agenda under lock and key.

"Fuck you," Owen spat, but he shook his head. "I kind of hate myself for the way I acted with him. I'm sure he doesn't remember, but I do and I'd like to make amends."

Ah, there it was, the whole truth. Bryan was proud of his friend for owning it.

"Doesn't sound like she wants help," Bryan prodded.

"Are all women stubborn? I mean, I thought I'd met my quota with my mother and Morgan and Stacie, but I think Shannon takes the cake."

Bryan laughed. Yeah, and if you added Jenny into the mix, that brought stubborn to a whole new level. "Good luck. Let me know if I can help."

"Thanks. Do me a favor though, keep it under the radar. Stacie doesn't know and I don't want to get her hopes up that she might see Logan again."

Bryan was becoming a master at keeping secrets. "Can do," he said, figuring this one had to be easier than the secret Morgan was forcing him to keep.

"So you gonna tell me about this girl?" Owen asked, turning the conversation in a direction Bryan didn't want to navigate to.

"I already did. There is no girl."

"Liar. Must be serious if you don't wanna brag."

Bryan grabbed the wrench from the tool chest and passed it off. May as well let the big mouth do the muscle work. That might get him to stop talking. "Must be nothing if I don't wanna brag. We gonna get this radiator installed or what?"

"Yeah, we better get to it before your booty call pulls you away."

Chapter 11

Morgan touched up her lip gloss and took the sample bottle of body spray out of her bag. Bryan liked coconut, so she'd hit Bath and Body Works to pick up the tasty lip gloss and coordinating spray. She lifted her thick hair to give a quick spray at her nape, then held the bottle further away to spray her breasts. One last spray on her belly and she was good to go. Bryan would pick up the scent and follow its trail like a hound sniffing out its prey. Man oh man did she ever like being Bryan's prey. Since her period had forced an unwanted reprieve from all things sex, she was eager to get back in his sites. Fortunately, she'd found someone to fill her Wednesday night shift at the clinic.

When the door to the ferry bathroom swung open, Morgan tucked the body spray into her bag and checked herself in the mirror. She was surprised to see Stacie gawking at her in the reflection, wearing her own look of surprise.

"Morgan, hey."

"Hey Stace." Shit. Morgan had specifically gotten on the five o'clock ferry knowing Stacie took the six o'clock boat to meet Owen. So much for best laid plans.

"I'm surprised to see you here," Stacie said, digging into her backpack.

"One of my classmates lives in Bremerton. We're studying tonight."

"Really? You smell pretty good for a study session."

"Beats smelling like the ferry," she countered.

Stacie gave her a long look in the mirror and Morgan wanted to squirm. She didn't like being assessed and she was pretty sure that's what Stacie was doing. "So you're not heading over to see Bryan?"

Great.

Morgan liked Stacie, she really did, but her pursuit of this topic was getting old. "No, of course not. You and Jenny really need to get over that. There's nothing going on with me and Bryan." Nothing at this second, anyway. As soon as Morgan walked through his door, all bets were off.

"Yeah, right. We see the way you two look at each other."

Morgan forced a laugh. "I think you're imagining things, Stace. Bryan and I don't look at each other."

"You know what, you're right. Lately, it's the way the two of you avoid looking at each other that's giving you away."

"I don't know what you're talking about," Morgan scoffed, pulling the thick straps of her purse onto her shoulder.

"I don't know why you're hiding it. Bryan's a great guy. You're terrific. You two are perfect for each other."

Bryan was great and if Morgan was interested in something serious, maybe she'd go for it. Serious, though, wasn't her deal.

In the short term, she needed to focus on grad school. When that was done, she'd have a rewarding career. She didn't need a man to fill some void. Happiness was defined by self, not by some man who couldn't keep the promise he made in front of God and family. Nope, marriage vows or even something permanent without the ring wasn't in the cards for Morgan. The sex was great, but beyond that, Bryan was just friend material.

Besides, dating was fun. When she and Bryan were done with their benefits, she'd get back to dating. Love was a pain she didn't need. Fun was good. Fun was safe.

Morgan wasn't naïve enough to think she wasn't carrying around scars from her childhood. Unfortunately, scars are permanent. Sure, they fade with time, but they're never really gone. You had to learn to live with them.

That's why Morgan was studying to be a midwife. She'd get to bring new life into the world. That was her calling. That's what would make her happy.

Right now, what would make her happy was a graceful exit. Unfortunately, she couldn't leave the bathroom and ignore Stacie. They were trapped on the ferry together, with another ten minutes until they sailed into port. Then Morgan was going to have to fake going off in a direction that wasn't toward Bryan's apartment.

"I'm going to go sit near the front. Maybe I'll see you when you're done in here," she offered.

"Sure," Stacie sang, her gaze still assessing as Morgan left the bathroom. Fortunately Bremerton was coming into view. It was such a pretty place. Morgan would love to live in one of the small houses along the water and watch the ferries come and go. The reality was, she'd never make enough money to afford such a place, but it was good to have dreams.

A smile crept across her face as she spotted Bryan's apartment building. Five floors up she spotted his balcony. A couple times late last summer they'd hung out there, grilling burgers and drinking beers. She'd learned a long time ago to ignore the desire that sparked whenever she was around him. Instead, she'd embraced the friendship they shared. She'd never imagined he'd been hiding the same desire. They'd been alone together more times than she could count, both at his apartment and at hers. Why had he never put the moves on her before?

Because of Owen. His loyalty to her brother was both endearing and annoying.

"Why are you scowling?" Stacie asked as she sat next to Morgan.

"I'm not." Last she knew, she was smiling. Then she got

thinking about how Bryan wanted to tell Owen about their hook up. *Gah.*

"So you haven't dated anyone in a while. Since, like Christmas. Well, except for that fiasco after the Super Bowl."

Why couldn't Stacie just let this go? "Owen attacked both Erik and Derek," Morgan pointed out. "It's no wonder I don't bring my dates around anymore."

"Maybe you should stop dating guys whose names rhyme with ick."

Morgan laughed, remembering Owen had said the same thing. "And maybe Owen should keep his fingers out of my chili." Her relationship with her brother was a double-edged sword. While she knew she could count on him for anything, his view on her acquaintances was frustrating.

"Listen, I'm going to stick my fingers in your chili, as you say, because you're my friend. If," she emphasized, though Morgan wasn't sure why, "there is something going on with you and Bryan, and everyone thinks there is, Owen is going to find out. How do you think he's going to feel when he finds out his best friend and his sister have been hiding something from him?"

Morgan didn't have to answer. Owen would be furious. He'd go all 1960's on Morgan and do who knows what to Bryan. That was the whole point of the secret.

When Morgan didn't say anything, Stacie continued. "He's going to feel betrayed. You know Owen doesn't handle betrayal well."

That was stupid. It wasn't as though what Morgan and Bryan were doing affected Owen. They were having sex, for Pete's sake.

"Well, I guess it's a good thing nothing's going on."

Stacie simply shook her head, obviously not believing Morgan for a second. She and Bryan were going to have to be more discreet.

"When you're ready to tell someone the truth, I'm all ears."

Morgan wasn't the type to kiss and tell, she never had been, but then she'd never been with anyone as incredible as Bryan.

Sometimes she felt like she was going to explode keeping all the deliciousness to herself. Unfortunately, telling Stacie was practically telling Owen.

Fortunately, it was time to disembark.

***

Brian bit back the groan when he walked into his apartment. He expected to find Morgan there since he'd told her where to find the hidden key. He didn't expect her to be making dinner...in that tattered denim skirt. She had the most amazing legs and with bare feet and olive skin disappearing beneath the frayed hem...well, damn she looked hot in his kitchen.

Bryan wiped the sweat from his brow and chained the door.

Did she know what the sight of her in that skirt did to him?

"What are you doing?" he asked gruffly. That tank top didn't leave much to the imagination, not that he had a brain cell left to think with.

"Big strong sailor needs his protein." She turned around and bit down on her lip, her eyes wide as she gave him a full body scan.

Bryan realized this was the first time she'd ever seen him in uniform.

His service khakis weren't anything to get excited over in his book, but apparently the look worked for Morgan. "See something you like?"

"Maybe." She released her lip and leaned back against the counter. "Do you?"

"Absolutely." He could have her naked in 2.4 seconds, but then he wouldn't get to savor every inch of her body. Hopefully she wasn't hungry because they weren't going to have dinner anytime soon.

Brian dropped his bag and closed the distance between them, pressing himself against her curves. He probably ought to lose the uniform before the thing got destroyed, but she was too tempting to walk away from.

He swallowed her giggle as he claimed her mouth. God, she felt so good, all soft skin and hot body. He held her tight, bending his knees so he could grind his erection between her legs as their tongues sought and took with a ferocity that had him wanting to strip her naked and forget about savoring her. When she looked this hot, and gave as good as she got, it was hard to control the need to drive right into her.

Breathing in her tropical scent, Bryan planted hungry kisses along her jaw, nipping at her lobe before finding that sensitive spot just below ear. Her little moan told him he found his target.

Her hands moved up his arms and down his chest, honing in on the buttons. "You look good in uniform," she purred. "So good. It's no wonder you have women throwing themselves at you all the time."

"I don't go out in uniform," he said, nipping at her neck and along her collar bone, eliciting another little moan.

"Oh, well, you should."

"You're the only woman I want throwing herself at me," he informed her as she continued to release buttons.

She tugged the shirt, along with the white t-shirt beneath, from his trousers. Her nails scraped up the center of his stomach to his chest where she splayed her hands and lit him on fire.

"I love all your muscles," she cooed. "I want to see you naked."

Yes. Hell yes.

But no. "Not yet," he growled.

He'd lose all control if they didn't have the barrier of clothes between them. He wanted her naked first so he could touch and tease and taste her. He wanted to watch her come, first from his fingers, then from his mouth. Then she could see him naked, just before he slipped inside her and made her come again.

Bryan let his hands wander over the fabric of her slinky tank top. The thing was so simple, just black with thin straps. Spaghetti straps, he thought they were called, but didn't really give a shit. They provided unlimited access to her skin, that's what he cared about.

He pushed the straps down, kissing the spot he'd just exposed, from her shoulder down her chest until he reached the hem. The fabric gave way easily, releasing her round breasts and allowing him to cup them. Damn, her nipples were already hard, tight pink buds that just begged to be licked and sucked. Who was Bryan to say no to that kind of invitation?

The pad of each thumb moved over and around, making them even harder. Someone groaned, maybe him, maybe her – who the fuck cared. She was so damn responsive, it only keyed him on, his mouth finally going to where his eyes had been focused. Her breath caught as his tongue swept across the perfect bud. His thumb continued to work the other side, then he switched, ravishing the same affection on the other side.

Her hands brushed over his short hair, encouraging him on, not that he needed encouragement. Damn, she was beautiful. He wanted more.

Still ravishing her nipples with his mouth, his hands wandered down the fabric and over the denim before finding the soft skin of her amazing legs. Her skin provided a nice contrast, soft and smooth and warm. He slid his hands back up, this time going under the skirt. When he squeezed her bare ass, he figured she was wearing a thong, but as he found his way to the front, he realized she was commando.

He released her nipple as his cock jumped in his pants.

"Oh, hell, Morgan, you're not wearing panties."

"You like?"

Dumb question. Yeah, he liked. He liked a lot.

She licked her lips, her eyes dark and intense as the fingers of both his hands explored and teased. God, the things he wanted to do to her.

The soft purr of her voice as he slowly caressed between her legs put him into a dilemma. Yeah, he wanted to make her come just like this. The more urgent need was to lose his pants and boxers and get inside her, deep inside, with those legs wrapped tightly around his waist as he drove into her over and over.

But to lose his pants, he'd have to stop touching her.

Fuck it. He could strip one handed.

Bryan wanted to maximize her pleasure, so he left his dominant hand between her legs and moved his left hand to release his belt. It was a difficult task even when he didn't have the lust-filled shakes, but Morgan made it even more difficult as she put her hand over his, stopping his motion.

"What's your hurry, sailor? Your ship about to sail?"

"Sweetheart, I'm sporting a submarine that's ready to dive deep."

"Mmmm…I love it when you talk dirty." Her tongue was warm as she traced along his jaw.

"I love it when you act dirty."

Morgan eased open his belt and wasted no time getting his trousers open. He had to leave the warmth of her soft, wet flesh to lose the undershirt before backing himself to the couch, pulling Morgan along with him. As he slouched, Morgan straddled his thighs, his hand once again delighting in all the pleasures to be found between her legs. She rocked against him, her own hands settling on his chest and giving her a little leverage.

Holy shit, she was going to ride his hand to orgasm. Bryan might just lose it right there in his pants.

He practically growled when some asshole knocked on the door.

"What?" he barked, not even thinking. He should have just ignored the damn thing.

"Hey, man. It's me."

Morgan's eyes opened wide at the sound of her brother's voice on the other side of the door. Before Bryan could say anything, she bolted for the bathroom, tugging her tank top back into place as she scurried.

He took a few deep breaths to wrestle down the frustration. "Hang on, man. I'll be right there."

Bryan followed Morgan to the bathroom, picking up his shirts as he went. "What are you doing?"

"Stacie saw me on the ferry today and she thinks there's something going on with us."

"There is," he pointed out.

"No shit, but we don't need to confirm her suspicions. If she knows, Owen will know and that'll be it for us."

He hated this. The sneaking around had been fine at first, but Bryan was done with it.

"Let's just tell him. He can't keep us from…" he wanted to say "seeing each other," but now was not the time to negotiate their status. He'd barely gotten her to admit they were involved. He imagined saying they were seeing each other would send her into panic mode. "Doing whatever we want to do."

"What I want to do is you, without Owen knowing. So I'll just stay right here until they're gone."

Bryan couldn't argue with her. Owen was at the door and would wonder what had kept Bryan from opening it.

"Fine," he muttered even though it was anything but. When he spotted Morgan's panties lying on the bathroom floor, he wanted to choke his best friend for showing up now.

Setting his belt back and slipping on his undershirt, Bryan had to recite the phonetic alphabet to soften the submarine in his pants. No way could he open the door to Owen, and most likely Stacie, while Morgan was stowed away in his bathroom and he was sporting an unholy sailor's mast. It took him until Lima, Mike, November before he was confident he could open the door without offending anyone. Bryan also threw out a prayer of thanks that his buddy didn't try to let himself in with his own key. If he had, Bryan would have to explain the chain too.

Deep breath, smile, then he swung the door open. "Hey man. Stace. What's up?"

"I missed you at shift change. You cut out early."

"Yeah, I didn't have anything to do." He had plenty to do, actually, but it all involved the hot woman hiding in his bathroom.

"You gonna let us in?" Owen asked.

"Yeah, sorry. I was just getting changed. Come on in."

Owen made himself comfortable on the couch and Bryan did his best to hide the cringe of guilt that ripped through him. Yep, he'd just been in that same spot, except his best bud's sister had been straddling his hips, getting ready to rock his world. Yeah, what a good friend he was.

It was obvious Owen didn't know what was going on. There was no way he'd be this relaxed if he knew his sister was here and not wearing panties.

"So what are you two up to?" Bryan asked.

"You said you wanted me to take a look at a computer."

Aw, shit. Bryan had totally forgotten about that. When he got the text from Morgan that she didn't have to work tonight, his mind stayed on one track and it had nothing to do with a computer virus.

"Is that Morgan's bag? What's she doing here?"

"Huh?" Brian asked, trying to play dumb. She had bolted for the bathroom so fast, she obviously forgot about her bag. She was probably more concerned with slipping those panties back on. "Oh, yeah, she's in the bathroom. Computer's over there." Bryan nodded at the desk on the other side of the room. "I'm going to get out of this uniform."

He had a million maneuvers for avoiding the subject. The good thing about most of the guys he hung with, they didn't like small talk. They really were like dogs…throw a bone or toss a ball, and squirrel! They were completely distracted. The trick worked with Owen, at least long enough for Bryan to buy more time and come up with a plan.

On his way by the bathroom, he put on a show. "Hey Morg, your brother and Stace are here."

He imagined she was cussing under her breath, but the bag was obvious and there was no point denying she was there, especially if Stacie had seen her on the ferry. Besides, the bathroom wasn't the smartest hiding place in his small apartment. If either Owen or Stacie needed to hit the head, Morgan was busted.

Bryan slipped on a wife beater and loose jeans before he headed back out to the living room. Morgan was scooping up her bag. "Thanks for use of the bathroom. I really hate public bathrooms. Do you have any idea how many germs fester there? Ugh. It's disgusting. I'm going to go meet up with my date."

Owen perked up from the desk in the corner and didn't delay his inquisition. "Date? With who? Where are you two going? How'd you meet him?"

Bryan didn't think it was possible, but the scowl she'd already been wearing deepened. "None of your business. None of your business. And oh, hey, none of your business."

"Morgan, come on. I'm not trying to be a dick. It's about personal security. Someone should know the who, what, when, where. Just in case. You got me on speed dial, right?"

"Yes, big brother, I have you on speed dial. As for the rest, I'm fine. Bryan has the necessary details."

Stupendous. He should have known she'd throw him under the bus.

"Before you go," Owen started, not seeming to care that Bryan had any made up details of Morgan's non-existent date, "you've been avoiding me. We need to talk about Mom."

"What's there to talk about? She's getting married. I'm happy for her."

Bryan nearly laughed. Her expression and tone were a complete contrast to her words.

"I know this is stirring shit up for you," Owen said. "Mom told me you were bitchy on the phone."

Morgan laughed, but there was no mirth. It felt like a replay of Sunday when she'd first gotten the news from her mother. "I had my period, so I was being bitchy."

All the color drained from Owen's face and Bryan felt it swarm his own face. Yeah, he'd been present for the early arrival of the monthly curse, but damn, he didn't expect Morgan to be so open about it with her brother.

The smile on her face revealed her intentions, though. She'd wanted to shut her brother up and it looked like she'd succeeded.

"I'm outta here," she sang as she spun around in a playful pirouette and headed to the door.

"Whoa! You have a tramp stamp?" Owen drawled.

"Hey," Bryan called across the room. He tried to stay out of the brother-sister rants, but there was a line you just didn't cross. "Have some respect. That's your sister."

"Yeah, my sister with a tramp stamp." Owen sat back in the chair and crossed his arms, assessing Morgan who was once again scowling at her brother.

Despite that, she could hold her own with her brother, so it was probably safer if Bryan backed off. He didn't want to fall under suspicion by rushing to Morgan's rescue.

"It's a tattoo, Owen. It's a symbol for life and healing, not a tramp stamp."

"Dad had tattoos."

Morgan crossed the room like a storm trooper and slapped Owen across the face. The contact echoed throughout the room and Bryan felt his eyes widen with shock as Stacie gasped.

"Don't ever, *ever* compare me to him."

Bryan had seen the siblings argue on occasion. It wasn't often, but it was never cutthroat. He wasn't sure what had spurned Owen to verbally attack his sister, but Bryan didn't like it. It took all his willpower to keep his feet planted firmly in place rather than swooping in to rescue Morgan.

She turned back toward the door and pushed her skirt down, further revealing the art. Bryan had seen it up close and personal and he thought it was sexy as hell, especially once he knew what it symbolized. The tension coursing through the room now, though, kept him from getting aroused at seeing all that skin and ink.

"Jesus Morgan," Owen spat.

"Don't cuss at me either," she snarled over her shoulder

Owen held up his hands in surrender. "I was just giving you a hard time. Don't be so sensitive." It hadn't sounded like playful banter. Owen's attack had been mean.

Morgan gripped the door handle. "I won't be so sensitive when you stop being so insensitive."

"Hey. I'm sorry, okay." Owen pushed out of the chair and crossed to where Morgan stood. The anger rolled off her in waves, putting Bryan on high alert. She hated being rescued, but if Owen was going to continue being a dick, Bryan was ready to intervene. "You're right, I never should have said that."

Owen put his arms around Morgan, wrapping her in an affectionate hug Bryan had seen them share often. Morgan didn't reciprocate at first. "I'm a little tense about Mom and this guy too. I shouldn't take it out on you."

That seemed to loosen Morgan up a little and she hugged him back. Bryan let out the breath he didn't even realize he'd been holding.

When Owen let go, he kept a hand on the door. "So tell me about this date. Is it a first date? You're not sleeping with this guy right? Because, you know, with a tramp stamp and all, guys might think you're easy." He winked when he said it, but Bryan knew Owen would want all the details of her date. Owen likely knew Morgan wouldn't give up any of it. She didn't like her brother trying to keep her on a short leash.

Morgan rolled her eyes, but it seemed more playful than annoyed. "Don't worry, Owen. I've been out with this guy before and he's not a keeper."

Okay, Bryan really hoped that wasn't her way of taking a crack at him.

"If he's not a keeper, why go out with him at all?"

"Because it's fun. Catch you guys later." Owen stepped back to let her out. Before the door closed, she stuck her tongue out at Bryan.

Little temptress.

He wanted to follow her out, find out if she was coming back, but that'd be too obvious. She'd played her cards well, although hearing the word date spoken from her mouth, even if it was just a ploy, sent a surge of jealousy pulsing through his veins. Yeah, they were just messing around, but he still didn't like the idea of some other guy putting his hands on her.

Instead of chasing her down, he gave her a minute before sending a text. *U cmg bck?*

"Can I get you guys anything?" Bryan asked, heading into the kitchen where the dinner Morgan had started was still sitting on the counter. She'd been chopping vegetables before they'd gotten distracted.

"This guy doesn't have a firewall or virus protection. This is going to be ugly." Owen was completely wrapped up in his work at the computer. Sluggish computers were his specialty. When Bryan's neighbor, knowing Bryan worked in computer security, asked if he'd take a look at it, Bryan had happily agreed. He liked Paul and liked keeping up positive neighbor relations. He would have figured out the problem eventually, but Owen could find it a thousand times faster. "I'll have a beer if you got one," he threw in, probably as an afterthought.

Stacie joined Bryan in the kitchen. "Sorry about the interruption. I figured Morgan was here, but I couldn't talk him out of coming," she said quietly.

"She was just using the bathroom," Bryan insisted, keeping the cover because that's what Morgan would want.

Stacie gave him a knowing smile. "You guys are so full of shit."

Great. If Stacie was cursing, she likely wasn't taking her meds, which meant her brain-to-mouth filter might not be working. She was being subtle now, but would that be the case after she left?

"Believe what you want," Bryan shrugged. He had to play dumb because anything else would reveal his and Morgan's dirty little secret. Not that he cared. Hell, at this point it would be a relief to have the secret out. Unfortunately, Morgan was always true to her word and he feared if the secret did get out, they'd be through. It was stupid, but he wasn't ready to let her go.

"On the ferry, Morgan told me she had a study group here in Bremerton. Just now, she said she had a date."

Well, fuck.

"Maybe she lied on the ferry so you wouldn't interrogate her about the date," Bryan suggested, trying to think fast.

"Right, because my interrogations are way more intense than Owen's."

She had a point, but what could Bryan say. He held out the beer to her. Fortunately she took it without further discussion and delivered it to Owen. Bryan popped one open for himself and took a long swig before his phone beeped. The message from Morgan read *U btr mk it wrth my whl.*

Would he ever make it worth her while.

Bryan peeked out of the kitchen to where Owen was working his magic on the computer. He hoped it wouldn't take too long. Bryan replied to Morgan's text. *I promise.*

Stacie had made herself comfortable on the couch with her sketchpad. To avoid any further assumptions from her, Bryan joined Owen at the computer.

"There's a butt load of spyware on here man. That's what's slowing things down." Owen scribbled on a notepad Bryan had left on the desk. "So who's my sister dating?"

Great, now Bryan had to play out another rouse. "Uh, just some guy she knows from school."

Owen pushed back from the desk. "I've made some notes. You know how to clean it up, right?"

"Yeah, I can manage. Thanks. You've probably saved me hours."

He pulled Stacie into his arms. Bryan never thought much of the warm, easy affection the two shared, but seeing the two of them now sent pangs of jealousy racing through him. He wanted that. It was foolish and crazy, but so was this whole situation with Morgan.

"No problem. So what are you up to tonight?"

Bryan settled onto the couch and put his feet on the wooden table. "Just gonna hang."

"Come out with us. We'll crash Morgan's date."

Yeah, that'd be fun. More like impossible, since she didn't actually have a date. "What are you, seventeen?"

Owen laughed. Bryan focused on that instead of the way Stacie was studying him. "Come on, you like messing with her as much as I do. This is almost too easy. Unless you're just covering for her. She did tell you where she's going, right?"

"Yeah, and that doesn't mean I'm telling you."

Owen raised one eyebrow. "Putting my sister before me?"

Bryan chortled with guilt. He'd been putting Morgan first for a while now, all so he could keep sharing a bed with her. "Keeping a promise."

"When'd you turn into a pussy?" Owen teased, but Bryan didn't find it amusing.

Okay, now he'd had enough. Bryan pushed off the couch and stepped over the table to get in Owen's face. "You know what, fuck you, man. You're sister's a mature, independent woman. She's capable of making her own decisions and keeping herself safe. She doesn't need you all up in her business and I don't need you riding my dick."

Owen raised a hand in surrender. He seemed to be doing that a lot tonight. "Chill out, man. It's all in good fun."

"Well, it's not my idea of fun."

Stacie stepped between them and whispered something in Owen's ear before giving Bryan another one of those glances that held too much knowledge. Despite what she thought she knew, he was grateful she intervened because his temper was spiking. When had Owen started being such a dick to his sister? He'd always been

191

possessive, but Bryan had never seen him be mean.

"You need to get laid," Owen drawled. "That booty call never came through for you, did it?"

Bryan checked his watch. "Ferry's coming in soon. You ought to be on your merry way so you don't miss it."

"Come on, Owen. Let's let Bryan be." Stacie gave his arm a tug, but Owen didn't budge.

"Did I miss the memo on being uptight? You and Morgan both need to learn to take a joke."

Nothing Owen had said was funny. "Maybe you're the problem. You've been acting like an ass ever since you walked in here tonight"

Owen just stood there, staring at Bryan like he had three heads. What he'd said wasn't off the mark. His friend had been acting like an ass. He'd told Morgan the situation with his mother had made him tense. Bryan also realized he was dealing with that situation with Logan's mother too. Maybe it was all getting to him.

Before Bryan could offer up an apology, Owen shook his head. "You're right. Sorry, man." Owen held out his knuckles.

Bryan bumped them, even if it was reluctantly.

"We good?" Owen asked.

"Yeah, man, we're good." It's not like Bryan could stay mad at him.

Bryan fell back on the couch as soon as Stacie opened the door. The friendly long-haired cat that'd been hanging around rushed into the apartment. She was probably hungry. Bryan usually fed her when he came home from work. It probably wasn't a good idea, but there was something about her that had him acting out of character.

Sounded like a certain brunette.

"You got a cat?" Owen asked.

"Nah, she's just a stray." As he said it, Natasha, as Bryan had affectionately named her, jumped onto his lap.

"She looks pretty cozy for a stray."

She didn't have a collar and Bryan had asked around, but no one wanted to claim her. He'd taken to calling her Natasha because she was just too sweet and pretty to be called Cat. "She's been around since I came back from Colorado. No one seems to know where she came from.

"You want me to put her out?" Owen asked.

Bryan gave the cat a long stroke and was rewarded with a rhythmic purr. "Nope, I'll handle it."

As soon as they were out the door, Bryan succumbed to beating himself up for being so uptight, as Owen had pointed out. Morgan could handle her brother. In fact, she could handle him better than anyone. She didn't need Bryan coming to her rescue, especially when Owen was only trying to mess with her. It's what brothers and sisters did. Hell, Bryan had grown up messing with is little brothers all the time.

Bryan's hand must have stilled because Natasha nudged him. When he started stroking her fur again, she curled into a ball on his lap. He didn't normally have any affection for pets. Puppies were cute, but who didn't think that? He'd never committed to a pet because orders could come down at any time and if he went on a ship, what would happen to his furry companion?

The same thing that would happen to a woman. She'd find someone new, or at least temporary while he was at sea.

Yeah, Bryan was a cynic when it came to relationships. He'd seen plenty work, but he'd seen enough fail to know that wasn't the path for him.

He knew why he was on the defensive when it came to Morgan, but he needed to get over it. She wasn't long term. Hell, she'd made it clear on more than one occasion they were friends with benefits. It seemed that at every turn Bryan was trying to make it more than it was. With Morgan, that was a losing battle.

His tension was most likely from the stress of sneaking around, or more specifically, almost getting caught. If Owen and Stace had shown up five minutes later, it would have been a nightmare. Then again, the secret would be out.

When he heard the knock on the door, he barked out another "What?" Then he heard the key and watched the lever move. He should have been happy to see Morgan enter his apartment.

Her smile was beautiful as always. "Who's your friend?"

"Natasha. She's a stray. I feed her once in a while."

Morgan laughed as she kicked the door closed. "Natasha?"

"I'm pretty sure she's a former Russian assassin working for the good guys now." As if the cat disagreed, she jumped off his lap and slinked around Morgan's ankle.

"Has nothing to do with how pretty she is." Her smile and voice were filled with amusement as she gave the cat a few affectionate strokes and gave Bryan one hell of a view of her perfect cleavage. "Anyway, I saw them leave. Watched them get on the ferry, actually. Coast is clear."

"Morgan–"

"Don't Bryan." Her smile dissolved, as did the humor in her voice. "I know what you're going to say. Just don't."

"I'm lying to my best friend. Do you know how many times that guy has had my back? And how do I repay him? By doing his sister behind his back."

Morgan let the cat out and locked the door, sliding the chain into place, before tossing her bag on the floor. When she slipped out of her sandals, Bryan couldn't help notice her toenails were painted pink, the same color as her lips. Her long legs moved slowly across the floor. By the time she reached the couch, her tank top was gone and hell, she wasn't wearing a bra. How had he missed that little detail earlier?

As if he were a marionette, his hands moved to the soft curves of her breasts when she straddled him on the couch. Her skirt lifted and he saw she'd lost the panties again...if she'd ever put them back on.

"Dammit, woman, you're going to wreck me."

"That's my plan," she purred. "At least for tonight."

She caressed his arms, her hands soft and warm, washing away the tension with every stroke. He wanted to talk, to convince her it was time to tell Owen they were together, for her to admit they were together, but Bryan knew that would get him exactly nowhere. Yeah, best to let his libido win this battle.

He smoothed his hands up her thighs and under the denim. It was like Déjà vu. She was just as wet and warm as she'd been before Owen showed up, just as responsive as he slid his fingers against her wet heat.

Morgan's hands traveled down his chest, one finger playing with a little a hole in his shirt. "Do you like this shirt?"

Bryan shrugged. "It's cloth. It serves a function. I wouldn't say I have any particular affection for it."

"Good." With both hands, she dug her fingers into the hole and ripped the shirt apart.

Worn out cotton was his new best friend.

And damn, so was her mouth. She trailed hot kisses all over him, starting at his jaw and working down his neck to his chest. Her hands scraped across the hair there before she tongued his nipples.

Her lips were soft, yet firm and confident when they touched his skin, making him want more. When she started working his pants open, he wanted to help to speed things along, but he couldn't move, enraptured by the feel of her mouth.

The anticipation of what she was going to do to him created a storm of sensations throughout his body.

He lifted off the couch and helped her slide the jeans and boxers off his hips. Then he wriggled out of them as her hands got busy on his skin again. As if knowing how painful his erection was, she took him gently in her hand, a subtle stroke with her fingers. When her lips reached his stomach, he knew his fate.

"If I let you do this, I'm not going to last long once I'm inside you."

The caress of her warm breath was erotic as hell as she continued to travel south.

"You're a little tense. I'm just trying to relax you."

He loved her relaxation techniques. Her mouth surrounded him and he no longer felt the throbbing pain, just the pleasurable warmth of her mouth. Bryan's fingers tangled in her thick hair as he threw his head back in total surrender.

Chapter 12

Morgan loved that she could basically turn this big, strong sailor into a puddle of mush. The smile on his face spoke volumes to the pleasure she'd just lavished on him. He was definitely more relaxed now than he had been when she'd walked in. Maybe now he wouldn't want to play true confessions.

"You're amazing," he sighed as she straddled his lap again. It'd take a while for him to recover, but she hoped he'd continue with his fingers the way he had been before they were interrupted. "Did that really just happen?"

She couldn't keep from laughing. "Do you really have to ask?"

His hands squeezed her hips. "You realize I'm at your mercy, right? Anything you want, it's yours: a sports car, a trip to Hawaii, a yacht."

All of those sounded wonderful but there was something she wanted that was more immediate. "How about a mind-blowing orgasm?"

"I just had one."

Morgan slapped his chest. "I meant for me."

Bryan growled his approval as he pushed off the sofa, holding her tight as he carried her across the room.

"What are you doing?" she laughed, loving the feel of being

wrapped around him and held so tightly in his arms.

"I'm taking you to bed now." His voice was raw and rough.

"The sofa isn't working for you?"

"Sweetheart, the couch worked just fine, but I want to make sure you're good and comfortable so I can make coming back worth *your* while."

She had no doubt he'd keep his promise. Now that he wasn't thinking about Owen anymore, she knew the next part of the night would be all about her. They'd been doing this for months now, one or two times a week, for the most part. Occasionally, they managed to hook up more than that. No matter the frequency, Bryan wasn't a selfish lover. He always made sure it was worth her while. That's probably why she kept coming back.

That, and the fact that the arrangement worked. Morgan didn't demand anything of Bryan and he didn't ask for anything more from her. They went out occasionally, but it didn't feel like dating, even though he always insisted on paying. They were friends, had been ever since Morgan had visited her brother in Norfolk and met Bryan. They both looked out for Owen when he needed it, but outside of her brother as a common bond between them, she just really enjoyed spending time with him.

When Bryan set her down on the bed, she made a move to take her skirt off, but he stopped her.

"Leave it on," he commanded. She almost chuckled, but the way he looked at her, the desire so obvious in his eyes, her emotions were overcome with her own need to feel his mouth on her.

"If I leave the skirt on, I can't see what you're doing." She loved to watch, especially when his gaze shifted to hers and he had fire in his eyes.

"Then just lay back and enjoy it."

Unexpectedly, he took one foot in his hand and started massaging it with a firm touch. "Your toes match the color of your lips. Did you do that on purpose?"

Morgan hadn't even noticed. She'd actually treated herself to a pedicure a few days ago and picked a nice summer pink. Though the flavor of her lip gloss and the matching body spray was contrived, she couldn't say the same for her toes. "It was the prettiest pink at the spa the other day."

"I like it."

Big strong sailor liked pink toes. That might be funny if he wasn't being so sweet. Morgan relaxed and let him work his magic massage on her foot. She felt herself almost doze off and was grateful he switched to the other foot before she was completely lost to the relaxation.

After a while she felt his hands move up her legs. The massage on her calf and thighs was significantly shorter than the time he'd spent on her feet. That was fine. She was anxious for his kiss.

His fingers found her first and he moaned his approval when he felt how wet she was. His mouth finding her wasn't subtle at all. One moment he was looking at her, the next he was kissing, licking, sucking at her. His whiskers had grown in enough to add a contrasting friction. She loved the weekends when he didn't have to shave, the rasp of his stubble was an erotic pleasure.

Not being able to see him through the denim was as exciting as watching him. She closed her eyes, losing herself completely in the feel of him.

Morgan felt the orgasm stir to life and her hips lifted off the bed on their own power, desperately searching for more friction where Bryan continued to kiss her. Then she felt his hands squeeze the inside of her thighs, a pleasurable pressure point for sure, and the orgasm was no longer stirring. She cried out as the pleasure over took her.

When the spasms stopped she realized Bryan had sprawled out beside her. He held out a condom as she rolled toward him. "I want you on top of me."

She wasn't sure how she was going to muster the bone structure to do what he wanted, but where there was a will, there was a way.

She managed to roll the condom on with minimal effort and

feeling his arousal motivated her. She was eager to feel him inside and live the pleasure all over again.

***

The new Captain America movie had been better than he'd expected. Maybe that was because it felt like a date. The theatre had been crowded and there weren't six seats next to each other anywhere in the theatre. Morgan and Bryan had taken the two spare seats in the back corner. Owen and Stacie sat up front in the middle and Jenny and Ty were about five rows in front of Morgan and Bryan, near the aisle. Morgan had refused to make out with him during the trivia questions, but she'd let him fondle her leg. She'd even looked intrigued when he told her he wished she'd worn that rag of a denim skirt so he could slide his hand underneath and slide into her warmth.

They'd shared a bucket of popcorn and crate of Milk Duds. Bryan managed to cop a feel a couple times, not even earning him a slap.

When the movie finished, they all grabbed a beer at a nearby pub and raved about the action. Bryan overheard Jenny whisper something to Ty about a Captain America/Peggy Carter role play. Owen must have caught it too because he soon whispered something in Stacie's ear that had her blushing and downing her beer.

Then they all left.

Owen dropped Morgan at her place first since they were in North Seattle and her apartment was between there and downtown. Then he took Bryan to the ferry. Bryan thought about calling Morg, getting on the bus and spending the night, but something about the way his little stray feline had acted when he left prompted him to head home. She'd tried to get in his apartment before but only when he was going in, not coming out. The way she bolted in and disappeared, he worried something or someone had hurt her.

His new assignment loomed too. He had to tell Morgan sooner rather than later that he'd be going out on a ship soon because Owen would hear about it on Monday. News traveled fast among their crew and Bryan knew Morgan wouldn't want to hear it through the grapevine.

The ferry seemed to troll across the sound at a snail's pace. The sky was dark with no moon, but the city lights cast a lively glow over the water. Bryan missed the darkness of the sea where there was no light pollution to dim a starry, moonless night. He couldn't imagine going three more years in the navy without being on a ship. It had already been five years and that was nearly unheard of. Yes, he loved Puget Sound, but if he'd wanted to stay landlocked his entire career, he could have joined the army.

His heart was torn now though and wasn't that perplexing. Yes, he wanted to go out on a ship, but leaving Morgan behind wasn't going to be easy. As the ferry swooshed across the water, he thought of texting her, to tell her he missed her already. That was the kind of sap she hated and Bryan wasn't sure he should let himself succumb to those feelings. His ship would sail soon – at least he hoped – and this thing he and Morgan had going would end. He hated the ache in his chest at just the thought, but this was his life. He was a sailor first. Nothing, no one, would ever change that.

Not that Morgan wanted to. She was doing a better job at keeping this casual than Bryan was. He laughed as the Seattle skyline disappeared. Falling in love was for pussy-whipped Romeos. Bryan never thought himself capable of the emotion. Morgan, though, she was changing everything. She stirred stuff in him that should scare the shit out of him. The fact it didn't surprised the hell out of Bryan. That didn't mean he'd act on it. An attempt at forever with Morgan would be futile. She wouldn't have it and Bryan wasn't willing to give up the chance to go to sea one last time.

Once the ferry hit dock, he walked off the boat with purpose, eager to check on his feline friend. He turned on the lights as soon as he stepped in and was surprised to find she didn't greet him. He looked under the couch and in the bathroom, to no avail. She wasn't under the bed or curled up under his blankets. He heard a soft purr and went to the corner where his laundry basket was half full. On the pile of tee-shirts, shorts, boxers and socks lay his little friend, and hell, five little fur balls suckling at her.

Natasha meowed, a sweet little sound that invited him to meet her babies. He gave her head a gentle stroke and she nuzzled his hand and meowed again.

He grabbed his phone from his pocket, calling the only person he could think of who knew anything about babies.

"Midnight booty call?" Morgan answered with a smile in her voice.

"Not exactly. Natasha had babies."

"Natasha? Your cat?"

"She's not my cat, but yeah."

"Where is she?"

"In my dirty laundry basket. I don't know what to do. Can you come check on her? Make sure they're all okay."

Morgan laughed. "I'm a nurse, not a vet."

"Close enough for me. Please, Morg. I don't know a thing about cats or babies."

"You realize it's going to take me a couple hours to get there."

"I know."

"Fine. But only because you sound so pathetic. Just let her be. Mommy's have good instincts about how to care for babies."

Nearly two hours later, Morgan was knocking on his door, thank God. Her smile was radiant even though he knew she was laughing at him. "You look a little pale, sailor."

"I've never had to deal with anything like this before." He didn't have pets growing up. They moved every few years and his parents took turns being deployed. They both said the boys were enough of a responsibility. Bryan supposed that was true. He and

Beau and Blake were hell on wheels on an easy day.

"Lead the way," Morgan said. Bryan took her hand and showed her to his bedroom. Memories of the last time she'd been there washed through him and he had to focus on Natasha and the babies to keep from pushing her onto his bed and reliving that night.

"Well, hello Mama," she cooed, giving Natasha a gentle stroke. "You have beautiful babies."

All five kittens had similar coloring to their mother and Bryan couldn't help wondering if the father had been purebred as well. When Natasha had first made an appearance, he knew right away she was a Siberian because he'd dated a woman once who had one. He figured she had to belong to someone, as beautiful and friendly as she was, but it had been a month and no one seemed to claim her. Bryan was a sucker for a pretty girl, apparently, because he'd taken to giving her tuna and chicken and a little milk here and there.

"They all seem fine," Morgan said, turning to him. "Not that I'm an expert. I did a Google search on the way here. You're going to need to get a litter box and food for Natasha. She'll take care of the babies for the first few weeks. You should call a vet tomorrow."

"Yeah, yeah. I've already looked up vets and shelters."

"You're not going to put her in a shelter, are you? She's so pretty and she obviously adores you."

"I don't know a thing about cats."

"Well, learn. She chose you, Bryan. You need to respect that."

Bryan liked the cat, but kittens? It's not that he wasn't a responsible guy, but this was a kind of responsibility he never pictured himself having.

"You're not going to pass out, are you?" It was only when Morgan wrapped herself around him that he realized how unsteady he felt. "Come on, big, strong man. Let's grab a shower and go to bed. Tomorrow we'll get them set up in something a little more appealing than your dirty laundry."

God, the woman was amazing. She got him undressed and in the shower and even though he could have done it himself, he let her take care of him. He felt like a major pussy, but somehow the miracle of birth, even though cats had been doing it for centuries, had really gotten to him.

The care she took with him had his heart nearly leaping out of his chest. The hot water felt good, but her hands on him, lathering up the soap and rinsing it off was the most incredible thing he'd ever felt. They'd shared a shower enough times for Bryan to be aroused by just her proximity, but she didn't kiss or fondle him. Despite that, her touch was just as arousing.

He got into bed with the towel still wrapped around his waist and watched Morgan slip into one of his tee-shirts. "I'll be right back," she said, giving the kittens an affectionate glance before she left the room. He discarded the towel and pulled a blanket up. He was hard as granite, but sex right now seemed inappropriate somehow. Bryan had found himself in a situation he didn't know how to handle and Morgan had swept in like Nurse Nightingale and taken care of everything. Thanking her by ravaging her amazing body seemed a bit lewd and entirely selfish. It was strange, but Bryan was more interested in holding her.

She finally returned with a frothy drink and a sandwich. "You need protein," she said, handing him the glass, which he recognized as a protein shake. She took half the sandwich after sliding the plate onto his lap.

"Thanks for coming to my rescue," he said after taking a long drink.

Her muffled laughter still had Natasha peering at them over the edge of the laundry basket, as if to tell them to quiet down and not wake the babies. "What can I say? I'm a sucker for babies."

He wasn't sure if she was referring to the kittens or him and decided not to pursue it. He'd already admitted to himself what a pussy he was over this furry crew. He didn't need to explore that revelation with Morgan. It might weaken his cave man status.

With the sandwich and shake devoured, Bryan moved the glassware to the bedside table and pulled Morgan to his chest. He wrapped an arm around her and lay there content, watching the kittens and enjoying the quiet moment. He started to drift off and thought he felt her chuckle, but exhaustion claimed him before he could defend his manhood.

When Bryan awoke the next morning with a very warm body on top of his, he realized his manhood had never been in question.

***

Morgan could hardly believe Bryan had conked out without even laying a hand on her. The man lived and breathed sex. Considering how good he was at it, and that she was the recipient of his attention, she wasn't complaining. She'd come to his apartment expecting a little reward for her nursely efforts, but seeing him completely emotionally wrecked over the birth of kittens had her thoroughly amused.

And ridiculously turned on.

Thank God for morning erections.

Not caring whether he was fully awake, she tossed her tee-shirt aside and rolled on top of him. His body was warm and hard, all those hours he spent in the gym making him worship-worthy.

The erotic dream that starred the hunky sailor still unconscious beneath her is what had woken Morgan. She didn't imagine it'd take much to wake him and as she rubbed against him like a cat in heat, the rest of his body stirred to life.

"Morg," he groaned, so much gravel in his voice he had to clear it.

"I want you," she simply said, and kissed him with the fervor of her need. His hands moved to her hips, the alpha in him taking over and moving her in a rhythm that somehow made him harder.

"You're wet," he said, that gravel still rasping his voice. "You have a sexy dream?"

She had and he played the starring role. Regardless, after how

205

cute and vulnerable he'd been last night, she was sure she'd have woken up wanting him anyway.

Slinking her body across his, she whispered "yes" in his ear before she took a little nibble. He was inside her on her next slide down his erection and she gasped at the alluring invasion. She loved this chemistry they shared, how well they fit together.

"I love it when you're like this," he said against her neck, his lips and tongue burning their way over her skin. He moved slowly, driving her insane, until he was – *yes, right there* – kissing her breast.

They moved together so perfectly. Though she didn't want to think about it, the thought of life after Bryan flashed through her mind. Would she find someone else who didn't want anything more than what she had to offer and who made her feel so…alive?

His hands slid up her back, bringing her back to the moment. He liked to be in charge, but sometimes so did she, so she grabbed his arms and moved them over his head.

"So hot," he mumbled, letting her do whatever she pleased.

"I love it when you talk dirty," she confessed, hoping he'd take the cue. His mouth curved and he kissed her before murmuring – *oh, God, yes, do that* – the naughtiest things against that sensitive spot just below her earlobe.

The alpha sailor couldn't stay bound for long. In a move that was worthy of an Olympic gymnast, he flipped them both over. She'd expected him to continue with his naughty ministrations, but as he moved slow and sure in and out of her, his voice turned reverent, telling her she was beautiful. That kind of poetic admiration usually didn't work for her, but maybe it was the miracle of the kittens or Bryan's vulnerability that had her wrapped up in the moment.

Morgan had no will to fight it because – oh, yes – it was all about her. She hadn't been with a lot of men, but Bryan was the most giving lover she'd ever known.

She tried to quicken the pace, but Bryan continued to move

slowly. One arm slipped under her back to angle her hips up while the other skimmed down her leg, hooking her knee as it moved back up. She hooked her other leg over his hip and he groaned his approval but didn't speed up.

"Faster," she encouraged.

Bryan kissed her, but didn't obey. "Just let me make love to you, Morg."

He'd never said those words to her before. When it came to sex, he veered to the side of crude, but coming from Bryan, it always made her body tingle with anticipation. He had a way with words, though, and whether it was dirty or sweet, she loved it.

It didn't take long for her to get lost in the slow rhythm, her release screaming through her like a Midwest tornado, Bryan following her over the edge.

She was completely undone, wishing she could wake up like this every morning. It was a ridiculous thought. She didn't do forever and neither did Bryan. That's why this worked. They were a perfect fit for as long as their circumstances would allow.

He kissed her, a soft caress that had a little too much emotion in it and Morgan wondered if he was still reeling from the kitty drama of last night.

"I've never done that before," he said, looking into her eyes as though he was trying to see into her soul.

"What's that?"

"Not used a condom."

Her eyes widened and she mentally slapped herself. Yes, she was on the pill, but that was only 91% effective at preventing pregnancy and zero percent against disease. Not that she didn't trust Bryan, but he had a hell of a past.

"Get off me," she demanded, needing distance, seclusion, someplace to bang her head against a very hard surface and knock some sense back into that stupid brain of hers.

"Morg–"

"Don't, Bryan, just don't." Damn, damn, double damn! What

had she been thinking? Well, duh, obviously she wasn't. She'd never had sex without a condom, NEVER, and she hadn't planned to start. Not today. Not ever.

What if she got pregnant?

Oh, damn, she couldn't even fathom. What would Dr. Merrill think if she called and asked him to prescribe her an emergency contraceptive? No, no, she couldn't do that. Her own stupidity wasn't an excuse to do something so drastic. Plus, she'd never be able to face her boss again.

But, pregnant! God, please don't let her be in the nine percent.

"You are on the pill, right?" he asked, concern washing away all that sentimentality.

"Yes, of course, but, this was so not smart. Would you please get off me?"

She pushed at his chest and pulled her hips back and even though he was complying, she somehow felt empty as he left her body.

Stomping out to the bathroom, she felt bad when Natasha glared at her, as if telling her not to wake the babies.

She cleaned up and scowled at her reflection, trying to figure out what the hell had come over her. Morgan wasn't particularly sentimental. She liked to have a good time, but she was responsible. No way was she going to end up stuck with some guy because they'd been stupid in the throes. No, she'd witnessed her brother's heartache, and worse, the abuse her mother bared for years. That was not for Morgan.

Not that Bryan was just some guy. They were friends. In fact, except for Owen, he was her longest-standing friend. She hadn't stayed close with anyone from high school and even though she was connected with some of her college friends on Facebook, they weren't the kind of friends she'd turn to in a crisis.

Bryan was. And this was a crisis. So maybe she should act like an adult and talk to him about it instead of running away and hiding in the bathroom.

A splash of cold water felt nice but didn't stop her heart from racing. She was a nurse, for Pete's sake, she should be able to talk about contraception with the man she'd been boinking for the last few months.

She startled when she opened the door to find him standing there. He'd put on shorts, though she suspected he was commando. That thought made her all warm and gooey again.

He held out the tee-shirt she'd discarded not too long ago and she slipped it on. "I'm sorry. I was just a little shocked."

"Shocked that I've never had sex without a condom or shocked that you just did?" She made no secret about her feelings on birth control. Anyone who knew her knew she was an advocate for protection.

"Both, I guess." But that wasn't the truth. "I obviously wasn't thinking this morning."

He pulled her to him and stroked her hair. His heart was loud as thunder against her ear, his skin warm. She scraped her nails through the hair on his chest, loving how rough it felt.

"Sweetheart, it's okay. I've always used a condom and I have a physical every year. If it makes you feel better, I'll get you a copy of my medical records." She didn't say anything for a long time, just held on to him and tried to make sense of why she'd had such a lapse in judgment. Then again, maybe it was best not to analyze it too deeply.

"I'd never hurt you," he murmured and she knew that. This wasn't about anything other than the risk of pregnancy.

"I know and I trust you," she confessed because she wanted him to know. Above all else, he was her friend and even if he'd been too many women to count, she knew he took care of himself. "It's just that the pill isn't infallible. I don't know if super fertility runs in the family or if that's just Owen's burden, but it's not something I'm willing to take a chance with."

He pulled back, his hands keeping a firm grip on her arms as he gave her that soul-searching gaze again. "Then why did you?"

She had no idea. The thought of a condom hadn't even crossed her mind. She was hot with need, wanting him as though she was a love-struck lunatic. Except she wasn't love-struck. Morgan didn't do love. Even the thought of falling in love had bile rising up her throat. Usually. For some reason, it wasn't now and the hailstorm of emotions threatened to short-circuit her brain. "I don't know," was all she could say.

That seemed to be enough for Bryan as he pulled her into his arms again and just held her.

Chapter 13

"They're too young to cuddle, but you can ooh and ah as much as you want. Be sure to give Natasha lots of loving too. She's very proud of her babies," Morgan explained to the crew who had come to meet the kittens.

Morgan had been amazing. She'd taken care of him last night, something Bryan wasn't accustomed to. As the oldest of three brothers, he learned early to be a caregiver, wanting to give his mom a break whenever he could. Plus, his brothers seemed to listen to him and they shared a mutual respect. The skill had come in handy when Owen needed taking care of after his divorces. Bryan had even enjoyed the opportunity to take care of Morgan a little bit when she was in the midst of finals and when she'd had to deal with that asshole of an abuser at the clinic.

So it was different being on the receiving end. With Morgan as the caregiver, though, he liked it more than he would have thought, especially as she snuggled with him on the bed while they kept an eye on Natasha and the babies.

As she directed their friends to the spare bedroom, where she'd helped Bryan create a more suitable nest for the kittens than his dirty laundry, she was confidant and authoritative and Bryan wanted her more now than ever.

Or maybe that had something to do with what happened between them that morning.

God, she'd felt good. Amazing. When she slid over him, he didn't question it. She was a Nazi when it came to birth control, so if she wasn't demanding it, he figured she had everything under control. He knew she was on the pill, so he let his need dictate that he keep his damn mouth shut.

Even though she seemed horrified after, he still didn't regret it. All those things he'd heard about sex without a condom…well, damn, they were true. It wasn't just the lack of condom. They'd made love. There were no other words for it. It wasn't a fun romp or a manic roll in the sack. She'd felt so good and had so completely undone him that he'd made love to her.

Yes, he was waxing poetic. If he'd heard the words from Beau or Owen, he'd call them pussy-whipped Romeos. Somehow, though, he now understood. It was a deeper connection, something so far beyond just physical. He and Morgan had always had chemistry, there was no doubt there, but this morning, there had been more.

He wanted to make love to her again, only slower and longer this time. Not because he was horny, which of course, he was because he always was when she was around. No, he wanted her now because he wanted to feel the power of that connection with her again.

Unfortunately, she'd done her best to avoid being alone with him after their little chat. He made breakfast while she took a shower because he knew she needed space. Then she cleaned up the kitchen while he took his shower. Then she'd insisted on calling the vet, who was willing to make a house call on a Saturday. The kittens and Natasha had received a clean a bill of health. He said he'd have his staff check records for a Siberian female and would also have them call other Bremerton vets if their records turned up empty. Natasha was a beauty, and so incredibly affectionate, the doctor was sure someone would remember her.

That tugged at Bryan's heart. Somehow, over the course of the last few weeks, she had gotten to him. He didn't want to find her owner and maybe it made him a selfish ass, but he hoped she'd been abandoned. He had no right to want to keep this cat, but for some reason didn't want to let her go.

Kind of like the woman who was keeping watch over her.

Damn him straight to hell, but Bryan had fallen in love with not just Natasha, but Morgan too. He could deny it to hell and back, but it'd be a lie. He'd fallen and damn if he knew what to do about it.

"Did you name them?" Holly asked, giving each Natasha a stroke on the head as the babies cuddled with their mother. All the while, Morgan scratched Natasha's chin, cooing and telling her what a wonderful mama she was.

Morgan laughed and Bryan's heart suffered another tug. "Well, Bryan has the hots for Black Widow, hence Natasha, so since they were born on the same day as the Winter Soldier release, we've named them in honor of the movie. This is Falcon, and this pretty girl is Peggy, then we have Fury, Bucky, and finally Cap."

There was no "we" in the naming. Morgan had insisted on the Captain America theme and Bryan had no argument. Naming the kittens really had been the last thing on his mind.

"Only one girl?" Stacie asked, pushing Holly aside and taking her turn.

Bryan laughed. "No, Bucky's a girl too."

"But you're too pretty to be a Bucky," Stacie cooed. Not so long ago, all this maternal fuss would have put a stitch in his side, but he was right there with them, loving these precious fur balls for the miracles they were.

Christ. Falling in love and loving these fur balls and their ridiculously cute names? He was so far off his game he needed a good solid dose of testosterone injected straight into his main vein.

Owen shot him a suspicious glance and Bryan decided it was time to do something manly. Scratching his balls seemed a bit obscene, so he opted for plan B. "Anyone want a beer?"

The women ignored him, as did Ty who was just as caught up in the furry cuteness. Bryan lurched out of the room and hit the kitchen for that brewski before he dropped onto the cool leather of his sofa and took a long drink.

Owen joined him, sans beer, and without the sitting. No, instead, he loomed in front of Bryan, arms crossed over his chest, biceps flexing.

Fuck.

"So, buddy," Bryan didn't miss the sarcasm in that label. "How long have you been banging my sister?"

Owen's voice was steady. In fact, everything about the man was completely controlled. Bryan had seen him like this before, and recognized it for what it was, the calm before the fucking shit storm.

It was as though he'd already pulled the pin and was just patiently waiting for the grenade to explode, knowing full well it would hit the target dead on.

Fucking. Hell. Bryan would welcome a black hole right now. Maybe a meteor approaching the earth at a catastrophic trajectory. Anything to keep from having this conversation.

He wanted to lie. In fact, he could hear Morgan's stern voice in his head commanding him to do just that. It would be so easy to deny it all. To anyone else, Bryan might be able to lie and still look at himself in the mirror. He couldn't do it, though. Not to Owen. A lie of omission was one thing. Lying to his best friend's face, it was wrong.

"I'm not just messing around with her, man." Morgan might think that's what was going on, but Bryan couldn't deny the thing making his heart race.

Love.

"Son of a bitch!" Owen took two long steps across the room and lifted Bryan off the couch, the cotton of his tee-shirt fisted in his best friend's hands.

"How long?" Owen demanded.

"A while."

"How long?" Owen asked, his voice strangled.

It was time to face the music. Bryan had always known his and Morgan's secret would get out at some point. Jenny and Ty had been watching them closely since the Super Bowl and Morgan had informed him both Jenny and Stacie had inquired repeatedly about their status. And Stacie knew, even though Bryan had never confirmed her suspicions.

"December."

The punch didn't surprise him. Owen still held Bryan's shirt with his left, his right giving Bryan an upper cut that had him seeing stars. He took a cross to the nose before Owen thrust him back onto the couch.

Bryan didn't much care that blood was spewing from his face. He deserved it, after all. He'd deceived his best friend, betrayed him, over and over again, for months. Even though Bryan knew the shit would eventually hit the fan, he'd hoped it wouldn't be a public event. Any minute, their friends would come out of the spare bedroom to let Natasha and the babies rest. They'd want to know why he was bleeding. Morgan was going to be livid. He'd rather take another upper cut than see the rage on her.

"Listen, man–"

"No, you listen. You need to end it. Walk away before it becomes a problem."

"It's not going to become a problem."

"No? What if she gets pregnant? What then?"

He almost laughed. "We're careful. Have you ever heard your sister preach about birth control?" Even this morning's slip wasn't completely unprotected. Yes, two methods were better than one, but damn, he liked being inside her without the condom and if she was going to insist on two methods, they'd have to find a new second.

Bryan didn't miss the wince on Owen's face, likely at the confirmation that he and Morgan were in fact having sex. Bryan would probably feel the same way if he had a sister. He was ready to take another punch when the voices from the bedroom moved closer.

"Holy shit! Why are you bleeding?" Morgan rushed to his side, immediately going into nurse mode.

"Yeah, buddy. Why are you bleeding?" The sarcasm seethed from Owen's voice like lava flowing from a volcano.

"I'm sorry, Morg," he whispered as she dropped onto the couch next to him and started checking his nose with clinical confidence.

"What do you mean, you're sorry?"

Realization tightened her expression and she practically leapt off the couch as though Bryan had a contagious disease. He hoped he did. If Morgan could catch the love bug the way he had, this might not end in catastrophe after all.

***

"I'm not going to let you turn my sister into a slut."

The Landry temper was already pumping through her veins and the only thing that had saved Bryan was Owen's lewd comment.

Before the shock of it wore off, Bryan was off the couch and had Owen pinned against the wall. "She's not a slut."

"Boys," Morgan intervened before it got ugly. The last thing she wanted to do was clean up her brother's and Bryan's blood. "Enough!"

No punches were thrown, but she could see the alpha tempers flaring between them. "Bryan. Sit," she commanded. "Owen. Back off."

Bryan was bigger, but she'd heard him say more than once that Owen fought dirty. Something he'd learned from fighting their father, she was sure.

Neither one of them obeyed her commands.

"This is between me and Bryan," Owen drawled.

"Actually, I'm pretty sure it's between *me* and Bryan. You need to get your fingers out of my chili."

Owen's eyes flashed to her, the rest of his body still in a stand-off with Bryan. "So you are screwing around with him."

It wasn't a question therefore, Morgan chose not to answer. She wasn't sure what had been spoken between the two of them after they left the kittens to grab a beer, but it didn't matter. She wouldn't give Owen the chance to kill Bryan because she wanted the honors. She'd warned him what would happen if her brother found out and look who was bleeding all over his tee-shirt.

"You know what," she said, throwing her arms in the air as the two of them remained locked in a grudge-match. "You two kill each other. I have better things to do."

***

Bryan took the most direct route to the ferry. Since his apartment building was on the waterfront, it took him only about ninety seconds to get there, but Morgan was nowhere to be found.

Fuck.

He hadn't wanted her to leave, but Owen's comment had riled him up and Bryan decided it was better to let the siblings cool their heels away from each other. The ferry seemed the most logical destination for Morgan since it was the quickest way back to Seattle. Since she wasn't there he hoped maybe she'd calmed down and gone back to his apartment.

Bryan walked along the boardwalk toward the Turner Joy at the end of the pier. He even took a quick walk around the gift shop, but still there was no Morgan and he doubted she'd use the historic navy ship as an escape. He turned back to the pier and checked Harborview Park and Starbucks, but came up empty. Where the hell had she gone?

Slinking back to his apartment, Bryan hoped Morgan was there and the rest of the crew had vacated. Since the ferry wasn't due for another thirty minutes, the chances of his friends being gone were slim.

This day had turned into a complete *Whiskey Tango Foxtrot*, from Morgan putting distance between them to Owen's assumption and now to Morgan's disappearance. Bryan wanted to hit rewind and have a do over. This time, he'd keep his trap shut about the lack of condom and not invite his friends over to see the kittens. Hell, he'd even pass on the vet visit and just keep Morgan busy in his bed all day.

Ice would be good. His entire face throbbed and Bryan was sure he looked like he'd been to war, returning after having lost the battle. Owen sure packed a mean punch.

Everyone was lounging in the living room when he returned. Staci and Owen sat together in a chair while Jenny, Ty, and Holly occupied the couch.

Stacie gave him a sympathetic look as she got up. "Let me get you some ice."

"You just couldn't let it be, could you?" Bryan wasn't the kind of man who was aggressive toward women, but right now he wanted to strangle Stacie.

"I didn't say anything," she insisted.

"Right. You and your BFF there have been bugging Morgan for weeks."

"And apparently she's been lying for weeks." Jenny launched off the couch and stepped in between Bryan and Stacie, her arms crossed. She was tiny, but she had the whole intimidation thing down.

"You two knew?" Owen asked.

Well, shit. Bryan thought for sure Stacie was the one who'd put the idea in his head. If she hadn't, how did–

"How did you know?" Bryan asked, directing his attention at Owen. Maybe that'd redirect Owen's anger too.

The scowl spoke volumes to Owen's mood, as did the way he had his arms crossed tightly over his chest as he sat on the couch. "I didn't. It was just a hunch. I was hoping my instincts were off."

Bryan laughed without mirth, skimming his hand across his short hair. When had he and Morgan given themselves away? They'd tried to be discreet, but obviously that hadn't worked.

Of course, if truth be known, Bryan was relieved to have the secret out. Now if he could just find Morgan. She wasn't answering the phone or replying to his texts. Not surprising. When her temper flared, she steered clear of anyone she could maim.

"You found her and ended it, right? Morgan's on the ferry back to the city and you're going to keep your grubby paws off her."

"No and no. I didn't find her and even if I did, it wouldn't be to end it. We're consenting adults. You can't tell either one of us what to do."

"You lied to me," Owen pointed out.

Bryan shook his head, for that was worth. "I never meant to. I mean, I never meant for anything to happen between us either. It just did."

"I don't want to hear your pansy ass excuses. She's my sister, man. You shouldn't have crossed that line."

"Maybe not, but I told you, we're not just messing around. I care about her."

"Right, and what happens when you get deployed? That's what you're waiting for, isn't it, for your ship to sail? What happens with you and Morgan then?"

"I don't know. We'll figure it out."

"I'll tell you what happens. Morgan won't wait for you. She's got daddy issues that have a longer lifespan than your man-whore habits. She's just using you because she knows you don't do serious relationships."

Bryan refused to believe that was true. Maybe that's how it had started out, but something had grown between them. Bryan wasn't the only one whose heart had gotten involved. Morgan might be more reluctant to admit it, but he felt it. It's why she had trusted him enough to forget the condom.

"It's time for you to go," Bryan said and held open the door. Stacie urged him to go and Bryan appreciated her intervention. Jenny, Ty, and Holly, who'd been quiet during all the drama, followed suit, Holly offering him a sympathetic glance as he closed the door behind her.

***

Natasha's vibrant purr was in stark contrast to her penetrating stare. Bryan shifted in the chair, uncomfortable with having his soul fully exposed by a fur ball.

"Stop staring at me like that," he insisted, but Natasha neither blinked nor balked. She had a way of tormenting his psyche, forcing him to question his motives and regret the bad decisions he continued to make.

The cat looked angry and if she didn't sound like a buzz saw cutting redwoods, he'd think she was.

The enigma of cats.

Her kittens suckled with rapt fervor and Bryan knew her purr was motherly love, not any affection she'd reserved for him. She refused to look away, boring a hole into his soul. Those yellow eyes saw things, things he'd never imagined he was capable of feeling but was now helpless to hide.

Natasha saw it all. She was smart like that.

She'd adopted him, so she must have seen something in him long before he knew it was there, some locked-up emotion he'd only ever shared with Mom and Pop and his brothers, and the few friends who were close enough to be family. The love she saw, though, that emotion she was exposing with her feline super powers, was so much more than he'd ever felt before.

As her searing stare turned his defenses into ash, Bryan knew there was only one thing to do. He'd have to reciprocate, figure out a way to let Natasha into his life. He'd like to say that military life didn't afford opportunities for pets, but he'd been in Bremerton for nearly five years now. Of course, his ship was about to sail – finally – but still, he'd find a way to adopt her back because somehow he couldn't imagine not having her in his life.

Keeping the kittens wasn't an option. Maybe he had enough love to share, but definitely not the patience. That wasn't a problem, however, since each of his friends had already laid claim to each of the babies. They'd have good homes, within his tight-knit extended family – so long as Owen hadn't disowned him as a friend, not that Bryan could blame him if he did. It was clear that Stacie had fallend in love with Bucky, though, and Owen, being the pussy-whipped Romeo he was, would do anything to make Stacie happy. Bryan suspected the intuitive feline mother already knew that, so her gaze implored him to open his heart not to her, but to the other woman who had been making it beat for years.

"I think I'm in love with her," he admitted to the cat. She blinked her acknowledgment and he could practically hear her say, "no kidding, dumbass." Bryan laughed, a mere mortal in the eyes of the cat, a dumbass who hadn't recognized, or more cowardly, hadn't been able to admit what was so obvious.

He crossed the room and squatted to give her a gentle pat. "You're wise beyond your years." Natasha blinked again, then licked her paw and commenced to giving herself a bath. She was obviously satisfied with his admission and he figured if he had the cat's approval, he'd better stop being a dumbass and go win Morgan's heart.

To do that, he had to make sure she wasn't holding a grudge about him giving up their secret to Owen. More than that, though, he needed to make sure she was alright. She hadn't answered her phone – not a big surprise – but even though she was predictable, Bryan was going to go out of his mind with worry. He spied the digital clock in the corner of the room. The ferry would be leaving in twenty minutes. He had plenty of time to get the Ducati out of the parking garage and make the boat. If Morgan wasn't at her apartment, he'd wait, however long it took, just to make sure she was okay.

***

Six texts and two phone calls from Bryan. Four texts from Holly. One from Jenny. Two from Stacie.

Nothing from Owen.

She should have known he'd be waiting for her at her apartment. He had a key, after all, and he wasn't one to let things rest.

She wasn't even surprised when she walked in to find him sitting on the sofa.

When she'd gotten back to Seattle, Morgan took a slow walk down the waterfront before hopping on a bus to Greenlake. The walk had calmed her a little, enough for the stress of school to start eating away at her. Today was meant to be a study day. She had a test on Wednesday and needed every spare moment to study for it. Not that she minded helping with the kittens, but her life seemed to be spiraling out of control. First the fiasco of not using a condom, then Owen's little tantrum and his alpha stand-off with Bryan.

Making like he wasn't even there, Morgan went into her bedroom to change into yoga pants and a big tee-shirt she'd stolen from Bryan. On her way to the ratty old papasan chair she'd found at a yard sale and loved more than any other piece of furniture (except, maybe, Bryan's giant bed), she grabbed a pint of Ben and Jerry's Karamel Sutra, because, well, there ought be some Sutra somewhere in her life. Plus, she was only indulging to spare her brother his life…because whatever he had to say was going to make her lethal if she didn't have a sweet distraction.

"Bryan's always been there for me. After Daphne. After Kristina. There's nothing he wouldn't do for me."

Morgan let the ice cream and caramel melt on her tongue as she digested Owen's words. This wasn't something she didn't already know, but of course, there was a point brewing somewhere. "I know. He's a great friend." That was one of the best things about Bryan was how good of a friend he'd been, not just to Owen, but to her too.

"I'd do the same for him. I've never had to because he's never put his heart out there. If it ever happens, *when* it happens, I'll be there for him. Drop of a hat. Doesn't matter where I am or what I'm doing. I'll be there for him."

"I know that."

"He's more than just my best friend. He's my brother. And you, you know you're more than just my sister. You're my best friend, too."

"I know, Owen. I love you too."

"Yeah, then why are you screwing around with him?"

Because he gave the best orgasms in the world. Because she'd lusted after him for twelve years. Because he was safe.

But she couldn't say any of that to Owen. He believed in love and marriage and family. Even though that whole concept had failed him twice already, he kept going back for more. Morgan thought he got it right with Stacie, but that was Owen's dream, not hers. Morgan didn't want to be at the beck and call of a man who would eventually resent her for the life he was stuck in. "What I do with my life is my business. Just because you're my brother doesn't mean you can butt your nose in."

"Do you have any idea how many women he's been with?"

Morgan fought the urge to cringe. Bryan didn't even know how many women he'd been with, but she knew he hadn't been with anyone else since last fall and that's what mattered. They were involved, somehow exclusively, and even though she didn't want to define it further, she was glad there wasn't any other woman in his life or his bed. "I don't care," she said because it was the best answer she could come up with.

"You can do better."

"He's your best friend–"

"And he's a man-whore, Morgan. He's just using you."

She hated that label. Yeah, she'd used it on more than one occasion, mostly to distance herself from Bryan, but ever since he'd told her he didn't like it, she'd stopped. "Maybe I'm using him."

Owen's fisted hands hit the cushions of the sofa on each side of his legs. The Landry temper was brewing in him too. Good thing she had the ice cream, otherwise her apartment might erupt in a full scale war.

"That doesn't make it right." He gave a quick nod in her direction. "He didn't leave that here when he was on his way to bang some random chick, did he?"

Morgan eyed the shirt, the one that Owen had bought off some guy's back to give to Bryan. "No. He left it here after spending the night with me."

Owen's lip curled and she was sure if Bryan were in the room, Owen would clock him again. She really hoped he'd put ice on his nose after she left. He was going to have one hell of a bruise anyway, but the ice would help.

"You lied to me," Owen murmured so low it was almost imperceptible.

"If you knew about me and Bryan, you'd go all *Father Knows Best* on me."

"I do know best."

Morgan coughed, "Divorced twice." Cough-cough.

"Subtle." He shook his head, but she saw a smile creeping past his serious front. Before he let the humor seep its way into this very uncomfortable conversation, he shook it off and pinned her with another *Father Knows Best* glare. "You know it's not going to last. When it ends, it's going to cause problems. Not just for you and not just for him. Think about the position it puts me in."

She nearly fell out of the papasan with laughter. "Oh, that's right, because it's all about you. Excuse me."

Aw, but poor Owen didn't find it funny. "You didn't want me to date Daph. You were best friends until I crossed that line with her."

"I didn't want you to date her because she was a bitch, not because she was my friend."

"But you weren't friends with her once we started dating."

"Don't even try to compare your friendship with Bryan to me and Daphbitchne. She and I would have lost touch right after graduation if you hadn't married her."

"And what am I supposed to do when you and Bryan call it quits? I can't pick sides."

"Then don't. Bryan and I are just having fun. No one's going to get hurt."

Owen pursed his lips again, shaking his head in that disapproving way that reminded Morgan of their mother. She took another bite of ice cream to keep from reaching out and smacking the expression off his face.

Unfortunately, when he opened his mouth, it wasn't any better than the expression. "Do you have any idea how slutty that makes you sound?"

She'd had enough with the slut comments. It was time to throw some of his own plays back in his face. "At least I knew his name the first time I slept with him." That was more than he could say for him and Stacie.

And apparently he didn't like being dragged into the gutter because he shot off the sofa, his controlled appearance evaporating like rain on a scorching sidewalk. "Stacie and I love each other. We're living together. It's a committed relationship, Morgan, not an arrangement you can pay for on the streets."

Morgan didn't like the way he loomed over her, the bad ass, know it all big brother talking down to his little sister. She pushed out of the chair and even though he was half a foot taller than her, she stood up to him and craned her neck. "If you allude to me being a slut one more time, you are going to regret it." She'd never had to defend herself against Owen, but living in fear for years had been a great motivator to learn some quick self-defense techniques. She had no problem giving him a knee to the nads and she had a pretty potent right hook according to her kickboxing instructor in Lafayette.

Owen took a step back, but tight quarters provided by her living room furniture didn't allow him to gain much distance. "What you're doing with him, it's not right. It's not healthy, for either of you. You need to knock it off."

"Or what? You going to take me over your knee and spank me? Because Bryan does that and frankly, I like it."

Anger flared in Owen's eyes and she had to bite back the satisfying grin. If he was going to play the jackass card, well, she was throwing down the bitch card. "He's really good with his hands. Did you know that? Oh, and that mouth." Morgan fanned herself with both hands.

His lips pursed as he pointed at her like she was a naughty puppy. "You. Need. To shut it."

"No. I don't," she snapped back, mimicking his tone and clipped words. "You can't tell me what to do, or in this case, *who* to do."

His knuckles were white and his face was red. "Shut up, Morgan. Stop talking like that."

She got right in his face. "You already called me a slut. Why not live up to it."

"Back off, Morgan." He gave her a gentle shove, putting distance between them again.

"Why? Because I'm right?"

He shook his head so vigorously she knew he was coming undone. "No, because you're acting like Kristina."

And that was the final straw. Morgan's right hand made contact with his left eye before she even realized what she was doing.

Chapter 14

The yelling was hard enough to listen to and maybe he was crossing a line by eavesdropping, but Bryan needed to know Morgan was okay. He also needed to know he hadn't thrown away his friendship with Owen. Morgan knew how to push her brother's buttons and Bryan suspected that's what she was doing. Well, until his last comment.

When the cussing commenced from both of them, Bryan figured it was time to intervene. Her front door wasn't locked, so he let himself in. Morgan was cradling her right hand and by the way Owen had his hand to his face, Bryan was guessing she'd clocked her brother a good one.

Bryan choked on a laugh. "Everything alright in here?"

Morgan glared at him, wrath tightening her normally soft features. "Who the hell let you in?"

Well, so much for a warm greeting. "The door wasn't locked and it sounded like a warzone in here." He crossed the room and took her hand gently in his. "You need some ice for this."

"Get me some while you're in there," Owen groaned.

"Get your own ice," Morgan shot back. "Preferably at your own place."

Owen followed them into the kitchen, undeterred by Morgan's

seething anger. "Where the hell did you learn to punch like that?"

Bryan grabbed a plastic bag from the drawer and filled it with ice from the box in the freezer. He placed it on Morgan's hand, but she handed it over to Owen. Bryan choked back the laugh. These two couldn't stay mad at each other, they were just too tight. Even though she was still shooting daggers from her dark eyes, the nurse in her would make sure her brother was tended to first. Not wanting Morgan to suffer, Bryan got to work on a second bag.

"Toby Dubois. He teaches a kickboxing class for women at the Lafayette Fitness Center."

Bryan didn't know who Toby Dubois was, but given the way Owen laughed, he knew the guy. "I'll have to drop him a message and let him know he did good. Maybe next time you can try open handed."

"Maybe next time you can try not being an asshole."

"I'm looking out for you." Owen shook his head as he gave Bryan an imploring glance. "One or both of you are going to get hurt."

Bryan had a feeling it was going to be him, but it wasn't enough of a deterrent to make him walk away.

When no one responded, Owen just shook his head at them. "I'm gone," he said, bee-lining it for the door.

"Hasta la pasta," Morgan muttered, her lip curling in a snarl.

Owen didn't bother to acknowledge her.

Bryan followed Morgan into the living room and settled onto the couch as Morgan curled up in the papasan. "You alright?" he asked.

Morgan was stewing – never a good thing – her lip still curled as she cradled her hand and the icepack. "He makes me crazy. I'm not a little girl anymore. Is he ever going to realize that?"

"He can't help wanting to protect you. It's who he is."

"Says the guy with the black eye," she chortled.

"I deserved it."

"He did have some choice things to say about you."

Of course he did. Bryan was a bastard. He'd slept with his best friend's sister knowing the guy wouldn't approve. It was a betrayal that was probably unforgivable. It was too late to take it back, even if he had wanted to – which, for the record, he did not. Morgan was, well, she was worth the risk. "Oh yeah? What'd he say?"

"That I can do better."

That's it? "You can," Bryan agreed. He believed that not just because Owen said it. Morgan could do a thousand times better than a sailor who'd been riding desk jockey for the last few years, sleeping with any girl who looked like she might be a good ride.

"He also said you're a man-whore."

Bryan laughed. You know, because he hadn't been called that a thousand times before. "Yep."

"I thought you hated being called that?"

"I do, but he didn't say anything that isn't true."

"*Isn't* true?" The horror in her voice at the present tense was somehow reassuring, and didn't that just make Bryan even more of a selfish prick.

"Well, *wasn't* true." Christ, it'd been nearly six months since he was with someone other than Morgan. He'd been with her for nearly five. Unofficially, that qualified her as his longest ever relationship. "I haven't been with anyone else, Morg, I swear."

"We've been over this. You don't owe me an explanation." She was trying to distance herself again. The tactic made Bryan's chest ache. What the hell did he have to do to get her to admit there was something more between them?

"I *want* you to know. It's only been you."

"If that's your way of trying to coax me to forgive you for telling him, you know I'm not that easy. We had an agreement, Bryan. You broke it and I want to know why."

Just as he knew he was going to have to face Owen again, Bryan also knew he was going to have to face Morgan. He was already nursing a black eye and based on how bad Owen looked when he left, Bryan knew Morg could inflict some serious pain too. He just hoped she believed him and didn't view his explanation as a copout. "He knew," Bryan sighed, realizing Owen had been bluffing. "Or at least suspected. He brought up the topic, so I figured Stacie had said something. He admitted it was just a hunch."

"A hunch? You have better instincts than that. Why didn't you call his bluff, deny it?"

"Because I can't lie to him, Morg. He's like a brother to me."

"And you've never lied to your brothers?"

"To their faces, no. I wouldn't do that to Owen either."

"Stupid male loyalty," she mumbled.

Right, because loyalty was reserved for one gender only. "You females have it too." Hell, he'd seen it in Jenny when she stepped between him and Stacie. "You know, we're both adults. We're responsible for our own decisions. I don't need his permission and neither do you."

"No, but look how he overreacted."

"I don't really blame him. You're his little sister."

She crossed her arms in a huff. "And I can take care of myself."

Bryan laughed. "You proved that. He's got a nice shiner."

Morgan tried to hide the smirk, but Bryan didn't miss it and it caused him to chuckle. There was a bit of the devil in her, something Bryan loved about her. What he also knew was at some point, guilt would set in. She and her brother were tight, as tight as Bryan was with his brothers.

"You've got a pretty decent shiner too. Did you ice it?"

Between having two brothers and being a young, stupid sailor surrounded by other young, stupid, and drunk sailors, he'd had enough black eyes in his life to know that rule of thumb. "I did."

She sprung out of the chair like someone had just lit her ass on fire. "Well, time for you to go. I've got things to do."

Bryan watched her head to the door.

"You want me to leave?"

"That's what I just said." Her voice was too cheerful, faking it cheerful.

"You're still pissed."

"I told you, if Owen found out, we were done. So thanks for stopping by and I'll see you around."

Bryan didn't move. "We're not through," he insisted.

The fake smile disappeared as she crossed her arms and narrowed her eyes. She looked so much like her brother when she pissed, it made Bryan laugh.

"I'm not kidding. We had an agreement. You broke it."

Bryan pushed off the sofa and crossed the room slowly. Her expression softened except for her eyes, which sparked with desire. Her arms dropped to her sides and that was just perfect. As Bryan reached her, he took her wrists gently in his hands and eased her against the wall. "I didn't agree to anything." Bryan spoke softly across her ear, nearly groaning when he felt her breath catch.

As he pressed his body into hers, he felt the temperature rise a thousand degrees.

"Bryan," she whispered and there was no denying the desire in that breathless plea.

"Remember that first night? Right here against this wall. We started something that night and it's not even close to being over."

Her breath caught again, cranking up Bryan's libido to the nth power.

"Let me go," she growled.

Bryan eased back enough to see the scowl which matched the tone of her voice. "Morg–"

She gave him a subtle shove and even though it wasn't enough to actually move him, Bryan stepped back. "I want you to leave."

Well, this conversation had done a fast one-eighty. "Fine. I'll leave. I need to check on the kittens anyway."

Morgan stayed where she was while Bryan made his exit. He moved slowly, waiting for her to change her mind and call him back in, but after he closed the door, the abrupt click of the lock caused his heart to sank into his stomach.

***

Because he was a glutton for punishment, Bryan headed straight for Owen's. After he knocked on the door, Owen nearly tore it off the hinges opening it.

"Unless you're here to tell me this whole thing with you and Morgan is a practical joke and I've been punked, then I don't have a fucking thing to say to you."

That wasn't the greeting Bryan had been hoping for, but it was the one he'd expected. "I'm sorry I didn't tell you, but I'm not sorry for what's happening between us."

Owen just shook his head and when he took a step back, Bryan thought he was being invited in, until the door slammed in his face.

Bryan knocked again, but to no avail. "I can knock on this thing all night," he called through the wood. "I'm not leaving until we talk this out."

Owen had always had his back, since the first day they met. Bryan hadn't grown up with a best friend. With both parents in the navy, they moved every few years, so any friendships formed were temporary. The only lasting friendship he'd ever had was with his brothers. He'd arrived in Norfolk at the same time as Owen and they'd both been assigned to the computer security detachment. It was Bryan's second assignment, but his first assignment had kept him on a ship for the better part of two years. So he and Owen found their way together, a couple newbies learning the ropes. Owen was married to Daphne at the time and Hailey was born shortly after they arrived at the naval station. Daphne didn't make life easy for Owen and even though Bryan had never been around kids, he liked spending time with Owen and his baby girl.

After several minutes of pounding a steady rhythm on the door, it opened. "Come in," Stacie said. "He's brooding on the couch. I'm going to go to the pet store and scope out what we need before we bring Daisy home."

"Daisy?" Bryan questioned.

"Bucky," she sighed, shaking her head. "She's too pretty to be called that, so I'm renaming her Daisy Buchanan. You know, from The Great Gatsby."

"Oh," Bryan said, pretending he knew what the hell she was talking about. He recognized the title of the book, and was pretty sure he'd read it in high school, but that was a damn long time ago. "So you're adopting one of Natasha's kittens?"

"Oh, definitely. If you don't mind, of course."

"No, that's great. You can have them all if you want."

Stacie laughed. "Jenny and Ty are adopting Peggy and Holly said she wanted one, but can't decide between Falcon and Cap. I'm willing to bet money she takes both. That just leaves Fury. You can probably sweet talk Morgan into taking him."

Bryan wasn't sure he'd ever be able to sweet talk her into anything ever again. "Have fun shopping," he said, stepping back to let her though. He was happy to know the kittens were claimed, though something tugged at his heart thinking about letting them go. He'd never had pets because he moved around too much, but in a few years, deployments and moving every few years would be a thing of the past. He'd always thought he'd get a dog, but had never considered cats.

Kicking the door closed gently, he stepped into the apartment and slipped out of his sneakers before heading to the living room. Owen's condo had an open living space. The kitchen was separated from the living room by a dining table. Owen was stretched out on the couch, an open book in hand.

"Exactly what is happening between you and my sister?" he asked without looking away from the book.

"I don't know," Bryan admitted, sitting in black chair that matched the modern-style couch. He was perpendicular to the couch, face to face with the cover of Owen's book.

Bryan looked around as the seconds ticked by, taking in the artwork and photos he'd seen a thousand times. His friendship with

Owen had never once been on the line and Bryan hoped it wasn't now, but as the clock on the wall continued to tick, hope was replaced with fear.

"I care about her," he finally said when the silence was too much to take.

Owen clapped the book closed, his mouth tense and eyes narrowed, obviously assessing Bryan. "Are you in love with her?"

It was a question Bryan should have been expecting, but for whatever reason it kicked his heart into overdrive and lit up every nerve ending in his body. "I think so."

"You *think* so? What the hell does that mean? You either are or you aren't."

Bryan pondered that, knowing it was true. Only pussies *thought* they were in love. Real men would admit it. Own it.

Of course, Bryan had spent his entire adult life thinking he wasn't capable of such a thing. He'd never been interested in a serious relationship, never wanted a family. He liked his freedom, to come and go as he pleased. He could work on rebuilding cars and spend money however he wanted. He didn't have to answer to anybody. It had been a good life, but now it wasn't enough. He needed Morgan like he needed his next breath.

"Then I am."

Owen tossed the book on the table and laughed. "You have no idea what you're getting yourself into, do you?"

All Bryan could do was shrug. He saw the humor of the situation – the man-whore had fallen in love with his best friend's sister, a woman who wasn't capable of loving him back. Despite how ridiculous it was, he couldn't bring himself to laugh along.

When Owen finally got over his damn self, he shook his head at Bryan. "Does she know?"

Now it was Bryan's turn to laugh. "I'm trying to take things slow." More like he was a chicken shit but he trusted Owen to read between the lines.

Owen lifted a single brow, sliding his feet to the floor and resting his forearms on his legs. "Slow? Don't you think it's a little late for that?"

"It's a lot harder to break through the emotional barriers than the physical ones. You know that."

"Yeah, I guess I do." Owen shook his head again. "You're going to get hurt."

"It's nothing I can't handle."

"I'm going to remind you that you said that when you're drowning in a bottle of bourbon."

"That's your poison, my friend. I'll take the Crown. Straight up."

"I'll side with her you know, when things go south with you two."

"As you should." Bryan didn't have any delusions. He had brothers and knew firsthand that blood was thicker than water. "But you're not the only one protecting her. You ever get in her face with words like slut and tramp again, it won't be her fist that's leaving a mark on you." Bryan tapped his own black eye, just to remind Owen of the one he was sporting courtesy of his little sister.

"Tough guy."

"I could take you, man. You piss me off enough and I could take you." Bryan hoped to never be in that position, but no way could he let Owen talk to Morgan like that again.

"I don't like this, but I appreciate that you're looking out for her. She packs a mean punch. Makes me proud."

"Yeah, your eye is looking pretty this morning. How are you going to explain that at the shop?"

Owen laughed and nodded at Bryan's face. "Same way you're going to explain yours. Bar room brawl. Bastard was huge. Meaner 'an a hungry gator on a hot day."

"So you probably don't want me to rat you out, tell everyone you were beat up by a girl?"

Owen chortled, pinning Bryan with a stern look. "When I tell everyone that you were bangin' my sister behind my back, I'll get all the support."

"True that. So we're good, man?" When he'd been on the outs with his brothers, letting it go was this easy, but for some reason he hadn't been expecting that from Owen, especially since Bryan had been the one to cross the line and betray his friend.

"We're not even close to being good. I can't keep you from doing whatever it is you're going to do, but don't expect my blessing."

"What about your friendship?" It was a hard question to ask, but Bryan had to know.

"I'm going to need some time to figure that one out."

It wasn't what Bryan had hoped to hear, but the truth was he'd crossed a line and had to accept the repercussions. "I didn't mean for any of this to happen. It just did."

Owen's mouth stretched in a thin line, as though he was weighing Bryan's words. When Owen finally stood, Bryan stood with him, hoping to find some sort of acceptance or even forgiveness. All he saw was a pain Owen had worn in the past, when he'd been betrayed by his ex-wives. It nearly tore Bryan apart knowing he'd been the source of the betrayal this time.

"You can see yourself out," Owen said, moving past Bryan and onto the balcony.

Bryan hung his head and headed to the door, unsure if it hurt more to be dismissed by the woman he loved or by the best friend he'd betrayed.

***

"Men suck," Morgan grumbled as she crawled out of bed after another restless night. It'd been a hell of a week, filled with moody, ungrateful patients, and lectures and labs that may as well have been spoken in Swahili.

Five days had passed since she kicked Bryan out. Five days had passed since Owen walked out. No calls. No texts. Nothing.

Five flippin' days. Not one damned word from either one of them.

Not that it was unheard of to go five days without out talking to either one of them, but after the way they each left on Saturday, Morgan couldn't believe neither one of them had called or stopped by. They both owed her a good grovel filled with apology and whatever bribery they saw fit to win her affection back.

She'd accept some good grub from her brother. Bryan could be way more creative with his groveling.

But no, they had to be stubborn or maybe just stupid and not make the first move. Well, to hell with them. She couldn't keep on like this. Her grades were suffering enough without this added distraction. Dr. Merrill had even inquired about her attitude, saying she seemed off, not her usual happy self.

She blamed Bryan. Those holy wow orgasms had become something she craved. He ruined their perfect arrangement by confessing his sins to Owen, who went all overprotective brother on her.

Stupid men.

She heard the unmistakable sound of a Mustang's engine revving, quickly followed by its silence. Owen, she thought, rushing to the door and peering out the window. Yep, there he was, climbing out of the sporty car, a smile on his unshaven face.

Dread filled her, much like it had as a child when her father came home from work. He was all smiles, filled with a warm affection that they knew would last only until the first glass of bourbon was down. Then the fun began.

Morgan had dumped his bourbon down the sink once, hoping he wouldn't care, would find another way to take the edge off the day. She nearly got beaten for it. The only reason she didn't was because Owen confessed. She was only ten at the time and hadn't learned how to fight back at that point. Even though Owen was only eleven and a skinny little boy, he was willing to take a beating for his sister.

The guilt from having hit him last weekend stirred the tears to life as she retreated to the living room. She knew it'd hit at some point and finally seeing Owen made it bubble up like blister on sunburned skin.

He knocked on the door, lightly at first and after a few minutes he knocked again with a little more fervor. "Be careful what you wish for," she grumbled as she headed back to the door. Yes, she'd wanted him to grovel, but it seemed like a much better idea in theory than in reality.

The reality of it was she needed to apologize to him as much as she needed him to do the same. She just hoped he wasn't here to lecture her.

When she opened the door he didn't say hello. "I'm an asshole."

Morgan laughed at his greeting. "I know."

Without missing a beat, he pulled her against him, a warm hug that filled her heart. She loved her brother. Even though she knew she loved her mother by default, the affection had never been there between them, nor with her sisters. But she and Owen had always been close.

"Do you want something to drink?" she asked as she stepped back from his warm embrace. "Coffee? Tea? Juice?"

"What are you having?"

"Green tea. I have to study today." She had a test next week and wasn't anywhere close to being ready for it. The drama of the weekend had kept her distracted, but now with Owen's apology, maybe she could focus on her studies.

"I'll have that too."

Morgan turned on the electric kettle and got the cups ready as the water boiled. The silence was filled with tension as she anticipated what he might say. He was here on a peace offering, of that she had no doubt. But was he going to make demands of her to stop seeing Bryan? Despite kicking him out on Saturday, she didn't want to stop seeing him and no matter what Owen's stance was, he couldn't make her.

When she delivered the tea, she sat in the chair across from him. This was her own posturing. Normally they sat next to each other on the sofa, but she needed to stay on the defensive and it was easier to do that with a little distance.

Owen sat back on the sofa and rubbed his forehead. Then he sat forward. "I'm sorry, Morgan. I really am. I know that you're not a, you know."

"What, in the light of day you can't say it?"

"I'm not Dad. I'd never hurt you."

"You did hurt me. You're more like Dad than you care to admit. I bet you went home and threw back some bourbon that night, too."

"Actually I got on the tread mill and ran twelve miles. I asked Stacie to stay at Jenny's so I could be alone, but she refused. She wouldn't even let me sleep on the sofa. She made tea, too." Owen took a long sip. Morgan had never known him to be a tea drinker, but he'd changed a lot since Stacie came into his life. Funny how love could change people like that. Not that Morgan knew, or ever would. Even though she loved her brother and sisters, she could never love a man. Not after her parents had shown her what love could do to people.

"I know you're not a slut," Owen finally said. There was a sadness in his eyes, regret, she realized – recognized, really, since she was feeling it too.

"I'm sorry I hit you."

Owen laughed. "I guess I don't need to worry about you as much as I do. You pack a mean punch."

"I've been taking self-defense classes off and on for years. I've never used it before."

"That wasn't self-defense. That was pissed off."

It was pissed off, but only because she was defending her own honor. "So you're okay with me and Bryan?"

Morgan wasn't surprised when he shook his head. "No, not in a million years, but that's my problem and I have to deal with it."

"He's a good guy." Not that she needed to tell her brother that. Bryan was his best friend. He knew what an honorable person he was.

"I know," though his voice didn't sound convinced of that. They worked together and she wondered if they had reconciled this week. "I'm more worried about how you're going to wreck him than anything else."

"Bryan?" She laughed, expecting Owen to laugh along with her. When he just sat there, looking at her like someone had killed his puppy, she shook her head. "You can't be serious."

"Morgan," he paused like he wanted to say something but couldn't find the words. "Be honest with me. Do you love him?"

"No," she blurted. That was a bit too abrupt, so Morgan tried to shrug it off. "I know that's what you're hoping, at least to justify us having sex, but it's not that kind of relationship with us."

"I wouldn't be so sure of that," Owen grumbled.

"What are you talking about?"

Owen puckered his lips, obviously contemplating something.

"Bryan and I are just friends," she reminded him. "Don't make it out to be more than it is."

Shaking his head, Owen let out a long sigh. Morgan was sure if it was acceptance or resignation. It didn't matter. She didn't need his approval to live her life and if she wanted to keep on sleeping with Bryan, she could.

"Just be gentle with my boy, k?"

***

The beep on her phone pulled Morgan out of her text book. A ridiculous hope made her heart beat faster and for the first time this week she wasn't disappointed.

Bryan's text was short, but it filled her with anticipation. *You home?*

She responded immediately with a simple *Yes.*

Good. Answer the door.

As she read the message, there were three firm thumps at the door. Morgan breathed in a deep breath, not wanting to seem too anxious or excited, but she still hurried to the door, taking another deep breath before she opened it slowly.

Bryan wore a navy t-shirt and loose-fitting jeans, holding a pizza box and a movie. "Need a study break?" he asked.

"Dinner and a movie, without getting out of my sweats? You bet."

This was the kind of thing Bryan had always done. Before December, he'd sometimes crash out on her sofa after a movie night instead of trying to catch the last ferry.

"I didn't bring any drinks, but I can run back out if you need me to."

"All I have is iced-tea," she said, stepping out of his way to let him into the apartment. Bryan headed straight for the kitchen and dropped the pizza box on the counter.

Morgan pulled the iced-tea out of the fridge while Bryan grabbed a couple plates.

"You're not very predictable when it comes to pizza, so I got half meat-lovers half veggie-lovers."

"Ooh, nice. I'll have one of each."

Once they were set with pizza and drinks, Morgan settled onto the pappasan and Bryan took a seat on the sofa.

The pizza was exactly what she needed, well, that and Bryan's company. She'd spent the morning in the books before working an afternoon shift at Dr. Merrill's family practice. When she came home, she'd plunged right back into the books again. Owen's visit had been a relief and even though she was able to concentrate a little more, she was still missing Bryan.

"How are the kittens?" she asked. It sounded like small talk, and maybe it was, but she had missed those little fur balls too.

"I can't believe how fast they grow. They haven't opened their eyes yet. I was worried at first, but I Googled it and learned it can take a whole week before that happens. Natasha's a great Mom."

The reverence in her voice made Morgan's female anatomy contract with longing.

"Can I come see them this weekend?" she asked.

"Of course. You don't have to ask, Morg."

"I haven't heard from you all week," she said between bites of pizza, finally acknowledging the big fat elephant in the room.

"You kicked me out Saturday, remember?"

"Yeah, but–" But what? She had kicked him out and she'd been mad at him for giving up their secret to her brother. Now, though, Owen seemed to have accepted it and yeah, okay, it would be nice not to have to sneak around.

She moved from the papasan chair to the sofa, cuddling up next to him. Bryan's arm went around her automatically, pulling her against his chest. She peered up at him, one finger gently stroking his face.

"Your eye looks like shit." Yep, more small talk.

Bryan laughed, giving the bruise a gentle stroke with his fingers. "It doesn't hurt as much. I figure all the pretty colors means it's healing."

Morgan dropped her half empty plate on the table and moved onto the couch, snuggling up to Bryan and placing a gentle kiss next to colorful bruise.

"He hit me here too," Bryan pointed at his jaw.

She kissed that spot. "Anywhere else?"

"If you must know, I still hurt all over."

Chapter 15

The sweet sound of Morgan's laughter never failed to kick Bryan's heart up a few gears. "So I guess you're up for having manic sex and forgetting this whole fiasco happened?"

Bryan hadn't liked staying away all week, but he figured Morgan needed some space and he was still trying to get back in Owen's good graces. The guy had hardly said two words to Bryan all week. "I like the part about having manic sex, but I'm not sure we can forget what happened."

"I dare you to try." He loved the mischievous way her lips curved.

Bryan never turned down a dare, but there were important issues to discuss.

"About Owen," he started and was immediately pinned with a stifling glare.

"I don't want to talk about Owen."

"I need to make things right with him."

She turned away, her arms crossing and a pout protruding her luscious bottom lip. Even when she was a brat, she was hot as hell.

"He was here this morning, apologizing."

That was good news. Maybe his friend was finally cooling off. Of course, he'd make amends with his sister long before he'd forgive his best friend's betrayal.

"He hasn't talked to me all week. I'm not sure how to gain his trust again."

"Is that why you ignored me all week?"

"I didn't ignore you. I thought you needed some space, so I gave it to you."

"And then just showed up without warning."

He stroked her arm with a lazy caress. "You're the one who always preaches about us being friends. I don't want to step back from where we were, but if all I get is your friendship, I'll take it."

"How noble," she teased, giving his nipple a squeeze through his shirt.

Bryan pulled her back against him, unwilling to let the brat in her turn this conversation against him. Though, admittedly, he'd screwed up. "You make it sound like a bad thing."

She shook her head against his chest. "Actually, even though it can be annoying at times, it's probably one of your more endearing traits." She relaxed her arms, one hand splaying across his chest. It was like she'd applied one of those heart restart paddles he'd seen on TV, kicking his ticker into overdrive.

He was torn between trying to talk to Owen again and staying right here with Morgan, making sure he hadn't screwed up this relationship too. Owen was important to him, but so was Morgan.

Of course, he'd tried all week to talk to Owen and all he got in response was the cold shoulder. The Landry's sure knew how to hold a grudge. Bryan was grateful Morgan seemed to be more forgiving than her brother, but he still needed to earn Owen's trust back.

If he left Morgan now, though, this relationship they'd built over the past months, and hell, years, would be facing a firing squad. Maybe she didn't want to admit how involved they were, but she certainly wouldn't take kindly to being second in this fiasco.

"So what are my other endearing traits?" he asked with a hint of amusement in his voice.

"You're smart," she laughed.

"What else?"

"You're a pretty good cook. You're probably the sweetest guy I've ever met. You proved that with Natasha. I can tell you're a good brother and I've heard you on the phone a few times with your mother, so I know you're a good son, too."

He was glad she thought all those things of him. It proved their friendship was still intact and that what they shared wasn't just about the amazing sex. Speaking of…

"When I have my ego stroked, I prefer to hear how good I am in bed. Or how big I am. Or how good I am in bed."

Her laugh kicked his heart into high gear again. "I'm pretty sure I tell you that every time I have an orgasm."

Bryan couldn't hold back the cocky smile that spread across his face and was glad Morgan wasn't facing him to call him on it. He wasn't the kind of man who needed his ego stroked. He'd been with enough women to know he was good in bed. He could tell the difference between faking it and honest to God pleasure and more often than not, he brought the woman he was with to that happy and satisfied destination. Hearing it from Morgan, though, yeah, he liked that. Craved it, even.

"You get one of those nurse's uniforms yet?" he teased.

The little slap that landed on his chest didn't hurt and only edged him on. "I'm a nurse every day. I can't play one in the bedroom."

"You need to learn to compartmentalize, sweetheart. I'm totally willing to play sailor for you." The first time she'd seen him in uniform, man, the way she looked at him practically set him on fire.

"You look good in your uniform – beats scrubs any day of the week."

"I think you're scrubs are sexy as hell." The way they clung to her ass and draped around her breasts. The fact there was no panty line, leaving him to wonder what she wore beneath. Yeah, sexy.

"Sailor is sexy." Her finger was circling his nipple over his shirt, springing the giant sailor in his pants to life. She must have noticed because her hand wandered south, giving his erection the same attention. "You get to fire torpedoes and launch submarines, and sink your battleship inside of me."

"Keep talking naughty like that."

Morgan laughed. "You're so dirty."

"I am. So tell me what naughty nurses do to dirty sailors. Sponge baths? Or maybe tongue baths. I think I might need one of those."

She pushed away, pinning him with a look that was more amused than angry. "I don't know if you deserve any kind bath. I'm still kinda pissed that you swooped in to rescue me."

Well, at least she wasn't thinking about him giving up their secret anymore. "I wasn't rescuing you. I was saving your brother's ass."

"Oh, is that how it played out?"

"You gave him a black eye, Morg."

"I'm going to feel guilty about that when I wake up in the morning."

"Then maybe I'll keep you up all night so you don't have to worry about waking up."

"What'd you have in mind?"

"For starters, my tongue wants to play battleship. Then we'll figure out what to do with my submarine."

***

Morgan looked completely relaxed as Bryan kissed his way north. Usually his three-fer special consisted of getting her off with his hand, then his tongue, then by planting himself inside her. But tonight all the innuendo had him going straight for the intimate kiss. He loved the taste of her, the way she felt against his mouth. He could have kept at it all night, but she was begging him to stop.

Playing dirty sailor was definitely a satisfying adventure with Morgan. He couldn't talk her into the slinky little nurse's uniform with white fishnet stockings, but outside of that, she was receptive to his suggestions.

"I want to come inside you again," he confessed, nipping her ear and kissing the soft lobe.

Her sigh was sweet music. "You do that every time."

"No, I mean without a condom."

Surprise flashed in her eyes. "That's just about the dumbest thing I've ever heard you say. Not to mention irresponsible."

They'd done it just that morning, and she'd confirmed she was on the pill, so he wasn't sure why it was so dumb.

He wanted to tell her how he felt, that he'd fallen for her, but this hardly seemed the time. She'd see it as a desperate plea to get his way, which maybe it was. It would also have her jumping overboard on this little ship they were sailing on. With what had happened with Owen earlier, the deck was stacked against Bryan. Better not to show all his cards, not yet.

"It's best not to complicate things since we're not exclusive" she added.

Bryan felt like they were back at square one. How many times had he told her he hadn't been with anyone else? Aw, hell, was she seeing someone? Avoiding that question, he simply suggested, "We could be."

"Okay, that's the second dumbest thing you've ever said."

Dammit. He had to know. "Are you seeing anyone else?"

"No."

And thank God for that. Of course, they were naked. His body was hovering over her. If she was seeing someone else, would she really admit it now?

Yeah, she would. One thing about Morgan was she didn't lie.

Okay, so she'd been lying about their relationship, but that was different. She wouldn't lie about something as important as this.

"Neither am I," he admitted again. "And I don't want to. So why not make it official." After all, the only thing holding them back was Owen not knowing. Now everyone knew.

"Okay, Owen's little pep talk or whatever it was is definitely going to your head."

"Morg..." he sighed, frustration preventing him from presenting a strong argument.

"Things are good, Bryan. Why do you want to change that?"

"I'm not changing anything. You're not seeing anyone. I'm not seeing anyone. We're already there. We just haven't put the label on it. It makes sense to now."

"No, it doesn't."

"What are you afraid of?"

She tried to push him away, but he didn't budge. "Bryan, come on. We're just having fun. It's not a relationship."

"Look, we don't have to keep this a secret anymore. Owen knows. We spend most of our free time together anyway. Having dinner or drinks. Going for a ride on the Ducati. You can deny it all you want, but the fact is we're not just having sex."

She threw her head back, hopefully in defeat. "You suck."

He took a nipple into his mouth and let go only after she couldn't hold back the moan. "You've never complained about that before."

"Okay, fine. Yeah, it'll be nice to not have to pretend in public. But we're not having unprotected sex."

"You're on the pill and like I told you this morning, I've never once not used a condom. I'm clean."

"You're thirty-four and you've been with how many women? How is it possible you've never slipped up or been so desperate you didn't bother?"

Those words shouldn't have hurt because she was only speaking the truth, but somehow, he felt tainted.

"You know my best friend? The guy who had a habit of knockin' girls up? Yeah, I've never been interested in being trapped like that. If there's one thing I've learned over the years, it's not to trust a woman who jumps into bed too quickly, especially after she finds out I'm a sailor. I'm not interested in offering a free ride."

She smiled and relief flooded his chest. "Smart and sexy."

"Who'da thunk, huh?" he quipped

He loved the way she laughed. "How do you know you can trust me?" she asked.

Morgan preached safe sex as casually as if she were talking about the weather. As an OB nurse and aspiring midwife, she'd seen enough scared, single women give birth. Not to mention the situations her brother had gotten himself into.

"You're smart and responsible, and most of all, you respect yourself and your body. Plus, you're brutally honest. If you say you've never had sex without a condom, I have no reason not to believe you."

She stared at him like he had three heads. "Don't you fall in love with me, Bryan Curtis."

Her words were like taking a bullet to the brain. Bryan had no idea where it had come from and it was ricocheting around, disrupting every clear thought and sending him into a panic.

"I – why would you say that?" Because, duh, he already had and there was no going back.

"Sex without a condom means you're looking for something more than I'm willing to give. We aren't forever, Bryan. Maybe we're exclusive now, but you're going to go out on a ship and I'm going to go back to dating for fun and when you get back, you'll resume your previous lifestyle."

Fuck. This was not what he wanted to hear. He had no intentions of going back to his previous lifestyle. Easy sex didn't seem like a whole lot of fun right now. Any sex, really, unless it was with Morg.

He rolled off her, his erection completely deflated. Resting his arm against his forehead as though in distress, he shook his head. "I'm going out on a ship, Morg. But when I come back, I'd like to pick up where we left off."

"That's not what I want." Her voice was barely a whisper.

"Why not?" He knew the answer, but prayed he was wrong.

"I'm not interested in marriage or anything that resembles marriage. We're having fun, Bryan. I don't want to ruin that with plans for the future that won't pan out anyway."

Bryan didn't say anything. He couldn't. Everything he was starting to want was exactly what Morgan didn't want and the woman was stubborn and determined. She would never give in, not if he proclaimed his love, not if he begged, and especially not if he demanded.

"What's your beef with marriage anyway?"

"What's yours?" she countered. It was a good question. He was just as opposed to the union as she. Well, he had been, anyway. Now, he wasn't so sure. At least he could stick with the story that had been his truth his entire adult life.

"I'm married to the navy," he said. "Most women don't like bigamy."

"You can be in the navy and be married. It works for lots of people."

"Yeah, well, I've seen it fail enough to know it wasn't something I wanted." He hoped she didn't call him out on the past tense. He hadn't wanted it. Then he'd gotten stupid and fallen for her. Now he wanted everything.

She rolled onto her side, her head perched on one hand, her other hand lazily tracing through the hair on his chest, waking up the giant sailor.

"So tell me how you've lured so many women into bed. False promises?"

He hated talking about his past sex life with her. Why couldn't she look forward instead of letting the past trap them. "I never lie just to get someone in bed. If she isn't interested in what I have to offer–"

"A roll in the hay and a quick exit?"

She really thought highly of him, didn't she? "It's not always a quick exit. Anyway, if they're looking for something long term, I let them know straight up I'm not offering that. It saves the awkward good-bye in the morning and I don't like sneaking out."

Morgan laughed, showing her doubt. "Women lie, Bryan. They may agree to what you're offering, but that doesn't mean they aren't hoping for more. You've got a lot to offer. It's why woman flock to you."

Was that a compliment or a hit? Or maybe she was placing herself amongst the women who lied about what they wanted.

"So are *you* hoping for more?" Bryan tried not to sound hopeful when he asked.

"No. I'm the exception to the rule."

Bryan wasn't so sure about that, but maybe it was just wishful thinking. "So what exactly is it that I have to offer?"

"Didn't I already stroke your ego once tonight?" she asked, her hand moving down to stroke his other ego.

"I like hearing it." From you, he wanted to add, but decided to keep that little tidbit to himself. He was already teetering on the edge of telling her too much and he knew it would not end well if he did.

"You're hot." She gave his erection a little squeeze, enough to make him groan. "You're also smart and easy to talk to. You're the type of guy that would rescue a damsel in distress, which most women like."

"But not you."

"No, not me. You also have a very admirable career. You're a hero. Women like that, too."

"I'm not a hero, Morg. I sit behind a computer and protect old data."

"Yeah, and what would happen if someone got ahold of that old data?"

"Lots of bad things."

"So you're a hero."

"Whatever. People may see it that way, but that doesn't make it true. Guys on the front lines are the heroes." Bryan wasn't comfortable being labeled a hero, especially when he didn't have to dodge bullets or IEDs or whatever other horrors terrorists came up with these days.

"Fine, but all the other stuff is true."

Bryan wasn't interested in talking about his redeeming qualities. Yeah, so he'd asked the question, but the hero bullshit always made him uncomfortable. With her hand wrapped around his very eager sailor, he was ready to get back to the initial question. "You gonna let me come inside you, or what?"

"Definitely not."

"Why not?"

"Because we don't have that kind of relationship."

So much for the straight up answer he was looking for.

"And exactly what kind of relationship would that be?"

"Sustainable. Serious. Committed. Neither one of us wants that, so we shouldn't allow our sexual exploits to lead us down that road."

"I think we can trust each other enough to skip it, Morg. You're on the pill and we're both clean. It'd be a great way to send me off with a bang before I ship out."

"What do you mean, before you ship out?"

The skipper had come to Bryan on Wednesday, detailing a new computer security program the Department of Defense had implemented for all ported ships. Rather than wait for deployed ships to port, they wanted to implement the new program at sea. They were sending in a team to conduct training, implement, and test. He'd be gone anywhere from three weeks to three months, home for one, and back out again. They expected the implementation to take eighteen months, which really meant two to three years because there would be issues that weren't accounted for.

"I told you, I'm going out on a ship."

"You're going to war?" The horror on her face nearly strangled his heart.

"Not war, sweetheart. Just helping with some new computer programs."

"You're going out on a ship. A ship that's deployed. That sounds like war to me."

"It's a routine deployment. It's not a big deal."

"No, not until Russia or Korea decides to launch a nuke."

"If anyone decides to launch a nuke, it doesn't really matter where I am, all hell is going to break loose."

"You want this, don't you?"

"Morg, I don't want to leave Puget Sound, but I've been at Bremerton for nearly five years. It's a fluke I haven't gotten orders out of here. By the time this program is fully implemented, I'll have less than two years until retirement. They won't send me anywhere with that little time left. These TDYs pretty much guarantee I won't get orders to another duty station."

"It's dangerous and crazy."

A routine deployment wasn't dangerous or crazy, but the world was a volatile place, so it could get dangerous and crazy quicker than a ship could pull anchor. "Obviously, there's always a risk." The risk wasn't just at sea or in a hostile country though. It was just a couple months ago when that news helicopter crashed in Seattle. "Hell, there's a risk just living in the city. I could be struck by a bus on my way to the ferry. Those people who were in that helicopter had no idea that was their last day. That's why I want all of you, Morg – flesh to flesh."

Morgan smiled and shook her head. "You could charm a cobra back into his basket, couldn't you?"

"Is that a yes?"

"No. At least not tonight. We need two forms of birth control and if we're going to forego the condom, we need something else."

It wasn't exactly what he wanted to hear, but it was progress. He'd make a trip to the drugstore tomorrow and buy every contraceptive on the shelf to use as a secondary if it meant he got more of this incredible woman.

Chapter 16

"Okay, I can't watch another tear jerker like that. Damn that Nicholas Sparks anyway," Holly sniffled.

Morgan couldn't agree more. She hated when Jenny was in charge of bringing movies. She either picked the sappiest love story or the most heart-wrenching tragedy. Nicholas Sparks' movies typically delivered both.

"Let's play truth," Stacie suggested.

Suppressing a groan, Morgan realized this was better than watching another movie from Jenny's collection. Holly looked terrified.

"Maybe we shouldn't," Morgan suggested. She didn't really have anything to hide now that her relationship with Bryan was public knowledge, but Holly had plenty of things she didn't like to share and Morgan wouldn't encourage a game that her friend wasn't comfortable playing.

"Oh, come on," Jenny chided. "Don't be a spoilsport."

"Says the woman who has no secrets," Morgan responded.

"Oh, I have secrets. That's not what this is about. Nothing too personal. Just sex stuff."

Holly nearly choked on her drink.

"How is sex stuff not too personal?" Morgan questioned.

Stacie ignored them all, pulling four shot glasses from the cupboard and grabbing the vodka they'd used to mix mudslides.

"You lied to us about Bryan." Jenny crossed her arms and gave Morgan that don't-mess-with-me look. "You owe us."

Morgan didn't owe anyone anything, but she'd been stressed from school and that ridiculous Nicholas Sparks movie hadn't done anything to loosen her up. Maybe a good game of truth was just what she needed. However, it could be the last thing Holly needed. Even as she was thinking this might be fun, her protective instincts went into overdrive. "You okay with this, Holl?"

Holly shrugged. "If it's just sex stuff, I don't have much to share."

"Great. I don't have much to share either." Unless it got personal about Bryan, then she'd have plenty to share. Actually, now that she thought about it, she'd wanted to share for months about her escapades with Bryan. Maybe this would be fun after all.

Stacie poured the shots and explained the rules. "Okay, so we each get to pick a topic. You have to reveal your own truth about it. If you don't answer, you drink. Who wants to start?"

Everyone pointed at Stacie, which made her laugh.

"Alright, huh. How old were you when you lost your virginity? Holly."

"Uh, seventeen," Holly confessed, a blush brightening her alabaster cheeks.

"Me too," Jenny sang, her pride a complete contrast to Holly's modesty.

And seventeen, wow. Not that Morgan thought it was young, but it made her feel like a nun. "I was twenty-four."

Jenny's eyes widened, which was no surprise to Morgan. She knew they all thought she was a little slutty given the way she dated. She didn't particularly care what they thought because she knew the truth. She'd never been easy and even though she wasn't interested in anything long-term, she wasn't quick to jump into bed with anyone. Okay, so maybe Bryan was the exception, but honestly, she'd lusted after him for twelve years before they did the deed, so technically, it wasn't fast or easy.

"Twenty," Stacie added.

"Morgan wins the old hag award!" Jenny called out and the other three threw back their shots. Morgan wasn't sure if she was supposed to or not, so she threw hers back too and Stacie refilled their glasses.

"Holly, you're up," Stacie said.

"Biggest guy. I'm talking length and girth, not height and weight. And actual penetration." Okay, well, Holly didn't mess around when she played this game.

Smiles lit up everyone's faces.

"Christian Fox," Jenny sighed, her eyes going all dreamy.

"From the chess club?" Stacie asked.

"That be him."

"Never would have guessed," Stacie said, looking a little surprised. Since the two of them had been roommates in college, Morgan figured that's where they knew the guy from. Frankly, by the way Jenny and Ty couldn't keep their hands off each other, Morgan expected to hear about him.

All eyes turned to her and she felt the heat rush to her cheeks before the truth passed her lips. "Uh, Bryan." It was weird to talk about having sex with Bryan to other people. Of course, the secret was out and everyone knew, so there was no point hiding it.

"Oh, do tell," Jenny urged.

Details. When was the last time she'd shared that kind of information? Never, maybe. Well, this was girl's night in and Bryan was worthy of talking about.

"Uh, well, I can wrap both hands around him and not cover him completely." God, she hoped he didn't catch wind of this little game. Then again, if she was praising the *giant* sailor below his waist, he likely wouldn't object.

Stacie giggled. "Owen, too. He's huge. I mean, like, wow huge. Scared the Fates out of me the first time I saw him." She sighed and got that same dreamy expression Jenny had had. "But he knows what he's doing, so it's fantastic."

That was more than Morgan really needed to know about her brother, but she supposed it wasn't fair to ask that Stacie not share.

"Jason Phillips," Holly cut in, thankfully changing the focus. "He was scary big and it hurt like hell. I thought it would only hurt that first time, but after the third time, I actually started avoiding him."

"Was he your first?" Jenny asked.

"Nah, it was a few years ago."

"Is he why you gave up men?" Stacie asked. By now everyone knew Holly was off men and apparently into women, but no one seemed to care.

"No, I gave up men because my last boyfriend beat me up."

There was a collective sound of moaning, then Stacie raised her glass. "We need to drink on that one."

After the glasses were empty, Stacie went back to filling them.

Morgan was a little shocked Holly had shared that little bit of information, but maybe that was a testament to the friendship she was building with each of them.

"Numbers," Jenny said, taking her turn. "How many guys, or girls," she appended, nodding at Holly, "have you been with?"

"Four. All guys," Morgan added.

"Two. Though, honestly, Greg was so boring I'm not sure he should count." Stacie explained.

"Sorry, girlfriend, if there was penile penetration, it counts," Jenny informed her before turning to Holly.

"Uh, I'm not really sure," Holly said. "I'm sure I could figure it out if I thought long and hard, but I don't take it long and hard anymore."

"Are you serious?" Morgan asked, then wished she hadn't. Honestly, it wasn't her business if Holly couldn't keep count, but the shock factor of her admission disrupted Morgan's tact-filter.

"About not taking it long and hard, yeah," Holly laughed. "But actually, I know how many people I've been with. It's five; four men, one woman when I was a freshman in college."

"So even though you're not taking it long and hard, you're not currently seeking the pearl in the bearded clam?" Jenny's face was stone-cold serious as she waited for Holly to answer. Meanwhile, Stacie choked on air and Morgan bit back a laugh.

"Well," Holly said on a sigh, "I'm not sure if Morgan's clam is bearded, but I did try hitting on her, as I'm sure you've all heard, and that didn't really work out, so I've decided to be intimate with my vibrator until I can get over my man issues."

Morgan hadn't told anyone about the pass Holly had made at Gasworks Park, and even though Bryan had been witness to it, she had trusted that he hadn't said anything either.

"I had no idea," Jenny said in perfect harmony with Stacie's "Really?"

"Yeah. Apparently, Morgan is really into dark-haired sailors with really big, you know, sailors in their pants."

Morgan laughed at her analogy knowing full well Holly had no idea she and Bryan often referred to his assets as the *sailor*. It was probably an obvious analogy for someone in the navy.

"Well, I bet you would have had a chance if Bryan wasn't already sinking his battleship in Morgan's...huh, clamshell." Stacie finished her quip with very little confidence, turning it into more of a question than a statement. Since she hardly ever swore and typically used literary analogies, Morgan figured she had little experience in this type of conversation.

"Bearded or not, I'm not into any sort of seafood. No offense, Holl," Morgan attested.

"None taken," she held out her glass and they exchanged a loud clank before the two of them downed their shots. Jenny wasted no time refilling their glasses. "Though, I do like eels. Long and really hard eels, not diced and grilled. I prefer them alive and wriggling." Holly's voice held a distinct longing. She'd said she needed to get over her man issues, maybe she was well on her way.

"Do people really grill eels?" Stacie asked, missing the euphemism.

"In Louisiana, we'll grill anything." It was true. Morgan had eaten more vermin than she'd care to remember. Some of it was good. Some of it was pure voodoo.

"Speaking of electric eels, all hail the glory of the vibrator," Jenny chanted, holding up her shot glass and obviously making an effort to avoid talking about grilled vermin. After everyone clinked, while repeating the chant, no less, another shot was tossed.

"Four for me," Jenny said, holding out her glass for a refill.

Everyone else followed suit and when Stacie was finished pouring, Morgan stepped up to the plate.

"First guy you ever went bareback with," Morgan said. This was a chance to find if she was being overly cautious or if she was justified in analyzing Bryan's request.

"Greg," Stacie groaned. "I was on the pill and since I'd made him wait two years, I gave him a break on that."

"Justin," Holly held up her glass and took a drink. "First time I had sex. No condom. I was a pretty stupid teenager. I haven't really smartened up much when it comes to men. That's another reason I avoid them."

"Ty," Jenny said. "We were planning to move in together, so I went on the pill and we said good-bye to the condoms. Made spontaneous public sex a little easier!"

"Given how much spontaneous public sex the two of you have had, I don't think the condom requirement really made much difference," Stacie added.

"Never for me," Morgan lied. Yeah, she'd started this round, but now she wasn't willing to follow through, at least not honestly. She was curious about everyone's perception of the topic, though, because left to her own analysis, not using a condom spelled T.R.O.U.B.L.E. Exclamation point.

"Never?" Jenny asked.

"No." Morgan wanted to affirm it with another 'never' but

found she couldn't take the lie that deep.

"How is that even possible?" Stacie asked.

"I'm a safety girl. No condom, no sex. You've met my brother, right?"

"Fair enough," Stacie said, her head nodding as though the thought of getting pregnant was the last thing she wanted. Morgan could drink to that.

"So tell me though, just hypothetically." Please, please, please let them think this hypothetical. "What does it mean when a guy wants to have sex without a condom?"

"He wants to mark you."

"He's in love with you."

"Damn."

Stacie, Jenny, and Holly's harmonious responses didn't help Morgan's predicament.

"Okay, thirty seconds," she pointed at Stacie. "Go!"

"It's a sign he wants more. It's his way of marking you, you know, like a tom cat. He wants to leave a piece of himself behind so you'll think twice about sleeping with someone else." That definitely applied to Bryan. Morgan suspected him wanting to be exclusive had more to do with keeping her from other men than anything else.

Morgan turned to Jenny. "If we're talking about Bryan, and let's be honest, we all know you are, it's a sign he wants more. He's fallen hard and this is his way of saying it without using words. Couple that with the marking thing and it's all pretty obvious. The man wants to own you, in the best way possible."

How was there a best way of being owned? Morgan had no interest in that. Her father had owned her mother and there was nothing good about that situation. It was exactly what Morgan wanted to avoid.

Morgan was interested to see how Holly was going to break the tie here, but all Holly did was repeat her previous response. "Damn."

"You don't have anything more than that?"

"My last boyfriend refused to use a condom then beat me up when I got pregnant. So yeah, 'damn' is all I got."

"Are you on the pill?" Stacie asked.

"Oh, this isn't about me. I, uh, had a patient who was asking and I wasn't really sure how to answer since, I've never, well, you know." Stumble on your words much?

Dammit, she sounded like an idiot, only confirming to her friends that she was in fact, talking about Bryan. May as well take another plunge.

"So what does it mean when you forget to use a condom?"

"Shut! Up!" Jenny said and slapped Morgan's arm. "No one asks a theoretical question during a girl's night if she doesn't need advice. Give us the scoop."

Morgan's lips were feeling a little loose and her head a little fuzzy. The vodka was obviously kicking in and what the hell, it was girl's night and she did need advice. "I'm on the pill. You guys know I believe in doubling up, especially after watching my brother back himself into a wall."

"Twice," Stacie added.

"Exactly." Morgan pointed at Stacie. Oh, hello dizzy spell. This was why she avoided vodka. Making her best effort to keep her eyes from darting around, she finally gave up and closed them. "So I'm on the pill and I always use a condom. But, like, I'm not really sure what happened, but last Saturday we, well, we kind of forgot to use one. And now Bryan wants to forget to use one every time and I don't think I can do that."

"Forgot to use a condom? You don't just forget," Jenny pointed out and a week ago Morgan would have agreed, but she truly had not realized what had happened until Bryan brought it up.

"Honest to God, cross my heart and hope to die," Morgan made the signals with her hand and held it up as though swearing some sort of oath. "I truly forgot. I just, well, I wanted him so bad, and you know, it didn't cross my mind to double up."

"You're in love with him," Stacie sighed.

"No. No, absolutely not. I don't do love. Owen got all those genes."

"Don't sell yourself short." Stacie slurred.

"Yeah, you love like crazy," Holly added.

Jenny laughed. "They're drunk. Listen to me, girlfriend. I see the way you look at him. That's not just lust. It's happily ever after."

"I'm going to throw up," Morgan finished, pretending to gag. She was absolutely, positively NOT in love with Bryan. "He's hot and he was being all vulnerable after Natasha had the babies. And you know how I am with babies. It's my life. So I clearly had a moment of weakness."

"Hot and vulnerable? Sounds like true love to me," Jenny followed up and Morgan really wanted to smack her. Didn't matter who brought the subject up. No one was saying what she wanted to hear, that it was okay to have a moment of weakness and it really didn't mean anything.

"Bryan gets around," Morgan reminded them. "He's not a keeper."

"Got around, from what I hear," Stacie said.

"You mean he's not sleeping with anyone else?" Jenny asked.

"He says he's not," Morgan said. She believed him, trusted him, but she didn't need to add that little tidbit to this conversation. No, this was supposed to be about Bryan's intentions, not her weakness.

"He told Owen the same thing," Stacie admitted.

"He's in love with you," Jenny sang, and as if they were singing Row, Row, Row Your Boat, Stacie and Holly joined in tandem.

Morgan wanted to throw herself off the West Seattle Bridge. Bryan had been acting strange, but the worst part was that Morgan liked it. She liked that vulnerable, sweet side and she liked his Knight in Shining armor side, which was the most mind-blowing part. Normally she didn't like being rescued, but with Bryan, she welcomed it.

The problem was, Morgan couldn't do what Jenny referred to as a happily ever after. Love changed people, made them do crazy things. Plus, DNA was a powerful thing. She'd proved last weekend – when she'd given Owen a black eye – she was half Landry. The other half was a docile, submissive side she refused to acknowledge. Better to deliver a punch than take one.

The lovey dovey version of Row, Row, Row Your Boat was followed up with Morgan and Bryan kissing in a tree. She didn't bother waiting for Stacie to pour another shot. No, instead Morgan did what any desperate Landry would do – she grabbed the bottle and took a swig straight from the spout.

Chapter 17

Morgan had been grateful for the slow night. Her professor had offered a retake after she'd bombed her last test and Morgan needed all the study time she could muster. She'd tried to find someone to work her shift at the clinic, but just her luck, there wasn't a single person who could fill in. So here she was, nose deep in her text book in room number eight.

"We need this room," Derek said. "And we need you."

"What's going on?" Morgan clapped the book closed and hopped to her feet.

"Woman in labor. Pre-term. Dr. Sisco is already in a C-section and you're the most experienced mid-wife we have."

"I'm not a mid-wife yet," she reminded Derek, who had decided delivering babies wasn't his thing and was going to withdraw from the program when this quarter was finished.

"Close enough. No one else has any experience delivering babies and this baby is coming fast."

How was it possible she was the only person in this clinic who could deliver a baby? She'd never gone solo before. She'd assisted Dr. Merrill three times. That was it. Assisted. Three times.

Her anxiety was building. Doubt wasn't something she normally danced with, but it seemed to be a frequent partner lately.

"I've gotta scrub," she informed Derek. "Are you scrubbing in too?"

"Connie said she would. I'm going to prep the room first and then I'll scrub in.'

Good. Morgan needed the moral support. "What about Holly?"

"Holly can't."

"Of course she can. It's quiet. We have no other patients."

"It's a domestic." Derek's voice was low, as if he didn't want to tell her the whole situation. "It's the woman who took a baseball bat to her husband."

Oh, shit.

"Is the husband here?"

"No. She drove herself."

Morgan groaned. She'd never experienced labor, but she'd seen enough women in labor to know driving wasn't a smart decision.

As she scrubbed, Morgan focused on her breathing, trying to keep her blood pressure at a manageable rate. The last time she'd seen this woman, she'd just beaten her husband up with a baseball bat. The husband was drunk, but had talked about payback. Morgan worried this pre-term labor was a result of that. Thank God he wasn't here. Of course, that didn't mean he wouldn't show up.

"We're all set," Derek informed her.

Morgan started through a mental checklist of what they would need. "You have the fetal respirator?"

"Check. We've got it all. You are going to rock this."

Morgan wasn't so sure of that. "Call the nearest hospital," she couldn't even think which one was closest, "and let them know the situation. We'll have to transport ASAP. Also, make sure security is in place. The husband does not get into this clinic, do you understand me?" Morgan could deliver a baby and she could handle an abusive man, but she couldn't do them both at the same time.

"Got it, but there's no time to transport. The baby's coming."

Morgan continued through the mental checklist of everything she knew and needed to do. With a trauma like this, the mother could hemorrhage. Morgan had absolutely no experience with that.

"Did you start an IV?" she asked as Derek walked with her back to the birthing room.

"Yes."

"We need to watch for hemorrhaging in the mom and make sure the baby is breathing. Respiratory is our highest priority."

"Got it."

Derek knew all this and was likely just appeasing Morgan as she went through her check list verbally.

She twisted her shaking hands together, trying to calm them and slow the rush of adrenaline. "Did someone at least alert Dr. Sisco?" There was no way they could pull the doc out of surgery, but if she knew there was another fetal emergency, she might hasten her pace.

"Holly's on it," Derek affirmed.

When Morgan walked into the room the woman was crying. "Our anesthesiologist is in surgery," Connie was explaining. "You're going to have to do this without an epidural."

"I can handle the pain," the woman said calmly despite the tears. "Just make sure my little girl is okay."

The comment tugged at Morgan's heart even though she didn't want to feel sympathy for this woman. She'd let her husband do this to her by staying with him, not just endangering herself, but also the baby. Morgan fought back the memories of her childhood, of all those times her father came home drunk and angry, taking his aggressions out on her mother. Morgan couldn't understand why the woman had never left.

Her own respiratory system was threatening to go into arrest, so Morgan focused on the task at hand. She had to deliver this baby. There were a million things that could go wrong, and she'd face those if the situation arose.

Morgan took a quick look at the chart, noting the mother's name was Amanda. Then she got into position, mentally blocking out the memories that continued to flood her brain and the speculation of how this woman had gone into labor.

"Amanda, I need you to focus on your breathing. Aside from the contractions, are you having any other pain?"

"My stomach hurts," Amanda groaned.

Morgan looked at the monitor and saw that the woman's heart rate was elevated. "How's her blood pressure?"

"It's low," Derek said, his voice sounding grave. "Her pulse is racing."

Morgan palpated Amanda's abdomen and found it hard. She was showing all the signs of placental abruption, at least according to the text book. "We need to monitor the baby, get the fetal monitor," she ordered, knowing if there was a placental abruption, the baby could exsanguinate and no way could Morgan risk the baby losing all her blood.

"Is my baby okay?" Amanda asked.

Connie and Derek were busy placing the pads on Amanda's belly. "What happened to send you into labor?" Morgan asked.

As if a vacuum had sucked all the air out of the room, everyone stilled for a moment and Morgan realized her voice had been harsh. Amanda continued to take deep breaths in and let them go in long exhales and Morgan wasn't sure the woman would admit to what had happened.

"Josh shoved me down the stairs. I lost consciousness and when I came to, he was gone and my water had broken."

"How long ago did this happen?" Morgan asked a little less harshly, trying to keep her anger in check.

"I don't know how long I was out, but as soon as I came to, I drove straight here. I live in Lake City, just ten minutes from here."

Morgan wanted to lecture the woman and find out if she was finally going to get help, but this wasn't the time. With the fetal monitor all set up, they could now monitor the baby. The heart rate seemed normal, then Amanda cried out and the baby's heart rate dropped.

"Blood pressure dropped," Derek said, though the beeping of the monitor gave a clear indication of that.

If this was a placental abruption, a C-section would need to be performed to keep Amanda from bleeding out and to keep the baby from exsanguinating. As Morgan checked to see how dilated she was, she could see the baby's head crowning.

Shit. Shit, shit, shit!

There was no turning back at this point. The baby was coming. She just hoped Amanda's uterus would clot quickly enough to prevent too much blood loss.

Amanda with your next contraction, I'm going to need you to push."

"It hurts," she cried.

"I know, but your baby is coming and you need to help her. Keep breathing and when I tell you to, push."

***

When Bryan got out of the shower, his phone was beeping with a vengeance. He had two missed calls from Owen and a text. The text simply read Call me ASAFP. He checked his voice mail to find the same message.

This couldn't be good. It had been a week and a half since Owen found out about Bryan and Morgan and the guy still wasn't talking to Bryan. He hoped the urgency was Owen declaring his forgiveness, but that seemed unlikely.

Bryan hit Owen's number and his buddy didn't even say hello. "Is Morgan with you?"

"No, man. She's working at the clinic tonight."

Owen uttered a string of curses that would have made Bryan proud if Morgan wasn't the topic at the moment. "She left. There was some sort of trauma and when it was finished, she walked out. Didn't even take her phone. Holly called Stacie to see if she'd shown up here."

"What the hell happened?"

"Holly can't talk about it, HIPPA or some shit. She sounded worried though and I don't like that Morgan is MIA."

Bryan didn't like it either. He had no idea where she'd go if she was upset because he'd never known her to get upset. "I'm going to look for her," he said.

"Holly tried her apartment and she's not answering. I'll go over just to make sure she isn't there. Let me know when the ferry hits Seattle."

Thank God Owen wasn't telling him to back off because no way could Bryan not be involved if Morgan was in trouble.

Looking at his watch, he realized a boat was about to leave. Bryan shouldered the phone so he could put on socks and sneaks. "There's one leaving in about two minutes. I'll run for it, but that means I won't have my own transportation."

"Stacie's staying here in case Morgan shows up. Come over and grab the keys to her Jeep. I'm taking the Mustang."

"Roger that," Bryan said, disconnecting. Without even untying his sneaks, he slipped them on and headed to the door. He nearly ripped the thing off its hinges in his rush, only to find Morgan standing outside.

Her hair was a tangled mess and her eyes were red and puffy.

"Morg," Bryan sighed, relieved to see her. But then she sobbed and it was as though a damn burst because she leaned into him and starting bawling.

His arms wrapped around her and he rested his cheek on the top of her head. Bryan had never seen her cry and just like any dumbass man, he didn't have a clue what to do. So he just held her and let her cry it out because it seemed that was what she needed most.

An eternity later, when the sobs finally subsided, she stepped back. "Sorry," she said, wiping her eyes and cheeks with the back of her hands.

"No need to apologize." He stepped aside and signaled to his apartment. Morgan walked in and looked around as if she'd never been there before. "What do you need? A beer? Coffee? Hot cocoa?"

Morgan laughed. "Just some water. Can I use your bathroom?"

"Of course. You don't have to ask."

While she disappeared into the bathroom, Bryan got her a glass of ice water and grabbed a couple ibuprofen from his stash behind the sink. He didn't have any chocolate, but made a mental note to keep some handy in case this situation ever happened again. Women always seemed to appreciate that. She was probably hungry, so he called in an order for Chinese delivery. Then he called Owen.

"She's here," he said when his friend answered.

"Is she alright?"

"She's upset. I don't know what's going on yet, but I'll keep you posted."

"Do that," Owen commanded in a harsh tone.

There was a long pause and Bryan wanted to say something, but what? He'd deceived his best friend – a man who didn't take kindly to betrayal – and there was no undoing it.

Finally Owen breathed a long sigh into the phone. "Take care of her," he finally said, his words a hell of a lot less harsh.

"You know I will," Bryan promised just before the line went dead.

When Morgan finally came out of the bathroom, she looked exhausted. He handed her the water and the ibuprofen and she smiled as she took them. "I didn't know where else to go," she said as she settled on the couch.

Bryan sat next to her, extending his arm so she could nestle against his body. "I'm glad you came here. Do you want to talk about what happened?"

"I'm done," she said quietly, her head resting against his chest and her hand on his stomach.

"What do you mean?"

"Done with school, done with the clinic. I'm not cut out for this."

"You're quitting?" This was all Morgan had talked about since she'd moved to Seattle. She wanted to focus her career on delivering babies, so she was going to school to become a midwife and wanted to do that exclusively.

"Yeah, I'm quitting," she sighed.

"Tell me what happened tonight," Bryan urged, hoping Morgan didn't jump on the stubborn horse and refuse to talk.

"Remember that guy that came in a couple months ago? His wife had beaten him up with a bat?"

"I remember." Goddammit, if that guy had laid a hand on Morgan, Bryan would hunt him down and tear him apart one limb at a time.

"Tonight it was his wife. He pushed her down the stairs and sent her into pre-term labor. Dr. Sisco was performing a C-section on another patient, so I had to deliver the baby."

She took a couple deep breaths and Bryan held her tighter. Then he realized she was crying again. "Is the baby okay?"

"She's fine. She went into distress briefly, and I thought we might lose the mother, but everything turned out fine. By the time we got the baby cleaned up, Dr. Sisco was out of surgery and took over."

"Then why do you want to quit? Sounds like you did everything right."

"I panicked. All I could think about was how her husband had said she was going to pay for beating him up. I tried to get her to go to a women's shelter, but she wouldn't. And then this. I just – dammit, I just can't handle this. I thought I could, but school is hard and I failed a test and now this. I just can't do it." She was bawling again and Bryan wished he hadn't pushed her, but she couldn't quit because of one asshole.

He lifted her chin, forcing her to look at him. "You're the strongest, smartest, most determined woman I know. You're a great nurse, Morg. Everyone has a bad day on the job now and then, but this is what you were meant to do. Don't make any hasty decisions in the heat of the moment."

She shook her head. "It's not hasty. I've been thinking about it for a while. My job at Dr. Merrill's office isn't dependent on the degree program. I like it there. That's what I want to do."

Bryan didn't believe that for a second. She was passionate about being a midwife. He didn't figure school was easy, but she was smart.

What she really needed right now was to cool down. Some laughter, comfort food, and mind-blowing sex, followed-up with a good night's sleep would help get her into a better frame of mind. Tomorrow, when tonight's trauma was a thing of the past, she'd have a fresh perspective on her future.

He grabbed the tablet computer sitting on his table. "I've got something to show you."

"Pics of naked girls aren't going to help right now," she quipped. At least her humor was coming back.

"This is better than porn."

"Better than porn? Must be good."

Bryan navigated to the link where there was a list of a hundred epic autocorrect fails. He'd nearly pissed himself laughing so hard and given Morgan's wry sense of humor, he was confident this would take her mind of things.

When it came up, Bryan handed her the tablet.

She chuckled at the first couple, but within a minute, her whole body shook with a laughter that echoed throughout the apartment.

Morgan was wiping tears from her face when she put the tablet down several minutes later. "Oh, that was classic. I haven't laughed that hard in a long time."

"What was your favorite?" Bryan asked, already suspecting based on how hard she had laughed.

"Without a doubt, the one with the dad. *I'm eating your mom out for dinner.*" She just about fell off the couch laughing again. "Oh God, that was funny. *No, I'm eating your mom out for dinner.*"

In perfect stereo, Bryan said along with her, *"Thanks, Dad. That clears it up."*

The knock at the door stifled her laugher. "Oh, I hope we aren't disturbing the neighbors."

Bryan knew it was the Chinese food, but couldn't help think of other ways he'd like to disturb the neighbors with some noise. After he paid for the food, Morgan smiled at him, her expression tugging at his heart. "You ordered dinner?"

"Comfort food," he corrected.

"You're a keeper," she chuckled.

Once the Chinese food was spread out on the table, they dug in. Morgan ate as though famished and he was glad she wasn't pushing the food around on her plate like some women did when they were upset. This wasn't the healthiest meal, but sometimes comfort food did more to nourish the soul than a healthy meal could do for the body.

She helped him clean up and when the extras were all in the fridge and their plates were in the dishwasher, he turned to find her looking him over. "Thank you for that. For everything."

"Is there something else you need?" he asked, hoping he was reading her expression correctly.

"You," she said before grabbing his hand and heading to the bedroom.

***

When Morgan had gone into Bryan's bathroom to wash her face, she'd stumbled upon his stash of alternate contraceptives. He had everything from sponges, to spermicidal foam, to suppositories. Before tonight's fiasco, she'd been thinking about his request not to use a condom. In fact, she had thought about little else, including school. That was one reason she'd failed the test. The other reason was even more obvious. She'd been wrong in this career choice. Delivering babies had her too emotionally charged. Yeah, sure, she knew not every birth would be as complicated as the one she had tonight, but there would be others like this. As much as Morgan wanted to believe she could compartmentalize her own memories, it was obvious she couldn't. And now, every time she had to deliver a baby, she would remember her first time and it wasn't a memory she wanted to keep.

Then there were the memories of being in bed with Bryan. Those were memories she most definitely wanted to hang onto. Though she didn't want to explore Bryan's reason for not wanting to use a condom, she did want to make him happy. This was something he wanted and he knew Morgan's stance on doubling up. Since he'd gone the extra mile, she'd helped herself to the foam. It wouldn't protect her from STDs like a condom would, but she trusted Bryan, so being infected wasn't the issue.

Actually, being infected with a sexually transmitted disease would be easier to deal with than what Bryan had already infected her with. God, was she really feeling the L word for him? Someone needed to develop an antibiotic that could put the kibosh on that.

Bryan was all about the foreplay tonight, probably in an effort to make her forget about what had happened at the clinic. She liked it when he was this sensual, but knew what was coming next. He was going for what he boasted as a three-fer. He'd just brought her to orgasm with his fingers, now he was going to make her come again with his mouth before he brought her to a third climax with actual intercourse. She wasn't sure oral sex was a good idea with the contraceptive foam already in place.

When he finally got her out of her panties, he knelt between her legs and just looked at her. His hungry stare always made her feel incredibly sexy, but recently his gaze had been more reverent, making her feel beautiful. Loved.

"You can't go down on me tonight," she informed him, but her tone was so harsh she wished she could rewind and start again.

"Why not?"

"Because I used a spermicide. I don't want to poison you."

"A spermicide?" He was clearly perplexed, maybe hopeful. Morgan was in such turmoil herself, she was doing a lousy job of reading Bryan's emotions.

"I found your stash in the bathroom," she explained. "So…we don't need a condom."

His eyes widened just before one corner of his mouth lifted. Yep, he clearly understood and that smile had Morgan aching for him.

Bryan moved slowly, bracing his hands on either side of her head as he caressed her lips with his. The kiss was so sweet, as though he were thanking her. Morgan didn't want to think about the emotion of the kiss, she just wanted to feel him inside her.

He was still on his knees so she reached down to stroke his erection. She held him firmly, just the way he liked and he groaned against her mouth.

"I want to go slow. You're not making it easy."

"I want you in me," she said. Last time they'd had sex without a condom, she'd been so overcome with needing him she hadn't even realized what they were doing. This time, she wanted to feel it, to really experience her flesh wrapped around him.

His lips moved along her jaw and her neck before skimming across her breast. His tongue took the lead on her nipple. "I love your body," he said before claiming the other and driving her insane.

He took his time, rubbing his erection against her core with teasing strokes until he finally slid inside her. His movements were so incredibly slow and sensual. She wasn't sure if she could really differentiate between this coupling and when he'd used a condom, but it definitely felt more intimate. That probably had to do more with knowing nothing separated his skin from her flesh.

"You feel so good." His pupils were dilated, making his eyes dark and causing the light to reflect off them in intense sparks.

"So do you. I like it when you move slow like this."

"Yeah? What about when I go like this?" He moved his hips in a slow circle as he pushed deep inside her.

She couldn't bite back the moan as a tingle surged low in her belly. It was the awakening of another orgasm and she was surprised how quickly it came to life.

Bryan continued to press, slow and deep, hardly withdrawing from her depths at all. As his breaths got deeper, carrying a primal echo on them, she became even more aroused. She loved how much he was enjoying this.

He kissed her again, this time demanding her mouth open as he pushed his tongue inside. Morgan brought her knees up so he could go deeper and he hooked an arm under one leg, stretching her and angling her hip to increase the friction. He groaned and broke the kiss.

"Look at me when you come," he said, but it wasn't his usual commanding voice. The softly spoken request made her heart beat even faster.

"You have a beautiful smile."

She couldn't respond. Her breaths were frantic as the pleasure climbed. She moved her hips, wanting more and he groaned again. "I can't hold out much longer." His voice was like gravel as he held on to the quickly fraying tether on his control.

"Faster, Bryan. Please."

He finally gave in to her pleas, which was probably what he'd been waiting for and moved in and out of her with a ferocity that matched her need. She wanted to close her eyes and just feel, but the way he looked at her had her completely focused on him. He felt so good, she wanted to do whatever he asked, but getting lost in his eyes proved there was more happening between them than just sex.

She let go of that thought as the orgasm reached its peak and took her over the edge, Bryan murmuring her name as he followed.

***

"I need your place," Jenny demanded as she pushed Morgan out of the way. The woman was normally the model of high-end business fashion, but her hair was soaking wet and wind-blown and she wasn't even wearing a raincoat despite the stereotypical Seattle spring day.

"Geez, Jenny. Come on in. Feel free to drip wherever you please."

"I know right," she agreed, wringing out her hair right there in the foyer.

Morgan looked at her like she had three heads.

"Ah, shit, sorry. Can I have a towel?"

A little late for that, but Morgan was keen to prevent any further flooding in her apartment. "What's going on? Why are you out in this weather?" She was completely soaked, her jeans clinging to her legs while her big sweatshirt dripped with rainwater. Jenny rarely went out in public in such casual clothing, and Morgan feared she was about to deliver some really bad news.

"I can't get any privacy. Ty's everywhere. He's at the condo. He's at work, which is weird since we don't work together anymore. Then he's at Stacie's. Everywhere I turn, there's Ty."

Given the way the two of them clung to each other, Morgan wasn't sure why this was a problem. "Isn't that how it usually works when you live with someone?"

"I know, I know, but I can't get any damn privacy." This antsy woman was not the Jenny Carter Morgan had come to know and call her friend since last summer. Usually the woman was the epitome of confidence and don't-mess-with-me, but now, Morgan hardly recognized the flustered mess standing in her foyer.

"Why do you need privacy?" she asked as she handed Jenny the towel she'd retrieved from the pile of laundry on her sofa.

Jenny held out a pregnancy test, her eyes wide and her lips

pursed.

"Oh." There was no need for further explanation. "How late are you?"

"Very. Like a month."

Morgan grabbed Jenny's wrist and commenced to taking her pulse, using the clock in the kitchen to time it. After thirty seconds, she dropped the wrist and asked, "Any other symptoms?"

"Like freaking out?"

Morgan laughed, but Jenny wasn't in the least amused. She looked terrified. "No, like nausea, dizziness, heartburn, overly emotional." Okay, she didn't need Jenny to confirm the last one since it was staring her squarely in the eye.

"No, nothing," Jenny responded.

Morgan raised a brow. "Not overly emotional?"

"I wasn't before today, no more than usual. But I can't keep ignoring the fact I haven't had my period. I mean, I actually had to fake it last week because Ty noticed. Can you imagine? Faking your period."

"Exactly how did you fake your period?" Morgan asked, intrigued that Jenny would go that far. She also found the situation amusing. Obviously, an unexpected, or worse, unwanted pregnancy was no laughing matter, but Jenny and Ty lived together and were planning their wedding for August. There were worse things than getting pregnant. What was amusing was seeing Jenny completely and totally flustered. Morgan needed a distraction like this. She'd taken the re-test and wasn't feeling at all confident about it. She was also mustering up the courage the tell Dr. Sisco she was quitting the program and wouldn't be volunteering at the clinic any longer.

Jenny moved to the mountain of laundry piled on the sofa. After pulling a pair of underwear off the top, she started folding. "I tossed out perfectly good tampons. Left the wrappers in the trash and flushed the other parts. Plus, I denied him sex and complained of cramps. I don't get cramps, so maybe that was pushing it, but I was desperate. Plus, I never deny him sex. I mean, that's like punishing yourself, right? He's a god, for crying out loud. But if I'm pregnant, he'll smother me. He might deny me sex."

"Is that why you don't want him to know?" Morgan grabbed the next pair of undies off the pile. She didn't need help, but she wasn't about to tell Jenny to go away. The woman apparently needed something to do.

As carelessly as she shook her head, she looked like an out-of-control bobblehead. Morgan would have to remember this the next time she was stressed to the hilt and needed a good laugh.

"He's already bugging me about kids and it's months until the wedding. He's been ready forever. I'm a career woman. I always knew we'd have kids, but I just figured I'd be thirty-five or some shit like that. The agency is just starting to take off. I'm not ready for a baby. Oh, these are cute."

Jenny held up the rainbow panties Bryan had bought her when she'd sent him shopping for the essentials after unexpectedly getting her period. Fortunately, Jenny proceeded to fold them without requiring further explanation.

When the pile of laundry had transformed into neatly folded piles on the table, Morgan said, "Why don't you just chill out for a minute. Can I make you a cup of tea?"

"Yeah, tea's good. That'll make me pee, right? Cause this girl doesn't pee on command."

Morgan didn't know a lot of women who could pee on command. "Yeah, tea will help with that. Did you call Stace?"

Jenny nodded. "She's on her way, sworn to secrecy." Jenny made an X over her heart and kissed her index finger before pointing it upward, as if she was sealing the secret with some sort of silent solemn vow. "I knew I could trust you. You're good at keeping secrets. Plus, you're a nurse, so you're sworn to confidentiality, right?"

"For my patients, yes. That doesn't apply to taking pregnancy tests in my apartment, but don't worry, I can keep a secret."

"Thanks. Whatever the result, we're going out after, my treat.

We're either going to get completely hammered because I'm not pregnant or we're going to O.D. on chocolate and chai."

Sounded like a good plan.

"Oh, can you call Holly? Strength in numbers, girl power, you know, all that."

Morgan wasn't sure that was a good idea. What Holly hadn't revealed during their Truth and Drink game was that when her ex had beaten her to a pulp, she'd had a miscarriage and now wasn't able to have children. Morgan wasn't sure Holly would want to be present when Jenny found out, good or bad. Morgan laughed a little, wondering which was good, a positive or a negative.

"I have to pee. Oh, I'll do this now." Jenny grabbed the box and headed to the bathroom and Morgan got busy carrying her laundry to the bedroom. She didn't figure lingering at the door would help Jenny's performance, but she couldn't resist the urge to give a quick listen each time she walked by. When the toilet flushed, Morgan figured it was a successful trip. Now she just had to wait for Jenny to announce the result.

Chapter 18

"Morg? Hey, you here?"

Bryan knew where she hid her spare key and she'd told him he was always welcome to let himself in if she wasn't home. He liked that she didn't have anything to hide, that she trusted him to be in her space without supervision.

It's not like he was going to rifle through her underwear drawer or anything. Tempting, but it just wasn't his style. He'd rather see them on her anyway, just before they landed on the floor.

He actually liked this feeling, like he was coming home to her. Bryan had never lived with a woman, so the warm feeling was surprising. Of course, he'd been getting that warm feeling a lot lately – every time he thought about Morgan.

Her apartment wasn't as tidy as usual. Laundry was folded but left in piles on the table in front of her couch. When he went into the kitchen, he found dirty dishes in the sink. It looked like she had left in a hurry. He wondered if one of her patients was giving birth. Although last time she'd talked about work, she'd said that June was going to be a busy month but there weren't many births expected before then. Maybe she'd been called in to the clinic. That happened on occasion. Morgan hadn't mentioned quitting the clinic or school again, so Bryan hoped she wasn't following through now that she seemed to have calmed down.

They were supposed to meet here, and even though he was early, she had said she'd be home at three. Bryan decided to give her a call and see where she was at. They were doing that more these days, calling instead of texting. He liked hearing her voice.

"Helllllloooo," she sang into the phone."

"Hey. I'm at your place."

"Oh, dammit. I totally forgot we were meeting up."

He preferred to call it a date, but Morgan was still having issues with those terms. "What's going on?"

"Emergency retail therapy with Jenny and Stace."

"Whose emergency?"

"Ah, it's just a girl thing. Don't worry about it. Listen, I really don't want to blow them off. Can we meet up later?"

"You going to make it worth my while?" he asked.

Morgan laughed. "Don't I always?"

"Buy a sexy nurse uniform while you're shopping. That's how you can make it up to me. Don't forget the white fishnets."

"In your dreams, buddy."

"It's a fantasy, not a dream."

"Are you going to hang at my place or should I call you when we're done?"

"I think I'll head over to your brother's. Why don't you just meet me there."

"Excellent. Bye-bye."

She was gone before Bryan could say bye. Morgan sounded pretty cheerful, so if she was out having emergency retail therapy, he had to figure it was either working or it wasn't her emergency.

He decided to tidy up for her. She liked things clean, so seeing dirty dishes in the sink, a package of snack crackers left open, and the block cheese on the counter seemed really strange. There seemed to be three of everything, so it was obvious the girls had a case of the munchies before they headed out shopping.

After everything was in its rightful place – well, except for the laundry because he really wasn't comfortable rifling through her dresser – he decided to hit the head. It wasn't a long drive to Owen's, but no point being uncomfortable. And maybe some of Morgan's unmentionables were hanging in the shower.

The open box on the vanity had Bryan's heart stopping in his chest. The letters on the box were small but what they spelled was larger than life. Hell, it was practically lit up in neon. Catching a glimpse of the stick on the back of the toilet had his deadbeat heart dropping into his gut.

This was bad news. Morgan having some retail therapy, leaving her apartment in complete disarray, and a very scary box and even scarier stick lurking like a predator in the bathroom.

Using just two fingers, he lifted the stick and peered at the pink plus sign.

Ah, hell. Did that mean what he thought it meant?

The directions had been opened and were on the edge of the tub. Still holding the stick, he lifted the instructions with his other hand and tried to focus. The tiny print wouldn't come in to focus, but it mattered not because there were pictures. Plus sign equaled pregnant.

The stick bounced off the vinyl floor as the instructions floated a bit more slowly to the same destination. Bryan wiped the sweat from his brow and tried to breathe.

Plus sign equaled pregnant.

Morgan was pregnant.

How…

Well, that was a dumb question, even in his current state of disbelief. He knew how. Morgan hadn't only preached about birth control, she'd cited statistics on failure rates for various methods. That's why it was important to double up. So had two methods failed or had she gotten pregnant that morning after the kittens were born?

No wonder she needed emergency retail therapy.

When Bryan caught his reflection in the mirror, he was as white as his dress uniform. If he'd been wearing it, he could have doubled for Casper.

Holy. Shit.

Morgan was pregnant.

He stumbled back through the bathroom door, the closet door opposite the bathroom stopping his backward momentum. The floor stopped his downward slide.

Morgan. Pregnant.

He should be upset about this. He'd never had sex without a condom for one reason, he wasn't stupid. Women couldn't be trusted. He didn't want to get anyone pregnant and he didn't want to pick up any bad juju. That was one thing he and Morgan had in common. She was all about safety. She talked about it like someone might talk about the weather. Oh, it might rain today, bring your raincoat. And don't forget your condoms, too, just in case.

Damn, she was on the pill. She'd even insisted on using a spermicide. So how in the hell could she have gotten pregnant?

There was a simple answer. The Landry's were fertile. Very fertile. Owen had gotten Daphne pregnant in high school. He'd always thought he got Kristina pregnant too, but apparently she'd lied about that to trap him into marriage. That didn't negate the fact it had happened when he was eighteen, though.

As freaked out as he was, Bryan wasn't pissed. He'd never pictured himself having kids. That was because usually marriage went along with that and he had never been interested in that institution either. The fact was he was in love with Morgan. Marriage hadn't been a thought, but as he imagined her walking down the aisle in a white gown, her belly swollen with their child, he liked the idea of having a family with her. He'd seen her at work at the clinic, calming a screaming kid, soothing a crying baby. She'd be a great mom.

Bryan would have to learn to be a great dad. He didn't know how, but he'd figure it out – for her, for them.

He pushed himself off the floor and headed out. He needed to talk to someone about this and there was only one place to go.

When he got to Owen's, Ty was there. They were playing Call of Duty. This was good. Ty added another layer of security, maybe. Though not likely. Owen was not going to be happy but Bryan couldn't keep another secret from his best friend.

***

"You're pregnant?" Owen asked. "How could you be so stupid?"

Morgan looked from Owen to Bryan, who was as white as a ghost. "I'm not pregnant."

Bryan moved to her. "It's okay, Morg, I'm a little freaked out, but I'll do right by you. We can get married. Everything will be fine."

Get married? Do right by her? What was this, 1952? "I'm. Not. Pregnant."

"I saw the pregnancy test in your bathroom. It was positive."

"I told you this would end in disaster," Owen preached to her before turning his anger on Bryan. "I oughta rip your balls off for touching my sister."

Morgan avoided looking at Jenny. Obviously she wanted to keep the pregnancy scare a secret since she'd opted to take the test at Morgan's apartment instead of at her own place.

"There will be no ball-ripping. It wasn't my test. You know I always double up on the birth control. Besides, the test wasn't positive." That's why they'd gone out for drinks and ended up at the mall. Jenny loved to shop. Morgan had heard about the closet full of new, never worn clothes that was a result of Jenny's therapy sessions. Seemed like a co-pay with a therapist would be cheaper and take up less real estate, but to each her own.

"It was positive," Bryan insisted, still pale and wide-eyed. If she wasn't so annoyed, she might think it cute.

"Baby?" Owen asked Stacie, hope in his eyes. That was a change from when he'd gotten Daphbitchne pregnant. It had taken him weeks to get used to the idea of being a dad. Even though she wasn't around when Krisbitcha claimed she was pregnant, Owen had called her and she'd heard the regret in his voice. None of that reflected in his expression now.

Stacie laughed and gave him a quick kiss. "Sorry. Not mine."

Before the question could be turned to Jenny, Morgan spoke up. "One of my classmates came by. She needed a private place away from all her roommates. I guess she was so relieved she didn't clean up after herself."

"Oh, for crying out loud," Jenny moaned. "I'm not going to let you lie for me, Morgan." Then she turned to Ty. "It was my test, but it was negative."

Ty's eyes grew round with surprise. "You thought you were pregnant? Why didn't you tell me?"

"Because I was a little freaked out. I'm not ready for a baby."

"But we're not–"

"No, we're not," Jenny interjected. "It was definitely negative."

"There was a plus sign," Bryan insisted again. "I read the directions. Plus sign equals pregnant."

Gah, men were such idiots. Morgan tossed her bags across the room and walked over to Bryan, smacking his chest. "You moron. The test only holds a valid sign for a few minutes. If you leave it lying around, the sign can change. That doesn't change the result."

"Any chance the test was wrong?" Ty waggled his brow.

"No." It was Jenny's turn to do some chest smacking, but even that gesture didn't wipe the goofy smile off Ty's face. "We went down to the clinic and had one done there. Negative." Jenny had been so relieved, but something had lingered and Morgan suspected it was guilt. Jenny and Ty were partners, after all, and this was something you didn't keep from the man you were about to marry.

Morgan was relieved she'd never have that kind of complication in a relationship.

"What made you think you were pregnant?" Ty asked. She could hear the disappointment in his voice, but Morgan was glad he wasn't pissed off at Jenny for taking the test on the sly.

"That's not a conversation I want to have in mixed company."

Morgan walked out to the balcony to give them some privacy if they wanted it. Of course, there was still a room full of people. Morgan, however, needed some air. Things had taken a turn for the unexpected when they'd walked into Stacie and Owen's condo. She didn't appreciate being bombarded by her brother before she had even stepped all the way into the condo. She certainly didn't appreciate Bryan making assumptions about things he knew absolutely nothing about.

"Morg," she shouldn't have been surprised to hear his voice behind her.

"Knock, knock," Morgan demanded as she turned to him, her arms crossed firmly over her chest.

"Morg–"

"Knock. Knock."

Bryan let out a long sigh and shook his head, but he played along. "Who's there?"

"1952."

"Morg–" he groaned.

"19. 52."

"1952 who?" he conceded.

"1952 called and wants its oppression of women attitude back. There's no room for it in the twenty-first century, dipwad."

"Wanting to marry you because you're pregnant isn't oppression of women." His voice was thick with that alpha attitude Morgan normally found sexy, but right now Owen wasn't the only one who wanted to castrate him.

"Do you even hear yourself?"

"It's responsible, not oppressive."

"You're an ass," she said, turning back to look out from the balcony. The city was alive with cars and buses motoring around the streets and people walking, some with purpose, some at a leisurely stroll, to wherever their destination was. Morgan wished she was among them instead of being trapped on the balcony by the source of her angst.

"I saw the test and I–"

"And you assumed. Didn't you ever learn not to assume?"

"Like you said, I'm an ass."

This was a nightmare and exactly what she didn't want. Bryan making assumptions and worse, making decisions for her. They were supposed to be having a good time. This wasn't a serious relationship. He'd be going off on a ship soon and she needed to reclaim some control in her life. Bryan had become a distraction she didn't need.

They were too cozy, too comfortable. The sex was great, but it had become too intimate, too personal. Morgan blamed herself. She'd slipped that one morning, had sex with him without a condom, and then she'd given in to his request to do that again. Yeah, she'd still insisted on using a second method of birth control, but that didn't delineate the intimacy that came with not using a condom.

Their relationship was getting out of control. It had been going on for five months now, making it the longest relationship she'd ever had with a man. Morgan was feeling things she had no business feeling and she knew Bryan was too. Everything was snowballing out of control.

"I think it's time to call it a day," she said, still looking out at the city.

His hands settled on her shoulders, giving her a gentle squeeze. The gesture was sweet, squeezing her heart too. "Yeah, sure. I'll take you home."

Morgan shrugged her shoulders and side-stepped out of his

grasp before turning to face him. "I don't mean today. I mean us. We both know this isn't going anywhere. Maybe we should quit while we're ahead."

Confusion tightened his expression. "Who says it isn't going anywhere?"

"Come on, Bryan. You're a womanizer and I'm not interested in getting married. You were ghost white when you thought I was pregnant."

Now anger flashed in his eyes. "I'm not a womanizer. Just because I haven't been serious with anyone doesn't mean I can't be. I was freaked because I don't know the first thing about being a dad. That doesn't mean I don't want to be."

"Since when?" Morgan's heart seized up in her chest. She didn't want kids. She loved them, but had never had any desire to have her own. That's why she'd chosen to be a midwife. She got the joy of bringing children into the world without contaminating them with her Landry blood.

"Since you."

No.

No, no, no.

This was bad. This was so, so bad.

"I love you, Morg. It scares the hell out of me, but it's true. I'm in love with you." She wasn't sure why the words had surprised her since she'd been wrestling with those emotions herself, but hearing them was like taking a slap to the face. The fog that had kept the emotions safely at bay cleared now, the reality more than she could handle.

Morgan pushed past Bryan and stepped into the condo, heading straight for the door.

"Morgan," Bryan called after her, his booming voice echoing throughout the condo.

Morgan turned to her brother as she passed him. "He stays."

If there was one thing she could count on, it was Owen to protect her.

***

Owen grabbed Bryan's arm, jerking him to a halt. "What'd you do?"

Bryan just shook his head. Of all the damn stupid things he'd ever done. Why couldn't he just keep his mouth shut?

His first mistake, falling in love with his best friend's sister. His second, telling her.

"Let go of me," he demanded, trying to shrug out of Owen's hold. The bastard was slightly smaller, but damn he was strong.

"I let go, you stay. Otherwise, I'll bust your ass. Hell, I might bust your ass anyway."

Their eyes met and Bryan made a silent promise to his best friend. Owen always had his back, no matter what. The only exception was when it came to Morgan. Sister trumped best friend any day of the week.

When Owen let go, Bryan went to the fridge and grabbed a beer. Frustrated, he cracked the top open with his teeth. What good was dental if you never used it?

"Guess you made an ass of yourself thinking she was pregnant?" Owen said as they sat at the bar. Stacie sidled up to Owen, patting Bryan's shoulder. Ty and Jenny had disappeared.

"It was a safe assumption," Stacie said. "Morgan lives alone and you guys hump like rabbits. The test being hers made sense."

Owen groaned, most likely at the hump like rabbits comment. "Off your meds, Stace?" Bryan asked. She had a tendency to lose her tact if she didn't take her medicine regularly.

"Just stating the facts as they've been told to me. Morgan gets all giddy when she talks about you."

"Yeah, well, she won't be doing that anymore." She'd gone as white as he'd been when he dropped the L word. *Idiot*. He knew it would happen, which was why he'd been keeping it to himself. That damn pregnancy test had given him diarrhea of the mouth.

"What'd you do?" Owen asked again, dread in his voice.

"Something really fucking stupid," Bryan admitted.

"You didn't."

"I did."

"Did what?" Stacie asked, furrowing her brow.

"Dumb ass here is in love with my sister. If I know my boy, he just told her."

"Oh," Stacie sang in a low voice of doom and gloom. Everyone knew Morgan's stance on love...it was a wasted emotion. Use that energy and passion to save the world. Don't be stupid enough to give it all over to one person who will end up abusing you. Yeah, she had Daddy issues, alright. Bryan wished Emmanuel Landry was still alive just so he could kill the bastard with his bare hands. Not just for what he did to Owen and Morgan's mother, but for the scars he left on his kids.

"Well, you got your wish, man. It's done. We're through." Bryan nodded at Owen who simply shook his head.

"If I thought it could work, I'd have been happy for you two, but she's a train wreck."

"Morgan is not a train wreck," Stacie said in Morgan's defense. "How can you say that about your sister?"

"Because she is," Bryan agreed. Morgan made no secret of it. "God, I'm an idiot."

"You're just now figuring that out? Should have kept your tiny little dick in your pants and none of this would have happened."

Bryan's first instinct was to correct Owen on the size comment, but his ego wasn't what needed stroking right now. Owen had accepted what was happening between them and was even starting to talk to Bryan again. Wanting to continue to rebuild the trust between them, Bryan knew he had to tell Owen first. If he found out Morgan was pregnant from anyone else, Bryan knew the damage would be irreparable. He'd never even considered that Morgan wasn't pregnant. *Dumbass.*

"You two are morons," Stacie proclaimed. "Don't you see why

she ran? She's in love with you, too."

Jenny was the one who was all into happily ever-afters. Apparently Stacie was now buying into that concept. Since Morgan wasn't a believer, he didn't see this ending happily for him.

"I've seen the way she looks at you, especially when you're not paying attention," Stacie added.

He knew how she looked at him too. He'd seen it, had convinced himself she loved him. That was great except for one little problem: Morgan would never admit to it.

And that was complete bullshit. If Bryan could man up and admit his feelings, Morgan could do the same.

"I'm going to find her," he said to Owen. "You can try to stop me, but you can't keep me away from her forever."

"Go," Owen growled, "but if you hurt her, I hurt you."

Bryan had no doubt that was true.

By the time he got to the bus stop, she was gone, so he headed around the corner to where he'd parked the Ducati. He'd likely beat her back to her apartment. He just hoped she was heading straight there.

When he knocked on her door there was no answer. He could let himself in, but given the circumstances, he figured that would be pushing his luck. So he'd give her an hour. After that, he'd have to decide if he was going to leave or wait inside.

He didn't have to decide. Twenty-seven minutes later, Morgan came strolling up the walk, her head hung low.

"Why are you here?" she asked as she pushed by him.

"Morg, we need to talk." It sounded so cliché, but Bryan was in new territory here. Bryan had had girlfriends who told him they loved him, but he'd never been the one to utter it. His response had always been simple and clear. He didn't feel the same and it was best if they end the relationship now. Not unlike what Morgan had said to him. The difference was he knew she felt the same. She was just too damned stubborn to admit it.

"You said enough," she said, unlocking her door and stepping in. He was surprised by that. She'd run off on him less than an hour ago, ordering her brother to keep Bryan hostage. Now she was letting him into her apartment. Bryan didn't want to hope this was progress, but he'd take even the small victories.

She stopped and looked around, obviously surprised the place was clean. She shook her head and headed to the bathroom. That was one place Bryan hadn't tidied up.

Five minutes later she returned to the living room, dropped into the papasan chair she loved and picked up a giant textbook.

Bryan had still been standing behind the couch waiting for her to return. He decided to settle on the couch, but Morgan acted like he wasn't even in the room.

"Are you just going to ignore me?"

She clapped the book shut and gripped it while letting out an exasperated sigh. "What do you want?"

Tension filled the room like a thick fog moving in from Elliot Bay. Bryan couldn't stand it, especially knowing he had caused it. "Morgan, come on. We agreed we wouldn't let things get awkward."

"Yeah, well you changed that rule when you…"

Her words trailed off because she would never say the word love, not even if referring to him saying it. He needed to change that.

"When I fell in love with you," he finished. "Yeah, I guess I did."

"I know what game you're playing. You can keep saying the words, but it's not going to change anything for me. I don't do L word and you know it. That's why it worked with us. You don't do the L word either."

"I'm not playing at anything." Bryan pushed off the couch and pulled Morgan out of the chair. Her hair was soft as silk as he tangled one hand in the lengths. He couldn't keep his other hand from caressing the soft skin on her arm. "Do you know how hard it is for me to be alone in a room with you and not have my hands all over you?"

Her breaths were heavy and her eyes focused on his lips. She wanted him just as much as he wanted her. At least he had that playing in his favor.

"It doesn't have to be over." When he pressed his lips to hers, she didn't kiss him back. He caressed her gently, not forcing his tongue into her mouth despite the urges driving him. Still, her lips didn't move. When he finally gave up, she dropped her head, leaning against his chest.

"I'm a good person, Bryan. I know I've got issues, just like anyone, but I'm a good person. I'm not going to string you along or pretend you never said the words. I can't be with you knowing you feel the way you do."

"It doesn't have to be complicated. I know you feel it too."

She shook her head against his chest. "This was supposed to be fun, uncomplicated. We were just supposed to be a couple friends having a good time. All this other stuff wasn't supposed to happen."

That was progress, right? She wasn't exactly admitting to how she felt, but she wasn't denying it either.

She pushed away and crossed to the kitchen, her arms wrapped around her waist as though she was in pain. "You're going out on a ship. I can't be the woman who sits by and keeps the home fires burning while you're off saving the world. It killed me every time Owen deployed. We had to rely on his stupid wives to give us information and you know how reliable they were. I'm not even related to you. I'd be the last to hear if something happened to you. I can't live like that."

"I'll be able to stay in touch, Morg. There's email and Facebook and Skype. There are a lot more options now than when Owen was deployed."

"It's not that easy."

"It is." Bryan insisted. "If we love each other, we can make it work."

"You assume too much."

"I know you love me, Morg. I see it in your eyes and I feel it when you touch me. You just need to admit it."

She laughed, but it wasn't filled with humor like the laugh he loved to hear from her. This laugh held no mirth, just a few decades of angst Bryan knew came from her childhood.

"I know you love me, Morgan," he said again, hoping to get her to say it.

She started shaking her head. Bryan closed the distance and gripped her shoulders. "Say it. Tell me you love me."

She pushed him away, tears pooling in her eyes. "Get. Out."

"Morgan–"

"Get. Out," she repeated. Bryan saw the anger in her expression, but something else played across her face that he couldn't quite place.

"If you don't leave, I'm calling Owen."

"I'm not afraid of your brother. Besides, you hate being rescued, so I'm calling your bluff."

"I do hate being rescued and Owen knows that, so when I do call him, he'll come running without hesitation. And you have to remember, Bryan, he grew up protecting me. You said it yourself, he fights dirty."

Fuck. Bryan knew that was true. There wasn't anything Owen wouldn't do for his sister, especially if she was calling for reinforcements.

He had no idea what had just happened, but if she wanted him to leave, he had to. He didn't want to hurt her or push too hard.

As he reached the door, her words shattered his heart. "We're done, Bryan. Don't call. Don't come over. I don't want to see you anymore."

Bryan didn't believe that. He'd triggered something and he'd give her some space to sort through it, but he didn't believe for a second that they were through.

Chapter 19

Bryan scrolled through his contacts to Owen's number. Right below it on the list was Serenity. He spied the name, realizing he'd never gotten around to deleting it after the Super Bowl. What the hell did that say about him?

Maybe it was meant to be. He was sure if he called Serenity now she'd be a sure thing. She certainly seemed more than willing a few months ago. Bryan could simply explain he'd been involved with someone, which was why he didn't call, but now he was on his own again.

If Serenity wasn't interested, Bryan knew it wouldn't take much effort to find another pretty and willing woman to take his mind off his troubles. The pretty bartender who had served him the warming beer was blonde and flirted freely. He could nurse a few more beers, over tip, and wait for her shift to end. That had worked for him before. At this very same bar, actually. He hadn't seen that bartender since she'd kicked him to the curb before he even got his clothes back on. He never did find out what her issue was, but it wasn't his problem. There were plenty of pretty women to choose from in Seattle, ones who didn't offer the complication of love.

That's the way it had always been for him. When one relationship ended, he simply moved on to the next. There was no heartache on his part and certainly no regret.

Now, though, he was wading in foreign waters. He'd never had his heart broken, not once in his whole life. Bryan wasn't sure what that said about the kind of person he'd been, but sitting at the bar now, nursing a beer he didn't really want, he realized how much he'd changed since that first night with Morgan. Maybe it had been a slow road to love or maybe he'd been there all along. Hell, he'd spent years messing around with blonde women just to avoid any similarities to Morgan.

He was such an ass.

Bryan hit delete on Serenity's contact information and hit send on Owen's number.

"You better be calling with good news," Owen warned.

"I know you're going to side with your sister, but I could really use a shoulder right now."

"That's big of you to admit," Owen laughed.

"Yeah, I'm turning over all kinds of new fucking stones lately."

"Where you at?"

"O'Neil's."

"Gimme ten."

Bryan was still nursing the same beer when Owen walked into the pub seventeen long minutes later. Watching the clock probably wasn't a good idea, but it beat thinking about Morgan.

Owen clapped him on the shoulder and took a seat on the bar stool next to him. "I'm sorry about Morgan, man."

"Sorry you slept with her or that you fell in love with her? Or that she's a bigger train wreck now than she was before?"

"Everything. I just never expected it to end up like this."

Owen ordered an ice water. "I know she cares about you, man. But if she's not willing to change, there's nothing anyone can do."

"I know she cares. I just don't understand why she can't say it."

"It's my father. He'd get drunk and demand that my mother tell him she loved him. And she did. Tell him, that is. I don't really think she loved him. For a long time, I didn't get it. Then after

Hailey was born, I figured it out. She was protecting us. If she did what he said, he'd leave us kids alone. And man, he had his eye on Morgan. I think Mom knew it. So she let that bastard do whatever he wanted to her just to keep him away from Morgan."

Bryan knew the elder Landry had had his eye on Morgan. Morgan had told him that her father had come after her once. What he didn't know about their family situation, though, made him a complete asshole. "Fuck."

"Yeah," Owen agreed, but Bryan knew his friend didn't realize what he was agreeing with.

"No, man. I think I might have sent her over the edge." Bryan raked his hand across his short hair, wishing it was longer so he had something to tug on.

"What did you do?" Owen asked, anger already stirring in his voice.

"I tried to force her to say it, to tell me that she loves me."

Bryan totally expected to eat a knuckle sandwich. In fact, he deserved it. Instead of feeding him one, Owen just sat there glaring. "You just won asshole of the millennium."

No doubt. Bryan pushed out of the chair. "I need to find her."

Owen blocked his path. "No. You need to stay the hell away from her."

"I may have just scarred her for life. I can't leave her like that."

Owen's stature stiffened, if that was possible. Bryan felt like he was in the land of the giants, peering up at the looming gatekeeper who had the power to break him in half with no effort. "You go near her and you're only going to fuck her up even more. Where is she?"

"I left her at her place."

"I'll go. You need to go home."

That was the last place Bryan wanted to go. "If I don't fix this, it makes me an even bigger asshole."

"You can't fix it, not right now. Let me talk to her."

"Tell her—" Tell her what? That he was sorry? That he was an asshole? Both those were true, but relaying it through Owen seemed like the pussy thing to do.

"I'll make sure she's alright," Owen said, giving Bryan a sympathetic pat on the shoulder. "Seriously, bro, go home. You don't want to be hanging out in a bar right now stewing over this. Believe me."

Owen was right. Bryan wasn't sure what had brought him to the pub. He was trying to avoid any place that made him think of Morgan, but that just about covered all of Seattle and a good chunk of Puget Sound. He couldn't avoid his apartment forever and since he was going out on a ship soon, he could go through his gear and make sure he had everything in order. That was as good a distraction as any.

He called to Owen before his friend walked out of the pub. Owen paused and Bryan crossed the room quickly. "Thank you. I know I betrayed your trust, but, well, thank you." Bryan held out his hand and Owen paused only briefly before taking it in a firm grasp.

"I don't like how it all played out, but I know you care about her. It's actually kind of nice to see you fuck up for a change. Maybe it means I'll get a reprieve."

Bryan chuckled at the sarcasm, grateful his friend – his chosen brother – wasn't holding a grudge.

***

Morgan hadn't been back to the clinic since she'd delivered that baby. Holly had brought her bag and phone by and Morgan had called in sick for her last two shifts. Her day couldn't really get any worse, so may was well bite the bullet and tell Dr. Sisco she was done.

When she walked in through the front door, she saw Amanda sitting in the waiting room, holding her daughter snug in her arms.

The woman stood and crossed the room to Morgan. "I never got a chance to thank you. The doctor explained how serious the situation had been and that your quick action saved me and Angelica.

"I was just doing my job," Morgan said, sliding her finger under the baby's fingers. "Angelica is a pretty name."

"She's my angel," Amanda sighed, gently bouncing the baby in her arms. "We've been staying at the women's shelter. They gave us a private room and the staff there has been helping with her, since I don't have a clue what to do."

Morgan's heart stopped beating. She was relieved the woman had found a safe place. "Are you filing charges?" she asked.

"I did, before I even left the clinic. The police have been to our apartment several times because the neighbors called it in, so there's quite a history. I have a lawyer and everything. I'm not going to let him hurt me or Angelica again."

"Good," Morgan said, wishing her mother had done the same all those years ago.

"Thank you," Amanda said again.

"I didn't do anything," Morgan admitted.

"You took me aside and gave me that card. No one's ever done that before. I was scared to be alone, I still am, but I can't let my baby grow up like that."

Morgan blinked back the tears and took a deep breath, focusing on the baby's face to avoid Amanda seeing too much in her eyes. "I'm glad you got help," Morgan finally said, slowly pulling her finger out from the baby's strong grasp. "I have to go."

She retreated a few steps and practically ran out of the clinic. Morgan was grateful her apartment was only a few blocks away. As she tried to unlock the door, her shaking hands fumbled with the keys. When the damn lock finally turned, she grabbed the spare key from its hiding spot and closed the door firmly behind her, sliding the chain into place for extra security.

Her apartment seemed dark and gloomy, but Morgan didn't want to open the curtains. She didn't like the thought of anyone being able to peer in. Besides, she totally intended to close her eyes and not open them until the feeling of spiraling out of control had dissipated.

Curling up in the papasan, she cradled her legs and took a deep breath in. It didn't have the calming effect she'd been hoping for and when she released the breath, it came out in a sob.

Fifteen years she'd lived in an abusive household. She'd never cried because she was too scared her father would beat her for it, just as he had her mother. What had started as fear turned into resentment as she realized her mother had chosen to love the man who abused her rather than leave and find a safe place for herself and her children.

Maybe it made her a horrible person, but she was jealous of little baby Angelica whose mother had finally been smart enough to leave and find help. Angelica wouldn't grow up the way Morgan had, living with fear and resentment.

The knock at the door startled her. Since she wasn't expecting anyone, Morgan figured it had to be Bryan. She was grateful she'd taken the hidden key and chained the door because he was the last person she wanted to see. Morgan couldn't escape the memories of her father, or those of her mother. It was a stark reminder of the life she didn't want for herself, only confirming she had to make a clean break from Bryan now before it got way too complicated.

When the lock clicked open, Morgan realized it wasn't Bryan at all. It had to be Owen since he was the only other person who had a key. Unless he'd given his key to Bryan, in which case her brother would soon be nursing another black eye.

"Morgan, you here?" Owen called when the chain snapped tight.

Owen's voice sent an immediate calm surging through her body. He'd always protected her, kept her safe. More than once he put himself between her and his father and he took a beating for it.

Morgan moved out of the chair quickly. She released the chain and opened the door, falling against Owen as soon as he stepped inside, unable to control the sobs.

He hugged her tight, petting her hair. "It's alright, Morgan. It's alright."

"I hate her, you know. I hate her for loving him." She had told Bryan she didn't hate her mother and maybe it was a horrible thing to admit, but having all those memories flash through her mind stirred more feelings than Morgan could adequately label. She just couldn't fathom how her mother had not just stayed with the man who threatened and abused her, but how she'd loved him, proclaiming just that every time the man demanded it.

"She didn't love him," Owen said, still stroking her hair. "She loved us."

Morgan shook her head, aware she was leaving tears and snot on her brother's shirt, but unwilling to do anything about it. "She said it. All the time. Every time he told her to, she said it."

Owen gripped her shoulders and held her away, looking at her with an intensity she hadn't seen in years. "She was protecting us. If she didn't do what he wanted, he would have come after us."

Maybe that was true, but that didn't mean the words her mother uttered weren't true. Hell, she continued to talk about the man years after he'd died, as if he'd been some sort of saint. "How do you know that?"

"Because I'd do the same thing for Hailey. I'd let someone torture me if it meant protecting her."

"I still hate her. She should have left. There must have been shelters or friends or something."

"She was afraid of him. He threatened to kill us if she left."

"How do you know that?" Morgan had never heard her father say those words. He'd handed out plenty of threats, but never to that extreme.

Owen sat on the sofa and Morgan sat next to him, needing the security of having her brother close. "I used to spit on his grave," he shook his head as he said it, as though he couldn't believe he'd done such a thing. Morgan was surprised. Even though he never spoke fondly of their father, he never spoke ill of him either. With Owen, he simply stated the facts as history had dealt them. "Every time I went home, I'd run through the cemetery and spit on his grave. The last time I was there, I was doing my usual run and Ma was there, sitting on the grass, crying. I was pissed at first. I mean, how could she go there like that, after everything he'd done to her? But she told me it was just to make sure he was really dead. She has nightmares about him, that he's still alive, so she has to go to the cemetery to remind herself he's rotting in hell. Her words, not mine."

"She said that? Really?" Then why was she always talking about the sweet man he'd been before the abuse had started?

"She didn't love him, Morgan, at least not during our lifetime, but she does love us. You should talk to her. Then maybe give Bryan a chance to apologize. He didn't know and he feels terrible."

"He told you?" Why that surprised her, she didn't know. The two of them were best friends, so they probably talked about everything. She just couldn't picture these two big, strong men talking about women troubles.

"Yeah, he told me. Are you in love with him?"

Morgan couldn't answer that question. How could she say yes and let Bryan walk away? Because that's what she was doing. There was no way she could ever look him in the eye again. She certainly couldn't speak the words he wanted to hear.

Yep, Daddy issues were a bitch. Even if they weren't, well, he was going out on a ship. He was heading out into the big blue ocean to make sure the navy was equipped with the latest technology. If he was on a ship when Russia or North Korea decided to start World War II, she probably wouldn't ever see him again. Damn men and their hero complexes. Why couldn't they just sit behind a desk where it was safe?

"This isn't what I wanted," she mumbled, more to herself than to her brother.

"Love isn't convenient. It doesn't come around because we want it to. I know it's cliché, but it really does hit when you least expect it."

Morgan had never expected it. She had goals and she had scars. Both of those factors had kept her focused on what she needed to do to be happy. Of course, up until he'd started throwing emotions into the mix, she had been happy with Bryan.

"I need some time to think. Would you let me borrow your car so I can get out of the city?"

"Sure." He pulled the keys out of his pocket and put them on the table. "I can take the bus home. Where you going?"

"I don't know. Maybe just for a drive. Maybe up to Deception Pass. Just someplace where I can clear my head."

Owen grabbed her hand and gave it a squeeze. "I never thought I'd see Bryan fall for someone. Honestly, I didn't think it was possible. But he's wrecked over you, Morgan. If you're not going to be with him, at least be gentle with him. He's a good guy, the best I know. I don't want to see you hurt him."

The last thing she wanted to do was hurt Bryan, but she wasn't sure she had it in her heart to love him the way he deserved.

Chapter 20

The mountains seemed distant, a blur behind tears she couldn't rescind. When she blinked, their majesty came into focus, if only briefly, reminding Morgan the world was so much bigger than just her heart. The rocky sand gave way to the smooth beach she'd walked on with Bryan. She felt the same panic now that she'd felt then, except this time her panic had been confirmed with his words.

He loved her.

Morgan stopped next to a small tidal pool. The rain had stopped and the brilliant reflection planted her feet, not unlike the roots of the trees that had lined the beach for decades. Her own reflection stood as clear, but the confidence reflecting off those waters was as backwards as the image itself. She might look the part, as she strived to do no matter the circumstances, but Morgan wasn't confident about anything. She felt like she was in flux, lost between the life she'd built and the one that was blossoming like a wildflower.

Bryan loved her.

She'd heard the words before. Men tended to say what they

thought a woman wanted to hear, except Morgan had never longed for that emotion. She'd spent her life avoiding it, not wanting to fall prey to false hope and desperation.

Not wanting to be like her mother.

But now, everything she thought she knew had been smudged and blurred. Morgan had called her mother, just as Owen had suggested, and asked her some direct questions. Candace sounded surprised, but she'd conceded, telling Morgan everything she'd never expected to hear.

Her mother hadn't loved her father, at least not during those abusive years. She had only proclaimed those words to keep her abusive husband focused on her and away from her beloved children. After his death, she only talked about the good man he'd been, hoping to replace the horrible memories with a happier image of their father.

Morgan kicked sand across the tidal pool, rippling the water and distorting her image.

Never once had her mother told Morgan she loved her, but Morgan had never said it either. At first, she'd kept the words to herself out of fear, then because of a misdirected rebellion that she figured all teenagers went through. As an adult, it had been out of spite. It had never bothered her before, but now, even after she'd finally said it before she hung up with her mother, Morgan was riddled with guilt over her selfishness and naiveté.

The water stilled again and Morgan studied her reflection. She'd never thought herself capable of love, not the kind shared intimately between a man and a woman. Truth be told, she never really believed it existed. Bryan had changed everything. Over the course of the last several months, even though their relationship was supposed to be about having a good time and nothing more, he'd someone eased his way into her heart, making her feel, really feel, for the first time in her life.

The tide was rolling in, the water cold as it covered her bare toes. The tidal pool got lost in the waves, but what it had revealed pounded in her chest.

Bryan loved her and the beat of her heart told her the truth she hadn't wanted to acknowledge. She loved him too.

But the man was bull-headed, an alpha to the core. Her biggest fear was something she had no control over nor had the ability to predict. Her father had once loved her mother, according to Candace's often-told fairy tales. Circumstances had changed him, turned him into a mean drunk who couldn't deal with life and took out his aggressions on the people he was supposed to love. Morgan never wanted to be in the position her mother had been in.

Bryan Curtis, however, was nothing like her father. Alpha to the core, yes, but his alpha tendencies had only ever protected Morgan, not been aggressive against her.

Even when he'd demanded she tell him that she loved him, it wasn't a threat. Bryan knew what was in Morgan's heart and was just trying to get her to see it too.

But how could she face him after that? Morgan was embarrassed by her reaction, but she was also ashamed of it. For years she had lived with false assumptions. They had molded her. Would it be that easy to change and embrace what Bryan had to offer instead of run from it?

Morgan didn't know forgiveness. It wasn't something she'd ever sought or practiced. Looking at the waters extending across the Strait of Juan de Fuca, she knew the tide didn't know forgiveness either. The water's ebb and flow was based completely on science. That was something Morgan understood. Anatomy was simple, each part of the body had a function, all of them doing their jobs to keep the body alive. The heart pumped blood through the body, collecting de-oxygenated blood and feeding oxygenated blood into the arteries so as to feed cells throughout the body. The process was quite simple and logical.

A broken heart meant it wasn't pumping blood the way it was supposed to. Scientifically that made sense to Morgan. When people spoke of a broken heart, however, they weren't talking in scientific or medical terms. It was emotional, psychological, and she'd spent her whole life avoiding that aspect.

Now, though, she understood. That ache that people always talked about, she had it. It was like a lead weight on her chest, making it difficult to think about anything else. If she didn't know better, she'd think it was heart burn or maybe even bronchitis, but it was nothing that could be explained with a medical diagnosis. She was aching for Bryan, because she was in love with him.

A month ago, even a week ago, she'd been compelled to ignore it. The problem was, the ache had only grown as time passed. It had only been hours since Bryan uttered those terrifying words, but as time continued to pass, the ache only grew stronger.

She knew from her friends' experiences the ache would eventually fade and disappear altogether. She just had to be strong enough to get through it. Otherwise, she was going to have to muster the courage to face Bryan again and tell him what he wanted to hear.

Her phone rang, pulling Morgan from her thoughts. The caller ID revealed it was the clinic. That was something else Morgan had to figure out.

"Hello," she said, a slight question in her voice since she had no idea who was on the other end.

"Hi Morgan. This is Dr. Sisco."

Shit. Morgan was supposed to meet with the doc today to discuss withdrawing from the program.

"Hi Dr. Sisco. I'm, huh, not going to be able to make our appointment today."

"That's good," the doctor answered, "because rumor has it you were considering leaving the midwife program. After your performance last week, I think that would be a huge mistake."

Her performance last week had felt like a debacle. Yes, Amanda's body had done what it was supposed to, her uterus clotting to prevent any blood loss. The baby came out so fast that her distress was quickly alleviated. Dr. Sisco had arrived in time to deliver the placenta, relieving Morgan of her duties. Morgan had left the clinic in a panic.

"I panicked after the baby was delivered," Morgan admitted. "I don't think that makes for stellar performance."

"Not from my perspective. Connie and Derek both filed reports and the exam room camera recorded everything. You did everything right, Morgan. It wasn't a textbook birth, but you handled it with expertise."

"I'm not sure I can handle any more abuse cases." It was a confession she wasn't sure she'd ever be able to put words to, but now that she'd said it, she felt as though a huge burden had been lifted. "I grew up with an abusive father. I thought I could compartmentalize it, but I think I proved myself wrong on that front."

"Everyone deals with trauma in different ways and everyone has different reasons for wanting to bring babies into this world. You are a competent nurse and a good person. I would like you to finish out the quarter before you make any decisions that could alter your career path."

"I appreciate your support, but balancing work and the clinic and school is harder than I imagined."

"I'm sure we can work something out here at the clinic and with Dr. Merrill. It's my understanding he has a significant number of patients giving birth this summer. We may be able to petition the scholarship board to count the time you spend assisting with those births toward your scholarship requirements."

Less time at the clinic would help, but Morgan also suspected sorting things out with Bryan would help her to focus on what she needed to do to earn her degree. She was almost halfway through the program. It really would be ridiculous to quit now. "That'd be great," Morgan finally agreed.

"Good. I'll schedule a time to meet with you next week and I'll ask Dr. Merrill to join us. Then we can petition the board."

When Morgan disconnected, she found the clouds had cleared

and the sun was shining brightly in the sky. It was as though the universe was speaking to her and for the first time in longer than she could remember, Morgan didn't feel like the walls were closing in around her.

***

It had been the longest three days of his life. Bryan had given Morgan the space she needed and he'd hated every minute of it. He'd rather have been with her, cooking something up for dinner, lounging on the couch and watching a movie, making love. God, even sharing in every milestone those little fur balls achieved. The kittens' eyes and ears had opened and Fury had even taken to hissing whenever Bryan checked on them. Bryan was proud of the little guys, but it was hell not sharing it with Morgan.

Damn, he'd missed her.

She seemed back to her usual self, flirting with some asshole over by the pool tables. Bryan had been staring at her for the past twenty minutes, but she refused to look at him.

"Are you just going to sit there and let her walk away?" Owen asked. He'd suggested Bryan lay low for a couple days to give Morgan some time to process everything that was happening. Owen was sure she was in love with Bryan too and she'd come around on her own. Now hearing his friend ask that question, he wondered if Owen was so sure of his sister.

"You told me to sit tight."

"And now I'm saying don't sit for too long. She's here. You're here. That's pretty good math."

Yeah, those numbers added up and he damn sure was sick of waiting.

"I'm going to fight for her." Bryan pushed off the stool and crossed the bar to where Morgan was flirting excessively. He didn't know if this was another one of her gay friends running cover for her or an actual date. Either way, he didn't give a shit. He had something to say.

When she turned around, the smile he knew she'd been faking dropped from her face.

"I love you," he said, loud enough for everyone in the bar to hear.

"Bryan–"

"No," he said, putting up his hand. "I've served this country for 17 years to protect the rights most people take for granted. I've never asked for anything in return, but right now, I'm exercising my rights granted by the constitution, the freedom to speak my mind. All I ask from you is the courtesy to hear me out. You don't even have to say anything and when I'm done, you can walk away and I'll let you." *At least for now.* He was getting on a ship in a month. If he didn't win her in this round, he had a couple months to prepare for the next round. He'd never give up, not when he knew she felt the same way he did.

She didn't move, just stared at him with those beautiful brown eyes. They revealed everything he knew she couldn't say, the horrors she'd overcome, the fear of living it again. All that was on the surface, but like the ocean that hides so many secrets far within its depths, her eyes also held something deeper, something he knew she didn't want to acknowledge for fear of losing control of the life she'd built.

There was so much love reflecting in those depths it nearly shattered his heart.

He couldn't not touch her and as his hand cupped her cheek, Morgan closed her eyes and nestled against his palm. A single teardrop found its way to his thumb, as if pleading with him to not take her down this road. Maybe he was being selfish, or maybe he just knew without a shadow of a doubt they belonged together. Either way, he couldn't give in to that meager demand.

Brushing the tear away and inhaling a deep breath he whispered, "Look at me." As Morgan opened her eyes, he hoped the resolve in his eyes was powerful enough to wash away her fear.

Seventeen years in the navy had taught Bryan to compartmentalize during tense situations. Even though he was very aware that all eyes in the pub, at least in the vicinity of the pool table, watched them like sentries on guard duty, and that Owen had followed him across the bar, he focused on the woman in front of him.

"I love you, Morg," he said again, keeping his voice low. "I think I've loved you since the first moment you looked up at me with those incredible brown eyes. You were sweet and innocent back then and I've watched you grow into the most amazing woman, so strong and independent." He chuckled and shook his head. "And stubborn. You are so damned stubborn." Her stubborn nature was a paradox. He loved her for it, but he hated that he had to wade through it without a lifejacket.

"I wasn't there when you were a kid. I didn't witness what you and Owen had to go through. I never experienced your fear or dread. If I had been there, I would have fought for you. You, your mom, your brother. I would have died fighting for you if that's what it took to keep you safe." Her eyes widened but Bryan couldn't tell if it was shock or horror. He kept driving forward.

"I wasn't there, Morg, but I'm here now. I'm willing to fight for you now, to help you find forgiveness and move beyond the fear. I know you're scared and I know you're too stubborn to admit it and I'm not asking you to. I'll never ask you to. I'll never even ask you to admit you love me, because I don't need the words. I see it in your eyes every time you look at me." He took her hand and placed it against his chest. "I feel it every time you touch me."

"Bryan,"

"No," he said, shaking his head. He wasn't ready to hear her objections. "Just let me finish."

He took another deep breath knowing this was it. He had to put it all out there without demanding anything from her.

"We're good together. I can't imagine going on the way I was.

You make me want to be a better man. All I see is a future with you and I know you see that too. I know it, Morg, which is why I can't just walk away. I want to marry you, spend the rest of my life loving you and fighting for you. You're the only one for me. The *only* one. If I could have just one thing, one wish in the whole world it'd be that you take a chance on me, on us. That you take a chance on yourself."

Bryan sucked in a deep breath and held it. The woman was a rock, she stood there, tears pooling in her eyes, but even after he'd just poured his guts out in front of her and half of Seattle, she wouldn't let the tears fall. Bryan let the breath out and turned away, feeling more defeated than he'd ever felt in his life.

"Nice speech," she bellowed across the bar. Great, she was going to let sarcasm drive her response.

"I meant every word," he said as he continued toward the door.

"You're right," she called when he'd taken a few more left-right-lefts. Her words stopped him, but he was too scared to face her. "I am scared. I watched my mother pledge her love to a man who beat her over and over again. I swore I'd never put myself in that situation."

He did turn now, and found tears streaming down her cheeks. He wanted to go to her, to wipe the tears away and hold her in his arms, but he knew she needed the space.

"You, Bryan Curtis, are not my father." She took in a deep breath and wiped the tears. "You love me and you'll fight for me. I know that. I knew that before you even said the words and if you'd given me two seconds, you would have heard me say that I love you. I've been too stubborn to admit it, too stubborn to fight for you – for us. I can't let you walk away just because I'm too scared to take a chance."

Bryan crossed the room, standing close but not taking her into his arms. "I love you, Morgan."

"I love you, too. I always have."

Bryan dropped to one knee, and grabbed her hand, placing it

over his racing heart. "I don't have a ring or a lot of fancy words, but you can feel the promise in the beat of my heart. Marry me, Morg. Be my wife, my partner."

***

"Yes," Morgan sobbed and dropped onto Bryan's bent leg. He caught her as she knew he would and kissed her as he held her firmly in place.

The thunder of applause echoed throughout the bar.

When he finally broke the kiss, he wiped the tears away. Owen moved in behind him and patted Bryan on the shoulder. "Nice speech."

"A speech suggests it was rehearsed. I was winging it."

"Well, you wing it well," Morgan admitted. She knew Bryan would be here tonight and wasn't surprised when he walked in the bar. She had rehearsed a speech, but she just couldn't find the courage to approach him or even look at him. Instead, she'd flirted with the guy she'd pummeled in her last game of pool just to avoid having to start the conversation. Even though she'd been grateful he had started it, she'd been terrified at what he might say, and what she needed to say to him.

"You've always been my brother," Owen said, a big smile on his face. "I couldn't think of anyone else I'd want to marry my sister."

"Me either," Bryan grunted, kissing Morgan again.

He held up his watch, showing it to Morgan. "We've got time to hit the courthouse before it closes."

She laughed. "Tomorrow. I don't want a lot of pomp and circumstance, but I do want to buy a pretty dress."

"Seriously? You'll marry me at the courthouse tomorrow?"

"Yes."

"No," Owen cut in.

Morgan couldn't stop the automatic eye roll. She should have known her brother's blessing was too good to be true. "You can't stop me from marrying him, big brother."

"I know, but I am going to put my foot down about the date. You need to invite Mom and Beth and Janie. Hailey, too."

She wasn't all that close with her sisters. The age difference made them more like aunts. And she definitely wasn't close with her mother, but maybe they could start mending that relationship now.

"Are you going to invite your family?" she asked Bryan.

He smiled. "Yeah." He laughed and shook his head. "They're not going to believe I'm getting married."

Morgan could relate. "I can hardly believe it."

"I get to give you away," Owen interjected.

"We can't wait too long. My ship sails in a month and I want you to be my wife before then."

"You're going to marry me then run away with your other wife."

Bryan laughed. "Yeah, but in three years, I'm all yours."

"You're worth the wait."

Epilogue

Morgan's heart was beating so fast she thought she might go into cardiac arrest. Her bridesmaids had left the tent ten minutes ago to take their places, leaving Morgan alone with her racing heart and fluttering belly. Yes, she was nervous, but it wasn't cold feet. All she wanted was to walk down the makeshift aisle on the beach and exchange vows with Bryan.

It was the craziest thing she'd ever done.

Apparently everyone agreed because they were all here – her friends, her sisters and their families, her mom and Will, who turned out to be a super nice man. Even Bryan's family had come and immediately welcomed her to the family. His brothers were serving as groomsmen and even though Owen was giving her away, he was also standing in as Bryan's best man.

The past two weeks had been a whirlwind of planning. Bryan took charge of booking a navy chaplain and a photographer, taking Morgan to the courthouse to get the marriage license, and making sure they could get married on the beach at Deception Pass. Jenny had taken charge of the dress shopping, finding discount bridesmaid

317

dresses in a pretty pale green for her, Stacie, Holly, and Hailey. Then she and Stacie and Holly had all planned a bridal shower/bachelorette party combo that included a night of dancing and buckets of daiquiris. The boys had even crashed the party and Bryan had given Morgan her own private male strip show. Finally, Owen had taken her shopping for a wedding dress, stating it was his prerogative as the big brother and "giver awayer" of the bride.

It had all come together so quickly, Morgan felt like it was a dream.

As she gazed at herself in the full length mirror Jenny had packed as a necessity, Morgan barely recognized herself. Her hair was pulled up in this fancy way that had it off her face but still hanging down her back. Since Bryan loved her hair, she didn't want it all pulled up and Jenny had played around with it until they'd come up with something that Morgan liked. Man, was there anything that woman couldn't do?

Her dress was a simple strapless style that hugged her curves and flared out at the bottom. Given the beach wedding and her own personal style, she opted out of the fancier styles with a train. She'd been lucky to find silver flat sandals with enough bling to make them special. Holly had handled getting the flowers, and Morgan held a simple bouquet of yellow and orange roses, just like the bouquet Bryan had given her for Valentine's Day.

The tent flapped open, startling her. She turned to find Owen staring at her with his mouth agape.

"I know, weird, huh?" she said, taking a deep breath in to try and calm her nerves.

"Wow," was all he said.

Morgan didn't usually need ridiculous affirmations, but she was way outside her comfort zone. "Wow good or wow bad?"

Owen wrapped his arms around her in a very affectionate embrace. Morgan held tight even though she was terrified of breaking into a fit of tears. Good thing her mascara was waterproof. When her brother finally let her go, he wiped a tear from his eye.

"Wow very good. I think my boy's going to pass out when he sees you walking down the aisle."

"Good thing I'm a nurse, then," she laughed, trying to lighten the mood. She didn't normally hide her emotions from her brother, but it wasn't her goal to be a blubbering bride.

"You ready to do this?" Owen asked, holding out his arm. He'd rented a tux even though she told him not to and he looked so incredibly handsome. He'd be the odd man out since Bryan and his brothers had planned to dress in their sailor uniforms.

Taking one last look in the mirror and finding absolutely nothing to fuss with, Morgan knew it was time. "I'm more than ready."

She took Owen's arm and they stepped out of the tent. Her belly continued to tumble as they stepped around and onto the red fabric they'd put down to create an aisle for her to walk down.

When they came around the final corner and she saw Bryan, her knees nearly buckled. He wasn't wearing the same uniform as his brothers. Oh, holy wow, no. He was wearing his fancy dress uniform and oh, for the love of Pete, did he look incredible.

"Wow," she said, hoping she didn't have drool running down her chin.

"He cleans up pretty good for a squid," Owen joked.

"Step it out, soldier. I want to marry that guy."

Owen laughed and they started their march, not as quick as Morgan had hoped, but seeing the fire in Bryan's eyes as she crossed the beach was motivation to keep the slow pace.

"You're beautiful," Bryan said when Morgan stepped up next to him.

"What, in this old rag?"

"It's going to be a rag by the time I'm done ripping it from your body."

Owen groaned. "Oh, for the love of–"

"You two seem eager to start," the navy chaplain interrupted Owen's rant. "Shall we?"

Both Morgan and Bryan nodded and ten minutes later the chaplain told Bryan he could kiss his bride.

"Wife," Bryan said, his smile filled with equal amounts of affection and possessiveness.

"Husband," she said, stepping closer to him.

Without further preamble, he pulled her against him and claimed her mouth in the most glorious kiss she'd ever had.

~

Continue reading for an excerpt from The Sound of Consequence,
the first story in the
Puget Sound ~ Alive With Love series.

THE HUM OF MORNING TRAFFIC woke her with a start.

Accustomed to living in a quiet neighborhood in Maine, it took Stacie Nightingale a few moments to remember that she was in downtown Seattle.

And that the warm body in bed with her was not her fiancé.

Correction! Ex-fiancé.

The weight of his arm was the first reminder of a nearly sleepless night. The ache between her legs was another reminder. She swallowed a chuckle, not wanting to wake the man who had her pinned to the bed. If only her best friend could see her now. Not only had Stacie had sex, something she rarely engaged in even with her ex-fiancé, but she'd actually enjoyed it, something she never did with said ex.

Stacie had intended to leave in the middle of the night, after the giver of multiple orgasms had fallen asleep. But here she was, exactly where she didn't want to be...still in this man's bed and unable to make a discreet escape.

A new relationship didn't interest Stacie. She had been curious about her sexuality, which was the main reason behind her uncharacteristic promiscuity. She'd indulged in the one-night stand to prove that she wasn't broken, that her inability to have an orgasm wasn't her fault.

She'd never had one with her ex. Until last night, she didn't know if she could have one. Now she knew better.

She could have multiple.

Orgasms.

With an s!

Now that that little mystery had been solved, it was time to get her new life started. She came to Seattle to write and paint. Leaving her stable teaching job and moving across the country to write children's books was quite the coup. Her mother was likely fuming, once again disappointed in the middle child who never lived up to expectations. But Stacie knew the bigger revolution was having a one-night stand with a man she didn't even know.

Memories of last night slowly seeped into her mind. The club. The cab. The elevator. Then…

The memories slammed her like a freight train at top speed. Their night had been better than fantastic. Their first kiss had exploded in a fiery dance, with Stacie's last ounce of control turning to ash and being carried away like smoke on a windy day. She'd never been kissed like that before, so passionately, so thoroughly. It had awakened her senses in a dizzying sensation of lust and need. She'd never wanted anyone with such a reckless abandon. Nor had she ever been wanted so fiercely. Or taken. Yeah, she'd been taken last night, over and over again. She'd also liked it more than she ever could have imagined.

Despite the lingering need, all good things must end, and she needed to get out before he wanted to talk. Conversation complicated things.

Pulling a technique from her past, one she'd used on her ex almost every night for the last six years, Stacie whispered, "You're snoring," hoping that was enough to get him to roll over and off her hair.

He licked his lips and moved his arm up to scratch his chin. "Sorry," he murmured, rolling onto his back.

Stacie wanted to smile as she eased her legs out of the knot, but she couldn't allow herself to get too confident. Just because this trick had worked on the only two men she'd ever slept with didn't mean they were anything alike. Her ex could sleep like the dead. She couldn't count on that being the case with this guy.

As she stood, the giver of multiple orgasms stretched his legs, kicking the sheet to the floor. It was obvious from the perfect curve of his pecs to the washboard ripples of his abdomen that he worked out. As Stacie's eyes moved further down his body, she bit down on her lower lip, remembering how their bodies had moved together, how he had felt inside of her.

He was big. Scary big.

She'd taken one look at his naked body and wondered how he was going to fit. His incredibly delicious mouth had stretched into a smile before he promised he wouldn't hurt her. It might have been some kind of sexual miracle, but he hadn't. He'd hoisted her off the bed and found his way inside her before they'd even hit the sheets.

Looking at him now, she understood why her body ached. The intimidation of his size had faded as he penetrated her, stretching and filling her with long, slow strokes. Even though he was still sleeping, that one amazing part of his body was wide-awake and once again larger than life!

Stacie swallowed hard, the picture-perfect male form stirring memories, invigorating a new dose of desire. It wasn't just the sex, it was the way he had looked at her. Whether it was the shape of his eyes or maybe the fire in them, she knew he had been looking at her, not through her like she was accustomed to. He was a distraction though. That's all. She couldn't afford to get involved with someone who would keep her from achieving her dream. There were stories to illustrate, paint to put on canvas. Sex was great, she now knew, but it wasn't the path to happiness.

She snapped out of the delicious daze and tiptoed around the large bedroom. She found her jeans near the door and stifled a laugh when there was no sign of her boring and practical cotton panties.

Leave 'em! Get the blazes out of here!

It was more important to expedite her departure than to leave with anything more than the essentials, so up went her jeans and with a button and a zip, she was officially commando.

Her shirt and bra were in the hall. Hastily pulling the black lace over her shoulders, she secured the front closure, not caring that the straps twisted. The memory of buttons popping flashed through her mind. There hadn't been time last night to open her shirt with grace and since it was torn from that little event, there was no point collecting the buttons.

Gripping the ragged fabric closed, she scanned the apartment in search of her purse. It was amazing how much this place looked like the condo she had moved into just days ago, from the location of the master bedroom to the open kitchen and living room just down the hallway. Everything was opposite, though, like a mirror image, and the furniture was different. The stacked boxes in the corner next to the gas fireplace made her wonder who was moving in. Or moving out.

Stacie grabbed the purse she'd carelessly dropped on the floor near the door and stepped into the hall. She was about to close the door when she heard the deep Cajun voice call to her, "Wait! Baby, wait! Come back!"

"Crap, crap, crap," Stacie whispered as she closed the door behind her. She couldn't wait for the elevator in case he ran after her, so she looked toward the stairs. The door across the hall caught her attention. An ivy welcome wreath hanging on the door read 'Live Laugh Love.' The apartment number read 5-C in brass plating.

Holy Heart of Darkness! She'd spent the night right across the hall from her own apartment!

Stacie scrambled for keys and managed to get inside the door just before her sexy Cajun neighbor made an appearance. Peering through the peep hole to make sure he hadn't witnessed her escape, Stacie's gaze followed the taut skin of his abdomen down to where partially fastened button fly jeans teased her, the stark angles of his hips making just enough of an appearance to keep her glued, breathing heavily at the little peep hole.

He disappeared from view, heading toward the elevator. That was good. That meant he hadn't seen her come across the hall. She steadied her breathing while waiting for him to reappear. Just one last glimpse and she'd get on with her new life.

It wasn't long before he came into view again and when he did, he paused in front of his door and looked straight at her.

Stacie gasped and held her breath. Could he know he was being watched?

The tingle she'd felt at the back of her neck last night once again flowed to every muscle like an electrical storm, awakening the sensuality she hadn't known she possessed. Need outplayed common sense as she continued to watch him, silently praying that he didn't try to open the unlocked door or knock on it.

Her prayers were answered when he shook his head and turned back to his door, closing it behind him.

"Where have you been?" Jenny's playful voice startled Stacie away from the peep hole.

Stacie turned the deadbolt and fastened the chain. Then she took a deep breath and turned to her friend, trying to get her heart to slow down. "Jeez, give a girl a heart attack, will ya!"

"A little jumpy?" Jenny Carter wore pajamas, a pink silk robe wrapped loosely around her petite body. The delicate slant of her Asian eyes narrowed as her full lips, a gift from her African-American father, angled into a coy smile. "So, whatcha been doin'?"

As if Stacie really needed to answer that question. Standing there, hair tangled, her shirt missing all its buttons, and no panties – though that last bit wasn't blatantly obvious to anyone else – not to mention the fact that she hadn't washed last night's make-up off. Well, it didn't take a genius to know what she'd been doing.

It was a classic walk of shame, though she hadn't heard that term since college and had never actually experienced one. Nope, ten years with Greg Johnson, the guy she started dating in high school, didn't lend way to a walk of shame. Of course, he was out of the picture. Now, so was the guy across the hall. That reality didn't keep her kiss-swollen lips from smiling, or her cheeks from blushing.

"If it was that good, then why are you home so early?" Jenny was always so perceptive. It was just one of her really annoying traits. Stacie wondered if all best friends were insightful and perceptive or if she was one of those lucky people whose best friend knew everything.

Making her way into the kitchen, Stacie glanced at the microwave clock. 7:15. Jeez, she might have gotten two hours of sleep. No wonder her head pounded. Releasing the grip on her shirt, she took a seat at the breakfast bar and watched Jenny get the coffee started. "I left before things got complicated."

Jenny looked back over her shoulder, her left eye brow arching with suspicion. "You mean you snuck out?"

Stacie spun around on the stool as if she was Diana Prince transforming into Wonder Woman. "I came here to start a new life. The boring school teacher with the stable, loveless relationship and the controlling parents got left behind in Maine. The exciting and creative writer and painter living in Seattle isn't interested in anything more than a one-night stand."

It was quite the revelation, but it was all true. Stacie had been under everyone else's control for far too long. It was time to take control of her life. Though having a one-night stand was a bit drastic, it felt good and in the moment, it was what she had wanted, so she wasn't going to allow herself to have regrets or get sucked into anything more with her neighbor.

Once Jenny got the machine working its percolating magic, she leaned back and took in Stacie's disheveled appearance with a crooked smile.

"Given the look of satisfaction on your face, I'd say you're off to a good start. So, how many orgasms did you have?"

One, two, five... "Holy, Aphrodite! Too many to count. I never knew sex could be..." Stacie could use a thesaurus at the moment, but there weren't any words to do her memories justice. "So amazing," she finished.

"That's because you've wasted the last ten years with Greg 'I always tuck my shirt in' Johnson," Jenny chided.

Wasted was a bit brutal. Maybe Stacie had squandered the last few years. She was willing to admit to that before she'd own up to the entire relationship being a waste.

Though it probably was. Greg was the epitome of boring, from his five dollar haircut to his khaki slacks, tucked-in alligator shirt, and penny loafers. Jenny had him pegged and Stacie was glad she had left him behind.

"So gimme the deets...name, sign, length, girth."

Stacie's body warmed. "He's got this incredibly sexy accent. Cajun, I think. He gets an A+ with extra credit on length and girth. I didn't really have a chance to get his name or sign."

"Holy shit!" Jenny's eyes widened with surprise. "You really did have a one-night stand!"

Stacie smiled, realizing how out of character her actions had been. That wasn't the only thing buzzing through her head though. "Last night wasn't the first time I'd seen him."

Combing fingers through her sex-tangled hair, Stacie hoped to free some of the knots and look at least half as put together as Jenny. Of course, the luxury of good genes was obvious in Jenny's straight, silky black hair that had likely never seen a tangle or a knot. Sometimes Stacie really hated her best friend.

"You got into town two days ago and last night was the first time you left the condo! How is it possible that you've seen him before?"

"Starbucks." Stacie gave up the battle with the relentless knots and folded her hands on the bar. "I spilled coffee all over him."

"Classic," Jenny laughed.

"Cliché," Stacie corrected. That whole scene had been embarrassing. It was the day after she arrived and it had taken ten minutes and a conversation she could barely track to finally order some fancy latte. Then she turned and dumped half of it all over the guy's white shirt. He seemed more concerned about her scalded hands than his shirt, but that didn't keep Stacie from running away in sheer humiliation. Fortunately a couple shots of Jägermeister had helped her get over that last night when she'd decided to dance with him at the club.

Of course, at the café she'd also been dealing with another episode of vertigo. It had hit while she'd waited for the drink, right after that funny tingle traveled up the back of her neck.

"This is Seattle, Stace. Meeting a guy by accidentally spilling coffee on him is perfectly acceptable. In fact, I'm sure the coffee hounds encourage such things. Love, or at least the potential for love, sells more products. Why didn't you tell me about this before?"

Stacie wasn't interested in love. What she had felt was complete and total lust. Maybe for some people that was an acceptable way to start a relationship, but that was something Stacie also was not interested in. Though it would be hard to forget both of their encounters. When she'd looked up from the coffee-drenched shirt, she found intense forest green eyes and luscious lips. Her body had radiated heat from where he touched her, and the fire spread everywhere. She had never felt an attraction like that before. Not by looking at a man, and certainly not by his touch. That was why after a little liquid courage, she had approached him at the club.

"Deets, Stace," Jenny urged, leaning across the breakfast bar, obviously hoping for a spicy twist. "What happened when you spilled coffee on him?"

"I left." Spilling coffee on someone had been beyond

embarrassing and being flustered by the physical attraction was equally unsettling. Plus, the vertigo made her dizzy and was often followed by a raging headache, so she'd run out of the café like a zombie was chasing after her.

"You left?" Jenny asked with a hint of disgust in her voice. "You didn't talk to him? He didn't buy you another coffee?"

Stacie slid off the bar chair and walked toward the sliding glass door as she laughed at Jenny's romanticism. Jennevieve Mae Carter was a shark when it came to marketing, but her thick skin and razor sharp teeth softened like a feather-filled pillow when it came to relationships. Even though her last serious relationship ended on a really sour note, she basked in everyone else's potential for the happily ever after.

Despite writing children's stories with happy endings, Stacie was more of a realist when it came to her own relationships. Turning away from the view of the Emerald City, she focused her attention back on her roommate. "No, I just left."

~~~

Photograph by BLC Photography

Susan Ann Wall lives in northern New Hampshire with her family. She sees the world in varying shades of purple and never passes on the opportunity to add to her collection of purple sunglasses or purple shoes. When she's not tapping away on her purple netbook, she enjoys kayaking and skiing with her three kids, drinking a nice cold one with her husband, and jaunting off to Bon Jovi and Kenny Chesney concerts.

You can find Susan online at:
www.susanannwall.com
Facebook: Author Susan Ann Wall
Twitter: @susanannwall
Blog: susanannwall.wordpress.com